Amos Cooper Dayton

Theodosia Ernest

Or, the heroine of faith

Amos Cooper Dayton

Theodosia Ernest
Or, the heroine of faith

ISBN/EAN: 9783337192198

Printed in Europe, USA, Canada, Australia, Japan

Cover: Foto ©Andreas Hilbeck / pixelio.de

More available books at **www.hansebooks.com**

THEODOSIA ERNEST;

OR,

THE HEROINE OF FAITH.

———————

PHILADELPHIA:

AMERICAN BAPTIST PUBLICATION SOCIETY,

1420 Chestnut Street.

Theodosia Ernest:

OR, THE HEROINE OF FAITH.

---◄●►---

INTRODUCTION.

DOUBTS SUGGESTED.

"MOTHER, have I ever been baptized?"

The questioner was a bright, intelligent, blue-eyed lad, some thirteen summers old. The deep seriousness of his countenance, and the earnest, wistful gaze with which he looked into his mother's face, showed that, for the moment at least, the question semed to him a very important one.

"Certainly, my son; both you and your sister were baptized by the Rev Doctor Fisher, at the time when I united with the church. Your sister remembers it well, for she was six years old; but you were too young to know any thing about it. Your Aunt Jones said it was the most solemn scene she ever witnessed; and such a prayer as the good old doctor made for you, I never heard before."

"But, mother," rejoined the lad, "sister and I have been down to the river to see a lady baptized by the Baptist minister, who came here last month and commenced preaching in the school-house. They went down into the river, and then he plunged her under the water, and quickly raised her out again; and sister says if *that* was baptism, then we were not baptized, because we stood on the dry floor of the church, and the preacher dipped his hand into a bowl of water, and sprinkled a few drops on our foreheads: and she says Cousin John Jones was not baptized either; for the preacher only took a little pitcher of water, and poured a little stream upon his head. Sister says she don't see how there can be *three* baptisms, when the Scripture says, "One Lord, one faith, *one* baptism."

"Your sister is always studying about things above her reach, my son. It is better for young people like you not to trouble yourselves too much about these knotty questions in theology."

"But, mother, this don't seem to me to be a knotty question at all. One minister takes a person down into the water, and dips her under it; another stands on the dry floor of the church before the pulpit, and sprinkles a few drops into her face; another pours a little stream upon her head. Now, anybody can see that they do *three different things;* and if each of them is baptism, then there must be three baptisms. There is no theology about that, is there?"

"Yes, my child, this is a theological question, and I suppose it must be a very difficult one, since I am told that some very good and wise men disagree about it."

"But, mother, they all agree that there is only one baptism, do they not? And if there is only one, why don't they just look into the Testament and see what it is? If the Testament says sprinkle, then it is sprinkling; if it says pour, then it is pouring; if it says dip, then it is dipping. I mean to read the Testament, and see if I cannot decide which it is for myself."

"Do you think, my son, that you will be able to know as much about it as your Uncle Jones, or Dr. Fisher,

who baptized you, or Dr. Barnes, whose notes you use
in learning your Sunday-school lesson, and all the pious
and learned ministers of our church, and the Methodist
Church, and the Episcopal Church? They have studied
the Testament through and through, and they all agree
that a child who is sprinkled is properly baptized."

"Yes, mother, but if the baptisms in the New Testament were sprinkling (and of course they were, or such
wise and good men would not say so), why can't *I find
it there, as well as anybody?*"

"Very well, my son, you can read and see; but if you
should happen to come to a different conclusion from
these great and learned men, I hope you won't set up
your boyish judgment against that of the wisest theologians of the age. But here comes your sister. I
wonder if she is going to become a theologian too!"

Mrs. Ernest (the mother of whom we are speaking)
was born of very worthy parents, who were consistent
members of the Presbyterian Church; and she had
grown up as one of the "baptized children of the church."
As she "appeared to be sober and steady, and to have
sufficient knowledge to discern the Lord's body," she
was doubtless informed, according to the directions of
the confession of faith, page 504, that it was "her duty
and her privilege to come to the Lord's supper." But
she had felt no inclination to do so until after the death
of her husband. Then, in the day of her sorrow, she
looked upward, and began to feel a new, though not an
intense interest in the things of religion. She made a
public profession, and requested baptism for her two
children.

The little boy was then an infant, and his sister was
about six years old, a sprightly, interesting child, whose
flowing ringlets, dimpled chin, rosy cheeks, and spark-
ling eyes, were the admiration of every beholder.

Twelve years had passed. The lovely girl had become a beautiful and remarkably intelligent young lady
The little babe had grown into the noble looking, blue-
eyed lad, with a strong, manly frame, and a face and
brow which gave promise of capacity and independence
of thought far above the average of his companions.

Theodosia and Edwin. How they loved each other!
She, with the doting affection of an elder child and only
sister, who had watched the earliest developments of his
mind, and been his companion and his teacher from his
infancy; he, with the confiding, reverential, yet familiar
love of a kind-hearted and impulsive boy, to one who
was to him the standard at once of female beauty and
womanly accomplishments.

Theodosia came in, not with that elastic step and
sprightly air which was habitual with her, but with a
slow and solemn gait; scarcely raising her eyes to meet
her mother's inquiring gaze, she passed through to her
own room, and closed the door.

The mother was struck with the deep and earnest
seriousness of her face and manner. What *could* it
mean? What could have happened to distress her
child?

" Edwin, my son, what is the matter with your sister ?"

" Indeed, mother, I do not know of any thing. We
stood together talking at the river bank, and just before
we left, Mr. Percy came up to walk home with her. It
must be something that has happened by the way."

The mother's mind was relieved. Mr. Percy had been
for many months a frequent and welcome visitor at their
pretty cottage, and had made no secret of his admiration of her accomplished and beautiful daughter; though
he had never, until a few weeks since, formally declared
his love. Mrs. Ernest did not doubt but that some
lovers' quarrel had grown up in their walk, and this

had cast a shadow upon Theodosia's sunny face. She
waited somewhat impatiently for her daughter to come
out and confirm her conjectures. She did not come,
however, and at length the mother arose, and softly
opening the door, looked into the room. Theodosia
was on her knees. She did not hear the door, or become
conscious of the presence of her mother. In broken
whispered sentences, mingled with sobs, she prayed:
"Oh, Lord, enlighten my mind. Oh, teach me thy way.
Let me not err in the understanding of thy word; and
oh give me strength, I do beseech thee, to do whatever
I find to be my duty. I would not go wrong. Help!
oh help me to go right!"

Awe-struck and confounded, Mrs. Ernest drew back,
and tremblingly awaited the explanation she so much
desired to hear.

When at length the young lady came out, there was
still upon her face the same serious earnestness of expression, but there seemed less of sadness, and there
was also that perfect repose of the countenance, which
is the result of a newly formed, but firmly settled determination of purpose.

Mrs. Ernest, as she looked at her, was more perplexed
than ever. She was, however, resolved to obtain at once
a solution of the mystery.

"Mr. Percy walked home with you, did he not, my
daughter?"

"Yes, mother."

"Did you find him as interesting as usual? What
was the subject of your conversation?"

"We were talking of the baptism at the river."

"Of nothing else?"

"No, mother; this occupied all the time."

"Did he say nothing about himself?"

"Not a word, mother, except in regard to the question whether he had ever been baptized."

"Why, what in the world has possessed you all? Your brother came running home to ask me if *he* had been baptized; Mr. Percy is talking about whether *he* has been baptized. I wonder if you are not beginning to fancy that *you* have never been baptized?"

"I do indeed begin to doubt it, mother; for if *that* was baptism which we witnessed at the river this evening, I am quite sure that I never was."

"Well, I do believe that Baptist preacher is driving you all crazy. Pray tell me, what did he do or say, that gave you such a serious face, and put these new crotchets in your head?"

"Nothing at all, mother. He simply read from the New Testament the account of the baptism of Jesus and of the Eunuch. Then he took the candidate, and they went down both of them into the water, and he baptized her, and then they came up out of the water. could not help seeing that this is just what is recorded of Jesus and the Eunuch. If so, then it is the baptism of the Scriptures; and it is certainly a *very different thing* from that which was done to me, when Dr. Fisher sprinkled a few drops of water in my face."

"Of course, my dear, it was different; but I don't think the *quantity of water* employed affects the validity of the baptism. There is no virtue in the water, and a few drops are just as good as all the floods of Jordan."

"But, mother, it is not in the quantity of water that the difference consists; it is in the *act* performed. One *sprinkles* a little water in the face; another *pours* a little water on the head; another *buries* the whole body under the water and raises it out again. Two apply the water to the person, the other plunges the person into the water. They are surely very different **acts**;

and if what I saw this evening was scriptural baptism, then it is certain that I have never been baptized."

"Well, my child, we won't dispute about it now; but I hope you are not thinking about leaving your own church; the church in which your grandfather and your grandmother lived and died: and in which so many of the most talented and influential families in the country are proud to rank themselves, to unite with this little company of ignorant, ill-mannered mechanics and common people, who have all at once started up here from nothing."

"You know, my mother, that it is about a year since I made a profession of religion. I trust that before I did so, I had given myself up to do the will of my Heavenly Father. Since then I have felt that I am not my own. I am bought with a price. It is my pleasure, as well as my duty, to obey my Saviour. I ask, as Paul did, Lord, what wilt *thou* have me to do? You taught me this lesson of obedience yourself; and I am sure you would not have me on any account neglect or refuse to obey my Saviour. If HE commands me to be baptized, and the command has never been obeyed, *I shall be obliged to do it.* And I trust my mother will encourage me in my obedience to that precious Redeemer she taught me to love."

One who looked into the mother's face, at that moment, might have read there "a tablet of unutterable thoughts." She did not try to speak them. We will not try to write them. She sat silent for a moment, drew her breath deeply and heavily, then rising hastily went to look for something in her daughter's room.

Theodosia was not only grieved but surprised at the evident distress which she had given her mother. While on her knees in prayer to God after her return from the river, she had determined *to do her duty,* and obey the

commandment of Jesus Christ, her blessed Saviour, what
ever she might find it to be. But she had *not* deter-
termined to be *immersed*. That river baptism, connected with the reading of those passages of Scripture,
had only filled her mind with doubts; these doubts had
yet to become convictions. The investigation was yet
to be made. The question, Have I ever been baptized?
had been prayerfully asked. It was yet to be conscientiously answered. But if the very doubt was so distressing to her mother, and so ridiculous to Mr. Percy
(as it had seemed to be from some remarks he made on
the way home from the river), how would the final decision affect them, if it should be made in favor of immersion! Yet, aided by power from on high, she felt her
resolution grow still stronger to please God rather than
those whom she loved better than all else on earth. *And
she had peace* verging almost on joy.

When her mother came back, Theodosia saw that she
had been weeping; but no further allusion was made to
the subject of Baptism, until Mr. Percy came in after
supper.

This young man was a lawyer. He had united with
the Presbyterian Society, to which Mrs. Ernest and her
daughter belonged, during an extensive revival of religion, while he was yet a mere boy. Since he had come
to years of maturity, he had constantly doubted whether
he was really a converted man, and often seriously re-
gretted the obligation that bound him to a public recognition of the claims of personal religion. He often
made it convenient to be absent when the Sacrament of
the Supper was to be celebrated, from an inward consciousness that he was an unfit communicant; yet his
external deportment was unexceptionable, and his
brethren regarded him as a most excellent member,
and one whose intellectual capacity and acquirements

would, one day place him in a condition to reflect great honor on the denomination to which he belonged.

He had already taken a high position in the ranks of his profession; and had come to the sage conclusion, that the possession of the heart and hand of the charming Theodosia was all that was required to complete his arrangements for worldly happiness; and having overheard her remark to her brother, that if what they had just witnessed was baptism, they had never been baptized, he hastened to her side, and on their way home exerted all his powers of raillery to drive this new conception from her mind.

As for himself, he had never had a serious thought upon the question. He had been *told* that he was baptized in his infancy, and took it for granted that all was right. He had very serious doubts about his ever having been converted, but never the shadow of a doubt whether he had been baptized. When he listened to the religious conversation of some of his friends, and especially of the young lady of whom we are speaking, he heard many expressions, which, to him, were meaningless, and seemed almost fanatical. They talked of sorrows which he had never felt; of joys, the source of which he could not understand; and strangest of all, to him, appeared that habitual subjection to the *Master's will*, which led them to ask so constantly, and so earnestly, not what was desirable to themselves or agreeable to those about them, but *what was required* by the command of Christ.

That one should do this, or that, under the conviction that to refuse or neglect to do so would *endanger their soul's salvation*, he could easily understand; but how any one could attach much importance to any act *not absolutely essential to obtain eternal life*, was to his mind an unfathomable mystery. He had himself determined to secure his *own soul's salvation* at any cost, and if he had believed that immersion would *insure salvation*, he would have been immersed a hundred times, had so much been required. But thinking it as easy to get to heaven without, as with it, the whole business of baptism seemed to him as of the slightest imaginable consequence.

"What difference does it make to you, Miss Ernest," said he, "whether you have been baptized or not? Baptism is not essential to salvation."

"True," she replied; "but if my Saviour *commanded* me to be baptized, and I have never done it, I have not obeyed him. I must, so far as I can, keep *all* his commandments."

"But who of us ever does this? I am sure I have not kept them all. I am not certain that I know what they all are. If our salvation depended on perfect obedience to all his commandments, I doubt if any body would be saved but you. You are the only person I ever knew who had no faults."

"Oh! Mr. Percy, do not trifle with such a subject. It is not a matter of jesting. I do not perfectly obey. I wish I could. I am grieved at heart day after day to see how far I fall short of his requirements. Oh, no. I do not hope or seek for salvation by my obedience. If I am ever saved, it will be by boundless mercy freely forgiving me. But then, *if I love my Saviour*, how can I wilfully refuse *obedience to his requirements?* I do not obey to *secure heaven* by my obedience, but to please *him* who died to make it possible for a poor lost sinner like me ever to enter heaven. I think I would endeavor to do his will, even if there were no heaven and no hell."

Mr. Percy did not understand this. If *he* had been convinced that there was no heaven and no hell, he felt quite sure that all the rites, and rules, and ceremonies of religion would give *him* very little trouble. It was only in order *to save his soul* that he meddled with re ligion at all; and all that could be dispensed with, without endangering *his own* final salvation, he regarded as of very little consequence. He read some portion of the Scriptures almost every day (when business was not too pressing). He said over a form of prayer; and sometimes went to the communion table, because he regarded these as religious duties, in the performance of which, and by leading a moral life, he had some indistinct conception that *he was working out for himself eternal salvation.* Take away this one object, and he had no further use for religion, or religious ordinances.

"I know," said he, "that you are a more devoted Christian than I ever hope to be, but you surely cannot regard baptism as any part of religion. It is a mere form. A simple ceremony. Only an outward act of the *body* not affecting the heart or the mind. Why even the Baptists themselves, though they talk so much about it, and attach so much importance to it, admit that true believers can be saved without it."

"That is not the question in my mind, Mr. Percy. I do not ask whether *it is essential to salvation,* but whether *it is commanded* in the Word of God. I do not feel at liberty to sin as much as I can, without abandoning the hope that God will finally forgive me. I cannot think of following my Saviour as far off as I can, without resigning my hopes of heaven. Why should I venture as near the verge of hell as I can go without falling in? My Saviour died upon the cross for my salvation. I trust in HIM to save me. But he says, 'If ye *love* me, keep my commandments'—not this one or that one, but *all* his commandments. How can I pretend to love, if I do not obey him? If he commands me to be baptized, and I have not done it, *I must do it yet.* And if *that* which we saw at the river was baptism, then I have never been baptized."

"And so you think that all the learned world are wrong, and this shoemaker, turned preacher, is right; that our parents are no better than heathens, and a young lady of eighteen is bound to teach them their duty, and set them a good example. Really it will be a feast to the poor Baptists to know what a triumph they have gained. It will be considered quite respectable to be immersed after Miss Theodosia Ernest has gone into the water."

"Oh, Mr. Percy," said the young lady (and her eyes were filled with tears), "how can you talk thus lightly of an ordinance of Jesus Christ? Was it not respectable to be immersed after the glorious Son of God had gone into the water? If my dear Redeemer was immersed, and requires it of me, I am sure I need not hesitate to associate with those who follow *his* example and obey *his* commandments, even though they should be poor, and ignorant, and ungenteel."

"Forgive me, Miss Ernest, I did not intend to offend you; but really the idea did appear exceedingly ridiculous to me, that a young lady who had never spent a single month in the exclusive study of theology, should set herself up so suddenly as a teacher of Doctors of Divinity. If sprinkling were not baptism, we surely have talent, and piety, and learning enough in our church to have discovered the error and abandoned the practice long ago. But pardon me. I will not say one word to dissuade you from an investigation of the subject. And I am very sure, when you have studied it carefully, you will be more thoroughly convinced than ever before of the truth of our doctrines, and the correctness of our practice. If you will permit, I will assist you in the examination; for I wish to look into the subject a little to fortify my own mind with some arguments against these new comers, as I understand there are several others of our members who are almost as nearly convinced that they have never been baptized as you are, and I expect to be obliged to have an occasional discussion, in a quiet way."

"Oh, yes. I shall be so happy to have your assistance. You are so much more capable of eliciting the truth than I am. When shall we begin?"

"To-night, if you please. I will call in after supper, and we will read over the testimony."

They parted at her mother's door. He went to his office, revolving in his mind the arguments that would be most likely to satisfy her doubts. She retired to her closet and poured out her heart to God in earnest prayer for wisdom to *know*, and strength to *do* all her Heavenly Master's will, whatever it might be; and before she rose from her knees, had been enabled to resolve, with full determination of purpose, to obey the commandment, even though it caused the loss of all things for Christ. The only question in her heart was now, "Lord, what wilt *thou* have me to do?"

True to his promise, Mr. Percy came in soon after supper, anticipating an easy victory over the doubts and difficulties which had so suddenly suggested themselves to the mind of his intended bride. He could not help admiring her more, and loving her better, for that independence of thought and conscientious regard for right, which made the discussion necessary; and it gratified his vanity to think how fine a field he should have to display those powers of argument which he had sedulously cultivated for the advantage of his professional pursuits.

How he succeeded will be seen in the next chapter.

THE FIRST NIGHT'S STUDY.

THE BOOK OF TESTIMONY.

THE QUESTION STATED.

MEANING OF THE WORD BAPTIZE AS SETTLED BY CHRIST HIMSELF.

VALUE OF LEXICONS.

A MOTHER'S ARGUMENTS.

THE DAUGHTER'S ANSWER.

2

FIRST NIGHT'S STUDY.

"NOW, Miss Theodosia," said he, "let us begin by examining the witnesses. When we have collected all the testimony, we shall be able to sum up on the case, and you shall bring in the verdict."

"That is right," said she, with a smile, the first that had illumined her face since she stood by the water. "'To the law and to the testimony; if they speak not according to *this word*, it is because there is no light in them.' Here (may it please the court) is the record," handing him a well-worn copy of the New Testament.

"Well, how are we to get at the point about which we are at issue? It is agreed, I believe, that Jesus Christ commanded his disciples, in all ages, to be baptized."

"Yes, sir, I so understand it."

"Then it would seem that our question is a very simple one. It is, whether you and I, and others who, like us, have been sprinkled in their infancy, have ever been baptized? In other words, *Is the sprinkling of infants, in the name of the Father, Son, and Holy Ghost, the baptism which is required in this book?*"

"That is the question," she replied. "I merely want to know if I was ever baptized. I was *sprinkled* in the church. That lady, to-day, was *immersed* into the river. If *she* was baptized, *I was not*. That is the point. There is but one baptism. Which is it? the sprinkling or the dipping?"

"Oh, if that is all, we can soon settle the question. Sprinkling and pouring and dipping are *all* baptism, Baptism is the application of water as a religious ordinance. It don't matter as to the *mode* of application It may be done one way or another, so that it is done with the *right design.* I see from what your difficulty has arisen. You have misapprehended the nature of the word baptize. You have considered it a specific, rather than a generic term."

"I don't know, Mr. Percy, whether I quite comprehend you. My difficulty arose from a conviction that the baptism, which we witnessed to-day, was just such a one as is described in the Scriptures, where they *went down into the water* and *came up out of the water*—whereas *my* baptism had nothing about it that at all resembled the scriptural pattern. Please don't try to mystify the subject, but let us see which was the real baptism."

"I did not design to mystify the subject, but to bring it into a clearer light. The meaning expressed by some words, is rather a *result* than an *act.* If I say to my servant, *go* down to the office, he may *run* there, or *walk* there, or *ride* there, and he obeys me, equally, whichever he does—so that he gets there, it is all I require of him. *Go,* then, is a *generic* or general word, including a possible variety of acts. If I say to him, *run* down to the office, he does not obey unless he goes in this specified manner. So we call *run* a *specific* term. That is very plain, is it not?"

"Certainly, Mr. Percy; I comprehend that."

"Well, then, I say that baptize *is a generic term.* Jesus Christ said, baptize all nations. He does not say whether you shall do it by sprinkling, or pouring, or dipping; so that you attain the end proposed, you may do it as you please. If he had said, sprinkle all nations;

that is specific, and his ministers must have sprinkled. If he had said *pour* upon them with water, that is a specific act, and they must all have poured. If he had said, dip them in water, then they must all have dipped. The word would have required it. But he used the general term baptize, which signifies *any application of water as a religious ordinance*, and of course it does not matter as to the mode. You may take your choice."

"But I should, even in that case," said she, "feel inclined to choose the *same mode that* HE *did*, and which the *early disciples did*. There must have been some reason for his preference. But how do you determine that the word baptize is a generic term, as you call it—having three or four different meanings?"

"Simply by reference to the dictionary. Look at Webster. He is good authority; is he not. He defines baptism to be the application of water as a religious ordinance. What more do you want?"

"But, Mr. Percy," said Edwin, who had been a silent, but very attentive listener, "the Baptist preacher told Mr. Anxious, the other day, that baptize and baptism were not English words at all, but the Greek words *baptizo* and *baptismos*, transferred into the English Bible and not translated. He said that King James would not permit the translators to translate *all* the words, for fear of disturbing the faith and practice of the church of England, and so they just kept the Greek word—but if they had translated it *at all*, it must have read *dip* or *immerse* instead of baptize."

"Very well, Edwin, but it is not likely that the Baptist preacher is much wiser than Presbyterian preachers, or Methodist preachers, or Episcopal preachers. If dip had been the necessary, or even the common meaning of the word, it is very improbable that it would have remained for this unlearned and obscure sect to have discovered it. Such statements may do very well to delude their simple followers, but they cannot be expected to impose upon the educated world."

"But, Mr. Percy, I have looked up the words in my Greek Lexicon, and I find *it is just as he said*—Baptizo *does* mean to immerse. Baptismos does mean immersion."

"Oh, as to that, I suppose you got hold of a Baptizo Lexicon."

"Well, here it is; Donegon's Greek Lexicon. You can look for yourself."

Mr. Percy (who, if he was not a thorough Greek scholar, yet knew enough of the language to read it readily,) glanced at the word where Edwin had marked it, and ran his eye along the cognate words.

"*Baptizo*—To immerse repeatedly into a liquid, to submerge, to soak thoroughly, to saturate.

"*Baptisis* or *Baptismos*, immersion; *Baptisma*, an object immersed; *Baptistes*, one who immerses; *Baptos*, immersed, dyed; *Bapto*, to dip, to plunge into water, etc."

He was astonished. The thought had never occurred to him before, that baptize was not an English, but a Greek word; and that he should look in the *Greek* Lexicon, rather than Webster's Dictionary, to ascertain its real meaning, *as it occurred in the New Testament.* He turned to the title page and preface for some evidence that this was a *Baptist* Lexicon, but learned that it was published under the supervision of some of the Faculty of the Presbyterian Theological Seminary at Princeton, N. J.; the very headquarters of orthodox Presbyterianism.

Here was a new phase of the subject. He could only promise to look into this point more particularly the next day; when, he said, he would procure several different Lexicons, by different authors, and compare them with each other.

"In the meantime," said Theodosia, "there is an idea that strikes my mind very forcibly; and that is, that *the Saviour himself has fixed*, by his own act, *the meaning of the word as he employed it.*"

"How so, Miss Theodosia?"

"Just in this way; suppose we admit that it had a dozen meanings before he used it, and that in other books it has a dozen meanings still, yet it is certain that *he was baptized*. Now, in HIS BAPTISM a certain *act* was performed. It may have been sprinkling, pouring, or dipping; but whatever it was, *that act* was what HE meant by baptism. *That act* was what HE commanded. His disciples *must so have understood it.* He gave (if I may speak so) a Divine sanction to that meaning. And when the word was afterward used in reference to his *ordinance, it could never have any other.* If he was immersed, then the question is decided; baptism is immersion. If he was sprinkled, baptism is sprinkling. If he was poured upon, baptism is pouring. So we need not trouble ourselves about the Lexicons, but can get all our information from the Testament itself."

"There is a great deal of force in that suggestion, Miss Theodosia. It is a pity you could not be a lawyer (And he thought what a partner for a lawyer she would be, and how happy it was for him that he had been able to persuade her to promise to become Mrs. Percy.) But while it is true that we *may* find all the testimony that we need within the record, yet it is important that we get at the *real meaning of the record.* And as that was written in Greek, I see no reason why we should not seek in the Greek for its true sense. If *baptizo* means to dip, and *baptismos* means a dipping, an immersion, we shall be obliged to rest our cause upon some other ground. There must, however, be some mistake about this. I will look into it to-morrow."

"I do not care what the Lexicons say," rejoined Theodosia, "I want to get my instructions entirely out of the word of God. I don't wish to go out of the 'record,' as you lawyers say."

"You are right in that; but how are we to learn the *meaning of the record?* If any document is brought into court, it is a rule of law, founded on common sense, that the words which it contains are to be understood in their most common, every-day sense, according to the usage of the language in which they are written. Now *this* document, the New Testament, it seems, was written in *Greek*, and we are in doubt about the meaning of one of the *words*. We go to the Lexicon, not for any testimony as to the facts of the case, but only to learn the meaning of a very important word used by the witnesses. Matthew and several other witnesses depose that Jesus and others were *baptized*. If they were present in court, we would ask them what they mean by that word, baptize. We would require them to describe, in other language, the *act* which was performed —to tell us whether it was a sprinkling, a pouring, or a dipping. But as we cannot bring them personally into court, we must ascertain what they meant in the best way we can; and that is by a careful examination of the words which they used, and the meaning that would have been attached to them at the time they used them, by the people to whom they were addressed. Now as the documents were written in Greek, of course they used words in the common Greek sense. And we must ascertain their meaning just as we would any other Greek word in any other Greek author; and that is by reference to the lexicons or dictionaries of the Greek language."

" Very well, Mr. Percy; you talk like a judge. But what if you find all the lexicons agree with this? What if they all say that the word means dip, plunge, immerse?"

" Why then, we must either admit that those who are said to have been baptized, were plunged, dipped, immersed, or deny the correctness of the Lexicons."

" But if you deny the correctness of the Lexicons in regard to this word, what confidence can we have in them in regard to other words? Brother Edwin is studying Greek, and as often as he comes to a word which he has not met with before, he finds it in the Lexicon, and so learns its meaning; but if the Lexicons are wrong in this word, they may be wrong in all. Is there no appeal from the authority of the Lexicons?"

" Certainly, we may do in Greek as we do every day in English studies; we appeal from Johnson to Webster, and from Webster to Walker, and from Walker to Worcester. If one does not suit us we may go to another."

" One more question. Are any of these Lexicons *Baptist* books, made for the purpose of teaching *Baptist sentiments?* If so, you know they might be doubtful testimony."

" On the contrary, the Lexicons are made by classical scholars, for the sole purpose of aiding students in the acquisition of the Greek language. I do not suppose any one of them was made with any reference to theological questions, and probably no one of them by a person connected with the Baptist denomination. It is certain most of them were not, and if they *all agree* in regard to this word, it must be conceded that they did not give it a meaning to suit their personal theological views. There are a number of them in the College library, and I will examine them all to-morrow, and tell you the result."

Mr. Percy went back to his office studying the new phase of the question presented in the meaning of the word. "If baptizo in the Greek means to dip, in its primary, common, every-day use, then Jesus Christ was dipped. Then every time the record says a person was baptized, it expressly says he was dipped. I wonder if it can possibly be so. If so, why have our wise and talented preachers never discovered it? or, knowing it, can it be possible that they have *systematically concealed it?*"

Theodosia retired to her chamber, where she spent a few moments in prayer to God for the guidance of the Holy Spirit, and then took her Testament and read how they were baptized of John *in the river of Jordan.* How Jesus, after he was baptized, *came up out of the water.* How they went down both *into the water,* both Philip and the eunuch, and he baptized him, and when they were *come up out of the water,* the Spirit of the Lord caught away Philip. She compared these statements with what she had seen at the river, and did not need any testimony from the *Lexicons* to satisfy her that John's baptism and Philip's baptism was immersion. Why else did they go into the water? Why else was it done in the river? Ministers don't go into the river to sprinkle their subjects now-a-days. There was no reason for doing it then. Must I then unite with this obscure sect and be immersed? Must I break away from the communion that I love so dearly—from all my friends and relatives? Must I part from my dear old pastor, who was, under God, the means of my conversion—who has so often counselled me, prayed with me and for me, wept over me, and cherished me as though I had been his own child? The very thought was terrible. She threw herself on her bed and wept aloud. Her crying brought her mother to her side. She

kneeled beside the bed, took the poor girl's hand in
both of hers, and bade her try to banish this distressing
subject from her thoughts. It was not worth while, she
said, for a young girl like her to set up her own opinions,
or even to entertain doubts in opposition to her minister
and others who had spent their lives in the study of
this very thing. As for herself, if her pastor, Mr. Johnson, said any thing was in the Bible, she always *took it
for granted it was there.* He had more time to look
into these things than she had. It was his business to
do it; and he was better qualified to do it than any of
his people. And of course, if sprinkling was not true
baptism, he would never have practiced it.

"But, mother," sobbed the weeping girl, "I must answer to *God*, and not to pastor Johnson. Much as I love
him, I trust I love my Saviour better; and if my pastor
says *one* thing, and Jesus Christ *another*, Mr. Johnson
himself has often told us to obey God rather than man.
I have no choice; *I must obey my Saviour.*"

"Of course you must, my child; but Mr. Johnson
knows better what the Saviour commands than you do.
He understands all about these questions. And he will
assure you that you have been properly baptized. I
know that he agrees exactly with Dr. Fisher, who baptized you, as you yourself well remember "

"I remember that he sprinkled a little water in my
face, mother; but if that was baptism which I witnessed
to-day, he certainly did not *baptize* me."

"Well, my dear, try and compose yourself, and go to
sleep; and I will send for our pastor to come and see
you to-morrow. He will soon satisfy your mind."

"I hope he may; and I will try to sleep. Good-night
mother."

THE SECOND NIGHT'S STUDY.

———◆———

IN WHICH THEODOSIA IS ASSISTED

BY MR. PERCY, THE PASTOR, AND THE SCHOOL-MASTER.

PRESBYTERIAN AUTHORITIES:

MR. BARNES;
OR, EXPLAINING SCRIPTURE BY SCRIPTURE.

THEODOSIA'S OPINION OF THEOLOGICAL WRITERS

MORE AUTHORITIES:

DR. McKNIGHT, DR. CHALMERS, JOHN CALVIN,
PROF. STEWART, JOHN WESLEY, &c.

PUNCTUAL to his promise, Mr. Percy came in soon after supper on the next evening, and found the Rev. Mr. Johnson, the pastor of their church, already there. He had called early to take a social cup of tea, having learned that Theodosia was "like to go crazy about these new-fangled Baptist notions."

He did not think she looked much like a maniac, however, though there was a deep and saddened seriousness upon her face. Nor did she *act* like a maniac, for never before had she seemed so respectfully affectionate to him and to her mother.

He had not said a word upon the subject of dispute, and seemed reluctant to approach it; but when Mr. Percy came in, it could no longer be postponed.

"I am very glad to meet you here, Mr. Johnson," said the young man. "Miss Theodosia and I had quite a discussion yesterday evening on the subject of baptism. She has taken a fancy that she has never been baptized; and I believe that I nearly exhausted my logic in trying to convince her that she had. I hope your arguments will be more effectual than mine."

"Really, my children, I don't know," said the old man, "what I may be able to do; I have never studied these controversies much; I think it is better to live in peace and let every one enjoy his own conscientious opinion. These discussions are apt to run into disputes and quarrels, and often occasion a great deal of ill

(33)

feeling. I have known them to divide churches, and even families. It is better to avoid them."

"But what are we to do with such lovely heretics as this?" said the young man, with a smile and a sly glance toward her mother. "She must be satisfied that she has been baptized, or you will have her running to the school-house next Sunday to hear that uneducated Baptist preacher, and ten to one, she will ask him to go down into the water and baptize her according to the New Testament model. She says she wants to be baptized as Jesus Christ was, and that was in the river, you know."

"Oh, as to that," rejoined the pastor, "there is no evidence that Jesus Christ was immersed in the river at all. It has been satisfactorily proved that he was sprinkled or poured upon; and it is very certain that sprinkling was practiced by the apostles and early Christians."

"Oh, I am so glad to hear you say that," replied the young lady. "You don't know what a load it has taken off my mind Do tell me *how it is ascertained* that Christ did not go into the river, and *what evidence there is* that he was sprinkled, and it was sprinkling which he commanded. You can't imagine how anxious I am to know."

Well, I don't know that I can call up *all* the evidence just at this time, and we would not have time to go over it, if I could; but you may be assured that there *is such evidence*, and that of the *most satisfactory character*, or else all the learned and talented theological scholars of the various Pedobaptist churches would not have continued, for so many ages, to teach and practice it."

"Certainly, I have no doubt the evidence exists, since you say so; but can't you tell me *what it is*, or show me *where to find it?* I shall never be able to rest in peace till I am convinced that I have been baptized. And if that which I witnessed at the river yesterday was baptism, I am sure I never was."

"Oh, don't be so confident, my daughter. There are more *modes* of baptism than one. That was, perhaps *one* mode (though of that I have some doubt). You were baptized by *another* mode. That *may have been* baptism. Yours *certainly was.*"

"Well, do please prove it to me some way, Mr. Johnson. What you say is something like what Mr. Percy said yesterday. He told me that baptize was a generic term, expressing rather a certain result than any specific act. I think that was the idea, was it not, Mr. Percy?"

"Exactly; and if so, I leave it to Mr. Johnson if the manner of reaching the result is not a matter of indifference."

"Certainly," said the pastor; "'baptism is the application of water as a religious ordinance.' It does not matter about the quantity of water or the mode of applying it."

"Yes; that is what mother said yesterday. And we looked in Webster, and found that such was, indeed, the present English use of the word baptize. But brother says baptize is a Greek word slightly modified, and transferred from the Greek Testament to the English. *It is the New Testament meaning in the time of Christ, and among the people for whom the Gospels were first written*, that we want, not the meaning that it *has acquired* in the English since its transfer to our language."

"You see, pastor, she is going to be hard to satisfy. She pleads her cause like a lawyer."

"No, no, Mr. Percy, I will not be hard to satisfy. I desire, I long, I *pray* to be satisfied. I can never rest

3

till I am satisfied. I only ask for *the evidence.* **You**
said yesterday that *baptizo* was a generic term meaning
to sprinkle, to pour, or to dip; but we found it in the
Lexicon, and it proved to be a specific term, meaning
only to dip. Not a word was there about sprinkling or
pouring. It was simply and only dipping. To-day, Mr.
Johnson tells me about several *modes*—but they are not
modes of dipping. And yet if the Greek word *baptismos,*
baptism, means *dipping,* then they must, in order to be
modes of baptism, be modes of dipping. But, Mr.
Percy, you have not yet told us the result of your
examination of other Lexicons."

" We can make nothing out of them. I am sorry to
say they all agree substantially with the one you have
in the house. If we trust to them we must grant that
the word means primarily and ordinarily to dip, to
plunge, to immerse. Of this there is no doubt."

" Then I am more perplexed than ever. You said
yesterday that in order to know what the act was which
the disciples performed and Christ commanded, we must
ascertain the precise meaning of baptize, as they employed it in the Greek language. You have examined all
the Lexicons (the highest authorities) and find they all
agree in saying it was dip, plunge, immerse. You admitted yesterday that if they should agree in this, the
question was settled. If they said baptize meant to dip,
and *baptismos* a dipping or immersion, then every time
we read that one was baptized, we must understand that
he was immersed. I thought that was a plain, straightforward case. I felt that I could understand it. Well,
now you say you have examined carefully the other
Lexicons, and they all agree with this. No one says
sprinkle, no one says pour—all say dip, and consequently the Gospel says that Jesus was *dipped* of John
in the river of Jordan. But then our pastor says that

he has evidence that Jesus did not enter the river at all, and that he was *sprinkled*, and not dipped. Of course he would not say it unless it was so, but I really don't understand how it can be so."

"I have some curiosity on that point myself," said Mr. Percy, evidently relieved to find that he could (for the moment, at least), take the other side of the question. "I find myself in a very close place. These Lexicons have killed me. I don't know what to say. I suppose, of course, there is some way to get around the difficulty; but I must leave it to our pastor to point it out. For my part, I submit the case."

"Really," said Mr. Johnson, "the question never presented itself to me in just this light before. You must give me a little time to consider about it. And in the meantime let me beg of you both that you will examine some of the standard writers upon the subject. I do not think you have done this yet. What have you in the house?"

"Not a book upon the subject, except it be the Bible, and I don't much care to read any other till we have examined that. If sprinkling is there, it ought to be so plainly taught that I can see it for myself. If I can't find it, I will always doubt if it is there," rejoined the young lady.

"True, my child," said the pastor; "but we often fail to see things at first glance, which are very evident when they have once been pointed out, and our attention fixed upon them. This is the advantage of using proper helps to understand the Scriptures. Those not familiar with the language in which they were written, and with the customs and manners of the people to whom they were originally addressed, will derive great assistance from judicious criticisms. I like, myself, always to read

a commentary on every chapter that I attempt to understand."

"Oh, as to commentaries, we have Barnes' Notes on
the Gospels, and on some of the Epistles. And we
have McKnight's exposition and new translation of the
Epistles. Uncle Jones admires these old volumes of
McKnight's very much, but they always seemed very
dry to me. I love Mr. Barnes, and have studied his
notes in Sunday-school and Bible class all my life."

"Mr. Barnes is a very learned and eminent divine,"
replied the pastor. "His notes have attained a wide
circulation, and won for him an enduring reputation.
You cannot follow a safer guide. Have you examined
him upon the subject?"

"I suppose," said she, "that I have read it a dozen
times, but I never thought any thing particularly about
it, and don't recollect a word."

"Suppose, then, you get his Notes, and let us look at
them a moment before I leave. I can stay but a few
minutes longer."

Edwin had found the volume while they were talking
of it, and now handed it to the pastor.

"I suppose we shall find it here, Matthew iii. 6, as
this is the place where the word baptize first occurs.
Mr. Percy, will you have the kindness to read it aloud
for our common benefit?"

Mr. Percy read: "And were baptized of him in Jordan, confessing their sins." "The word baptize signifies, originally, to *tinge*, to *dye*, to *stain*, as those who
dye clothes. It here means to cleanse or wash any
thing by the application of water. (See note, Mark
vii. 4.)

"Washing or ablution was much in use among the
Jews, as one of the rites of their religion. It was not
customary, however, to *baptize* those who were converted

to the Jewish religion until after the Babylonish captivity.

"At the time of John, and for some time previous, they had been accustomed to administer a rite of *baptism* or washing to those who became proselytes to their religion, that is, who were converted from being Gentiles." * * * " John found this custom in use, and as he was calling the Jews to a new dispensation, to a change in the form of their religion, he administered this rite of *baptism* or washing to signify the cleansing from their sins, and adopting the new dispensation, or the fitness for the pure reign of the Messiah. They applied an old ordinance to a new purpose; as it was used by John it was a significant rite or ceremony, intended to denote the putting away of impurity, and a purpose to be pure in heart and life."

Mr. Percy stopped reading, and looking up at Mr. Johnson, said, "Pardon me, pastor, but if Mr. Barnes were present here as a witness in this case, I would like to ask him a single question by way of a cross-examination. He says that '*Washing* or ablution was much in use among the Jews as one of the rites of their religion,' and yet he tells us that *baptism* was not in use *till after the captivity*. Must not baptism then have been something *new* and different from the washing or ablution?"

"And I," said Theodosia, " would like to ask a question too; perhaps pastor Johnson can answer it as well as Mr. Barnes. He says, when they received a convert from the Gentiles, they *baptized* him; John found this rite in use, and merely applied an old ordinance to a new purpose. Now, I want to know how this ordinance was administered. *What was the act* which they performed upon the proselyte? Did they sprinkle him, or pour upon him, or was he immersed? If this can be ascertained, it will of course determine what it was that

John did when he baptized. Can you tell us, Mr. Johnson, which it was?"

"Yes, my child; it is universally conceded that the Jewish proselyte baptism was immersion. I do not know that this has ever been denied by any writer on either side of this controversy. It is distinctly stated to have been immersion by Dr. Lightfoot, Dr. Adam Clarke, Prof. Stuart, and others who have espoused our cause."

"How then do you get rid of the difficulty? If, as Mr. Barnes says, 'John applied an old ordinance to a new purpose,' and that old ordinance was immersion, it is absolutely certain that John immersed. There is not room for even the shadow of a doubt."

"It would seem to be so, indeed," said the pastor. "I never thought of it just in that light before. But though it is admitted by all that the proselyte baptism was immersion, it is doubted by many whether it existed at all before the time of John. Some think it originated about the time of Christ, and that the Jews practised it in imitation of John's baptism."

"I do not see," rejoined Mr. Percy, "how it can make the slightest difference in the result of the argument, whether it was in use before the time of John, or was borrowed from him. If they immersed *before* the time of John, and he borrowed his rite from them, of course it was immersion that he borrowed. If they immersed *after* the time of John, and borrowed their rite from him, of course John immersed, or they could not have borrowed immersion from him."

"But if John immersed," said Theodosia, "then *Jesus was immersed by John.* This immersion was called his baptism. The disciples saw it, and spake of it as such; and ever afterward, whenever baptism was mentioned, their minds would revert to this act; and so, when Jesus said to them, 'Go and baptize,' they must have understood him to mean, that they should go and repeat on others the rite which they had seen performed on him. And not only so." added the young lady, "but Christ's disciples had themselves been accustomed to practice the same baptism under his own eye. If John immersed, they had not only witnessed his immersion of Jesus, but they had themselves immersed hundreds, if not thousands, under the personal direction of Jesus himself."

"That would certainly settle the question. But where did you make that discovery?" asked Mr. Percy, increduously.

"Oh, it is in the record," she replied. "Here is the testimony, John iii. 22, 23: 'After these things, came Jesus and his disciples into the land of Judea, and there he tarried with them, and baptized. And John also was baptizing in Ænon, near to Salim, because there was much water there; and they came, and were baptized.' And in the next chapter it says that the 'Pharisees heard that Jesus made and baptized more disciples than John.' Now John baptized and Jesus baptized. They both did the same thing; that is as plain as words can make it: as plain as though it said Jesus walked, and John also walked; or Jesus talked, and John also talked. Whatever it was that John did, Jesus was doing the same thing. If John's baptism was immersion, then Jesus and his disciples were immersing, and they immersed more than John."

"That is really," said Mr. Percy, "a complete demonstration. Don't you think so, Mr. Johnson?"

"Well, I must confess it looks so at the first glance. We must look into this matter another time. Let us, for the present, see what Mr. Barnes says further,

Please read on, Mr. Percy; I have not much more time to spare this evening."

Mr. Percy read on:

" The Hebrew word (*tabal*) which is rendered by the [Greek] word baptize, occurs in the Old Testament in the following places:—Lev. iv. 6; xiv. 6, 51; Num. xix. 18; Ruth ij. 14; Ex. xii. 22; Deut. xxxiii. 24; Ezk xxiii. 15; Job ix. 31; Lev. ix. 9; 1 Sam. ix. 27; 2 Kings v. 14; viii. 15; Gen. xxxvii. 31; Joshua iii. 15. It occurs in no other places; and from a careful examination of these passages, its meaning among the Jews is to be derived."

" Oh," said the young lady, " that is what I like; I like to find the meaning in the Scriptures, then I know I can rely upon it. Just wait a minute, Mr. Percy, if you please, till I can get my Bible and hunt out those places, and see how it reads. If it reads sprinkle, then it is all right—sprinkling is baptism; if it reads pour, then pouring is baptism; if it reads dip, then dipping is baptism. We will soon see."

" Let me read a little further, Miss Theodosia, and perhaps you may not think it necessary to examine the texts."

She had, however, got her Bible, and was getting ready to turn to each text in order, when he resumed as follows:

" From these passages, it will be seen that its radical meaning is not to sprinkle or to immerse. *It is to dip.* Commonly for the purpose of sprinkling or for some other purpose."

" What? Do let me see that. Pardon me, pastor, but what does the good man mean? It is not to sprinkle; it is not to immerse; *it is to dip!* Edwin, please get Webster's Dictionary, and tell us the difference between the meaning of dip and immerse."

"Here it is. Immerse is to plunge into a fluid. Dip is to plunge any thing into a fluid, and instantly take it out again."

"Why, Mr. Percy, that just describes the act of baptism which we saw at the river. It was not an immersion, strictly speaking, but a dipping, a plunging beneath the water, and a raising out again. 'It is not to sprinkle or to immerse; it is to dip! Commonly for the purpose of sprinkling, or for some other purpose.'"

"What are you laughing at, brother Edwin?"

"I was only thinking how a preacher would look, dipping a man 'for the purpose of sprinkling' him. But see! there goes my teacher, and I believe he is a Baptist. At any rate he goes to all their meetings. Let me call him in; he can tell us something more about these things."

And before any one could interfere, he had run to the door and hailed Mr. Courtney.

Seeing this, the Rev. Mr. Johnson arose, and reminding the company that he had an engagement at that hour, promised to call again and talk over the matter more, at another day, and took his leave, passing out just as the teacher was coming in.

"Mr. Courtney," said Mr. Percy, "perhaps you can help us a little. We were just looking at Barnes on Baptism."

"I did not know he had ever written on the subject, except some very singular remarks he made in his Notes on the third chapter of Matthew."

"It was those we were examining, and I infer that you do not think very favorably of his argument."

"I think he makes a very strong argument for the Baptists."

"How so?"

"Simply thus: It is an axiom in logic as well as in

mathematics, 'that things which are equal to the same
thing, are equal to one another.'   Now he states a very
remarkable and exceedingly significant fact, when he
he says that the Hebrew word *tabal* is rendered by the
word *baptize*.   It occurs, he says, fifteen times in the
Hebrew Bible.   Now when the Jews translated their
Scriptures into Greek, whenever they came to this word,
they rendered it *baptize;* and when our translators
came to this same word, they rendered it by the English
word *dip*.   It follows, therefore, since dip in English
and baptize in Greek are both equivalent to *tabal* in
Hebrew, they must be equivalent to each other.

"Mr. Barnes says further, that the true way to ascertain the meaning of this word among the Jews, is to examine carefully the fifteen places where it occurs in the
Old Testament.   I see, Miss Ernest, that you have the
Bible in your hand ; suppose you turn to those places,
and let us see how they read.   It will not take more
than a few minutes of our time."

"I had gotten the book for that very purpose, sir.   I
like this way of study, comparing Scripture with Scripture.   I always feel better satisfied with my conclusions
when I have drawn them for myself directly from the
Bible."

"Well, here is the first place, Leviticus iv. 6: 'And
the priest shall *dip* his finger in the blood.'

"The second, Leviticus xiv. 6: 'And shall *dip* them
into the blood of the bird that was killed over running
water.'

"The third, Leviticus xiv. 51: 'And *dip* them in the
blood of the slain bird and in the running water.'

"The fourth, Numbers xix. 18: 'And a clean person
shall take hyssop, and *dip* it into the water.'

"The fifth, Ruth ii. 14: 'And Boaz said unto her at

Theodosia Ernest

PAGE 45.

meal time, come thou hither, and eat of the bread, and *dip* thy morsel in the vinegar.'

" The sixth, Exodus xii. 22 : 'And ye shall take a bunch of hyssop, and *dip* it in the blood.'

" The seventh, Deuteronomy xxxiii. 24 : 'And let him *dip* his foot in oil.'

" The eighth, Ezekiel xxiii. 15 : 'Exceeding in *dyed* attire.'

" The ninth, Job ix. 31 : 'Yet shalt thou *plunge* me in the ditch.'

" The tenth, Leviticus ix. 9 : 'And he *dipped* his finger in the blood.'

" The eleventh, 1 Samuel xiv. 27 : 'And he (Jonathan) put forth the end of the rod that was in his hand, and *dipped* it in the honey comb.'

" The twelfth, 2 Kings viii. 16 : 'And he (Hazael) took a thick cloth, and *dipped* it in the water, and spread it on his face.'

" The thirteenth, Joshua iii. 15 : 'The feet of the priests that bare the ark were *dipped* in the brim of Jordan.'

" The fourteenth, 2 Kings v. 14 : 'And he went down and *dipped* himself seven times in Jordan.'

" The fifteenth, Genesis xxxvii. 31 : 'And they took Joseph's coat, and killed a kid, and *dipped* the coat in the blood.'

" The passage in the 2 Kings v. 14, is very remarkable, since it corresponds precisely in the Septuagint to the text in Matthew. The Septuagint says of Naaman, *Ebaptizato en to Jordane.* Matthew says of the people baptized by John, *Ebaptisonto en to Jordane.* Nobody has ever questioned the correctness of the translation in Kings. He *dipped* himself in Jordan; and had Matthew been translated by the same rule, it must have read, they were *dipped* by John *in Jordan.*

"But I fear this subject may be disagreeable to you. Mr. Barnes, I know, is a most eminent minister of your own denomination, and I ought probably to have avoided speaking thus in your presence."

"Oh, no, sir," said the young lady; "I want to learn the truth, the whole truth, and nothing but the truth, on this subject. I am glad to learn it from any source, and in any way. Perhaps you can assist us further; but let us see what further Mr. Barnes has to say."

Mr. Percy read again:

"In none of these cases can it be shown that the meaning of the word is to *immerse entirely*. But in nearly all the cases the notion of applying the water to a part only of the person or object, though it was by dipping, is necessarily supposed. . . . . It cannot be proved, from an examination of the passages in the Old and New Testaments, that the idea of a complete immersion *ever* was connected with the word, or that it *ever in any case occurred*."

"Stop, Mr. Percy," said the young lady. "Pray stop, and let me think a moment. Can it be possible that a good man, a pious minister of Jesus Christ, could dare to trifle thus with the holy Word of God? Oh, it is wonderful! I cannot understand it! He said just now, that the meaning of the word 'was to dip for the purpose of sprinkling, or for some other purpose.' To dip means to plunge any thing into a fluid, and immediately take it out again. To immerse means merely to plunge the object in the fluid. Whatever is dipped, therefore, is *of necessity* immersed, to the same extent that it is dipped; and yet he says these things which the Word says were dipped, were none of them entirely immersed."

"Do not think too hardly of him," said Mr. Percy. "An advocate who has a bad cause to sustain (I know from experience), is sometimes obliged to resort to just such a jumble, to cover the weak points of his argument."

"Perhaps," said Theodosia, "it might be excusable in a lawyer, though even of that I am doubtful; but that a minister of the holy Word of Jesus should thus stoop to 'darken counsel with words without knowledge,' is something I never conceived of till now."

"When you have become more familiar with the influence which passion and prejudice, and especially early education and church attachments, exert upon the minds of even the wisest and best of men," said Mr. Courtney, "these things will not appear so strange to you. Mr. Barnes doubtless believes that sprinkling is baptism. He was taught so in early life, and has for many years taught others so. To convince him of the contrary, would now be almost or quite impossible, and when any text of Scripture comes in opposition to this opinion, he can hardly help perverting or misunderstanding it. You desired to know the true meaning of the word baptize, as it was used in our Saviour's time among the Jews; and you applied to him for information. He told you very properly that you must go to those places where it occurs in the original of their own Scriptures, and pointed out to you the fifteen places, which he assures you are the only places in which it occurs. He has thus given the matter into your own hands. You turn to the places, one by one, and find that in fourteen out of the fifteen it clearly means to *dip*. That such is the case, he does not deny. He is obliged to grant that 'its radical meaning is to *dip*.' This, now, he has proved from the Scriptures themselves. But this overthrows his sprinkling, so he must get rid of its force. This he undertakes to do—1. By intimating that there is some important difference between dipping and immersion. 'It is not sprinkling nor immersion,' he says; 'it is dipping.' And then he tries to confuse the matter by mixing in the object, 'for the purpose of sprinkling, or for some other purpose,' as though the purpose modified the act performed. The baptism mentioned in these fourteen places was equally dipping, whether it was performed for the purpose of sprinkling, as when the priest dipped the hyssop; or for the purpose of smearing, as when the priest dipped the tip of his finger in oil; or for the purpose of cleansing, as when Naaman dipped himself in Jordan; or for the purpose of pollution, as when Job was plunged in the ditch; or merely for the purpose of wetting, as when Ruth dipped her morsel, or Hazael his thick cloth. The wetting, the defiling, the cleansing, the smearing, were not the baptism; they were not the dipping, but a consequence of it. The sprinkling was not the baptism, the dipping, but a subsequent and altogether a different act. Then to make 'confusion worse confounded,' he intimates some vast distinction between entire immersion and dipping. These things, said to be baptized in these fourteen places, he can't deny were dipped; but 'none of them,' he says, 'were entirely immersed.' But the extent of the immersion does not affect the meaning of the word. The word immersed expressed only the act of plunging the object into the fluid. The word dip expressed this act, and the additional one of taking it out again; and this, he said and proved, was the Scriptural meaning of baptize. As far, then, as they were baptized, they were dipped; and as far as they were dipped, they were immersed. We learn the extent of the dipping from other words, not from this one. If Naaman is said to have dipped himself, or Hazael the cloth, there is not the slightest reason to doubt that the whole person and the whole cloth were immersed. If Jonathan dipped the end of his staff, why the end only was immersed. It was immersed, however, just as much as it was dipped or baptized."

"But," said Mr. Percy, "what will you do with the hyssop, and the living bird, etc., that were to be baptized into the blood of the slain bird, and where Mr. Barnes says it is clearly impossible that they all should be immersed in the blood of the single bird."

"I simply say that they could be immersed in it as easily as they could be dipped in it. If you will turn to Leviticus xiv. 6, you will see that the blood of the slain bird was to be caught over running water; and as it rested on, or mixed with the water, these things could all be entirely immersed, if need be. You will remember, however, that in common language the whole of a thing is often mentioned when a part is only meant. I say, for instance, that I dipped my pen in ink, and wrote a line; you do not understand that I dipped more than the point—enough to take up the ink to write. If I tell you that I dipped my hair brush in water, and smoothed my hair, you do not understand that I dipped it in, handle and all, but only the bristles. So only enough of the cedar wood, and hyssop, and scarlet, etc., may have been dipped to take up enough to sprinkle with; but as much as they were baptized, so much were they dipped; and so far as they were dipped, just so far were they immersed. But it does not make any difference to Mr. Barnes or his sprinkling brethren, whether the dipping was partial or complete; for they do not dip their subjects of baptism at all, in whole or in part, for the purpose of sprinkling, or for any other purpose; and, therefore, if the Scriptural meaning of the word baptize is to dip, as Mr. Barnes has so clearly proved by Scripture itself, then they do not baptize at all.

"Oh, yes, I see now how it was," said Theodosia, "when Dr. Fisher performed this ceremony upon me.

He baptized his own hand; for he dipped that in the bowl, but he only sprinkled me; and therefore, according to the showing of Mr. Barnes himself, I have never been baptized."

"Do not put down the book yet," said Mr. Courtney. "Just turn to Matthew xx. 22, and you will find that Mr. Barnes has no more difficulty than the greatest Baptist in the land, in understanding the word baptism to signify not only immersion, but *complete* immersion, whenever it does not refer to the ordinance.

"'The baptism that I am baptized with.' On this Mr. B. remarks as follows: 'Are ye able to suffer with me the trials and pains which shall come upon you in endeavoring to build up my kingdom? Are ye able to be plunged deep in afflictions? to have sorrows cover you like water, and to be sunk beneath calamities as floods, in the work of religion? Afflictions are often expressed by being sunk in the floods and plunged in the deep waters.' (Ps. lix. 2; Isa. xliii. 2; Ps. cxxiv. 4, 5; Sam. iii. 54.)

"You see Mr. Barnes has no more difficulty than the translators of the Old Testament, in giving the word its true meaning—to dip, to plunge, to sink beneath the waters, etc., when it does not refer to the ordinance; but when it does, all is confusion and mystery."

"I begin to think," said Theodosia, "that theological writers are not to be relied upon at all. And I feel more than ever inclined to trust to the Bible alone, and study it for myself. When such a man as Mr. Barnes can be so far blinded by education and prejudice as to come so near the truth and not see it—to point out the way toward it so plainly, and yet refuse to walk in it, and endeavor to hide it from others by such a strange medley of words, I have no further use for any book on the subject but the word of God. I will study that; and it shall be my only guide. If I find that Jesus was sprinkled in Jordan, I will be content. If I find that he was poured upon, I must be poured upon. If I find that he was dipped, then I must be dipped."

"Oh, no, Miss Theodosia; you are decidedly too hasty. I have often found in court, that a witness whom I expected to testify in my favor, and who evidently desired and intended to do so, has nevertheless, on a cross-examination, given such testimony as was altogether favorable to the opposite party. But I did not abandon my client, and give up my suit. I sought for other witnesses. Our information on this subject is, as yet, very limited. There are other sources of evidence; let us examine them. Something may yet turn up to change your opinion of theological writers. Did you not say you had McKnight on the Epistles in the house?"

"Yes; and uncle Jones, who you know is one of the Elders in our church, says it is one of the best, if not the very best of commentaries."

"Well, let us see what he says. How will we find the place?"

"Take a concordance," suggested Edwin, "and look at every place where the word baptize occurs."

"That is a first-rate idea. Well, here is the first place. Romans vi. 4. Buried with Christ by baptism. In the note he says: 'Christ's baptism was not the baptism of repentance, for he never committed any sin. But he submitted to be baptized—that is, to be buried under the water by John, and to be raised out again—as an emblem of his future death and resurrection. In like manner, the baptism of believers is emblematical of their own death, burial, and resurrection; perhaps, also, it is a commemoration of Christ's baptism.'"

4

"Stop, Mr. Percy, are you sure you are not reading falsely?"

"Yes, I am perfectly certain. Here is the book, you can see for yourself."

"No; but I thought you must be playing some trick on me. At any rate, McKnight must have been a Baptist. No one who believed in, and practiced sprinkling, could have written in that way."

"Perhaps he was a Baptist. Let us look at the title page and preface, and see who and what he was. It appears from this, that James McKnight, D.D., was born Sept. 17, 1721. Licensed to preach by the Presbytery of Irwine of the Scotch Presbyterian church. Ordained at Maybole in 1753. Chosen Moderator of the General Assembly of the Presbyterian church in 1769, which position he held for more than twenty years. This brief history of his life, prefixed to the first volume of his Notes, informs us further, that he spent near thirty years of his life in preparing these Notes, and 'that the whole manuscript was written over and over, by his own hand, no less than five times.' They were therefore the deliberate and carefully expressed opinions of a most eminent and very learned Presbyterian Doctor of Divinity, and presiding officer of the Presbyterian church in the country where he lived. Of course he cannot be suspected of any bias toward the obscure and despised sect called the Baptists."

"Well, read on then. Theologians are mysterious men."

"That is all he says on this verse. But here is verse 5th. 'Planted together,' etc.

"The burying of Christ and of believers, first in the water of baptism, and afterward in the earth, is fitly enough compared to the planting of seeds in the earth because the effect in both cases is a reviviscence to a state of greater perfection.' "

" Surely, he must consider baptism to be a burial in water. But perhaps he thinks there were several baptisms, and that dipping was one form or mode, while sprinkling was another."

" No, for here is his note on Ephesians iv. 5. One Lord, one Faith, one Baptism

" ' Ye all,' says he, ' serve one Lord, and all have the same object of faith, and have all professed that faith by the same form of baptism.' "

" Has he any thing else on the subject?"

" Yes, here, on 1 Cor. x. 2, 'And were all baptized unto Moses in the cloud and in the sea.'

" ' Because the Israelites, by being hidden from the Egyptians under the cloud, and by passing through the Red Sea, were made to declare their belief in the Lord and his servant Moses, the Apostle very properly represents them as baptized unto Moses in the cloud and in the sea.'

" And here again—1 Cor. xv. 29—' Else what shall they do who are baptized for the dead.'

" ' Otherwise what shall they do to repair their loss who are immersed in sufferings for the resurrection of the dead.'

" And here again — Heb. ix. 10 — ' Divers washings (*Baptismos*).'

" ' With nothing but meats, and drinks, and divers *immersions*, and ordinances respecting the body.'

" One more place, and we have all that he says upon the subject.

" 1 Peter iii. 21, ' The like figure whereunto baptism doth now save us, etc.'

" The water of baptism is here called the anti-type

of the water of the flood, because the flood was a type
or emblem of baptism in three particulars :

"1. 'As by building an ark and entering into it, Noah
showed strong faith in the promise of God, concerning
his preservation, by the very water which was to destroy
the Antediluvians for their sins. So by giving ourselves
to be buried in the water of baptism, we show a like
faith in God's promise, that though we die and are
buried, he will save us from death and the punishment
of sin, by raising us up from the dead at the last day.'

"2. 'As the preserving of Noah alive during the nine
months of the flood, is an emblem of the preservation
of the souls of believers while in the state of the dead,
so the preserving believers alive while buried in the
water of baptism, is a prefiguration of the same event.'

"3. 'As the water of the deluge destroyed the wicked,
but preserved Noah by bearing up the ark, in which he
was shut up, till the waters were assuaged, and he went
out to live again upon the earth ; so baptism may be
said to destroy [or represent the destruction of] the
wicked, and to save the righteous, as it prefigures both
these events. The death of the wicked it prefigures by
the burial of the baptized person in the water, and the
salvation of the righteous by the raising of the baptized person out of the water.' "

"Well, Mr. Percy," said Theodosia, "what do you
make of this witness? Do you wish to cross-examine
him, or ask him any further questions?"

"Yes, I would like to ask the Rev. Dr. McKnight if
he practiced sprinkling for baptism ; and if he did, upon
what grounds he could sustain a practice so different
from his own exposition of the teachings of the Scripture."

"As Dr. McKnight has not answered in his writings,
and is not present in person, it may be satisfactory,"

suggested Mr. Courtney, " to inquire of some other rep-
resentative of the same church establishment. If you
have Dr. Chalmers' Lectures on Romans, you will find
the question answered."

" Yes, sister, don't you know mother bought Chalmers' Lectures only the other day? I will go and get
the book," said Edwin.

"Ah, here it is—page 152; Romans vi. 4-7. 'The
original meaning of the *word baptism, is immersion;*
and, though we regard it as a point of indifferency
whether the ordinance so named be performed in this
way or by sprinkling, yet we doubt not that the prevalent style of the administration, in the apostle's days,
was by the actual submerging of the whole body under
water. We advert to this for the purpose of throwing
light on the analogy which is instituted in these verses.
Jesus Christ, by death, underwent this sort of baptism,
even immersion under the surface of the ground, whence
he soon emerged again by his resurrection. We, by
being baptized into his death, are conceived to have
made a similar translation—in the act of descending
under the water of baptism, to have resigned an old
life; and in the act of ascending, to emerge into a second
or new life.' Here we have a distinct avowal of the
well-established fact that the meaning of the word baptism is immersion, and that the practice of the Apostolic church was conformable to this truth. But in the
very face of it we have the candid declaration 'that we
(Presbyterians) regard it as a matter of indifferency
whether the ordinance so named be performed in this
way or by sprinkling.' "

" But, Mr. Courtney, how can it be a matter of 'indifferency?' If the word means immersion, then immersion was what Christ commanded—then the 'ordinance so-called' is 'immersion.' How can immersion be

performed by sprinkling? Really, these theologians are a strange, mysterious people. I cannot comprehend them. Christ commands me to be baptized—baptism means immersion—then, of course, if he meant any thing, he meant immersion. But these great and good men tell me it is a matter of 'indifferency' whether I do what he commanded, or something else altogether different from it."

"Pardon me, Miss Theodosia; it is only when the theologians are in error, and blinded by their educational prejudices, or attachment to their church forms and dogmas, that they are so unreasonable and so mysterious."

"Yet I have been accustomed to think they could hardly be in error at all. I have taken it for granted, until yesterday, that what the ministers of our church said about the teachings of the word of God, was all true, as a matter of course. I can hardly believe now that it is not so. I can't understand how those, who are so wise, so learned, so pious, so anxious to know the truth, and who spend all their time in learning and teaching it, can be wrong; or how a simple girl like me, may differ from them and yet be right. I am afraid to take a single step in opposition to my pastor's teaching, though I see clearly (as I think) that I shall step upon the rock of God's unfailing truth! How can it be, that such good men talk one way and act another? How do they try to justify their 'indifferency' to the commands of Christ? They give some reason, do they not?"

"I think most of them don't trouble themselves on the subject: they think little, and care little about it— not deeming it essential to salvation. When they do think or read upon the subject, it is in order to quiet their minds, or reply to an opponent. They have the practice of their church, received by tradition; they take it for granted it is right. They are where you were a day or two since, when you took it for granted that the ministers of your denomination could not be wrong. They don't think *their church* can be wrong; and they twist, pervert, and torture the Scriptures, as you have seen Mr. Barnes do, or openly set aside their teachings as a matter of 'indifferency,' as we have seen Dr. Chalmers do, in order to continue *the usage of the church.*"

"But," asked Theodosia, "does not Dr. Chalmers stand alone upon this point of 'indifferency?' It surely is not common for the ministers of our church (who in learning and piety I have always thought had no superiors in the world) to speak of literal obedience to Christ's commandments as a matter of no consequence. To me it seems to border upon absolute impiety, almost upon sacrilege. I am in a maze of astonishment."

"If you will continue your investigations for a little time, you will cease to be astonished at almost any sort of assertions made by the advocates of sprinkling," said Mr. Courtney. "You will, for instance, find them admitting, in one sentence, that immersion was submitted to by Christ, and practiced by the Apostles; and in another, holding it up to the reprobation and abhorrence of every Christian as an indecent and abominable rite. But, in regard to your question. Dr. Chalmers, so far from standing alone, simply echoes the sentiments of Calvin, the founder of your church, and others of its most eminent supporters. 'It is of no consequence at all,' says Calvin, as quoted by Prof. Stuart, 'whether the baptized person is totally immersed, or whether he is merely sprinkled by an affusion of water. This should be a matter of choice to the churches in different regions, although the word baptize signifies to immerse, and the rite of immersion was practiced by the ancient church.' 'To this opinion,' says Prof. Stuart, 'I do most fully and heartily subscribe.'"

"Well, I declare! these Presbyterian Doctors of Divinity are the most mysterious of people to me. They freely admit that the meaning of the word is to immerse, or to dip, and that immersion was practiced by the first churches—(and of course, if such is the meaning of the word, it must have been practiced by the first churches, as they could not misunderstand the commandment). Yet they tell us that it is of 'no consequence at all' whether we obey the commandment or not. Do the other denominations opposed to the Baptist occupy the same position?"

"I cannot answer for all," said Mr. Courtney; "I can for some. I have here a transcript of some of the writings of Mr. John Wesley, who was the founder of the Methodists, the most numerous of the Pedobaptist sects in this country. He says, in his notes on Romans vi. 4—'The allusion is to the ancient manner of baptizing, by immersion.' And he relates in his journal, vol. 3, page 20, 'that Mary Welch, aged eleven days, was baptized according to the custom of the first church, and the rule of the church of England, by immersion.'

"On page 24 of the same volume, he says—'I was asked to baptize a child of Mr. Parker's, second bailiff of Savannah; but Mrs. Parker told me, neither Mr. P. nor I will consent to its being dipped. I answered, if you certify that the child is weakly, it will suffice (the Rubric says) to pour water on it. She replied nay, the child is not weak, but I am resolved it shall not be dipped. This argument I could not confute, so I went home, and the child was baptized by another.'"

"It would seem, then," said Theodosia, "that Mr. Wesley conformed his practice to his belief. He believed that baptism was immersion, and refused to baptize at all unless he could do it according to the word of God. I honor the man for his consistency."

"Still," said Mr. Percy, "it does not seem that he was influenced by the word of God, but by the 'Rubric.' The word of God makes no exception in favor of those who may be certified to 'be weak,' but yet on the authority of 'the Rubric,' or formula of the church of England, Mr. Wesley was perfectly ready to dispense with the dipping, and employ pouring, if the parents *would only certify.*"

"Moreover," added Mr. Courtney, "it seems, from his conduct afterward, that he felt as much at liberty himself to change the ordinance of Christ, as the makers of the Rubric had done; for when he organized his societies, and gave them 'the Discipline' as their organic law, he directed baptism to be performed by sprinkling or pouring, if the parties preferred it.

"And though Mr. Wesley once refused to baptize a person at all unless he could do it by dipping, 'according to the custom of the first church,' or under a certificate of weakness, his followers, by his direction and by authority of his Discipline, employ sprinkling almost exclusively, and call immersion a vulgar and indecent practice; although they will sometimes perform it to satisfy a weak conscience, rather than lose a member.

"Martin Luther, the great reformer and founder of the Lutheran church, evidently entertained the same opinion with the other noted Pedobaptists we have been speaking of. After speaking of baptism as a symbol of death and resurrection, he says, 'On this account I could wish that such as are to be baptized, should be completely immersed into the water, according to the meaning of the word and the signification of the ordinance, as also, without doubt, it was instituted by Christ.' Yet Luther is the father of a sprinkling church—the

Lutheran; and whether he did so or not, it is evident that his followers, like Drs. Chalmers and Calvin, regard it as a 'point of indifferency.'"

"That is sufficient, Mr. Courtney," replied the young lady; "I merely wish to know if the other denominations were guilty of the same inconsistency with our own."

After a little further conversation, Mr. Percy and Mr Courtney took their leave.

Mrs. Ernest, the mother, had, during the time of this interview, been sitting quietly in a corner, very busily engaged in hemming some ruffles. She took no part in the discussion, but as soon as the gentlemen were gone, she turned to Theodosia, and said—

"My dear child, I am perfectly astonished at your behaviour this evening."

"Why, mother," said the young lady, in amazement, "what have I done? I am not conscious of any impropriety."

"Do you think, then, that it is perfectly proper and becoming in you to talk as you did this evening about the good and eminent clergymen of our church? It made my flesh quake and my heart burn to hear that impertinent little Baptist pedagogue accuse such a man as Dr. Albert Barnes of perverting the scriptures and mystifying the truth. I wonder if he thinks a learned and pious Presbyterian minister, like Mr. Barnes, is more likely to be 'blinded by prejudice and passion' than an ignorant Baptist schoolmaster. You thought I was not listening; but, though I did not take any part in your conversation, I assure you I heard every word of it, and if. it had not been for the presence of Mr. Percy, I do believe I would have been tempted to order the fellow out of my house. How could you be so destitute of every particle of self-respect, and of all regard for your

own church—the church of your mother and your grand
parents, in which you was born and raised, as to permit
a man to talk in that way in your presence? I declare
I was perfectly ashamed of you! If that Mr. Courtney
ever shows his face in my house again, I do think I shall
insult him."

"Mother, what was it that Mr. Courtney said that
was so unbecoming and offensive? I am sure he seemed
to me only as one anxious to get at the truth."

"Why! did he not say that our preachers perverted
the Scripture? Did not he say that they set aside the
commandments of Christ as matters of ' indifferency?'
I wonder if he thinks he knows more about the Scriptures than Dr. Chalmers or Mr Barnes, or even the
weakest preacher in our church? I always heard that
the Baptists were an ignorant, bigoted, and intolerant
sect, and I believe it now more than ever. Just to think
that—"

"But, mother, please let me say one word. Mr.
Courtney did, indeed, intimate that Mr. Barnes had
mystified and perverted the Scripture, but did he not
prove it before he said it? It was Mr. Percy who read
in Mr. Barnes' notes that we must look in the Old Testament at those fifteen places, to learn the meaning of
the word baptize. We looked, and found that in fourteen of the fifteen, the action was dipping, and in none
of them sprinkling or pouring. It was Mr. Percy
who read that 'the meaning of the word is not to
sprinkle or to immerse, but it is to dip for the purpose
of sprinkling, or for some other purpose.' It was Mr.
Percy who read in Dr. Chalmers that 'we (Presbyterians) consider it a point of indifferency' whether the
ordinance of Christ is performed as he commanded, or
in some other way. Now, if Mr. Barnes does prove that
the word means ' to dip,' for the purpose of sprinkling,

or for some other purpose,' and yet tells us that it can be done by pouring, does he not mystify the subject by a strange medley of words? Was it so very wrong in Mr. Courtney to point out these self-evident prevarications of Mr Barnes, or the openly avowed disregard to the commandment of Jesus Christ and the practice of the Apostolic churches in Dr. Chalmers?

"If Presbyterians are guilty of such inconsistency, I am sorry for it, and ashamed of it, but I can't help seeing it when my attention is directed to it; and I really do not see how it could have been becoming in me to get angry with those who were so kind as to point it out to me. On this subject I feel that I would be willing to learn the truth even from an infidel or an idiot, if they could aid me."

"It is the part of a true friend," said the mother, "to hide a friend's infirmities, not to divulge and glory in them. And even if our ministers have done and said some thoughtless and silly things, it is not for a Presbyterian like you, to speak of them, or permit others to speak of them so contemptuously, in your presence. If you have no spirit of resentment, I'll let you know that I have, and Mr. Courtney too, if he comes here with any more of his Baptist abuse of our pious and learned ministers."

"But, mother, if our ministers are wrong (as being human they surely may be) how can it be wrong to point out their errors, and guard inquirers after truth from falling into them?"

"I don't say," replied the mother, "that it is wrong to point out any trifling errors, which they may have inadvertently taught; provided it were done in a mild, gentlemanly, courteous, and Christian manner. But is it kind, is it courteous, is it Christian-like, to accuse a great and good man like Mr. Barnes, of torturing, per-

verting, and mystifying the Word of God, to sustain
some church dogma or church practice? Do you call
that gentlemanly?"

"My dear mother, please don't be so angry with me; I
really can't see why we should not call things by their real
names. And I must confess that so far as I can understand the meaning of the words, Mr. Barnes does, on
this subject, mystify and pervert the language of Scripture, and Dr. Chalmers does clearly intimate that it is
no matter whether we do what Christ commanded in
this ordinance, or something else—which he did not
command. And I begin to fear that others on our
side of this controversy are in the same predicament.
Whether those on the other side are not equally inconsistent, I have yet to learn."

"Well, my child, I don't know what to do with you.
You have no more respect for the opinions of the learned
and excellent ministers of our church, than for those of
the most ignorant people."

"I am determined, mother, that I shall never trust
any more to the mere assertions of any man, or set of
men, except those holy men who spake as they were
moved by the Holy Ghost. Whatever I can find for
myself clearly put down in The Book, that I will believe.
Henceforth, the Bible is my only guide, and I will myself judge of its meaning for myself."

"But, my child, do you, can you, think that you are
as competent to judge of the true interpretation of the
Word as the great and good men who have given all
their lives to its study?"

"No, mother; but how if these great and good men
disagree? Must I turn Catholic, and so secure an
infallible priest? If I don't do this, I must maintain
my right to my own private judgment. I am accountable only to God; I will be guided only by his Word. I

thought you and pastor Johnson would have encouraged and assisted me in the investigation of this or any other question connected with my religious faith and practice. I know that he has always told us to examine the Scripture for ourselves—and 'each to be fully persuaded in his own mind.' "

" Certainly, my child ; but then we thought that your investigations would tend to confirm rather than shake your faith in our doctrines; but you seem to be losing confidence rather than increasing it. These studies seem only to disturb and unsettle your mind; and I fear, if you continue them, they will end in your separation from us all. How, then, can I help desiring that you should leave off these distressing investigations? Till you do so, I can hardly feel that you are my own dear Theodosia. You begin almost to feel like a stranger to me now. I declare, I believe you will break my heart." And, overcome by her maternal feelings, she burst into a flood of tears, in which the daughter freely joined.

THE THIRD NIGHT'S STUDY.

WHICH CONTAINS

THE TESTIMONY OF THE PASTOR'S WITNESSES,

TO PROVE THAT

JOHN DID NOT IMMERSE AT ALL,

AND THAT

CHRIST DID NOT GO DOWN INTO THE WATER,

BUT

WAS BAPTIZED BY SPRINKLING

ON THE BANK OF THE RIVER.

THIRD NIGHT'S STUDY.

THE Rev. Mr. Johnson had been the pastor of a large and wealthy congregation for more than twenty years. Most of the young people of his charge had grown up under his pastoral supervision, and old and young had been accustomed to regard his word as Gospel truth; and when Miss Ernest ventured to suggest that she had never been baptized, and asked him for the proof, it was probably the first time that one of the "baptized children of his church" had ever expressed in his presence any serious doubt of the full authority of his bare and unsupported word.

After the brief visit at Mrs. Ernest's which we have recorded, he went to his study and commenced the preparation of a sermon, which he hoped and intended should prevent any others of his congregation from any attempt to investigate this subject for themselves.

He did not propose in this discourse to mention the Baptists by name, or to make any attempt to refute, or even to denounce their opinions or practices. (To do so might direct attention to them, whereas he desired to divert it from them.) But he determined to describe, and denounce as degenerate and vile apostates, all those who, reckless of the obligations which had been placed upon them in early infancy, and all the thousand nameless ties which had, in childhood and youth, bound them to the church in which they had been born, and solemnly dedicated to God in baptism, in whose doctrines they had been instructed by parental lips, and into whose

5

communion they had been received by a public profession of their faith, and who should, after all, be induced by some new coming proselyter to abandon the faith of their fathers, and the communion of their own church, and break off like wandering stars, to be lost in the darkness of anti-Presbyterian errors

This course, he was confident, would be more effectual in preserving the peace and unity of his church, and the dignity of its pastor, than any attempt to reason about the doctrines of this obscure sect of Baptists, who had so suddenly begun to attract attention in his village. He would overwhelm the doubters and inquirers with such a storm of public indignation, that hereafter no one would dare to doubt; but in the meantime it was necessary, privately, to satisfy such doubts as had already been expressed.

When, therefore, he had arranged the heads of his discourse, he repaired to his book-case, and took down such authorities as would refresh his memory on the subject of baptism—especially in regard to the points of difficulty suggested by Theodosia and Mr. Percy. The examination of these occupied the time till in the night, and was resumed again the next morning.

Very early the next evening, having his mind fully charged with all the "*strong reasons*" upon which Pedo-baptist's are accustomed to rest their cause, he called on Mrs. Ernest and her daughter again.

"Well, madam," said he, "how has our conversation the other evening affected your daughter? I trust she has ceased to be so much distressed about these new notions as she was."

"Indeed, Mr. Johnson, she gets worse and worse, and I begin to think Mr. Percy is going the same way. I am so sorry Edwin called in that little Baptist school-master. It made my heart burn to hear them talk as they did about the good and pious ministers of our church. It seemed to me they had no more respect for a minister of the Gospel, or even a Doctor of Divinity, than they had for a house carpenter, or a French dancing-master."

"How so, Mrs Ernest? I am sure your daughter has been too well raised to speak disrespectfully of any minister of the Gospel, or permit another to do it in her presence."

"That is just what I told her. I said I was ashamed of her, and——"

"But pray tell me, madam, what has happened? What was said that was so improper?"

"Why, only to think that that little impertinent Baptist pedagogue had the impudence to say, sir, here in my house, that our ministers perverted the Scriptures, deluded their hearers, set aside the ordinances of Christ, and substituted others in their place, and I don't know what all. I was so angry I could hardly see."

"Is it possible! and your daughter heard all of this?"

"Yes, sir; and the worst of it is, I do fear, sir, she more than half believes it. You can't think how changed she is, sir! I never knew her to have a particle of self-will before. She was always so gentle and affectionate, and ready to yield every thing to any body; but on this subject she is very stubborn, and declares she won't believe a single thing but what she can see in the Bible for herself, even though she had it from your own lips, and all the rest of the preachers in our church.

"Oh, sir," she continued, sobbing (for her maternal feelings had begun to overcome her), "if you don't do something for her she will be lost to us all! Do try to show her *where that sprinkling is in the Bible.* If she can see it *there,* she will believe it."

Mr. Johnson was fully resolved to make her see the

sprinkling, if he could; but was not quite certain as to the *place* where he would find it; and before he had time to reflect much upon the subject, the young lady came into the parlor.

She seemed for the moment slightly embarassed, evidently from the conviction that she had been the object of remark, but greeted her pastor cordially and respectfully. It seemed to him, though she was paler than before, that she had grown more beautiful in the last few days. The unusual mental activity, the excitement of a new object of investigation, and the calm, yet firm and solemn determination to learn and to *do* her whole duty, had imparted to her eye a new and intenser light, and to her countenance a strange, unwonted brightness, as though the spirit, stirred to its inmost depths by these new impulses, and burning with celestial fire, shone through its covering of flesh, and illuminated her face with almost more than mortal radiance.

Could it be possible, he asked himself, that this lovely young creature could speak irreverently of sacred things?

Alas! how much her mother and himself had misapprehended the nature of her feelings. Never in her life had sacred things appeared to her so sacred. It was because those great and good men, whom she had been accustomed from her infancy to look upon with reverence, now seemed to her, themselves, to trifle with sacred things, that she could no longer regard them as she had done. The Word of God; the commandments of Jesus Christ; the ordinances of the Gospel; these were sacred things. Never so fearfully sacred as now. And what could she think of those, who, ministering at the altar of God, perverted and mystified his Word, to hide the truth from those who sought for knowledge? What could she think of those who counted the command-

ments of Christ, and the ordinances which he had instituted, a "*matter of indifferency?*" She had, indeed, in
some degree, ceased to reverence the (so-called) ministers of Christ, who could be so false to their sacred
obligations as to trifle with God's holy Word, in order
to sustain a creed or a custom of their church; but oh!
how deep, how ardent, how unutterable was her reverence for the Word itself! How anxious, how agonizing
her desire to know what it required her to believe and
to perform.

It may be that the pastor had some suspicion of the
true state of her mind in this respect, for when he addressed her, it was with an expression of unusual and
most respectful consideration. He felt instinctively that
she was not now to be rated like a school-girl, or convinced by unsustained assertions.

Indeed, he felt a strange restraint in the presence of
the earnest-hearted, strong-minded girl; and was revolving in his mind how he could best introduce the
subject which he came to talk of, when she relieved him
by introducing it herself.

"You did not have time the other evening," said she,
"to finish your remarks on the subject of baptism. You
told me, you will recollect, that there was good and
sufficient evidence to show that our Saviour was not
baptized in the river at all, and that he was baptized by
sprinkling, and, of course, if this was so, sprinkling is
the Christian baptism."

"You state the case a little too strongly, my daughter; I meant to say only that there is no evidence that
he was baptized in the river; and that the baptism which
he commanded (the baptism of the Gospel dispensation)
was performed by sprinkling."

"Please, Mr. Johnson, don't try to mystify me. Do
you mean to say that the baptism which Christ sub-

mitted to, and the baptism which he commanded, were two different things, and that one was immersion, and the other sprinkling?"

"Not exactly, my daughter; I only meant to say they might be different. John's baptism was not Christian baptism. It was the baptism of repentance, designed to introduce Christianity. It prepared the way for the Gospel, but was itself no part of the Gospel dispensation."

"And yet, Mr. Johnson, Mark says it was 'the beginning of the Gospel of Jesus Christ.' But it does not make any difference to me whether it was Christian baptism or not. I simply want to know about the act performed. John did something, which is called baptism. Multitudes came to him, and were baptized by him in the river of Jordan. Jesus also came to him, and was baptized in the river of Jordan. Then Jesus went himself into Judea, and there he tarried and baptized; and at the same time John also was baptizing in Ænon, near Salim; and Jesus baptized more than John baptized. These baptisms were confined to the Jews; but after his death, Jesus told the disciples to go and preach his Gospel to all *other* nations, and baptize them; and we learn from the Acts that they who gladly received the Word were baptized, both Jews and Gentiles.

"Now, what I want to know is this: when John baptized, he performed a certain act. When Jesus and his disciples baptized, did they not perform the same act? and when he commanded to baptize the Gentiles also, did he not command the same act to be performed, and did not the disciples perform the same act, in obedience to that command? The same word is used, does it not mean the same thing?"

"If it does, my child, it must mean something else

besides immersion, for in many of these cases of baptism, immersion was out of the question. In fact, it is very certain that John did not immerse those whom he baptized; though if he had, it would not follow that Christ commanded immersion. John may have done one thing, and Christ may have commanded something else."

"Very true, Mr. Johnson; he may have done it, but where is the proof that he did? My name might have been Susan, but then I would not have been called Theodosia. If he had meant another act, he would have used a different word."

"Not if the word might mean either one or the other. You know that we contend that the word baptize means to sprinkle, to pour, to wet, to wash,* as truly as it means to dip or to immerse."

"Well, Mr. Johnson, even supposing it does have all these meanings, the disciples must have understood the Saviour to use it (when speaking in reference to his ordinance) in some one of them, and that one would be fixed by his own example. What he received as baptism from John in Jordan, they would ever after consider to be baptism; and would necessarily suppose he meant that act when he used the word, even though it had a hundred meanings. But if you will pardon me for being so troublesome, I would like to know what proof there is that baptize in the Greek language has all these various meanings? We looked into a Greek Lexicon the other day to find the meaning of the word, and we could not find any thing at all about sprinkling or pouring among the definitions there."

"*You* looked in a Greek Lexicon. You can't read Greek, can you?"

---

* See Dr. Miller.

"No, sir; but brother Edwin is studying the language, and he found the word, and I could read the definition."

"And so you think you and Edwin are competent critics of a disputed point in the Greek language?"

"Oh, no! Mr. Johnson, don't laugh at me. If you knew how anxious I am to learn the truth, I am sure you would sympathize with me and assist me. We did not think we knew any thing about it, and that is the reason that we went to the Lexicon to learn. It is not Edward's opinion that I referred to, but that of the learned Prof. Donegan. And Mr. Percy has since examined quite a number of other Greek scholars upon the same subject, and he has not found that any one of them gives sprinkling as one of the meanings of baptize, though all agree in dipping."

"And so you, and Edwin, and Mr. Percy set yourselves up to teach such men as Dr. Miller and other learned theological writers of our church, the meaning of the Greek language! Don't you intend presently to write a commentary on the Scriptures? or a book of Practical Divinity? Edited jointly by Miss Ernest and Mr. Percy!"

The young lady looked at her pastor in astonishment. She blushed deeply; tears filled her eyes, and her utterance was choked. She had expected sympathy and assistance; she met with ridicule and rebuke. Poor girl, she did not know how hard it is for one who has long been accustomed to rule other minds, and have his bare assertion received as unquestionable truth, to be called on for *proof*. If he said baptize meant to sprinkle, what right had she, poor, simple girl, to doubt his word or ask for evidence? Why, even he, a minister of the Gospel, had never asked for proof when Dr. Miller said it. He had always taken it for granted that baptism was sprinkling, or such men as Dr. Miller would not have asserted that it was; nor would the church have enjoined or permitted it.

There was an awkward pause in the conversation, for Theodosia was too deeply mortified and embarrassed to know how to begin again.

Mr. Johnson saw that he had made a deep impression, though he did not feel quite certain of its nature. And he said, very mildly, " My dear child, don't pretend to be wiser than your teachers. I can solemnly assure you, as a Christian man and a Christian minister, that the word we render baptize does legitimately signify the application of water in any way as well as by immersion, no matter what the Lexicons may say; and if so, sprinkling is as much baptism as dipping. The quantity of water used does not affect the validity of the ordinance."

To this Theodosia did not reply. She felt that it was useless to ask again for proof; and if she did not feel disposed to trust even her pastor's solemn declaration in regard to the meaning of baptize, it was because she remembered that Dr. Barnes had proved it to mean "not to sprinkle," but "to dip;" that Stuart admitted this to be its prevalent and common signification; that the great Dr. Chalmers expressly asserted that its meaning was to dip, and that it was immersion which was practiced in the early churches; that McKnight and other most eminent and learned Pedobaptists all agreed perfectly with the Lexicons in giving immersion as its true meaning, and proving that such was the understanding and practice of the apostolic churches. What Baptists might teach she did not know, for as yet she had not read a Baptist book. She had common sense enough to understand that if there had been any sprinkling or pouring in the Word, such men as Stuart, and Chalmers, and McKnight, would have been sure to find

it and parade it before the world as a justification of
their practice. Though she was silent, therefore, she
was far from being satisfied.

Mr. Johnson, acting on the adage that "silence gives
consent," considered this point as settled; "and now,"
he continued, "if this be the case, if the word means
to sprinkle or to pour, as well as to immerse, it is evident that John might have dipped, and Christ *might*
have commanded sprinkling, and yet have used the same
word which is used to describe John's baptism. I might
rest the case here; but I will go farther, and assert that
John's baptism *was not immersion at all.*"

"Good evening, Mr. Johnson, I am glad to hear you
say that," said Mr. Percy, who chanced to come in 'at
the moment, and heard this strange assertion. "If we
can only establish that position we will throw the Baptists out of court."

"Nothing is easier done, Mr. Percy," said the pastor.
"It could not have been immersion, in the first place,
because immersion was impossible."

"Of course," said Mr. Percy, "if immersion was impossible, it could not have been immersion. What was
impossible could not have been done."

"Very well, then, that settles the question, for it was
clearly impossible for John to have immersed the thousands and thousands (not to say the millions) that re-
sorted to him for baptism."

"I don't know about that," said Mr. Percy. "In the
first place, we must determine just how many there were,
and then just how many John was able to dip. Do you
know how many there were?"

"Not precisely," said the pastor, "but there were
great multitudes. The Evangelist says, Jerusalem and
all Judea, and all the region round about Jordan, went
to him and were baptized. Now the population of Jeru-

salem itself was a prodigious multitude, and that of all
Judea added to it would surely be more than one man
could dip in the time of John's public ministry."

"But," said Mr. Percy, "it does not say that *all the
inhabitants went.* It says the *places* went; by which we
are to understand, that some of each place mentioned
went. Just as if I should say, that in the great politi-
cal Convention of 1840, all Tennessee was gathered at
Nashville to hear Henry Clay. I would not mean that
every man, woman, and child in the State was there, but
only that there were some from every part of it. Just
so, Matthew says Jerusalem came—that is, a great many
people from Jerusalem and Judea, and the country
round about Jordan came; that is to say, the country
as well as the city was fully represented in the crowd.
Besides, John did not baptize all who came. He positively refused the Pharisees and Sadducees, who composed a great part of the Jewish nation. I do not see,
therefore, that we have any means of knowing the exact
number of the baptized."

"But it can't be denied," said the pastor, "that it
was an immense multitude, too many for one man to
have immersed."

"Will you permit me to ask a question?" said Theodosia, timidly (for she had become almost afraid to
speak at all, since that suggestion of the pastor about a
joint editorship with Mr. Percy in a body of divinity.)
"Will you permit me to ask how much longer it
would take to *immerse* them, one at a time, than it would
to *sprinkle* them one at a time, in a decent and reverent
way?"

"We do not know," said the pastor, "that they *were*
sprinkled *one at a time.* They might have stood in regular ranks along the bank, and John taking a bunch of

hyssop might have dipped it in the river and sprinkled them by dozens as he passed along."

"Or," suggested Mr. Percy, "he might have provided himself with a large sized syringe or squirt gun, and filling it from the river have turned its stream along the ranks, as I have seen the boys do at school, sprinkling a whole bench of boys before the master could see who did it."

This was uttered with such a perfectly serious air that the pastor was obliged to receive it as an amendment to his own supposition, though he could not help seeing in what a ridiculous light it placed both the baptizer and his subjects; and surely, there is, in the narrative of the Evangelists, quite as much evidence of the use of the squirt as of the hyssop.

"There is another thought," said Theodosia, "which it seems to me, will obviate all the difficulty in the way of either a personal dipping or a separate sprinkling of each individual. The Evangelist says that Jesus made and baptized *more* disciples than John—and when the disciples were gathered together after his death, there does *not seem to have been a very great multitude.* So it is probable, I should think, that though great multitudes *came to John,* and great multitudes *followed Christ,* yet comparatively *few* brought forth fruit to justify *their baptism.* And besides this, as Jesus is said to have baptized, though he did not do it personally, but by his disciples, so John may have done a portion of *his* baptizing by *his disciples.*"

"Spoken like yourself, Miss Theodosia," said Mr. Percy. "That does indeed obviate all difficulty. The baptism, whatever it was, must have been a personal, individual transaction; and as it would take as long to sprinkle a person, and say over the proper formula of words, as it would to dip him, one is just as possible as the other, and either entirely practicable with the aid of the disciples. Don't you think so, Mr. Johnson?"

"No, I do not; but let it pass. I have another reason for believing that John did not immerse. It says expressly that he baptized in Bethabara, beyond Jordan—and in the wilderness, as well as at the much waters or many waters of Ænon, and at the river Jordan. Now, as there is no mention made of a river at Bethabara, or of a lake in the wilderness, it is fair to infer that no great quantity of water was required—and, consequently, whatever he may have done in Jordan, he did not immerse in Bethabara or in the wilderness."

"Why not, Mr. Johnson? I can easily understand that he was baptizing in the wilderness, Bethabara, and Jordan *at one and the same time.* The Jews (as I have learned in my Sunday-school lessons) called any sparsely settled place a wilderness; and Bethabara was a ford or a ferry-house, on the east bank of the Jordan. If the neighborhood was lonely, it would be said to be in the wilderness; and a baptism performed in the Jordan, at that place, might be said with equal propriety to be performed in the wilderness, in Bethabara, or in Jordan. Just as I might say that a person was baptized in Davidson county, or in the city of Nashville. though the act was performed in the Cumberland river, where it passes the city."

"Well," said Mr. Johnson, ' I do not insist on this point; and I leave it more readily, as I have an argument that is perfectly *unanswerable;* and that is, that John says himself that he *did not immerse*—over and over again he repeated this testimony: ' I indeed baptize you *with* water, but he that cometh after me shall baptize you *with* the Holy Ghost and *with* fire.' ' I am come,' he says, ' baptizing *with* water;' and again: ' he that sent me to baptize *with* water.' Now, when I want to know how John baptized, I go right up to the reverend man with the hairy garment, and ask him to tell me for himself. 'Did you baptize by immersion?' 'No, sir; I baptize *with* water, not *in* water. I was *sent* to baptize *with* water, not *in* water—as he that cometh after me baptizes *with* the Holy Ghost, not in the Holy Ghost, and *with* fire, not *in* fire. So I baptize *with* water, not *in* the water. I apply the water to the subject, not the subject to the water.'"

"There does seem to be some force in that," said Mr. Percy.

"To be sure, there not only *seems* to be, but there *is* a world of force in it. It is perfectly unanswerable, sir. I am willing to rest our cause on this one point alone. You can easily understand how one can sprinkle with water, or pour upon with water, but no one would ever speak of *immersing* WITH *water*."

Theodosia began to think of her pastor as she had done before his visit. He was not, after all, disposed to rest *every thing* on his bare word. He had the proof, and had produced it, and that, too, just as she desired, from the Book itself. Still there was a difficulty. If John did not immerse, why did he baptize in the river? Why did Jesus, after he was baptized, come up out of the water?

These were insuperable difficulties, but she knew not how to present them without seeming wiser than her teacher.

Mr. Johnson, seemingly satisfied with the victory he had won, was about to take his leave, although it was yet early, promising to call again soon, and show that there was no instance of immersion as baptism recorded in the whole New Testament.

"Not only is it true," said he, "that John did not immerse, but there is no recognition of immersion as baptism in the Book. Neither before the death of Christ, nor afterward, did the disciples ever dip the baptized person in the water."

"Please stop a minute longer," said Mr. Percy. "While we are on John's baptism, I want to ask a single question. If John did not immerse, why did he baptize in the river? If Jesus was not immersed, how does it happen that he had been in the water? If Philip did not immerse the Ethiopian Eunuch, for what reason did they go down both of them into the water, before the baptism, and come up out of it after it was done? Nobody in these days goes down into the water to baptize unless he is a Baptist."

"They did not go into the water, then," replied Mr. Johnson, "any more than we Presbyterians do now. There is no proof that John, or Jesus, or Philip, or the Eunuch, ever went into the water at all."

"How can that be," asked Theodosia, "when the Scripture says expressly that they were baptized 'in the river of Jordan,' and that Jesus 'came up out of the water,' and that both Philip and the Eunuch 'went down into the water,' and 'came up out of the water?'"

"I know it reads so in our version," said the pastor, "but in the original it reads *near* or *at the river*, not in it. And *down to the water*, not *into* it, and up *from* the water, not *out of* it."

"Were the translators of our version Baptists?" asked Mr. Percy.

"No, sir. It is well known that they were of the Church of England."

"Had they any motive to favor the cause of the Baptists?"

"None at all, that I can conceive of."

"How, then, did they come to make such blundering work?"

"I cannot tell; but if they had known that the Baptists would make such a handle of these little words '*in,* and *out of*,' I have no doubt they would have been more cautious. I hope now, Miss Theodosia, that your mind is relieved. I will try to see you again to-morrow, when we will finish the subject. For the present, I must bid you good-night."

Theodosia accompanied him to the door, to light him out, and glancing up the street in the opposite direction to that which he took, she discovered Edwin and Mr. Courtney returning from an evening recitation, and could not resist the desire to hear what the teacher might have to say about baptizing *with* the water at the bank of the river. She accordingly waited till he came by, and invited him in.

"Well, Courtney," said Mr. Percy, as he entered the parlor, "we have got you in a tight place now."

"Why? what has happened? Any thing wonderful? You look as though you thought so."

"Yes, sir. The truth is, Mr. Johnson *did* have some strong reasons, and he has brought them out on us to-night. He has in fact *proved* what he said, and what you seemed to think impossible; that John's baptism was *not* immersion, and that the Saviour never went into the water at all, but was sprinkled on the bank."

"Well, how did he make all that out?"

"From the testimony of John himself. John says that he baptized not *in* but *with* water. It is easy to conceive of sprinkling with water, but no one ever heard of immersing with water."

"Is that all?"

"Yes, that is the substance of the argument."

"Is it possible," said Mr. Courtney, "that a minister of Jesus Christ can take such liberties with the Word of God!!"

"What do you mean? Mr. Courtney. Is it not all so?" asked Theodosia, in alarm, for she felt that if her pastor had deceived her, even in this point, she could never trust the word of any one again upon this subject,

"Mr. Percy," said Mr. Courtney, "can you read Greek? But never mind, Edwin shall set us right."

"I can read a little, and, when in practice, could do as well as most of our graduates," said Mr. Percy.

"Well, then, you can judge if I attempt to deceive you. Now, what will you say if you find that John's assertion, so often repeated, reads in the Greek Testament, in every instance, I baptize you ' *in*' water, never ' *with*,' in a single case? What will you say if you read, not only that Christ was baptized ' *in*' Jordan, but '*into*' the river of Jordan?"

"Why, I will say that you have gained a victory over all the doubts and difficulties which remained in my mind, and I will be convinced that John immersed, and that Jesus was immersed by him in Jordan."

"And I," said Theodosia, "will be convinced that theologians are the strangest people in the world."

"Say rather, Presbyterian or Pedobaptist theologians, Miss Ernest, for the Baptists do not have to bear up and twist about under such a load of error and inconsistency, and can consequently afford to talk, right out, the truth, the whole truth, and nothing but the truth. They can afford to take the Bible, the whole Bible, and nothing but the Bible, with every word translated into plain English, and abide by its decisions. They shun no investigation, avoid no controversy, and have no need to change or keep concealed one single word of the holy record. But let us to our task, for it is growing late. Edwin, have you your Greek Testament here?"

"Yes, sir; and my Lexicon and Grammar."

"Please bring them in.

"Edwin, can you tell us what is the primary and ordinary meaning of the Greek preposition '*en*?'"

"It means *in*, sir; or within, with the idea of rest in a place." (See Bullion's Greek Grammar, p. 170.)

"What is the difference between *en* and *eis*?" •

"*Eis* signifies motion from without to within. *En* corresponds to the English preposition *in*—*eis* corresponds to the English *into*."

"I asked those questions, Mr. Percy, not on your account, but to satisfy Miss Ernest. You are perfectly aware (as every school-boy who has gotten through his Greek Grammar must be) of the correctness of Edwin's answers.

"Now be kind enough to take the Greek Testament, and find John i. 26—'I baptize with water.' How does it read?"

"It reads, '*baptizo en udati*,' *in* water, true enough."

"And so you will find it in every place. See the 31st verse, '*en*' again; so in the 33d, and every place where this expression, which your pastor so much relies upon, can be found.

"In any other Greek book, any school-boy would without hesitation, translate it, 'I immerse you *in* water.' 'I am come immersing in water,' etc. But now, if you will turn to Mark i. 9, you will find that the preposition is not '*en*,' but '*eis*.' So that Jesus is said to have been baptized or dipped, not merely *in* but ('*eis*') *into* the river of Jordan.

"Now these two words, *en* and *eis*, are the only words by which the Greek language could express, without circumlocution, the idea of going into, or being in a thing or place; and therefore, if neither of them says that the baptism was done *in* the river, I do not see how it *could* be said to have been done there.

"Now I grant that, very rarely, *en* does mean with, and that it sometimes, though very seldom, does mean at, or near; but neither of these is the primary, common, every-day use of the word. *En* means *in*, in Greek, as much as *in* does in English. *Eis* means *into*, in Greek, as much as *into* does in English."

"But, Mr. Courtney, there must be some foundation for Mr. Johnson's supposition, that *en* means *with*, or it would not have been so translated."

"Very true, Miss Ernest *En* does sometimes (though very rarely) mean *with* in the sense of the instrument— by which an action is accomplished. But when a man would found an argument on its having that meaning in every particular case, he must *first prove that such is* OF NECESSITY ITS MEANING IN THAT INSTANCE. If '*En udati*' necessarily meant *with* water—if that was even its *common*, primary meaning, as it would be naturally understood in any other book, or in connection with any other subject, then it might form the basis for an argument; but no school-boy would think of any thing else but *in* water, whenever he would see it; and, consequently, for a classical scholar, like your pastor, to form an argument upon '*with*,' as the common meaning of '*en*,' is indicative either of great carelessness, or wilful perversion of the Word of God.

"Here is a fact which will enable you to form some more definite conception of the nature of the case. Some very industrious gentleman has counted the places, and so ascertained that this little preposition '*EN*' occurs no less than two thousand seven hundred and twenty times in the New Testament. In about twenty-five hundred of these places, it is in our version correctly rendered IN. In over twenty other places, *in* would *better* express the evident meaning of the original. In only about forty places, out of over twenty-seven hundred, does it of necessity mean *with*, in the sense of the instrument or material with which any thing is done. The chances, therefore, are as twenty-seven hundred to forty, that an argument based on the word '*with*' (where it stands for the Greek word '*en*') will lead to a false conclusion, and the chances are as twenty-seven hundred to forty that an argument based on '*in*,' as the real meaning of the word, will lead to a true conclusion. I baptize you *in* water, or, if we translate both words, I immerse, or more properly, I *dip* you *in* water, is therefore the true reading."

"But why, Mr. Courtney, should our translators have employed '*with*' whenever '*en*' occurs in connection with baptize?"

"For the same reason, Miss Ernest, that they refused to translate baptize. They were forbidden by King James to change the ' Ecclesiastical words.' They must not teach immersion. But if they had said baptize '*in*' water, it would have been just as plain that there was no sprinkling or pouring in the ordinance, as though they had translated ' baptize' in the New Testament, in the same way that you have seen they did in the Old, in all the places where (according to Mr. Barnes) the word occurs.

"But they did not use '*with*,' in every case, because that construction would have been, in some instances, such a monstrous perversion, that every one could see it. They did not venture to say that the people were baptized WITH *the river of Jordan*, confessing their sins; or that Christ was baptized WITH *the Jordan :* or that John was baptizing WITH *the wilderness*. Mark i 4. It was only where the connection did not make the meaning clearly obvious to the unlearned, that they ventured to mystify the ordinance by the substitution of *with*, in the place of the common and primary meaning of the '*en*.'"

"If I do not forget," said Mr. Percy, "*with*, when signifying the instrument by which any thing is done, is in the Greek language, commonly expressed by '*dia*' construed with the genitive."

"Yes; but even if John had said '*dia*,' instead of '*en*,' the pastor would have had no sufficient basis for his argument; for even '*dia*' would have been a very slight, and very narrow, and very sandy foundation. It would only have told that it was *water*, and not oil, or mud, or sand, or any other instrument or material with which the baptism was performed. It would have said nothing at all about the *mode* of performing the act. If I say that the cloth of which my coat was made was colored *with* a solution of indigo, I don't even intimate that the solution was sprinkled on it or poured on it. The cloth was *dipped* in it. I only mean that it was dipped *in indigo*, not in logwood, or madder, or any other dye-stuff. If I say that the leather of which my boots are made, was tanned *with* an infusion of hemlock bark, I don't deny that it was dipped in the infusion, I only mean that it was hemlock, not black oak, or red oak, or any other kind of material that was used."

"Oh, yes!" exclaimed Edwin, who all the time had been a most attentive, though a silent listener. "I asked old aunt Chloe, the cook, only this morning, how she would get the feathers off the chicken she was killing for dinner. 'I will scald it,' said she, '*with* hot water.' And I went into the kitchen, and saw her doing it by *putting it into* the water. And big Joe, the butcher, when he killed our hogs last Christmas, loosened the bristles and hair *with* hot water, but he did it by *im-*

mersion, for he dipped them several times into the barrel and then pulled them out and scraped them."

"That will do, Edwin," said Mr. Percy, laughing. "I see we must give it up. If you won't give us any more illustrations, I will promise never to mention '*with*' again, by way of argument on this subject, as long as I live; and seriously, Mr. Courtney, I feel that I have reason to be ashamed of myself for having been so easily imposed upon by this mere semblance of argument, presented with so much parade, and such an air of confidence, by our pastor, Mr. Johnson. I shall soon begin, like Miss Ernest, to lose confidence in all teachings but those of the Bible, and in all teachers but my own judgment."   •

"These, sir, are your only safeguards," replied Mr. Courtney; "but it is well to remember, that, though God's word is infallible, our judgment may be biased by our feelings; and when we study the Word, therefore, we should pray for a *heart willing to receive*, and a *will ready to obey* all the commandments of our Heavenly Master. The difficulty with many persons is not so much that they *cannot understand* as they are *unwilling to obey*. You will, I fear, find it much easier to satisfy your mind that immersion is the only scriptural baptism, than to abandon your church connections, and submit to be baptized according to the commandment of Jesus Christ. But I must bid you good-night. It is time I was at home."

THE FOURTH NIGHT'S STUDY.

<hr>

WHICH BEGINS IN THE DAY, AND INCLUDES, AMONG OTHER
STRANGE THINGS,

THE PASTOR'S PROOF

THAT IMMERSION WAS NOT PRACTISED

BY THE APOSTLES

ANY MORE THAN IT HAD BEEN BY JOHN.

THE BAPTISM OF THE HOLY GHOST.

THE BAPTISM OF THE THREE THOUSAND.

FOURTH NIGHT'S STUDY.

ON the following day, the Rev. Mr. Johnson called at Mrs. Ernest's cottage soon after dinner. Mrs. E. was delighted with this evident token of his interest in her daughter's welfare. She had now given up all hope of inducing her to abandon the investigation; and was only anxious to get through with it as soon as possible. Much as she had disliked Mr. Courtney's remarks at the time of his first call, she made no objection to the second visit; and even went so far as to ask her daughter why she did not invite some of the Baptists to meet Mr. Johnson face to face, when she would see what would become of all their hard sayings about the "Ministers of our church."

"That little Baptist pedagogue," said she, "would no more dare to say such things as he did about Dr. Barnes, and Dr. Chalmers, and Dr. McKnight, in the presence of Mr. Johnson, than he would to put his head into the lion's mouth. He finds that he can twist you and Mr. Percy about his thumb just as he pleases, but let him come where Mr. Johnson is, or any body else who has studied this subject, and I'll warrant you he will be as mute as a mouse."

"Well, Miss Theodosia," said the pastor, as soon as the young lady came in, and had exchanged with him the compliments of the morning, "I proved to you last evening, I trust beyond the shadow of a doubt, that John's baptism was not immersion. And now, as I have an hour to spare, I will, if you can give me your attention, show you that we have quite as good ground

(93)

for believing that the Apostles did not immerse any more than John did; and that in fact there was never any such a thing as even a single instance of immersion as baptism mentioned in the sacred Scriptures."

(Theodosia was about to interrupt him, and ask some further explanation concerning the Greek preposition "*en*," and the English preposition "*with*;" but remembering the "Book of Divinity," and thinking it safer not to seem "wiser than her teacher," she continued silent. He went on, therefore, in blissful ignorance of the utter overthrow of all the beautiful edifice which he had so ingeniously erected the night before.)

"Now be kind enough to get your Bible, and turn to Acts i. 5."

"Yes, yes, Mr. Johnson," said the mother, "that is the way to study the subject. Show it to her in the Bible itself, for she declares she won't believe a single word but what she can see in the Bible with her own eyes."

"Well, then, here it is; just read it, my child."

Theodosia read, "For John indeed baptized with water, but ye shall be baptized with the Holy Ghost, not many days hence." And as she read, she could not help giving the passage, in her mind, the true rendering, "John indeed immersed you *in* water," etc.

"You see from this," resumed the pastor, "that not only John himself said that he baptized *with* water, but that Jesus Christ also declared the same thing. But that is not the point to which I wish now to direct your attention. We settled that point yesterday. (Yes! thought Theodosia, but it did not continue settled.) What I want you to notice now is the prophetic declaration in this text: 'Ye shall be baptized with the Holy Ghost not many days hence.' Now turn to the second chapter, and you will see the fulfilment of this prediction. When the day of Pentecost was fully come, they were all with one accord in one place, and then and there they received this baptism of the Holy Spirit. Now tell me how this baptism was performed. Just read the 17th verse and you will see. 'And it shall come to pass in the last days, saith God, that I will *pour out* of my spirit,' etc. And now read the 33d verse: 'Therefore being by the right hand of God exalted, and having received of the Father the promise of the Holy Ghost, he hath *shed forth* this, which ye now see and hear.' Here then you see that the influences of the Spirit are called a *baptism,* and they are distinctly said to be '*poured out,*' and to be '*shed forth.*' And from this it follows, as a matter of course, that baptism is *pouring* and *shedding forth* or *sprinkling.* I do not see how it is possible for any thing to be clearer or more convincing than this."

"Certainly," exclaimed Mrs. Ernest, the mother; "that must convince any body in the world. I should like to know what the school-master could say to that. I do wish, Mr. Johnson, you would preach a sermon on this subject, and just set the matter at rest."

"Pardon me, Mr. Johnson," said Theodosia, "if this argument does not appear so conclusive to me as it seems to you. I was reading this very chapter this morning, and the same difficulty came into my mind then which you have presented now. It was on my mind when I engaged in prayer, and it was not until nearly dinner time that I was able to see clearly how it could be that baptism *is immersion,* and yet the Spirit be said to be *poured out* in this most remarkable baptism. Now it is all perfectly plain."

"Well, Miss Ernest, will you please favor us with your explanations?"

"Certainly," she replied. "Mr. Barnes, in his Notes

on Matthew xx. 29, explains baptism in suffering and distress, to be an overwhelming of the soul with great and intense afflictions. 'Are you able,' he says, ' to be plunged deep in afflictions, and to have sorrows cover you like water, and to be sunk beneath calamities as a flood?' Now in this there is no literal immersion, but the sorrow is represented as covering and swallowing up the mind as water does the body in the act of baptism. It is a metaphorical but not a real baptism.

"So in the case before us. As Christ had told James and John that they should be immersed or overwhelmed by sufferings and sorrows, so now he tells all the disciples that they shall in a few days be immersed or overwhelmed by the influences of the Holy Spirit. That these influences should cover, overpower, and swallow up their *minds*, as the water in baptism did their *bodies.* It is no more a literal baptism than the baptism of suffering in Matthew. It is a metaphor; and the allusion is not to the *act* done in baptism, so much as to the *result ;* that is, the *swallowing up* and *overwhelming* of their minds by the flood of life, and light, and joy, and heavenly influence which that day came upon their souls."

If the mother was surprised at the temerity of her daughter in venturing to differ from her pastor (to her a most unheard-of event), yet her maternal pride was so much gratified by the force and beauty of her reasoning, that she could not be angry, and there was even a smile —a *very slight* smile of exultation, which crept along the curves of her mouth, as her daughter, with animated face, and a new and strange light in her soul illumining her eyes, entered into the discussion; and from this time forth (though she was determined never to be convinced that her pastor was or could be wrong) she could not help feeling secretly gratified whenever her daughter had the best of the argument; and she inwardly enjoyed the evident amazement and perplexity depicted in the Rev. Mr. Johnson's face.

He was amazed, that *one* of the "baptized children of his church" should have ventured not only to *differ* from his opinions, so forcibly expressed, but even to *reason* with him out of the Scriptures. He was perplexed, because he could not, for the moment, see what reply he could successfully make.

"Surely, Mr. Johnson," resumed the young lady, after a moment's pause, "you do not imagine that there was in this Pentecostal baptism any *real, actual, literal pouring out* of the Spirit, like water is poured out of a pitcher, or any literal sprinkling of the Spirit, as the minister sprinkles the water off from the ends of his fingers?"

"It does not matter at all," he replied, "whether it was literal or figurative, actual or metaphorical, the conclusion must be the same in any case. There is here clearly a baptism, a scriptural baptism; a baptism, too, of the Gospel dispensation; and this baptism was performed by pouring. Jesus Christ prophetically foretold that they should be baptized with the Holy Ghost; and when the prophecy was fulfilled, Peter says expressly that the Holy Ghost was poured out."

"But he does not say, Mr. Johnson, that the *pouring out was the baptism.* The Holy Spirit *cannot be* literally poured out, or sprinkled out, nor could the disciples be literally immersed in him, any more than they had already been; for he is, and always was, everywhere present, and had always surrounded them on every side. It was clearly impossible, therefore, that there could be any literal baptism, in any sense of the word, by sprinkling, pouring, or immersion. It was not the third person of the trinity, the Divine Spirit, that was poured out and shed forth, but the miraculous and wonderful *influences* of the spirit, operating on the hearts and minds of the disciples and others. And if these *influences* were so powerful, and so universal, as to surround and overpower the minds of the Apostles, they might most beautifully and appropriately be said to be immersed in them. The baptism of *the spirit* is a *soul* baptism, not a baptism of the *body ;* and the *minds* of the disciples are represented by Christ as about to be taken so completely into the control and direction of the Holy Spirit, that they would, as it were, be *immersed in it and swallowed up by it.* Such a baptism actually did occur. The minds of the disciples were thus overwhelmed and swallowed up by the wonderful influences of the Spirit of God ; and this is what, it seems to me, was intended by Jesus, when he said they would be immersed in the Holy Ghost."

" Well, as to that," rejoined the mother (whose heart had begun already to follow her daughter), " I can see that their bodies were immersed too, as well as their souls, for there came a sound as of a rushing mighty wind, and it filled all the house where they were sitting ; and of course it covered them all up, and entirely surrounded them, and they were in this way immersed in it."

" If the pouring," resumed Theodosia, encouraged by this open expression of her mother's approval, " if the pouring had any thing to do with the baptism at all, it was only by way of preparation ; for as water might be poured into a vessel preparatory to immersing any object or person in it, so the preparation of the Holy Spirit for these wonderful influences might be here called his *pouring out,* as such preparation is sometimes called a *coming down,* or an *entering into,* or a *springing up.*"

" I am ready to admit," said the pastor, " that these

Pentecostal influences were called a baptism by Jesus Christ *only in a figure.* I hope neither of you think me so silly as to be capable of believing that the *personal substance* (if I may speak so) of the Holy Spirit could be literally poured out or sprinkled. But while it is true that this baptism was a figure, it is equally true that our baptism is a figure also. It is designed to exhibit in an emblematical manner the cleansing and purifying influences of the Holy Spirit in our hearts; how very beautiful and appropriate is it, therefore, as the Holy Spirit is represented as being figuratively poured out in this baptism, that the water which represents his influences should be *actually* poured out on us when we are baptized."

"It might indeed," said Theodosia, "have been a very beautiful and appropriate emblem, and had our Saviour thought as highly of it as you do, HE probably would have appointed it. But HE seems to have preferred *immersion in water;* and this, while it may signify the cleansing of the Holy Spirit, equally well, or better than the other, signifies also our death and burial to sin, and our living again to righteousness; and it is thus that Paul explains it when he says, 'we are buried with him by baptism into death, that as Christ was raised from the dead, so we should walk in newness of life.' It serves also to remind us of the burial and resurrection of Jesus, and prefigures also our own coming death, burial, and resurrection."

"What Baptist book have you been reading to learn all that?"

"I found it, Mr. Johnson, in a Presbyterian book; in the Notes of Dr. James McKnight on the 6th of Romans. I have never read any Baptist book in my life, unless (as I greatly suspect) the Bible is a Baptist book."

"I fear—I greatly fear, my child," rejoined the pastor, "that you are running into very serious and alarming errors. I have exhorted you, and reasoned with you, but I fear my labors have been almost in vain. And now, before I take my leave, I feel it my duty solemnly to warn you before God, to take heed where you are going. I should be greatly pained, if we should find it necessary to expel you from the church."

"Expel me from the church! Why, Mr. Johnson, what do you mean? Have I been guilty of any improper conduct? What have I done?"

"Nothing as yet, my child. I am happy to say, you have always been a faithful and consistent communicant since you first approached the table of the Lord. But now I find you growing wayward and self-willed, whereas, the Scripture says, 'be not high-minded, but fear—and be in subjection to those who have the rule over you in the Lord.' As yet, you have only imbibed some false and injurious notions on the subject of one of the ordinances of the church. So far, this has not led you to any overt act of evil which could subject you to the discipline of the church, but if you persevere in this way, and especially, *if by your conduct and conversation you lead others* to distrust the purity of our doctrines, the propriety of our practice, and validity of our ordinances, it will become our painful duty to deal with you as a disturber of the peace and unity of the church."

The pastor uttered this significant warning with all due solemnity of countenance and impressiveness of manner, but it did not have the effect upon the young lady which he had expected. A week before this time she would have heard it with very different emotions. Now she had not only learned to fear God rather than man, but she had, upon her bended knees, solemnly resolved before her Maker and Redeemer that, in regard to this subject, she would both learn and *do* her whole duty, whatever it might cost her.

This was indeed an unexpected, and, to her sensitive spirit, a most terrible test of the sincerity and firmness of that resolution, but it did not cause her to waver even for one moment.

She did, indeed, turn deathly pale. Her chin quivered, and the light for a moment went out in her eye. It was but for a moment, however, and before he had completed the speech, the blood had come back to her face, and her eyes were suffused with tears, which, however, did not overflow; and perfect collectedness of mind and calmness of manner, though with a scarcely perceptible tremulousness of voice, she mildly replied :

"If it was your purpose, Mr. Johnson, to deter me from making a conscientious and complete investigation of this subject, and then governing my conduct by the written word of God, I beg you will remember that you have yourself instructed me that I ought to obey God rather than man—and this, God helping me, I mean to do, whatever may be the consequences to me or others."

"No, no, my child, you do not understand me. I desire you should be governed by the word of God; but I would have you remember that God has given you *teachers* to help you to a true understanding of his word. It is for this purpose that he has appointed us his ministers, to guide the young, instruct the ignorant, and make known to all what are the teachings of that word."

"But what if our ministers should chance to disagree? Am I to remain all my life in doubt, or take the matter into my own hands and decide for myself? Will the ministers answer for me in the day of judgment? You tell me, Mr. Johnson, that Jesus Christ

7

was sprinkled, but James McKnight, another eminent minister of our own church, a Doctor of Divinity, and for twenty years the Moderator of the General Assembly of the Presbyterian church in the country where he lived, tells me '*that Jesus submitted to be baptized, that is, to be put under the water and taken out again by John;*' and Dr. Chalmers, another most eminent minister of our church, tells me '*that the meaning of the word baptism is immersion;* Martin Luther, the great reformer, says expressly, that *it was immersion which was,* '*without doubt, instituted by Christ;*' and John Calvin, the father and founder of our Presbyterian church, distinctly states that '*the word baptize signifies to immerse, and the rite of immersion was practiced by the ancient church!*'"

"Yes, my child, but then do not all these great and good men, at the same time assure you that it is a matter of no importance which way the rite is performed?"

"They do, indeed; but that is only their own private or individual opinion. They don't even pretend that the word of God teaches that it is of no consequence whether we do what Christ commanded or not. I cannot think, like Dr. Chalmers, that it is a 'matter of indifferency,' or like Calvin, that 'it is of no consequence at all.' I dare not set aside the commandments of Christ for the doctrines of men; and if you will pardon me for saying it, I do not see how any minister of Jesus Christ can dare to teach such sentiments. If Jesus Christ commanded us to believe and be immersed, I surely did not obey that command by being sprinkled.

"Pardon me, Mr. Johnson, for talking so plainly, but you have driven me to it. You promised, this evening, to show me, out of the Scriptures, that the baptism of the Gospel dispensation was sprinkling,

and all you have done was to show me where the Holy
Ghost was, by a figure of speech, said to be *poured out*
on the day of Pentecost, and where Christ had
prophetically declared that they should, in some sense,
that day he *metaphorically* immersed in the Holy Spirit
—for you do not pretend that it was more than a mystical and *figurative* baptism which the Saviour foretold.
You did not, and you cannot prove, that this prophecy
referred to the preparatory 'pouring out' any more
than to any of the wonderful influences that follow the
outpouring.

"Now I had learned from ministers of our own church,
from Calvin and Chalmers, and as directed by Mr.
Barnes, from the word of God itself, that the meaning
of the word is a dipping or immersion. I knew that
when Jesus was baptized it was done in the river, as
immersions are now performed. And that when the
Eunuch was baptized they went down into the water,
and when the solemn rite was done, they came up out
of the water, just as they do in immersions now. I knew
that Paul called our baptism a *burial.* And that our
own ministers, as Chalmers and McKnight, explained
this as an allusion to the custom of the first Church, of
baptizing by immersion, and because, in the face of all
this visible and tangible evidence that the real and
literal baptism submitted to, and commanded by Christ,
and practiced by the apostles in the first church, was
immersion, I could not, on the authority of a mere
figure of speech, and that of doubtful application, believe it to have been pouring, you tell me I am wayward
and self-willed, and intimate that I may expect soon to
be dealt with as a disturber of the peace and unity of the
church."

"I think, Mr. Johnson," said the mother, "that you
were a little too hard on Theodosia about that. I never

could myself see much force in these figures of speech or metaphors as Theodosia calls them."

"Why, mother," resumed the young lady, "if Mr. Johnson will let me reason in the same way that he does, I will prove to him that the poor little boy of whom we were reading this morning, that was drowned in the river, was actually drowned on dry land by a few drops of water sprinkled on his face."

"I don't see how, my daughter; but here is the paper containing the account of the accident. I would like to hear you try."

"'MELANCHOLY ACCIDENT

"'It is our painful duty to announce that little Charlie Freeman, a sprightly lad about nine years old, of a most lovely disposition and extraordinary promise, the only son of his mother, and she a widow, was accidentally *drowned* this morning in the Cumberland river. We were one of those who recovered the body and bore it to the dwelling of the now doubly-bereaved mother. We cannot describe the sorrow with which this sad event has filled our hearts. We have just left the melancholy scene, where the heart-broken mother is sitting in the midst of a large circle of friends who are all *drowned in tears.'*

"Now, Mr. Johnson tells me that the disciples, on the day of Pentecost, were figuratively or metaphorically baptized *by pouring*, and if so, then he asks me to be-lieve that Jesus Christ must have been literally and actually baptized in the same way, that is, by pouring, in the river Jordan. This is the whole argument. Now I say here was a large circle of this poor lady's friends who were metaphorically said to be drowned in a little water running down their faces out of their own eyes; and if so, then the dear little boy must have been actually and literally drowned by a few drops of water running down his face."

"But you forget," said the pastor, "that the lad was said to be drowned *in the river.*"

"Not at all," she replied, "for so also Jesus Christ is said to have been *baptized in the river;* but you try to persuade me that he only stood upon the bank, and John took up some of the water of the river, and sprinkled it on his face. And some of our writers tell me that he might have gone a few steps into the water, and there, standing in the river, John took up a little water and poured it on his head out of a muscle shell, or a cup. So I will grant that this poor little lad may have gone to the bank of the river, and that some of the water of the river was thus splashed up into his face; or that he waded in a little way, and some other boy did the same, took up some water with his hand, and threw it in his face—but that he *must have been drowned by a little water running over his face,* is perfectly self-evident, for this is the *only* way in which the large circle of his mother's friends *could* have been drowned."

"I see," rejoined the pastor, "that your mind is already made up, and it is scarcely worth while to argue the subject with you any further. You have determined that you will not be convinced. But before I leave you to-day, I will suggest one more point for your consideration, which, if you are not already hardened in unbelief, can hardly fail to satisfy you."

"Oh no, Mr. Johnson, I am ready and anxious to be convinced. What have I to gain by believing that immersion is the only baptism? You have already intimated what I may expect from you and from the church which I have loved so dearly. I fear I have already lost in part the affection of my precious mother"—and her eyes filled with tears.

"No, my daughter," said Mrs. Ernest, "you have not lost my love, and I will love you still, do what you may. I know you are a dear, good, conscientious child, and would not for the world do what you did not believe to be right. If you leave us, my child, I can't help mourning over you, but I will love you still. But do listen to Mr. Johnson, my darling, and see if he can't convince you."

"Certainly, mother; if Mr. Johnson will show me *one single place* in the Word of God where baptism is called sprinkling or pouring (not in the way of a metaphor or a figure, but literally and plainly), I will be content. If he will show *one single* instance in which baptism is plainly said to have been *done by sprinkling* or *pouring*—not dimly and metaphorically, as those good ladies were drowned in tears, but actually and really, as the dear child was drowned in the river—I will ask for nothing more. But till he can *show it to me in the Bible,* I can't believe that it is there."

"As to that," said the pastor, "I can show you sprinkling and pouring oftener than I can immersion, for there is no such word as immersion used in the whole book."

"I know," said she, "that sprinkling and pouring are mentioned often enough, but not as baptism; what I want is the place where *they are literally said to be actual baptism.* I know that *immerse* does not occur in our version, because *dip* is generally used where the word baptize occurs; but if *baptism* means immersion, as Calvin, McKnight, Chalmers, and others of our ministers say it does, and as the lexicons of the Greek language say it does, then immerse occurs, in fact, *every time baptize occurs.*"

"Well, well, I see you are not to be easily satisfied on this point; and I have no more time to spare to-day. I was about to direct your attention to another argument in this same chapter, which will, I trust, set your mind at rest forever.

"You see here that there were no less than three thousand souls converted by Peter's sermon ; and all this vast multitude were added to the church that very day. Now *it is clearly impossible* that they could have been baptized by immersion, and, therefore, it must have been done by sprinkling or pouring ; and if so, then sprinkling and pouring must be the Gospel baptism. I consider this argument entirely conclusive. I want you to examine the record of the transaction carefully and candidly, and if you can believe that these three thousand people were all immersed, you can believe almost any thing. I will call again next week, and you can tell me what you think of it."

The Rev. Mr. Johnson, as he was saying this, arose and took up his hat to depart.

"Please tell me one thing before you go," said Theodosia. "You said *it was impossible* that these three thousand persons could have been immersed. Please tell me why."

"For two good and sufficient reasons," he replied. "In the first place, there was not *water* enough ; and, in the second place, there was not *time* enough. And either one of these circumstances was clearly sufficient to render immersion impossible. We will not discuss the subject any farther at present. Examine it at your leisure, and I trust, when I see you again, I will find your mind entirely satisfied. For the present, I must bid you good evening."

Mr. Johnson walked home, thinking what strange perversity it was in a young girl to venture to form an independent opinion on a theological subject, and to question the infallibility of *his reiterated assertions,* and even to undertake to argue the matter with her pastor.

The young lady took her Bible, and began to examine again the passages to which the pastor had referred in their conversation; but before she had made much progress, her mother required her assistance in some household duties, which occupied her attention till after supper.

Scarcely was supper over, and the table cleared away, when who should come in but her UNCLE JONES.

"Well, Theo.," said he, in his unceremonious way, "I am told that I am about to lose my niece, and that you are on the point of turning Baptist."

"Oh, uncle, don't say that! I shall not be lost to you or any of those I love, even though I should feel it my duty to be baptized. I will still be your own niece, and love you as well as ever."

"You will! Then your mind is about made up on the subject, I suppose?"

"Very nearly, uncle. I have some other points yet to examine, which were suggested by pastor Johnson this afternoon, and unless I find them more——"

"Some other points to examine! Suggested by the pastor! Do you, then, undertake to differ with your pastor; and talk about deciding for yourself in regard to one of the most difficult and complicated questions in theology?"

"Oh, please, uncle, don't be angry; and don't laugh at me. I know I am only a poor simple girl, but I am accountable only to God, and must be decided by my own understanding of his Word. What I can't find in the Scripture for myself, I can't be sure is there. If I don't examine for myself, how can I know any thing about it?"

"Can't you take your pastor's word for it?"

" Yes, if he will show me a 'thus saith the Lord,' as his authority."

" But can't you take it for granted that he has such authority, without his pointing to the chapter and the verse ?"

" It is God's Word, uncle, that I must obey, not man's. If it is in the Book, he can't object to *showing me where it is.* I want to see it for myself. The Apostle praised the Bereans, not because they took Paul's word for all he said, but because 'they searched the Scriptures' for themselves 'to see whether these things were so.'"

" But what if you come to a different conclusion from the pastor ? Do you think it will be wise to trust your own judgment, rather than that of the many great, and good, and learned men of our church, who have examined this subject more thoroughly, and under much more favorable circumstances, than you can hope to do ? Do you think it will be indicative of the humility required by the Gospel of Jesus Christ, for a simple girl not yet out of her teens, and without any theological education, to set up her *own opinions* against those of the wisest and best men of the age ?"

" No, uncle, I don't intend to set up my opinions against those of the great and good men you speak of. But I find that others, equally great and good men, after a careful examination of the subject, have come to a different conclusion; and that some of these same Doctors of Divinity in our church, while they practice one thing, and instruct us to do it, yet expressly declare that it was another and a very different thing which Christ commanded and the first Christians practiced. Now 'when the doctors disagree,' not only with each other, but with themselves, what is a poor, simple girl like me to do ? I can't study theology, *but I can study the Bible.* If sprinkling, as baptism, is there, I can see it. Pastor Johnson says it is there; other learned theologians say it is not. What can I do? I say to each of them, if sprinkling is commanded, show me where; if pouring is commanded, point out the place; if dipping is commanded, let me see it for myself. If I can't find it, and you can't show it to me, I won't believe it's in the book at all. I hope, uncle, you don't really think that I am proud or egotistical; I only want to know just what my Saviour requires. I will believe any thing, and do any thing, if you will only show me that *he* has said it or commanded it."

" No, my dear child, I don't think you are egotistical or proud. I admire your independence, and I wish every person, in every place, would in the same way search the Scriptures, and understand perfectly the grounds on which their faith and practice rests. It is not only the privilege, but the *duty* of every person, to examine and decide for themselves personally, what the Word of God requires. Religion is a *personal* thing. It requires *personal* obedience—and that, too, of the heart, which cannot be rendered without some degree of *personal understanding* of the Word. If you trust your conscience in any man's keeping, you place yourself in a dangerous condition. I am rejoiced to see you studying this subject for yourself. And indeed I was only trying your courage a little, when I affected to be surprised at your doing so. But seriously, my dear Theo., why did you not come to your uncle with your difficulties?"

" I did intend to consult you, uncle, before my final decision, but the question came up so unexpectedly, and our investigation has gone on so rapidly, that I have not yet had any very convenient opportunity; and besides, uncle, to tell the truth, I was afraid you would either be angry, or laugh at me.'

"You were! Well, then, I will disappoint you, for so far from laughing at you, I consider it a very serious and most important question; and instead of being angry with you, it will give me great pleasure to assist you in the investigation; and if I can't show you the sprinkling baptism in the Bible, I will be immersed myself. I will not be like those Doctors of Divinity you spoke of, who say one thing and practice another If Jesus Christ did not command sprinkling, I for one will neither teach nor practice it. I have felt for some time that it was my own duty to investigate this subject, and I will do it now—and with your assistance."

"Oh, uncle, don't talk of my assistance. I am but an ignorant, though anxious inquirer after the truth, and am obliged to call for help on others at every step. If I should speak of rendering assistance to you, I should indeed deserve to be called proud and egotistical."

"Well, well; any way, my child. If you won't help me, I will help you. Tell me just how far you have got along, what discoveries you have made, and where you are standing now—and then we will consider of the rest."

"It will be too long a story, uncle, to go over all the road that I have traveled. But I have learned that there is '*one Lord, one faith, and* ONE BAPTISM.' I have been inquiring whether that baptism is sprinkling, or pouring, or dipping. I have discovered that baptize, as it is used in the New Testament, is a Greek word, and must be understood as those who read and spoke the Greek language in our Saviour's time would understand it. Dr. Albert Barnes told me I could learn this by examining the fifteen places where, he says, the word occurs in the Old Testament. I hunted out each place, and found it meant 'to dip.' I looked in Webster's dictionary, and found that to dip in water, was to plunge an object into the fluid and instantly take it out again—

the very act which the Baptists perform when they baptize. I got Edwin to look in his Greek Lexicon, and he found that the word had the same meaning there—that baptism was immersion. I read McKnight and Chalmers on the 6th of Romans, and found that these great Doctors of Divinity in the Presbyterian church agreed in declaring the same thing; and further, that it was immersion that was practiced by the first church. I am told that Luther, and Calvin, and Doddridge, and a great many others of the most eminent of our theologians, teach the same things. And I have not yet found in the Word of God a single passage which leads me to any different conclusion. Unless, therefore, I should find, as pastor Johnson assures me I shall, that it was clearly impossible to immerse the three thousand that were added to the church on the day of Pentecost, I must be convinced."

"On what ground does your pastor think it impossible?"

"He says there was neither water enough, nor time enough."

"Well, how can you prove that there was?"

"It don't seem to me, uncle, that it is necessary that I should be able to prove it in any other way than by the mere statement of the Scripture that they were baptized; for if the word baptize means to immerse, then the book *says they were immersed;* and if they were immersed, there *must* have been time enough, and water enough, whether I can prove it or not. If I do not believe this, I make God a liar."

"But what if it can be clearly shown that there *was not* water enough, or time enough; then would it not be more reasonable to suppose the word has some *other meaning,* than to believe the record to be false?"

"Perhaps it would, but the pastor only *said* it. He

did not *try* to *prove* it. Nor do I see how it would be possible *now* to determine how much water there was in Jerusalem eighteen hundred years ago, even if we knew the exact number of gallons it would require to immerse three thousand people. I remember that we read in 2 Kings xviii. 17, about the '*upper pool*,' and in 2 Kings xx. 20, about the '*pool*' that Hezekiah made, and in Nehemiah about another '*fountain*' and '*pool*,' and in Isaiah xxii. 9, about the '*waters of the lower pool*,' and in John v. 2, about the '*pool of Bethesda*' that had five porches, and John ix. 7, about the '*pool of Siloam*.'"

"I think the pastor will be obliged to give it up, Theo., so far as the want of *water* is concerned; for in addition to this testimony from the Scripture, we have that of many distinguished travelers, who were, like ourselves, opposed to the Baptists; and yet all agree that Jerusalem was, and is, one of the best watered cities on the globe. Dr. Robinson, one of these travelers, speaks of 'immense cisterns now, and anciently, existing within the area of the Temple, supplied partly from rain water, and partly by the aqueduct,' and tells us also that 'almost every private house had a cistern in it,' p. 480. Speaking of the reservoirs, he says, p. 483—'With such reservoirs, Jerusalem was abundantly supplied, to say nothing of the immense pools of Solomon, beyond Bethlehem, which were no doubt constructed for the benefit of the Holy City.'

"'There are,' he says, 'on the north side of the city, outside the walls, two very large reservoirs, one of which is over three hundred feet long and more than two hundred feet wide, and the other nearly six hundred feet long by over two hundred and fifty feet wide;' and besides these he mentions the pool of Silom and two others as being without the walls. Within the walls he mentions 'the pool of Bathsheba,' 'the pool of Hezekiah,' and 'the pool of Bethesda.' The pool of Hezekiah he says was about two hundred and forty feet long by about one hundred and forty-four feet broad; the pool of Bethesda three hundred and sixty feet long by one hundred and thirty feet wide; and besides these he mentions an aqueduct and numerous other fountains. (Rob. Resh. in Pal. pp. 480 to 516.)

"But we might have known, without any of this testimony, that a city to which the whole male population of a vast and fertile country were required to resort several times a year, and whose religious ceremonial required such frequent ablutions as did that of the Jews at the time of Christ, would be abundantly furnished with the means of bathing, and consequently present sufficient facilities for immersion. Moreover, the water would not be destroyed by dipping in it; and therefore the same quantity that would suffice for one would do for a hundred. And it is evident that so far as the water is concerned, *any one* of these numerous pools, either in or out of the city, would have sufficed. But was there not another and more serious difficulty? These pools and fountains belonged to the Jews. The same men who hated and crucified Christ now had control of the water of the city and the suburbs, and is it probable that they would permit the disciples to use them?"

"Certainly they would," said Theodosia, "for in consequence of the wonderful events of this day, the Scripture says that 'fear came upon every soul,' and that the disciples 'did eat their meat with gladness and singleness of heart, praising God and *having favor with all the people.*' They gave them the Temple to preach in, and it is not likely that they would refuse the pools to baptize in."

"Surely," said Uncle Jones, "that must remove all

conceivable difficulty as to the water; but we may not find it so easy to arrange matters in regard to time. Time has always been a very unaccommodating old fellow; and a day among the Jews was only twelve hours from six in the morning till six at night, and if we can't get the three thousand into the water within that period, we shall be obliged to leave some or all of them out, and dispose of them in some other way."

" Well, uncle, I don't see why we can't dispose of *some* of them in some other way, for the Scripture does not say they were all *baptized* that day, but only all *added* to the company of the disciples; and *some* of them may have been baptized by John or by the disciples of Jesus Christ before his death, and now only come out publicly and consorted with the Apostles; and some might have gone up to them and joined their ranks that day and have been baptized afterward. As a person is now said to have joined the Baptists when he makes a profession of religion among them, and is *received by them for baptism.*

" But is it by any means certain that three thousand could not all have been immersed that day? It would not be hard to tell if we knew how much time there was; how many administrators there were; and just how many each one of them could immerse."

" Well, stop a little, Theo.; let us take up one point at a time. How many hours had they to go upon? though as to that, I don't see why it would not take about as long to *sprinkle* or *pour upon* them, one at a time, and reverently repeat the formula, ' I baptize thee in the name of the Father, and of the Son, and of the Holy Ghost,' as it would to immerse them; *but we will examine.* What says the record? It seems that when Peter commenced his speech, it was not yet nine o'clock in the morning, which, as the Jews counted from **six,** would be the 'third hour in the day.' How long before nine it was we cannot tell. We will suppose it was just nine, and there were, consequently, only nine hours remaining, before six in the evening, which closed the day. Peter's speech, as it is recorded, would not have occupied a quarter of an hour in its delivery; but it is said that he exhorted them with many other words; so we will suppose he spoke an hour, or we will say *two* hours. It would then be eleven o'clock. Now we will give them another hour to go to the water, so that it is twelve o'clock when the baptism begins. Now they must finish, you see, in six hours; so that is our limit as to time."

"Very well, uncle, we will consider it so, though really I can't see that Peter spoke even *one* hour, much less two. But now how many administrators were there?"

"This is a question," said Uncle Jones, "about which there is some difference of opinion. There were certainly the twelve Apostles, and many think also the seventy others whom Jesus sent out two by two—who must have been present, as Luke says 'they were all with one accord in one place.' If so, then there were eighty-two authorized administrators. But let us, first, to obviate all difficulties, suppose there were only the twelve, who would each have just two hundred and fifty persons to immerse. So on this supposition, the question is narrowed down to this—can one man immerse two hundred and fifty persons in six hours? I have felt some little curiosity on this subject, and when I have witnessed immersions, have taken out my watch, and observed the time. It has usually required about fifteen minutes to immerse twenty persons; provided the candidates march in two by two, to the place where the administrator is standing. This allowance of time permits the work to be done without any appearance of haste, and with the coolest deliberation.

"I have been told by several Baptist ministers, whose veracity I have no reason to doubt, that they have immersed large numbers at the rate of two in every minute, or sixty in half an hour. At this rate the twelve would have finished the work of this occasion in a little over two hours—two hours and ten minutes. If they only worked half so fast, and baptized but one a minute, they had time to get through, and more than an hour and a half to spare. They could each have stopped every half hour, and rested ten minutes, and then have gotten through in time."

"So, uncle, it is as I suspected, there is no difficulty as to time, even though only the twelve were engaged in the work; but if the seventy assisted, then how long would it take?"

"In that case, there would have been less than forty persons for each administrator, and of course it could have been done in less than half an hour."

"But, uncle, is it certain that any one besides the twelve were authorized to baptize?"

"Surely, Theo., others must have been, for it is evident that Aquilla, Acts xviii. 2, and Apollos, Acts xviii. 24, and Paul himself, Acts ix. 18, were baptized by *others than the twelve*. And Peter, when he had preached the Word to the household of Cornelius, did not baptize them himself, but directed it to be done by some one else—Acts x. 14. But whether this baptism was performed by the twelve, or by the twelve assisted by the seventy, does not now concern us, as we find there was no want of time in either case. And so you have found nothing in this case to change your opinion concerning the meaning of the word baptize. Now have you any other difficulties in your way?"

8

"Not that I know of now, uncle. The case seems to me to be perfectly plain. But perhaps you can suggest some other source of information which I have not yet explored."

"Indeed, my dear niece, I am myself in great perplexity upon this very question. I have been some time engaged in its investigation; much longer than you have, and have been compelled to come to about the same conclusions with yourself—though this is the first time I have ever mentioned it."

"Oh, uncle, is it possible? Oh, if I had only known this four days ago."

"Oh, yes. If you had known it, I suppose you would have been quoting Uncle Jones as high authority for your heretical opinions. But I beg you will not mention this, even to your mother, until I shall have finally decided the case. But tell me now, Theo., what do you intend to do?"

"There is only one thing, uncle, that I *can* do. I must obey my Saviour—I must be baptized. There is only one reflection that still casts a shade of doubt across my mind, and that is this: if it was immersion that Christ commanded, and the Apostles and first Christians practiced, how has it so universally been set aside, and sprinkling substituted in its place?"

"A very important point is that, my dear niece, and I hope you will come to no final conclusion till you have investigated thoroughly the whole subject in all its bearings. And be assured, if I can in any way assist you, I will be most happy to do so. But your friend, Mr. Courtney, is much more familiar with these subjects than I am. Suppose I mention your difficulty to him and request him to call to-morrow evening. Perhaps I may come with him "

THE FIFTH NIGHT'S STUDY.

WHICH CONTAINS

A VERY IMPORTANT DISCUSSION

ON A

VERY IMPORTANT QUESTION.

NEW CHARACTERS AND CURIOUS ARGUMENTS.

THE SACRED OR APPROPRIATE USE

OF

THE WORD BAPTIZE,

DISTINGUISHED FROM THE COMMON.

FIFTH NIGHT'S STUDY.

NCLE JONES was Professor of Languages in the College to which we have once or twice before referred. A frank, free-spoken man, with a clear head and warm heart, in which affection for his amiable, talented, and beautiful niece held no small space. Like most of the members of his denomination, having received his so-called baptism without his own knowledge or consent, he had never, until very recently, felt that he had any personal interest whatever in this subject.

He had been informed that he was baptized while yet an infant in his mother's arms, and whether it was properly or improperly done had been no concern of *his*. It had been the duty of his parents and their pastor to attend to that, and he had never inquired whether they did it illy or well.

A few days since, however, his attention had been directed to the subject by a somewhat singular occurrence. Mr. Courtney, the teacher, was spending a leisure hour at Prof. Jones's room, at a time when no recitation claimed the attention of either, and they were earnestly discussing some item of the morning's news, when two of the college students looked in, and seeing a visitor, were about to withdraw, but the Professor, with his characteristic kindness, called them back, and inquired in what way he could serve them.

After a moment's hesitation the younger, (whose name was Pearson) replied: "Oh, it is of no consequence, Professor Jones. Chum and I had a little dispute which we agreed to refer to you for decision, but as you are engaged we will call some other time."

"No, no," said the Professor, "come in and tell me now. I am quite at liberty. Perhaps Mr. Courtney will assist us, if there is any thing important to determine upon."

"Oh, no," said Smith (the other student), "it is of no great importance. We only wish to ask you what is the Greek word for *to dip.*"

"It is *embapto, bapto,* or *baptizo,* young gentlemen. Why did you not refer to your English and Greek Lexicon? That would have enabled you to answer the question for yourselves."

"We did refer to that," said Pearson; "but Smith was not satisfied with the Lexicon. He thought there must be some mistake. Now," he continued, "will you be kind enough to tell us what was the word which, among the Greeks, commonly signified *to pour?*"

"Certainly. *Cheo* signifies *to pour.*"

"Had the Greeks any words which commonly meant to sprinkle?"

"Yes, *raino* meant to sprinkle."

"Had they any word which meant to wet?"

"Certainly, *brecho* signified to wet. But tell me, young gentlemen, what is the object of these questions? You know the meaning of these Greek words as well as I do."

"Pardon me, Professor, but let me ask one question more. Did not the Greeks have a word which signified to wash?"

"Yes, they had several. *Louo* was used to signify a general washing, as by bathing, and *nipto* a partial one, as of the hands alone. The Greek language was perhaps even more copious in words of this sort than the

English. It had a word to express almost every manner of using water."

"Excuse me, Professor Jones, but I want to ask one
question more. Will you please to tell us whether *bapto*
and *baptizo* are not as properly, and as commonly rendered by *dip* as *cheo* is by *pour*, or *raino* by *sprinkle*,
or *louo* by *wash* ?"

"Certainly they are, except when *bapto* has its secondary meaning, to dye, to color, to stain. But now,
young gentlemen, you must permit me to turn questioner. I desire to know for what purpose you come
with such a string of questions to *me* ?"

"We hope you will not be offended, sir; but Smith
and I," said Pearson, "went last Sabbath afternoon to
witness the immersion; and have since had a little discussion on the meaning of the word baptize and its cognates, as used in the Scriptures in reference to the ordinance.

"We found the words in the Lexicon just as we
would any other words, and by this means, were, as I
thought, obliged to translate them by dipping or immersion.

"But Smith contended that there must be some error
in this, and that *baptismos* must signify a sprinkling or
a pouring, as well as a dipping; and since we could
find no authority for this in the Grammars or Lexicons
of the language, he insisted on coming to you about it."

"Certainly, sir, there must be some mistake about
these words in the Lexicons, for my father was a Presbyterian minister, and I know he was a good Greek
scholar, and yet he not only baptized by sprinkling,
but insisted that there was no such thing as immersion
ever spoken of for baptism. The president of this college and all the faculty are Presbyterians, and they all
approve of sprinkling as baptism—which they certainly

could not do if the very word baptism in the Greek signifies immersion. I cannot understand it, sir, if Jesus Christ meant to say sprinkle, why did he not use the word *raino?* If he meant to say pour, why did he not use the word *cheo* or *eccheo?* If he meant to say wet (that is, to apply water in any form), why did he not use the word *brecho?* As it seems to be certain, from the practice of the best and most learned clergymen of the world, that he did not and could not have meant dip or immerse, why did he use a word which commonly, if not always, meant to immerse? And which, as a matter of course, every one who read or spoke the Greek would understand to mean immerse? I wish, Professor Jones, you would be kind enough to explain this to us, sir, for Pearson has annoyed me about it till I have almost lost my patience."

The professor himself was somewhat annoyed by these questions, and the more so because they had been asked in the presence of Mr. Courtney, whom he knew to be a Baptist, and a thorough classical scholar. He was, however, too prudent to permit the students to discover his embarrassment, and only replied, " We often find it much easier to ask questions, young gentlemen, than it is to answer them—but in the present case, you have only to recollect that words often undergo a change of meaning in the lapse of time, or by transfer to other places, and your difficulties with all vanish. We may grant that dipping or immersion is the idea which was originally connected with these words—and so it is still in the classic Greek; hence this is what you find in the Lexicons of the language; but the Greek of the New Testament was not the pure classic Greek, but a sort of Jew Greek, if I may so speak, which had come into use in Palestine, and may have been different from the language as originally spoken and written; and as the writers of the New Testament were treating of a *new* system of religion, they would be very likely to use words in a new sense. And though it cannot be denied that the idea of submersion is almost always in these words as they occur in the classical writers, yet it does not of necessity follow that it must be in them as constantly when they are used by the evangelists."

"Thank you, sir," said Smith. "That is very satisfactory." And the young men took their leave.

When they were gone, Professor Jones, observing the peculiar expression of Mr. Courtney's countenance, was led to continue the subject. "You did not seem," said he, "to be as well satisfied as the boys were with my explanation."

"If you will pardon me for saying so, Professor, I do not see how you could be satisfied with it yourself."

"And why not, pray?"

"Because you have too much good sense to take it for granted that a thing is true only because it possibly may be true. You intimated, if you did not plainly assert to the young men, that these words, *baplo, baptizo,* and their co-relatives, signify to sprinkle, and pour, in the Greek New Testament, though you will admit that they never have those meanings in any other Greek book; and your sole and entire authority for this assertion, is the fact that some other words have changed their meaning, and therefore it was possible that these might have done so also. I grant that they might have changed, but there is not even the shadow of any evidence to show that they have really done so. Some men have applied to the Legislature and had their names changed; and so you and I might have done, but this is certainly no proof that our names have been changed. If you build an argument, or base an explanation on this change, it is **not enough** to suppose it to be possible that such a change *might* occur; you must prove it to be certain that such a change *did* occur."

"But you will grant," replied Professor Jones, "that it was at least probable, that as Christ was introducing a new order of things in religion, new words, or rather old words with new meanings, should be employed in describing this new ordinance."

"So far from granting that it was probable, I will prove that it was morally impossible; though, if it had been even probable, it would not justify your conclusions.

"What would you think of the common sense of that member of Congress who should treat the Constitution of the United States in the same way that you treat the Constitution of the Christian church, and earnestly and soberly declare that such words as war and peace, taxes and treaties, are not to be understood among us in their common and ordinary acceptation, as they are used by other writers, and as we find them defined in the dictionaries—but that war means want, peace means plenty, taxes mean tables, and treaties mean troubles? You would expect his colleagues to call him a fool. Nor would you think more highly of his wisdom, if he should reply, and defend himself by saying—that it is true these were common English words, the meaning of which had been fixed and known for many ages, yet America was a new country, and the Constitution was designed to usher in a new order of things, and nothing was more natural than that its framers should use words in some new and unnatural sense! And yet, this is precisely the manner of reasoning adopted by grave and reverend DOCTORS OF DIVINITY, when they attempt to expound the constitution which Christ gave his church. There is not a single word in the whole Greek language the meaning of which is more definitely fixed and more perfectly known than that of *baptizo*, and those derived from it. In any other book but the New Testament, no scholar ever hesitates about its signification. When Homer speaks of a smith baptizing a hatchet or huge pole-axe in cold water, to harden it, we have no difficulty in knowing what he means. We see the smith harden steel in the same manner now, by plunging it in the water.

"When Herodotus says of the Egyptians, that if they touched a swine, they went into the river, and baptized themselves with their clothes on, no scholar doubts they plunged into the water.

"When Diodorus Siculus says of a ship that it was baptized in the sea, no scholar doubts that he means to say the ship was sunk—merged in the sea.

"When Plutarch says of the Roman general that he baptized his hand in blood, no one doubts that he dipped his hand in the blood. And yet you know that in these, and many similar places, the very same word is used which is employed in the New Testament to denote the ordinance. You may take the whole range of Greek literature, up to the very time when the Gospels were written, and you cannot find one solitary instance in which these words are used to signify either sprinkling or pouring, nor any one in which they have not in them the idea of an immersion—literal or figurative."

"Yes, Mr. Courtney, but that was classic Greek. The Hebraistic Greek, spoken and written among the Jews, might have been different."

"So it might, Professor Jones, but as regards this word, it was not different, nevertheless. If there was any such thing as Jew Greek, you would find it in the translation of their own Scripture, made by seventy learned men of their own nation, and hence called by them the Septuagint. With this translation the Jews, in our Saviour's time, were more familiar than with the original Hebrew. It was this that Jesus quoted in his discourses. It was this that Matthew, and the other writers of the New Testament, refer to, and quote as the Law and the Prophets. This was the Greek which the Jews understood better than any other. If there was, therefore, any such thing as Hebraistic or Jew Greek it was in this book. Now, sir, you know very well that the idea of *dipping*, expressed by the Hebrew word '*tabal*' is in this Jew Greek uniformly rendered by '*bapto*' or '*baptizo*'—and these words are never used in any other than their common classical signification.

"And further still, Josephus, who was a Jew, lived among the Jews, and wrote the history of the Jews, lived and wrote just about the same time that the authors of the New Testament did, and if they wrote in the 'Jew Greek,' he did so also. He wrote for the same people, at the same time, and in the same language, and uses the same word again and again, but no one ever suspected that *he* meant sprinkling or pouring, or that he used it in any other than its common, classical sense. He invariably uses the word to signify sinking, submerging, or dipping. And besides all this, you will please to remember that the greater part of the New Testament was written, not for the Jews, but for the *Greeks*, to read, and, consequently, if the writers did not use Greek words, in their ordinary Greek sense, they would not be understood—but would, in fact, convey an absolute falsehood. Mark was written at Rome, for the Italians and strangers who read the Greek language there. Luke addressed his Gospel and the Acts to an individual in the Greek nation, for Theophilus is a Greek name. John was written in the very territory of Greece itself. It is evident, therefore, that even if there had been a peculiar *Jewish* use of the word, the writers of the Gospels could not have employed it unless they had explained, at the same time, that they did not use it in its common signification. If I say that I was immersed in the Cumberland river people who understand English will think I was plunged beneath the surface of the water—or else that I state what was not true; because this is the common every-day meaning of the word immerse in the language to which it belongs. So when these writers say Christ was baptized in the river Jordan, everybody that read Greek would understand that he was submerged in the river, for this was the common every-day meaning of the word baptize in the language to which it belonged."

"I must acknowledge, Mr. Courtney," said the Professor, "there is a great deal of force in what you say; and I really do not, at this moment, see how I can set aside your reasoning. I had no idea that so strong an argument could possibly be made in behalf of immersion. But is it not true, sir, that there are many places in the New Testament where the word *cannot possibly* mean immersion—or where it is at least much more *probable* that it means something else?"

"I have no doubt, Professor, that there are a number of places where it would seem much more *probable* to you that it has some other meaning, if it were not that the usage of the language has fixed its meaning to be immersion. It might seem probable to us that Jesus rode into Jerusalem on a war-horse, but the meaning of the words employed in describing his entry compels us to believe that he rode on an ass's colt. So, also, it might seem probable that the Pharisees only *sprinkled* the couches on which they reclined at their meals, but the *word* employed shows that they really immersed them, however improbable it might seem to one who was not aware of the extreme care which the superstitious Pharisees employed, lest some part of their furniture should escape the contact of the water, and so remain in its impurity.

"So, also, when he says that 'The Pharisees and all the Jews eat not when they come from market, except they first wash (*immerse*) themselves.' It might seem more probable that they only *sprinkled* themselves, or crossed their foreheads with holy water, or poured some drops upon the top of their heads: but the words employed declare expressly that they '*immersed*.' I will not refuse to believe God's Word, because he tells me of a circumstance that seems to me *improbable*. The Scriptures are full of improbable things, but I surely will not dare to change the meaning of the words used to relate them, in order to get rid of the improbability.

"This would be worse than infidelity itself. I believe just what God says, whether it were probable or improbable.

"But now if you tell me that *these things were impossible*, that is quite a different matter. If any persons or things are said to be baptized, that *could not possibly have been immersed*, then I must grant that the Scripture either asserts what is not true, or that it uses words in a new and unusual sense. Permit me to suggest to you, Professor, that it would not be an unprofitable study to investigate this point. Take a Greek Concordance, and turn to every passage where the word occurs; and if you find any impossibility in admitting the classical and common meaning, I will be prepared to concede something when we meet again."

"I thank you for the suggestion, Mr. Courtney. You have indeed thrown new light upon this subject. I am just now somewhat bewildered by it. I will examine more carefully, and tell you my conclusions."

It was on Monday that this conversation occurred, and Mr. Courtney was returning home, when he was

called by Edwin into Mrs. Ernest's, to assist the inves
tigations of Theodosia and Mr. Percy. It was now near
night on Thursday, and he had yet heard nothing further from the Professor on the subject; but just as he
was leaving his school room, a lad handed him the following note:

"DEAR COURTNEY:—I have been examining, as you
suggested, into the Scripture usage of the word '*Baptizo*' and its cognates. I am surprised and embarrassed
by the results. Difficulties in the way of sprinkling increase at every step; yet there are also some difficulties
in the way of immersion. Perhaps you can easily
obviate them. I had last evening a very interesting
conversation with my niece on this subject. She feels
that she has been greatly assisted by your advice and
suggestions. There is still, however, one point on
which her mind remains in doubt. It is this. If Christ
commanded immersion, and immersion was practiced by
the first churches, how came it to be so universally discarded, and sprinkling substituted in its place? This
question, I confess, presents a mystery to me also.
Will you do me the kindness to meet me at Mrs. Ernest's
to-night, and come prepared to enlighten our darkness
on this point? Yours truly,
"J. M. JONES."

This was a subject to which the teacher had recently
given considerable attention, and had collected a number of authorities among Pedobaptist writers, showing, not only that immersion was at first the universal
practice of all the churches, but also the very time and
place when and where pouring first, and sprinkling
afterward, were introduced instead of it.

He went home, therefore, and, after supper, selected

such books as he thought would be most satisfactory to his inquirers, and took them with him to the widow's cottage.

He found Uncle Jones already there, who was not long in beginning the discussion.

"I see by the pile of books you have brought," said he, "that you received my note, and have come prepared to remove, if possible, all our historical difficulties. Before we enter upon the history of the ordinance, will you permit me to mention some difficulties in the way of understanding the word baptize to signify immersion, whereever it occurs in the New Testament?"

"Certainly; for though I ventured to tell you (when we talked upon this subject last Monday), that you would not find any *impossibilities*, I did not even intimate that you would find no *difficulties*. But what are those which have troubled you?"

"It will perhaps save time if we take up the passages in order. I knew that *bapto* and *baptizo* were derived from the same root, and, in classical usage, had precisely the same signification, except that *bapto*, while it signifies to dip, signifies also to dye or color, which baptizo never does.* And I, therefore, found all the places where these words occur.

---

* "What," says Professor Moses Stuart, page 298—"What are the *classical* meanings of bapto and baptizo? Both these words mean to dip, to immerse, to plunge into any thing liquid. All lexicographers and critics of any note are agreed in this." And again, on page 288: "The original etymological root of *baptizo*, *bapto*, and also of the nouns and adjectives kindred with them, appears plainly to be the Greek monosyllable BAP. The leading and original meaning of which seems to have been dipping, immersing, plunging, soaking, drenching in some liquid; and as closely associated with this, the idea of dyeing or coloring, since this was done by dipping." And again: "The precise difference between bapto and baptizo is, that while they both

" I will first mention those in which there is no direct allusion to the ordinance, but where the word occurs, as it often does in the Old Testament, in connection with other subjects.

" Theodosia, get your Testament, child, and read them as I mention them, according to my memorandum. The first is Luke xvi. 24.

" 'Send Lazarus that he may (baptize) *dip* the tip of his finger in water and cool my tongue.' This seems plain enough; and so does the second, John xiii. 26, 'It is he to whom I shall give the sop when I have (baptized) dipped it; and when he had (baptized) dipped it, he gave it to Judas.' Nor did I find any difficulty with the third, Revelation xix. 13, 'And he was clothed in a vesture (baptized) dipped in blood.' But here in the fourth case, or Mark vii. 4, I find a difficulty. 'The (baptisms) washing of cups, and pots, and brazen vessels, and *tables.*' Now, so far as the cups, and pots, and vessels are concerned, the matter is made entirely plain by turning to Leviticus xii. 32, 'Whether it be any vessel of wood, or raiment, or skin, or sack, whatsoever vessel it be wherein any work is done, it must be *put into the water,* and it shall be unclean until evening, and so it shall be cleansed.' From this it is evident that the cups and other vessels were immersed, or '*put into the water:*' but the word translated table, may mean also a couch or bed, and how the beds and tables could be immersed, I do not so easily understand."

"And yet, uncle," said the young lady, " the same Scripture that speaks of the immersion or baptism of

---

agree in one common and original meaning, that of immersion or plunging, usage has employed bapto to express the idea of coloring, as well as the idea of dipping or plunging; while baptizo is not employed in the additional sense of coloring."

9

the cups, speaks also of that of the tables Whatever was done to the cups, therefore, was done to the tables too."

"Yes, Theo., and that is what makes me doubt if there was any immersion about it. The cups could have been dipped easily enough, but to dip beds and tables is quite another business."

"But, uncle, if 'putting into the water' was immersion, must they not have been immersed?"

"It would seem so, Theo., but I can't understand how it could be done."

"The difficulty will all vanish," said Mr. Courtney "if you will remember that the little stool to hold his plate which stood at the head of each guest as he reclined upon the floor, was called a table, and the mat or cloth which he lay upon, was called a couch or bed; and either of these could be immersed as readily as the cups. They had no massive mahogany tables, or beds containing sixty pounds of feathers, as we have. The poor invalid whom Jesus healed, did not probably evince any extraordinary muscular power when he *took up his bed* and walked away with it.

"But we have other testimony besides that of Mark on the subject. What if I show you from the writings of a learned Hebrew, that the beds and tables not only could be immersed, but that their immersion was habitually practiced by the superstitious Pharisees!"

"That will indeed remove every shadow of doubt,' said the Professor; "but have you indeed such testimony?"

"Certainly we have. There was a very learned Jew who wrote a very elaborate commentary on the Jewish customs and traditions. Dr. Adam Clarke, the great commentator, recognizes his authority, and calls him the 'great expounder of the Jewish Law;' and, as he comes thus 'properly vouched for,' I trust his evidence will not be disputed. This learned and eminent Rabbi, commonly called Rabbi Maimonides, says, in his commentary: 'Every vessel of wood, as a table or bed, receives defilement, and these were washed *by covering in water*, and very nice and particular they were,' he adds, 'that they might be *covered all over*.'

"If the article was very large and could not be dipped all at one time, it could still, according to the teaching of this great expounder, be easily immersed. For, says he, 'A bed that is wholly defiled, if he dip it part by part, it is pure. If he dip it in the pool of water it is clean, even though its feet are plunged in the thick clay.'

"Perhaps," continued Mr. Courtney, addressing Theodosia, "your uncle may find it easier to believe Maimonides than Mark, and if so, the tables are disposed of."

"The Rabbi's explanation does indeed remove all difficulties," said Uncle Jones; "but now look at the first part of the verse. 'The Pharisees and all the Jews except they wash their hands, eat not; and when they come from the market, except they (baptize) wash, they eat not; holding the tradition of the elders.' Now I can hardly think it possible that the Jews, whenever they came from market, dipped themselves all over in water, as the word (*baptisonti*) employed here, would intimate, if immersion indeed be the meaning of the word. It seems as though something else would be much more natural and likely to be done."

"Suppose it was more likely that they should do something else," replied Mr. Courtney, "can you not believe, on the authority of the Word of God, that the superstitious Jews would do very unlikely, improbable, and inconvenient things? It cannot be denied that it was just as *possible* for them to immerse themselves (*baptisonti*) when they came from market, as it was to wash their hands (*nipsonti*) on ordinary occasions, or before meals; but it is very easy to determine what it was which they actually did, since it was that which was required by the 'tradition of the elders.' What, then, was this tradition of the elders? Maimorides shall enlighten us here again. ' If the Pharisees,' says he, ' touched but the garments of the common people, they were defiled all over as if they had touched a profluous person, and needed *immersion*, and were obliged to do it; and hence when they walked the streets, they walked on the side of the way, that they might not be defiled by touching the common people. In a laver (they say) which holds forty seahs of water, every defiled man dips himself.'

"It was, therefore, we see, a veritable immersion which was required by the 'tradition of the elders,' as preserved in their nation and recorded by one of their most learned Rabbis; and though Doctors of Divinity find it very hard to believe the plain assertion of the Spirit of God, speaking by Mark, and fancy there must be some mistake or misunderstanding when he says the Pharisees immersed themselves; yet I have never heard that any of them hesitated to receive the uninspired testimony of the Jewish Rabbi, or proposed to give to *his* words new and unheard-of meanings to obviate the necessity of admitting that immersion was practiced by the superstitious Jews."

"I am very much obliged to you," said the Professor, "for laying the sin of my unbelief at the door of the Doctors of Divinity; and, to tell the truth, they are in some degree responsible for it, for I am doubtful if I should have seen these difficulties so plainly had I not looked at them through the theological microscope of

Dr. Miller, of Princeton, New Jersey. You have disposed of them so easily and so satisfactorily, that I am
almost ashamed to ask you for your opinion about the
divers washings in Hebrews ix. 10. These washings,
you know, are in the original called Baptismois or baptisms—were they not some of the many sprinklings
enjoined upon the Jews by the Levitical law?"

"Surely, my dear sir, if they had been, Paul would
have called them sprinklings. He understood the use
of the proper word for *sprinkle*, for he uses it in this
same connection where he speaks of 'the ashes of an
heifer *sprinkling* the unclean.' The baptisms were evidently something else, and another and altogether different word is employed to designate them—one word
refers to the *sprinklings* required by the law, the other
to the *immersions* which it commanded."

"But, Mr. Courtney, I have in some way received the
impression that the law nowhere commands any *immersions*. It commands sprinklings and ablutions, washings and purifications, but never in any case immersions
—so the allusion must be to some other cleansings than
to immersions."

"Permit me to say, Professor, that you could not
have received that impression from a careful study of
the law itself—you are probably indebted for it to a
Doctor of Divinity. Take your Bible, and turn to the
law, and you will read of immersions or *dippings* in
blood—dippings in blood and running water—dippings
in oil—dippings in the water of purification—and in the
practice of the Jews, many, if not most of the *washings*
mentioned in the law, were performed by *immersion*,
though this was not specifically required by the command. The ten lavers that Solomon made, were for
washing the sacrifices, and these were washed by *dipping* them in the water. The great sea which he made,

was for the priests to *bathe* in, 2d Chron. iv. 6. And this washing was an immersion. On how many occasions do you read, in the 15th of Leviticus, that one 'must wash his clothes, and *bathe* himself n water?' Are clothes washed without *immersion?* The vessels of wood, skin, etc., were required to '*to be put into the water*'—was not this an immersion? And if you doubt that the washing or bathing of their persons was immersion, we will learn from Maimonides what it was that they actually did in obedience to this law:

"'In their law,' says this learned Rabbi, 'whenever washing of the body or the clothes is mentioned, it means nothing else than the washing the *whole* body; for if any wash himself all over except the very tip of his little finger, he is still in his uncleanness.'

"That this was what the Jews understood by washing, is further evident from the case of Naaman. The prophet told him to go and *wash* seven times in Jordan; and it was regarded as strict and literal obedience when he went and '*dipped himself* seven times.'"

"I see, Mr. Courtney, that it is just as easy to find the 'divers immersions' as the 'sprinklings,' and I do not see why I should have been so easily imposed upon. I find I must be careful how I receive the assertions even of our Doctors of Divinity."

"Yes, uncle," said Theodosia, "I have determined that I will find every thing in the Bible *for myself*. It is the only way in which I *can* be certain it is there."

"We have now," said Mr. Courtney, examined every text in the New Testament where the word is translated, and not merely transferred in our version. In several of these places we find it is rendered 'dip,' as it is in the fourteen places mentioned by Dr. Barnes, where it occurs in the Old Testament. In all the other places it is rendered *wash*, and we have ascertained, in every case, that the washing was by 'dipping.'"

"But, Mr. Courtney, did not you ascertain this from Rabbi Maimonides, and not from the Scriptures themselves? I want my faith to stand alone upon the Word of God"

"No, Miss Ernest, we learned it from the word of God itself. I quoted the Jewish Rabbi to satisfy your uncle—because (if he will pardon me for saying so) he seemed to feel that some human testimony was needful to sustain the (to him) strange assertion of the Word of God, that the superstitious Pharisees immersed their tables or couches, and themselves, but we had abundant proof without the Rabbi's testimony."

"What was it, Mr. Courtney?—please call it to my mind again. The Bible argument is all that I care to remember."

"You are right, Miss Ernest—it is all you *need* to remember. You know we have on former occasions determined the meaning of the word baptism, by a variety of methods. We found it to be immersion or dipping. Now, your uncle admitted this, so far as regards *all other books but the New Testament*. Here he conceived it *might* have a new signification. I conceded that it might, but denied that it did; for the fact that a thing *may* possibly, or even probably, be true, *is no evidence that it is true*. Then to show that it *must* have a new meaning, he referred to three places where, in our version, it is rendered 'washing.' In Mark vii. 4, he said it seemed unreasonable to think that the Pharisees immersed their tables and beds (for the word 'kleina,' rendered *tables*, may mean couches as well); and therefore he thought he ought to give the word some other meaning.

"To this I might have merely replied, the Word of

God says the 'kleina' were immersed, and therefore it
was done.   I will not take the liberty to *change* God's
word because it states improbabilities.   But we were
very accommodating, and reminded him that whatever
was done to the tables, or 'kleina,' was the *same* thing
that was done to the 'cups' and other vessels, and then
turned to Leviticus and showed that *they* were 'put
into the water,' and of course the 'kleina' were 'put
into the water,' also.   This, I am sure, was proof
enough, without going to the Rabbi, to see *how* it was
done, and this was all Scripture proof.   We went to the
Rabbi only to 'make assurance doubly sure.'   Then
your uncle thought it more reasonable to believe that
the Pharisees did something else instead of *dipping*
themselves (as Mark says) when they came from the
market.

"I might have answered as before—God says they
dipped, and I will not dare to doubt it, though it be
improbable.

"But as the text says, they did it 'holding the tradition of the elders.'   I referred to the Jewish Rabbi
merely to learn what the 'tradition of the elders'
required on this point, and we found it was just what
the word expressed.

"In the third place, your uncle had conceived that
the *baptismois* or washings spoken of in Hebrews ix. 10,
could not be immersions, because some Doctor of
Divinity had told him there were no immersions; and
we went back to the Old Testament and found immersions in abundance—even without those rites which
are called 'washings;' but even these were immersions
also, as I have proved by the case of Naaman, and
referred to the Rabbi as confirmatory evidence."

"Very satisfactory, I declare," said the Professor,
laughing.   "You see, Theo., Mr. Courtney fully

appreciates the difficulties in the way of convincing your uncle.

"But let us see what he has to say about these other places which I have marked, and in which the word is used without translation, and refers directly to the ordinance itself. The first is Matthew iii. 5, 6, which reads of the baptism of the multitudes by John."

"In regard to that," said Mr. Courtney, "it will not be worth while to consume our time to-night—I will refer you to Miss Theodosia, who has examined it already. I will only say, that if you prefer '*washing*' as your translation of the word, there could be no quicker way for John to *wash* them than by dipping them in the water."

"The next place I have marked," said Uncle Jones, "is the 11th verse of the same chapter, 'I indeed baptize you with water, but he that cometh after me shall baptize you with the Holy Ghost and with fire.'"

"I trust you find no difficulty there," said Mr. Courtney.

"No," replied the Professor, "except that it presents a strong argument in favor of immersion. The original certainly reads (if we translate as we would in any other book), I immerse you in water, and he shall immerse you in the Holy Ghost and in fire.

"The next is the 16th verse of the same chapter— 'And Jesus, when he was baptized, went up straightway out of the water.' I find a strong argument for immersion in this also; for if they did not immerse, I see no reason for going into the water—or, if we read that he went up *from*, instead of out of, the water, I still see no reason for even going to it. We do not go to the river to sprinkle now—I can't think they did then.

"The next place I have marked refers to the 'much water' of Ænon, near Salim; and I think no one can deny that John selected that place for the convenience of baptizing; and so far as it has any bearing on the case at all, it favors immersion. No other place presents any difficulty not already obviated, till we come to the baptism of the three thousand. Here seemed to be some doubtful circumstances, till I talked the subject over with my niece last night, but all is now quite plain; but there are some other instances recorded in the Acts, where immersion does not seem to have been so proba· ble as sprinkling or pouring."

"Please don't speak any more about *probabilities*, Professor Jones," exclaimed Mr. Courtney. "You admit that '*baptize*,' the word used to describe this ordinance, means to immerse, as its common primary signification in every other book but this, and that the people who read the Greek language, would understand this to be its meaning in this, *unless some intimation was given* that it must *not* be so understood, or unless this meaning was morally impossible. And now you say it seems more probable that sprinkling sometimes occurred. Suppose it were more probable, does not Luke, by using this word *baptize*, declare that it was not sprinkling or pouring, but clearly and plainly a dipping? Will you dare to give the word a meaning that it never had before, and has not now, in any Greek book in the world, merely because you think it more probable that something else was done, instead of what Luke says was done? Show me a case where immersion was impossible, and it will have some weight."

"No, no, Mr. Courtney, the New Testament meaning of the word is the very point in dispute. I shall not allow you to beg the question on the very position about which we are at issue."

"I did not intend, nor do I desire to do any such thing. It is no begging of the question to object to your mode of settling it. This word was used hundreds of years before Luke wrote this book. Its meaning was as well fixed and defined as that of any word in the Greek language. Luke was writing to those who read, and spoke, and understood this language (and this word among the rest) in its ordinary sense, according to the familiar every-day usage of the people who employed it.

"We agree, and no critic or scholar of any note has ever denied, that the common, familiar meaning of this word was to immerse, submerge, to dip. This we have proved. But now we want to know in what sense Luke employs it. I answer, that the presumption is, that he employs it just as every other writer does; for if he does not, nobody will understand what he means. He must use words in the sense that other people use them, or other people will not know what he means; but as he wishes to be understood, and writes under the inspiration of infinite wisdom, he will use words thus. If this word, therefore, commonly and familiarly meant to immerse, then it was immersion that he meant when he used the word. To this you reply, that in some cases it *seems more probable* that something else was done, and not the act which this word describes; and you will therefore make it mean just what you think is *most likely* to have taken place. I object to this mode of deciding the meaning of a New Testament word. If we decide according to this rule, I can show you that Lazarus was never raised from the dead; for it is to me much more likely that he was only *asleep*, or in a sort of *trance*—and when Jesus called him with a loud voice, it only awakened him. You tell me, however, that the Scripture plainly declares, again and again, that he *was dead*, and that Christ *raised* him from the *dead*. But I have only to assure you that, though the word rendered dead does mean dead—destitute of life—in every other book, and in almost every other place in this book, yet in this particular place it is much *more probable* that it means asleep, or in a trance; and, therefore, dead cannot mean destitute of life. If I am at liberty to trifle in this way with any words of the Sacred Record, it ceases to mean any thing but what I, or you, or any other man may fancy it ought to mean. Every man may make it mean just what he pleases. But pardon me for talking so long—I did not intend it when I began. Go on with your references, and I will show you that there is not even a *probability* that it was any thing else but immersion that was performed in any single case."

"I was," said Uncle Jones, "just about to mention the case of Paul, who was baptized 'standing up,' and of course, it could not be by immersion, Acts ix.: 'And Ananias went his way and entered into the house, and putting his hand upon him, said, Brother Saul, the Lord, even Jesus, who appeared unto thee in the way as thou camest, hath sent me that thou mightest receive thy sight, and be filled with the Holy Ghost. And immediately there fell from his eyes, as it had been scales, and he received sight forthwith, and *arose and was baptized.*' Now the Greek word '*anastas*' here rendered *arose*, might very properly be rendered standing up; and if so, he must have been baptized standing."

"That, *if so*, Professor, is a very convenient phrase. Let us see how it will work in other places. We read in the Old Testament that 'David arose and fled for fear of Saul.' The same word occurs here. It may mean 'standing up;' and, *if so*, then David *fled standing.* So, also, in this passage, 'Saul *rose up* out of the cave and went.' It may mean '*standing;*' and, *if so*, then Saul went *standing* out of the cave. And in this, 'Saul *arose* and got him from Gilgal.' It may mean 'standing;' and, *if so*, then Saul went up from Gilgal 'standing.'"

"Yes," said Theodosia, "and when Ananias and Sapphira died that fearful death, the young men were *standing still* all the while they were winding up the body, carrying him away, and burying him; for it reads, 'The young men arose, wound him up, carried him out, and buried him.' (Acts v. 6.) Is it not the same word that is used in the original?"

"The very same, Miss Ernest—and so it is where the prodigal son says I will arise and go to my father —yet he does not mean to say that he will go 'standing up.' If you will be kind enough to get Barnes' Notes, you will find a very true and apposite explanation of this word. 'He *arose* and went to his father.' 'The word *arose*,' says Barnes, 'does not imply that he had been *sitting*. It does not refer to any change of position, but expresses the act of *setting out*, or *beginning* to do any thing. It was a common expression among the Hebrews to denote *entering upon* a piece of business.' Now, if Luke had said, he *sat still* and was baptized, it might have made some difficulty; but if he rose up, or prepared himself, he would do this equally, whether he was sprinkled or immersed. Immersion is quite as probable, so far as this word is concerned, as sprinkling, or any thing else."

"I must acknowledge that you are right," said Uncle Jones, "and you have convinced me so often that I am almost ashamed to mention another difficulty which has been suggested—and that is, that there is nothing said about a change of garment, or of their going out of the house; and then Saul was so feeble that it would seem almost cruel to make him walk half a mile to the river, before he even partook of any food. I judge, therefore, that the rite must have been performed in the house, and *if so*, it could not be immersion "

"There is your '*if so*' again. But suppose it was done in the house, are you sure that there was not a bathing-tub, or a tank, or some other means of immersion in the house? There is surely no evidence that there was not. How do you know that it was half a mile to the river? How do you know that there was not a fountain in the yard? Most rich men's houses in the East are provided with them. You simply read that he 'was baptized,' and every Greek reader would understand this to mean that he was immersed. If you should come down next Sunday to the Baptist church, and apply for membership, and be received and baptized—I would, as clerk of the church, record the facts —I would write that you came, made credible profession of faith in Christ, gave satisfactory evidence of genuine conversion, was received and *baptized*. I need not record that you put on suitable clothing—that you went to the river, or to the pool, or to the baptizing. Everybody would know that you were immersed, if I simply said you were 'baptized.'"

"Well, well, I see I have been making 'mountains out of mole hills,' but really the Doctors of Divinity, as you so kindly suggested a while ago, have much of the blame to bear. I am almost ashamed to go on with my catalogue of difficulties, lest I provoke both you and Theodosia to laugh at me for my simplicity."

"Far from it, my dear sir. It is not long since I stood just where you are standing now. I know from sad experience with how much difficulty the light of truth makes its way through the mists and fogs by which one's early education has surrounded him; and how slowly it dispels the clouds and darkness of long-established prejudices. It is rare indeed to find any

one educated as you were, and accustomed as you have
been from childhood, to think that whoever might be
wrong, the Presbyterians *must* be right, yet exhibiting
the candor to acknowledge error, and the conscience to
repudiate it so soon as it shall be clearly seen. I hope
you will not refrain from expressing even the shadow
of a doubt, if it keeps your mind from seeing clearly
the way of Christian duty as required in God's Word
What was the next case on your memorandum?"

"It was that of Cornelius and his friends. Peter
says, who shall 'forbid water?' And it seemed to me
more natural for him to use this expression, if the water
was to be *brought* to sprinkle them, than if they were to
be taken to the water to be dipped in it."

"But," replied Mr. Courtney, "Peter does not say
the water *was to be brought*. He only says, who will
forbid water (that is to be used in the baptizing of these
people)? It was simply equivalent to saying, who will
forbid their baptism? But the water might have been
brought to *immerse* them. What would hinder it? I
was present once when a Baptist minister said to the
sexton of the church, 'Let water be brought for the
baptism of six persons this evening'—would you deny
that those six persons were to be *immersed?* In re-
cording the event, I might have said, the water was
brought, and they were baptized—for they were actually
immersed in a tank prepared for the purpose under the
floor of the church. Now, if one of the deacons had
exclaimed, I forbid the water to be brought for the
baptism of these candidates, you must (had you been
present and reasoned as you do upon this passage) have
concluded that it was sprinkling, and not immersion at
all which was spoken of."

"I am satisfied, Mr. Courtney, and do not see any
thing in my next case (which was that of Lydia and

her household) that has not already been disposed of.
I was going to object that there was nothing said about
change of apparel and going to or coming from the
water—but I acknowledge that when I read in a Baptist
paper that forty converts were baptized one Sabbath
morning, I do not doubt they were immersed, and yet I
never see a word said about the clothing they wore, and
often nothing about the place where the rite was performed   So I will pass to the jailor's baptism, Acts
xvi. 33   The only difficulty here is, that as he was baptized *in the jail*, it is very improbable that it was by
immersion, since it is not likely there was any convenience for an immersion in an eastern prison."

"Suppose, Professor Jones, that you should read in
a newspaper that 'The poor wretch who was last week
sentenced to death for the murder of old Mr Gripall,
had made a profession of religion, and had been baptized
by Elder J. R. Graves, the editor of the Tennessee Baptist,' would you imagine that Mr. Graves had *sprinkled*
him? Not for one moment; you could easily believe
that the water was brought, and the immersion was done
in the murderer's cell, even though not a word was said
about the bringing it. As the jailor was master of the
prison, could he not have water brought, had it been
needful?

"But the truth is, the baptism was not done in the
jail.   Read the passage carefully   He sprang into the
prison, and he brought the Apostles out of it (30th
verse). Some say he only brought them *out* of the *inner
prison*. I say he brought them out of that, and into his
own house, for (32d verse) they spoke the word of the
Lord to all that were in his house. He took them into
his family apartments, and there they preached the
Word.

"And then (verse 33d) he took them somewhere else

where he washed their stripes and was himself baptized; and then (34th verse) he brought them back into his house, and set meat before them. You see, therefore, that it was not done in prison, though if it had been, it would have been no proof that it was not immersion."

"I wonder," said Mr. Jones, "that I had never seen the case in this light before. Now, since I have observed it carefully, it is all very plain; and I have found no other instance where the word occurs in its *literal* sense, and which presents any difficulties which have not been already considered.

"There is, indeed, the case of the Eunuch, who was baptized by Philip, but the narrative, in all the details of it, absolutely requires immersion to preserve the consistency and probability of the story. They went down into the water, and not the one, but both of them went into the water. Then Philip immersed him, and then they came up out of the water. I wonder that any Greek scholar should ever have doubted that they went into and came out of the water; for, if this is not what is said, it is because the Greek language could not express it. In any other book, no scholar would hesitate a moment thus to translate the passage. What is here said to be done, I must concede is precisely what Baptists are accustomed to do. And, but for one thing, I am convinced that *immersion is the only baptism.*"

"And what is that, pray?"

"Simply that I find baptism spoken of *figuratively* or *metaphorically* in such a way as to lead me to suspect it must be something else. Indeed, in Acts ii. 17, it is almost expressly said to be a pouring."

"No, Professor, baptism is *not* here said to be pouring, nor is pouring said to be baptism, though Doctors of Divinity have ventured such assertions.

"Christ *did* tell the disciples that they would be im-

10

mersed in the Holy Ghost—and Peter did speak of the Holy Spirit as being poured out—but neither of them said that this pouring was the immersion. It might as well have been any other of the wonderful things that happened that day, which could in any respect be compared to an immersion.

"But before we go further, let me say one word as to the value of figurative usage in determining the meaning of this or any other word.

"Common sense teaches us that the figurative and fanciful must yield to the real and actual. When, therefore, we have settled the meaning of a word by its real, literal, every-day usage, we cannot unsettle it by a figure of speech—a chance allusion or comparison. The fanciful must be governed by the actual. This is self-evident. Now, we have seen and settled that the literal meaning of this word is to *immerse*. And henceforth, whenever and wherever we find it *figuratively* employed, the allusion must be in some way or other to immersion or some circumstance attending immersion. On this alone will its beauty and appropriateness as a figure depend.

"Now, remembering this, let us examine the case in hand. The allusion cannot be to 'the pouring,' which itself is but a figure—for no literal and actual pouring of the third person of the Trinity *could* occur. The allusion was not to the manner of the Spirit's coming, but to the copiousness, abundance, and overwhelming nature of his influences; filling, overflowing, surrounding, and, as it were, swallowing up their souls. The Greeks often used the word baptized in this way; as baptized in debt, baptized in affliction, baptized in wine (that is, overcome of wine), baptized in iniquity, or as we would express it, *sunk* in iniquity. We use the word immerse in the same way, when we say of one that he is immersed in dissipation; immersed in business; immersed in politics, and the like; we simply mean by such expressions that the dissipation, business, or politics, controls and occupies all the powers and capacities of the man. We do not mean to say that they were *poured* on him, or *sprinkled* on him, but only that they exert an overwhelming influence over him. And just in this sense he told the disciples they should be immersed in the Holy Ghost."

"I thank you, Mr. Courtney, for that lucid exposition. I can hardly understand how the matter came to be so mystified in my mind as it has been till now. I will trouble you with but one other case, and that is where the Israelites are said (1 Cor. x. 2) to have been 'all baptized unto Moses in the cloud and in the sea.' If this was an immersion, you must admit that it was a very dry one, for the Scripture says expressly they went through on dry ground."

"Certainly, I will admit that it was a dry immersion, for it was a *figurative,* and not a real one. The baptism of the Holy Spirit, which we were just speaking of, was a dry immersion. The baptism in sufferings, which Jesus spoke of so touchingly to James and John, was a dry immersion. The figure in either case was not in the wetting, but in the overwhelming abundance of the Spirit in one, and of sorrow in the other. The allusion in this case is not so much to the *act,* as to one of the attendant circumstances. They did indeed go down into the sea, as one goes down into the water to be baptized. The water stood on each side of them and the cloud covered them—so that they might very appropriately and beautifully be said, in a figure, to be *immersed* in the cloud and the sea. But the chief allusion is to another and altogether different circumstance. As the Christian, by going down into the baptismal water, professes his belief in Christ, and takes upon himself a solemn obligation of obedience to the laws of Christ. So the Jews, Paul says, by going down into the sea, and walking beneath the cloud, professed their faith in Moses, and took upon them obligations of obedience to him. They were thus 'baptized unto Moses.' The main allusion is not to the act, but to the obligation of the ordinance. Would the figure be any more beautiful, or any more appropriate, if we should say that they were all sprinkled into Moses, or were all poured into Moses?

"Professor Stuart, on this passage, says: 'The suggestion has sometimes been made that the Israelites were *sprinkled* by the cloud and by the sea, and that *this* was the baptism which Paul meant; but the cloud was not a rain cloud, nor do we find any *intimation* that the waters of the Red Sea sprinkled the children of Israel at that time.'"

"It seems to me," said Theodosia, "that the idea of rain is absolutely precluded; for if it had rained upon them to any extent, the ground would have been *wet*, but it says expressly they went through on *dry ground*."

"That would seem to set the matter at rest, Theo., if it were not that the Psalmist, evidently speaking of this very occasion (Psa. lxxvii. 17, 18), says expressly, 'The clouds poured out water, the skies sent out a sound, thine arrows also went abroad; the voice of thy thunder was in the heaven, the lightnings lightened the world, the earth trembled and shook.'"

"But the Psalmist does not say, uncle, that these terrible manifestations of Almighty power were directed against the *Jews*—*they* went over dry shod. To *them* all was light and peace. But the cloud went and stood *behind* them, and troubled their enemies, the Egyptians. The thunder, and the lightning, and the great storm of rain were upon *them*, while the Israelites were passing on dry ground."

"Well, Theodosia, I give it up. I have no longer any ground to stand upon; and I may as well admit at once, that *immersion is the only act which is anywhere in the Bible called a Baptism.* I have, I think, now examined every place that could throw any light upon the subject; and really I can't find even a probability of any other meaning of the word in *any* case, while in many this meaning is established by most overwhelming proof."

"No, Professor, there is one place you seem to have overlooked, which is exceedingly significant; that is Romans, 6th chapter, where we are said to be *buried with Christ in our baptism.* Here the allusion is most evidently not to any attending circumstance, but to the act itself. We are buried in the water like one who is dead, and raised out of it again like one resurrected. So, we are to consider ourselves as having died to sin, and as having been brought to life again by Christ; but not to the same life of sin which we led before, but to *'newness of life'*—or a new life—a life of holiness and obedience. That the allusion here is to the act of immersion is so evident that none but the most determined and unreasonable cavilers pretend to deny it. I do not know of any single commentator, whose opinions are entitled to any respect, who has ventured to differ in regard to this point from Luther, and Calvin, and Doddridge, and McKnight, and Chalmers—who all agree that the allusion is to the ancient form of baptism by immersion, or, as McKnight expresses it, to the ordinance in which Christ submitted to be baptized—that is, to be buried under the water, and taken out again by John,' etc. (See notes on this place.)

"I see " said Uncle Jones. "The Scriptures do not

even leave 'a loop to hang a doubt upon.' The common and every-day use of the word requires immersion—the scriptural, and especially the New Testament usage of the word, requires immersion—the places where the baptisms were performed required immersion, for why else would they go into the water?—and even the figures and metaphors drawn from the ordinance demand immersion. What shall we say then? Must we not be immersed?"

"I can only answer for myself, uncle. If it was immersion which Jesus Christ, my Saviour, submitted to in Jordan, and which he commanded all his disciples to teach and to practice, I cannot hesitate about whether I will obey my Saviour—I shall be immersed the first convenient opportunity."

"I cannot yet speak so confidently," rejoined her uncle. "It may be, something will yet turn up to show the matter in some other light. I must take more time to consider, and this reminds me that we have not yet examined the history of the ordinance to see whether it is true in fact that sprinkling has been substituted for immersion, or whether, after all, it was not immersion that was substituted for sprinkling. I am under the impression that these Baptists are the same sect that sprung up about the time of Luther and the Reformation—sometimes called Anabaptists, but more frequently the Mad Men of Munster. I grant I have not investigated the subject very carefully, but I am certain I have somewhere seen or heard their origin in Europe traced back to that occasion, and in this country I have been told they owe their beginning to Roger Williams, who was not properly baptized himself, and consequently could not give valid baptism to any one else. Am I not right in these conjectures, Mr. Courtney?"

Mr. Courtney did not reply until after he had taken

out his watch and observed the time of night. "It is too late," said he, "to answer that question and others which will be suggested by it, to-night. Suppose we postpone the further consideration of the subject till another time."

"Very well," said Theodosia, who felt that she had sufficient food for one day's reflection in what had already passed. "Come round, both of you, to-morrow night. Come early and take supper with us; and meantime, Mr. Courtney, you may leave this great armful of old books. May be, I will indulge my womanly curiosity by reading their titles. I don't believe I have much relish for their contents, unless they should be vastly more attractive than their external appearance indicates. Why, some of them look as though they might be a hundred and one years old."

"Old documents are sometimes very valuable," said he, "especially in such a discussion as we are to have to-morrow night. You will be more interested in them than you imagine."

THE SIXTH NIGHT'S STUDY.

---◇---

IN WHICH THE QUESTION,

HOW CHRIST'S ORDINANCE WAS CHANGED,

AND

POURING FIRST, AND THEN SPRINKLING,

SUBSTITUTED IN PLACE OF IMMERSION,

IS FULLY EXAMINED, AND TRUTHFULLY ANSWERED,

BY THE SPRINKLERS THEMSELVES.

SIXTH NIGHT'S STUDY.

THE interest which so learned and excellent a Presbyterian as Uncle Jones had exhibited in the study of Baptism, together with affection for her lovely daughter, had so far removed Mrs. Ernest's objections to this investigation, that she had resolved herself to be present, and take some quiet part in the conversation, upon the introduction of sprinkling. Uncle Jones she knew was a sincere and pious man. He was also a man of good sense, sound judgment, and of very extensive information. And (more than all to her) he was a *Ruling Elder* in the Presbyterian Church. If, therefore, Uncle Jones had ventured to *doubt* about *his* baptism, she began to think her daughter could not have committed any very *deadly* sin in doubting about hers. And, as Uncle Jones had spoken very highly of the logical accumen and historical information of Mr Courtney, she could not see why she should not treat him with such courtesy as was due to an intelligent gentleman, even though he was a poor Baptist schoolmaster. As for his prejudices, which had led him to speak so disrespectfully of the Doctors of Divinity and eminent ministers of "our church"—he had probably received them in his childhood, for she had no doubt he had been reared among the ignorant and bigoted Baptists, who never knew any better, and from whom nothing better could be expected.

When Mr. Courtney came in, therefore, she was the first to welcome him, and express her pleasure that he had come so early. She exerted herself to entertain him till Theodosia came in, and then went to prepare a nice dish which had just come into her mind for supper. It was not long till the Professor came also; but not a word was said about the object of their meeting till after the table was removed—when Mr. Courtney introduced it by saying:

"If I did not misunderstand you, Professor Jones, you expressed some doubt last evening whether immersion was not first introduced as baptism by the Mad Men of Munster during the Reformation of Luther; and whether the Baptists of the United States did not receive baptism from Roger Williams, who was himself not properly baptized, and therefore could not legally baptize others."

"This is my impression, sir. I do not know exactly how I received it—perhaps I got something of it from reading D'Aubigne's History of the Reformation— perhaps I received it by hearing something of the kind from the pulpit. I am certain that I have seen or heard it somewhere, and that I thought at the time I had good authority for believing it—otherwise, I should not have given it a place in my memory."

"I have," replied Mr. Courtney, "seen and heard such statements many times from various sources. They are often recorded in Presbyterian and Methodist newspapers. They form a part of every controversy on the subject of baptism; and you may hear them almost as often as you hear a sermon or listen to a discussion on this subject. It was consequently very easy for you to receive and retain such impressions."

"And yet I suppose you will assure me that I am altogether mistaken, and have been grossly deceived."

"No, Professor Jones, *I will not assure you*. I do not like that mode of discussion. I will *prove* to you (if you wil. receive the testimony of the *most reliable historians*, or that of the most eminent of *your own writers* on this subject); I will prove to you beyond all possibility of doubt that those who make such statements are either most grossly ignorant or most perversely false."

"I hope, Mr. Courtney, you don't mean to say that *our ministers* preach falsehood, or that *our religious* editors make statements that are not true?" said Mrs. Ernest, who already felt her blood begin to boil.

"No, no, sister," said Uncle Jones, who knew her mood. "Mr. Courtney only means to say that our ministers and editors *are mistaken*, and that he can prove that they have made statements without having first carefully examined *all* the evidence."

"Pardon me, madam," said Mr. Courtney, "I did not intend to use any language which would give offence to any one present, and most especially to you. I was myself for many years a Presbyterian. I know the ministers of that order too well to doubt that, as a body, they are in knowledge and piety equal to any in the world. There are among them many who are now my warmest personal friends—men whom I love as Christian brethren—men whom I admire as great and valiant soldiers of the cross—men who love Jesus, and are devoting their lives to his work, and are doing great good in the world. And yet there are among them men who, upon this subject, rashly venture to make assertions which most clearly and directly contradict all historical testimony, and which, if there is any *truth* in history, must be admitted to be false."

"How can that be possible?" asked Theodosia. "How can a good man *dare* to say what is not *strictly true?*"

"I do not doubt, Miss Ernest, that most of them *really believe* what they assert. They are themselves deceived. They have been trained and educated in error. They have trusted to the assertions of others, who had an interest in deceiving them. They get impressions, just as your uncle did, from books, or papers, or lectures, or sermons, in which such statements are made. They take it for granted they are true—and so repeat them to others—and extend and perpetuate the falsehood, which would at once be evident, if they would go behind these statements and examine the *historical records for themselves.*

"It is, in part, for this reason, that I do not ask you to take *my word* for any fact to which I may request your attention. Nor will I ask you to receive the testimony of any *Baptist* historian; you shall have the record to read for yourselves, and that record made *in every instance* by an opposer of our poor and despised denomination. I will prove to you, first, that the Baptists in Europe did not originate at the time of the Reformation, but had existed from the very foundation of Christianity; and then I will show you that the Baptists in the United States do not owe their origin to Roger Williams, any more than they do to Lord Baltimore or Cotton Mather; and that the validity of their ordinance stands on much safer ground, in point of regular succession from the Apostles, than that of any of the Pedobaptist sects."

"That is right, Mr. Courtney," said Uncle Jones; "let us have one thing at a time. Bring up your witnesses."

"Well, I have them ready. But first, let us understand distinctly the point on which we are at issue. You understand that the Baptist denomination sprang up as a new thing about the time of the Lutheran Reformation, and owes its origin to those who were then called 'Anabaptists, or the Mad Men of Munster?'"

" Yes ; that was my impression."

" Very well. Now I will show you that this is so far from being true, that there has been, from the *very earliest ages* of Christianity up to the present time, a body of professing Christians who have always held, as we do now, that baptism is not valid unless it be preceded by instruction and *faith in Christ ;* and, consequently, that the *baptism of infants is no baptism at all.*

" I grant that this *body of Christian people* has not always been *called* Baptists ; but as they possessed the distinguishing characteristics of the Baptists, it cannot be denied that they *were* Baptists."

" No," said Uncle Jones, " if they were professing Christians, and gave evidence of the new birth, baptized only by immersion, and refused to baptize infants, or recognize such baptism as valid, they were doubtless Baptists, by whatever name they chanced to be called."

" Then we are ready to proceed with the case. The first witness I will call is the celebrated ecclesiastical historian, John Lawrence Mosheim, Chancellor of the University of Gottingen. He was, of course, *no Baptist,* or he could not have held such a position. His history was originally written in Latin, but has been translated into English by Dr. McLaine, of England, and Dr. Murdock, in America. This learned and reliable historian says : ' The sacrament of baptism was administered, in this (the first) century, without the public assemblies, in places appointed and prepared for that purpose, and was performed *by an immersion of the whole body* in the baptismal font.'

" Of the second century, he says : ' The persons that were to be baptized, after they had repeated the creed, confessed and renounced their sins, and particularly the devil and his pompous allurements, were *immersed under water,* and received into Christ's kingdom.' No sprinkling, and no infants, you see, thus far. They were such as could profess their faith, and they were 'immersed under the water.' *McLaine's Mosheim*, vol. p. 46–69.

"As a witness of somewhat similar character, I will now introduce the Pedobaptist Neander, whose 'Church History' and his 'Planting and Training of the Christian Church,' have given his name a world-wide celebrity.

"This eminent and reliable historian, in a letter to Mr. Judd, says, expressly, 'The practice of immersion was beyond doubt prevalent in the *whole church*. The only exception was made with the *sick*—hence called *baptisma clinicorum.*'

"And in 'The Planting and Training of the Christian Church,' he says: 'The usual form of submersion at baptism practiced by the Jews, was transferred to the Gentile Christians. Indeed, this form was most suitable to signify that which Christ intended to render an object of contemplation by such a symbol, viz.: the immersion of the whole man in the spirit of a new life.'

"So also says Coleman, another noted Pedobaptist author, the friend and exponent of Neander, who is regarded as high authority by the opponents of the Baptists, and who takes frequent occasion to express his aversion to their faith and practice—yet a regard for the obvious truth compels him to say, page 372, 'Ancient Christianity Exemplified.' 'The term baptism is derived from the Greek word *Bapto*, from which term is formed *Baptizo*, with its derivatives *Baptismos* and *Baptisma*—baptism. The primary signification of the original is to dip, to plunge, immerse. The obvious import of the noun is immersion.'

"Yet, in another place, he *affects* to regard immersion as a departure from the apostolic usage :

"'We cannot resist the conclusion,' he says, 'that this mode of baptism was the first departure from the teaching and example of the Apostles on this subject.' '*If it was* a departure from their teachings, it was the *earliest*—for baptism by immersion, unquestionably, was *very early* the common mode of baptism.'

"Again, page 396, he says: 'In the Primitive Church, immediately subsequent to the age of the Apostles, this [immersion] was undeniably the common mode of baptism. (The utmost that can be said of sprinkling in that early period is, that it was in case of necessity *permitted* as an exception to a general rule). This fact is so well established that it were needless to adduce authorities in proof of it. * * * * It is a great mistake to suppose that baptism by immersion was discontinued when infant baptism became generally prevalent. The practice of immersion continued even to the thirteenth or fourteenth century. Indeed it has *never* been formally abandoned, but is still the mode of administering infant baptism in the Greek Church, and in several of the Eastern Churches.'

"Here, also, is another Pedobaptist historian, Dr. Philip Schaff, Professor in a Pedobaptist Theological Seminary at Mercersburg, Pennsylvania. In his 'History of the Apostolic Church,' page 568, he says: 'Immersion, and not sprinkling, was unquestionably the original normal form [of baptism]. This is shown by the very meaning of the Greek words *Baptizo, Baptisma,* and *Baptismos*—used to designate the rite. Then again, by the analogy of the baptism of John, which was performed in the Jordan ["*en*"], Matt. iii. 6, compare with 16; also, *eis ton Jordanan* [*into* the Jordan], Mark i. 9; furthermore, by the New Testament *comparisons* of baptism with the passage through the Red Sea, 1 Cor x. 2; with the *flood*, 1 Peter ii. 21;

11

with a *bath*, Eph. v. 36; Titus iii. 5; with a *burial and resurrection*, Rom. vi. 4; Col. ii. 12; and, finally, by the general usage of Ecclesiastical antiquity, which was *always* immersion, as it is to this day in the Oriental, and also in the Græco Russian Churches, pouring and sprinkling being substituted only in cases of urgent necessity, such as sickness and approaching death.' ''

"Are you *sure*, Mr. Courtney, that these learned historians were not Baptists?"

"Most certainly I am. Their church connections are as well known almost as their histories. But even if they *had* been Baptists, I do not see how that would invalidate their testimony. I hope you do not think that Baptists cannot tell the truth as well as other people?"

"Oh, no, Mr. Courtney, forgive me—I did not mean that; but it seems to me so *very strange* that good men can say such things in their writings, and yet act as though they did not believe a single word of what they say. But perhaps the *first* historians of the church, from whom these men have borrowed their statements, were Baptists."

"Yes, Miss Ernest, the first historians and earliest writers on the customs and practices of the Apostolic Churches *were* Baptists. And it is to them we are really indebted for *all* our knowledge of the earliest ages. Matthew, and Mark, and Luke, and John, were Baptists—or else they might never have told us about those baptisms in the river Baptists tell about such things now. Paul was a Baptist, or he would never have compared baptism to a burial and resurrection. Peter was a Baptist, or he would never have compared it to the flood. All those New Testament saints were Baptists, as we have seen in our examination of the meaning of the *word* baptize. The very word made them Baptists. They could not be any thing else; and, after their day, the *Fathers* (as they are called), that is, the earliest writers among the Christians, whose works have come down to us, were all Baptists. It was near three hundred years before there were any professed Christians who were *not Baptists*."

"On what authority do you venture such an assertion?" asked Uncle Jones.

"I might say," replied the schoolmaster, "that I make it on the authority of your own most eminent and most reliable historians. I have it over the signatures of Roman Catholic, Episcopalian, Lutheran, Dutch Reformed, and Presbyterian writers, who, while they have been in full connection with those very establishments, all of which have (when they could) been the most virulent and cruel *persecutors* of the Baptists, and some of which are *even now* subjecting our brethren in Europe to fines and imprisonment, and confiscation of property, because they will not conform to the corrupt and corrupting superstitions which have been substituted by Popish authority for the ordinances of Christ—have nevertheless openly, plainly, and repeatedly declared, as historians, that the apostolic churches were, in their membership, ordinances, organization, and government, just such as the Baptist churches are now. I say, I might give this authority; but I will refer you to the same source from which they, as historians, derived their information. I say the Christian Fathers, for the first three centuries, were Baptists, because these Fathers say so themselves.

"*Justin Martyr*, who is counted among the earliest of the Fathers, writing to the Emperor, and giving him an account of the churches in his day, about one hundred and fifty years after Christ, says: 'I shall now lay before you the manner of dedicating ourselves to God through Christ upon our conversion; for, should I omit this, I might not seem to deal sincerely in this account of our religion. As many as are persuaded and believe that those things which are taught by us are true, and do promise to live according to them, are directed, first, to pray, and ask God, with fasting, the forgiveness of their sins. And we also pray and fast together with them. *Then we bring them to a place where there is water*, and they are regenerated in the same way that we are regenerated, for they are washed in the name of the Father,' etc.

"*Tertullian*, who lived somewhat later, says: ' When we are ready to enter into the water (and even before), we make our protestations before the minister and in the church, that we renounce the devil and all his pomps and vanities—afterward, we are *plunged* in the water.'

"And again, ' Those who are desirous to dip themselves holily in this water, must prepare themselves for it by fasting, by watchings, by prayer, and by sincere repentance for sin.'

" But it is needless to multiply authorities. It is the united testimony of *all* the Fathers who speak of the subject at all, that baptism was in these early ages performed only by immersion, except of necessity in the near prospect of death. And those who, under such circumstances, received pouring as a *substitute*, were never said to have been *baptized*, but to have been *poured* upon *as a substitute* for baptism.

" How any man, who has any character to lose, can in the face of all this testimony venture the assertion that sprinkling was practiced in the early churches, and that immersion is a modern invention introduced by the Mad Men of Munster, is more than I can comprehend," said Mr. Courtney. " Merle D'Aubigne, the Historian of the Reformation, the very man to whom the Munster Men are indebted for most of their present notoriety—D'Aubigne does not venture any such assertion On one point, he says, 'It seems necessary to guard against misapprehension. Some persons imagine that the Anabaptists of the time of the Reformation, and the Baptists of our day, are the same. But they are as different as possible. * * * It is but justice to observe that the Baptists of Holland, England, and the United States (says Fessenden, as quoted .by D'Aubigne), are essentially distinct from those seditious and fanatical individuals above-mentioned, as they profess an equal aversion to the principles of the rebellion of the one, and the enthusiasm of the other.'—Pref. to Hist. of Ref., p. 10. But I find I am summing up on the case before I have introduced all the evidence. I have referred to historians; I wish now to call your attention to the testimony of several of the most eminent and learned *theological* authors—writing, not as historians, but as theological disputants.

"I will first introduce Professor Moses Stuart, who was a citizen of our own country, and an eminent professor in one of your own theological seminaries.

"Here is his book. It was written in answer to the question addressed to him by missionaries in a foreign land, inquiring in what way they should translate the Greek words which in our version read *baptize* and *baptism*. It was evidently written with great care, and not without much previous study of the subject.

"After referring to a number of eminent and reliable historians in regard to the practice of the early church, he thus concludes: 'But enough—it is a thing made out,' says Augusti, viz. :—the ancient practice of immersion So, indeed, all the writers who have thoroughly investigated this subject conclude.

"'I know of no one usage of ancient times,' continues

Mr. Stuart, 'which seems to be more clearly and more certainly made out. *I cannot see how it is possible for any candid man who examines the subject to deny this.*'

"'In what manner then,' he asks (p. 362), 'did the churches of Christ from a very early period (to say the least), understand the word *baptizo* in the New Testament? Plainly they construed it as meaning immersion.'

"'We are left in no doubt,' he says again, 'about the generally received usage of the Christian church down to a period several centuries after the apostolic age.'

"Can any testimony be more explicit, or more satisfactory than this?

"But even Dr. Miller himself, the great champion of Presbyterianism, on this subject declares, 'That it is not denied that for the first few centuries after Christ, the most common mode of administering baptism was by immersion.'"

"Oh, that is enough, Mr. Courtney," said the young lady. "After such declarations by the most eminent historians, and our own theological professors, I am sure neither Uncle Jones nor any one else can entertain a shadow of a doubt. We will admit that the practice of the first church was immersion. I was satisfied of that from the Scripture itself, since this was the meaning of the word, and consequently it was immersion that Christ commanded. What I desire to know is, how the *change* was brought about, and sprinkling introduced."

"All in good time, Miss Ernest, we will come to that presently. Have a little patience. These theological discussions are very tricky affairs. I want to set this point so far beyond all doubt or disputation that no one will dare again to intimate that the Baptists originated in the time of Martin Luther.

"Here is what Martin Luther says about it himself. No Protestant will doubt that he is a competent witness. 'The word *baptize* is a Greek word. It may be rendered immersion, *as when we plunge something in water that it may be entirely covered with water*—and though that custom is *now abolished* among the generality (for even children are not entirely immersed, but only have a little water poured on them), nevertheless they ought to be completely immersed, and immediately drawn out, for the etymology of the word requires it.'

"Here also is what John Calvin, the very father and founder of the Presbyterian denomination, says: 'From these words (John iii. 23), it may be inferred that baptism was administered by John and Christ by plunging the whole body under the water. Here we perceive how baptism was administered *among the ancients, for they immersed the whole body in water.*'

"Here is also Dr. Whitby, a very learned and eminent divine of the Church of England: 'Immersion,' says he, 'was religiously observed by all Christians for THIRTEEN CENTURIES, and was approved by the Church of England. And,' he continues, 'since the change of it into sprinkling was made without any allowance from the AUTHOR of the institution, or any license from any Council of the Church [of England], being that which the Romanist still urgeth to justify his refusal of the cup to the laity: it were to be wished that this custom [immersion] might be again of general use.'

"This musty looking old volume is 'The History of the Bible, by Thomas Stackhouse, Vicar of Beenham, in England,' a celebrated Episcopal clergyman. He says: 'We nowhere read in Scripture of any one's being baptized but by immersion—and several authors have proved, from the acts of councils and ancient rituals, that this manner of immersion continued as much as possible to be used for thirteen hundred years after Christ.'

"The celebrated Prelate, Bishop Taylor, of the English Church, Vice-Chancellor of the University of Dublin, says in his famous work called 'Ductor Dubitantium:' 'The custom of the Ancient Churches was not sprinkling, but immersion, in pursuance of the meaning of the word baptize in the commandment, and the example of our blessed Saviour.'

"Here also is what that earnest-hearted man, Richard Baxter (the author of the 'Call to the Unconverted' and the 'Saints' Rest'), says: 'It is commonly confessed by us to the Anabaptists, as our commentators declare, that in the Apostles' times the baptized were dipped over head in water.'"

"Oh, please, Mr. Courtney, don't read us any more such testimony. Any one who would not be convinced by what you have given us, would not believe if you should give us ten times more. Do you pray go on, and show how, and where, and by what authority Christ's ordinance was changed."

"No, no, Mr. Courtney—I want to hear all the proof you have. Never mind Theodosia—girls always are impatient," said the mother. "I wish Mr. Johnson was here, so we could know what he thinks about these statements, though as for that, I suppose brother Jones knows nearly as much about it as a preacher."

"Excuse me, Miss Theodosia—I will not detain you much longer on this point; I have only a few other witnesses whose testimony I will urge at *this time*, though there is scarcely a historian of the early days of Christianity, who does not furnish us with proof. Not many years since, the King of Holland appointed two very learned and able men, one a Professor of Theology

In the University of Groningen, and the other Chaplain to the King, to examine into the origin and history of the Dutch Baptists. They wrote out the result of their investigations and published the work at Breda, in 1819 In this volume, prepared by these two learned members of the Dutch Reformed Church, Dr. Ypeig and Dr. J. J. Durmont, the authors, after tracing up the history of the Baptists, make use of the following remarkable language:

"'We have now seen that the Baptists, who were formerly called Anabaptists, and, in later times, Menonites, were the original Waldenses, and who have long, in the history of the Church, received the honor of that origin. ON THIS ACCOUNT, THE BAPTISTS MAY BE CONSIDERED AS THE ONLY CHRISTIAN COMMUNITY WHICH HAS STOOD SINCE THE DAYS OF THE APOSTLES, AND AS A CHRISTIAN SOCIETY WHICH HAS PRESERVED PURE THE DOCTRINE OF THE GOSPEL THROUGH ALL AGES. The perfectly correct external and internal economy of the Baptist denomination tends to confirm the truth, disputed by the Romish Church, that the Reformation brought about in the sixteenth century was in the highest degree necessary, and at the same time GOES TO REFUTE THE ERRONEOUS NOTION OF THE CATHOLICS THAT THEIR COMMUNION IS THE MOST ANCIENT.'

"Such was the impression which this truthful document made upon the Court, that the Government of Holland offered to the Baptist Churches the support of the State, which was politely but firmly declined, 'as inconsistent with their principles.'

"The celebrated Bishop Bossuet says: 'We are able to make it appear by the acts of councils and by ancient rituals, that for more than thirteen hundred years, baptism was administered by immersion throughout the whole church as far as possible.'"

"Now, if you have any further doubt, I will bring up these very acts of councils, and authentic copies of these same ancient rituals. They are still on record, and it is not difficult to avail ourselves of their explicit testimony."

"Oh, no, Mr. Courtney : these historians, and preachers, and bishops, were none of them Baptists. We all know that, and if the facts had not compelled them, they would, of course, never have made assertions so injurious to their own cause, and so directly opposed to their own practice. If they say that baptism was done by immersion for thirteen hundred years, of course it must have been so. If Mosheim and Neander, Bossuet and Taylor, Coleman and Whitby, Stackhouse and Baxter, all sprinklers themselves, and all opposed to the Baptists, make such statements, and even Drs. Miller and Stuart, our own most eminent writers on the subject, admit their truth, why need we spend any more time ?"

"But what then becomes of your uncle's opinion, that the Baptists originated about the year 1530, with the Mad Men of Munster?"

"Oh, I have given up that opinion (which indeed was not more than an impression) some half an hour ago. The testimony is irresistible. Immersion was most unquestionably the practice of the early churches; but I am now, like Theodosia, exceedingly anxious to know how it came to be universally displaced, and sprinkling universally adopted in its place."

"You are mistaken, Professor Jones, if you imagine that this change is by any means a *universal* one. It was made by the authority of the Pope, and is confined to the Roman Catholic Church-and its descendants. The Eastern churches—comprising a vast number of professing Christians— have never adopted sprinkling, but continue to practice immersion to the present day ; and as Professor Stuart truly states, call the Western churches 'sprinkled Christians,' by way of derision. If you have any doubt of this, I will prove it to you by the testimony of your own writers of most unquestionable authority."

"Oh, no, Mr. Courtney, I do not doubt it. You have convinced me so often, that I am now willing to take your word for any thing you please to assert."

"I thank you, Professor; but still I do not like to deal in assertions. In regard to this point, however, the proof will come in by the way—together with that on the time and manner of the change."

"Do, then, Mr. Courtney, go on with that," said the young lady. "You don't know how provoking it is to be kept so long in suspense."

"Well, here is the testimony. I will leave the story to be told by some of the most celebrated members of the sprinkling churches. You will, of course, not doubt their truthfulness. Here is the Edinburgh Encyclopædia, edited by the learned and celebrated Sir David Brewster. Let us read what he says on the subject. In the Article on Baptism :

"'The first law for sprinkling was obtained in the following manner : Pope Stephen II., being driven from Rome by Astolphus, King of Lombards, in 753, fled to Pepin, who a short time before had usurped the crown of France. While he remained there, the Monks of Cressy, in Brittany, consulted him whether, in case of necessity, baptism performed by pouring water on the head of the infant would be lawful. Stephen replied that it would. But though the truth of this fact should be allowed, which, however, some Catholics deny, yet pouring or sprinkling was admitted *only in cases of necessity.* It was not till the year 1311, that the Legislature, in a council held at Ravenna, declared immersion or sprinkling to be indifferent. In this country (Scotland), however, sprinkling was never practiced in ordinary cases, till after the Reformation; and in England, even in the reign of Edward VI., immersion was commonly observed. But during the persecution of Mary, many persons, most of whom were Scotchmen, fled from England to Geneva, and there greedily imbibed the opinions of that church. In 1556, a book was published at that place containing the form of prayers and ministration of sacraments, approved by the famous and godly learned man, John Calvin, in which the administrator is enjoined to take water in his hand and lay it on the child's forehead. These Scottish exiles, who had renounced the authority of the Pope, implicitly acknowledged the authority of Calvin; and returning to their own country with John Knox at their head, in 1559, established sprinkling in Scotland. From Scotland, this practice made its way into England in the reign of Elizabeth, but was not authorized by the established church.' "

"Do let me look at that book a moment," said the Professor. "It is very strange that I should have been told, as I am sure I have been by some of the learned clergy of our church, that sprinkling was what was practiced from the earliest ages, and that immersion was attempted to be introduced in its place by the Anabaptists of Germany about the year 1530—when in fact immersion had been always the practice, and it was sprinkling that was substituted by John Calvin, the founder of our church. *Can it be possible that Doctors of Divinity will impose such falsehoods on their people in order to sustain the practice of the church?* I cannot understand it."

" Perhaps you want more testimony before you can

believe it," said Mr. Courtney; "and here is ample confirmatory proof in the plain and explicit declarations of
the famous Dr. Wall."

"Please tell me," said Theodosia, "who was Dr.
Wall? I have often heard of him, and I know that he
wrote one or more books on baptism, but whether on
our side or yours, I have never been informed."

"Dr. Wall," said Mr. Courtney, "was a minister of
the Episcopal, or English Church, and after the publication of his work, the satisfaction it gave was so great,
that in a general convocation of the Episcopal clergy,
held February 9th, 1706, it was ordered 'that the thanks
of this house be given to Mr. Wall, Vicar of Shoreham,
in Kent, for the learned and excellent book he has lately
written concerning infant baptism.'"

"Then he must have written against the Baptists, if
his work was approved by the clergy of the Episcopal
Church."

"Of course he did, and his book is considered to this
day the ablest defence of infant baptism which has ever
been written."

"Well, what does he say about the introduction of
sprinkling? Does he agree with the Encyclopædia,
which you have read? Where is the passage which
speaks of it? Please read it for us."

"'France seems to have been the first country in the
world where baptism by affusion was used, ordinarily,
to persons in health, and in the *public* way of administering it. It being allowed to *weak* children (in the
reign of Queen Elizabeth) to be baptized by aspersion,
many fond ladies and gentlemen first, and then, by de-
grees, the common people, would obtain the favor of the
priest to have their children *pass* for weak children, too
tender to endure dipping in the water. As for *sprinkling,* properly so called, it was at 1645 just *then begin-*

ning, and used by very few. It must have begun in the disorderly times after forty-one. They (the Assembly of Divines in Westminster) re-formed the font into a basin. This learned Assembly could not remember that fonts to baptize in had been *always used by the primitive Christians* long before the beginning of Popery, and ever since churches were built; but that *sprinkling,* for the purpose of baptizing, was really introduced (in France first, and then in *other Popish* countries) in times of *Popery,* and that, accordingly, *all those countries in which the usurped power of the Pope is,* or *has formerly been owned,* HAVE LEFT OFF DIPPING OF CHILDREN IN THE FONTS; but that all other countries in the world which had never regarded his authority, *do still use it;* and that basins (to sprinkle out of) except in cases of necessity, were never used by Papists, or any other Christians whosoever, till by themselves.'—*Hist. of Infant Baptism,* part 2d, chap. 9.

"This," said Mr. Courtney, "is Dr. Wall's account of the first introduction of sprinkling; and you see that it confirms the truth of what I told you, that it was introduced by Popery, and is confined to the countries where Popery prevails, or has prevailed. The Protestant sects borrowed it from the Catholics. Now look at page 403 of this other volume, by the same author, and read the passage I have marked.

"'The way that is ordinarily used, *we cannot deny to have been a novelty,* brought into this Church (the English) by those that had learned it at Germany, or at Geneva. And they, not contented to follow the example of pouring a quantity of water (which had there been introduced instead of immersion), but improved it (if I may so abuse that word) from pouring to sprinkling, *that it might have as little resemblance to the an cient way of baptizing as possible.'—Def. of Hist. of Infant Baptism*, p. 403.

"If you consult the Edinburgh Encyclopædia, the British Encyclopædia, and the Encyclopædia Americana, article Baptism, you will find a complete history of the whole subject, the truthfulness of which you will feel no disposition to question. You will there learn that in England the Westminster Assembly of Divines had a warm discussion whether immersion or sprinkling should be adopted. But by the earnest efforts of Dr. Light-foot, who had great interest in the Assembly, sprinkling was adopted by a majority of *one*. The vote stood—twenty-four for immersion, and twenty-five for sprinkling. This was 1643 years after Christ. The next year an Act of Parliament was passed, requiring the parents of all children born in the realm to have them sprinkled; and in 1648, some four years afterward, an Ecclesiastical Council, held at Cambridge, Massachusetts, adopted sprinkling in the place of immersion; and, in May of the same year, the Legislature of that State passed a law making it a penal offence for any one to *say* that infant sprinkling was not good and valid baptism."

"That is surely sufficient," said Uncle Jones, "to satisfy any candid mind, but yet I can hardly believe it, for very astonishment."

"What is there so surprising," replied Mr. Courtney, "in the fact that men should change Christ's ordinances? They did the same thing before our Saviour's time; and he had more than once occasion to reprove them, because they taught 'for ordinances the commandments of men,' and 'made the Word of God of none effect through their traditions.'"

"It is not," replied the Professor, "so much the *fact* which fills me with astonishment, as the care which is evidently taken by ministers of religion in our church to *conceal the fact*, and make on our minds the impression that sprinkling, instead of being merely *allowed by the Pope*, was actually commanded by Jesus Christ, and was commonly practiced by the church till the Baptists undertook to introduce immersion. But, if I do not forget, some of our writers have contended that there was sufficient testimony in the writings of the early Fathers to show that sprinkling was really employed at a very early day. Is it not possible that Sir David Brewster, and Dr. Wall, and Professor Stuart, and all those other great names, including Martin Luther and John Calvin themselves, may have been mistaken, and that sprinkling was, after all, the practice of the early church? Did not Cyprian, one of the ancient Fathers, expressly declare that sprinkling was practiced in his day, and was considered valid baptism? I am sure I have received such an impression from some source."

"You probably received it from some Doctor of Divinity—they are accustomed to make such impressions, but Cyprian says no such thing. The case to which you allude presents the very first instance on record in the whole range of ecclesiastical history in which it was thought possible to substitute any other act for the act of immersion. The facts have been preserved by Eusebius, one of the Fathers, and the historian of the early churches.

"It appears that a certain man, named Novatian, was taken sick, and was apparently nigh unto death. In this condition he became, as many others have done, greatly alarmed about his condition; and, professing faith in Christ, desired to be baptized. But he was too weak to be taken out of bed and put into the water. The water was, therefore, poured around him in his bed. He afterward recovered, and devoting himself to the ministry, applied for priestly orders, and the question arose, whether one thus 'poured upon' in his bed could be accounted a Christian? Now, it is evident, if pouring or sprinkling had been a common mode of administering the ordinance, this question would never have been asked.

"Cyprian was written to upon this subject, and he replied, giving it as his opinion that the grace usually conferred in baptism, might be received by such pouring. In other words, that, though this was not baptism, for it is not called baptism, *perichism* ('perichutheis'), from *peri*, around, and *cheo*, to pour—yet he considered it a valid *substitute* for baptism. This was some time in the third century after Christ. That such substitution was not common, and had received no general sanction from the church, is evident from the well known fact that the Monks of Cressy, in 754, wrote to the Pope, Stephen II., inquiring, 'If it be lawful in case of necessity, occasioned by sickness, to baptize an infant by pouring water on its head from a cup, or the hands?' To which the Pope replied: 'Such a baptism, performed in such a case *of necessity*, shall be accounted valid.' 'This,' says Basnage, 'is accounted the first law against immersion.' The Pontiff, however, did not dispense with immersion except in case of extreme necessity. This law, therefore, did not change the mode of dipping in the public baptisms; and it was not till five hundred and fifty-seven years, that the legislature, in a council at Ravenna, in 1311, declared immersion and pouring indifferent."

"Pardon me, Mr. Courtney, if I seem querulous; but did not ORIGEN, another of the Fathers, speak of baptism as a pouring, when relating the history of the flooding of the wood, and the sacrifice by the prophet Elisha in his contest with the prophets of Baal? Does he not call this *wetting* a baptism?"

12

" He does indeed, Professor.   He calls it a baptism in the same way that the writer of the book of Daniel calls the *wetting* of Nebuchadnezzar a baptism.   He was *baptized* in the dews of heaven.   The word in the Hebrew is *tabal*, which no one ever doubted signified to dip or to immerse.   He was dipped in the dews of heaven—a most beautiful, though hyperbolical, figure of speech, expressing the idea that he was as *wet as though he had been dipped*.   The allusion in both cases is to the *wetting*, not to the act by which the wetting was occasioned."

" I am glad," said Uncle Jones, ".that you mentioned that passage in Daniel, for I confess it has been a stumbling stone to me ; yet you set aside all my other Scriptural difficulties so easily, that I was almost ashamed to mention it.   I was going to tell you that baptize must signify something besides immersion, because it was *impossible* that the deposed monarch could be actually immersed in dew."

" If you had told me so, I would have proved to you," said Mr. Courtney, " that *dip* does not mean *to dip*, or to submerge, because Milton, a standard English writer, represents one as saying that he is dipped all over in the perspiration of his own body :

'A cold shuddering dew dips me all over.'

' If Daniel had been translated as he should have been, His body was *dipped* in the dews of heaven,' everybody would have recognized the force and beauty of the figure, as we do in Milton.   It would have been like that expression which represents the good land of Canaan as '*flowing*' with milk and honey ; or, like that which represents God as *pouring out* blessings till there should not be room to receive them.   Such hyperbolical figures are extremely beautiful, and are common in all languages.

"Nebuchadnezzar is said to be dipped in dew, and Origen says the wood and the sacrifice were immersed in water, to express the completeness of the soaking or drenching which they received."

"Yes," said Theodesia, "Edwin made use of the word *ducking* last evening in the same way. You recollect, Mr. Courtney, the lad who pulled the bucket of water over on his head in school yesterday, so much to the amusement of all the boys. Well, Edwin, in relating the circumstances, said that the little fellow got a good '*ducking*.' By which he meant, of course, that he was as wet as though he had *dived* in the water *like a duck*. It would have been equally proper to have said that he got a good '*dipping*,' and yet neither ducking or dipping means to pour upon—they are diving and plunging still."

"Well, well, Theodosia," said the mother, "that is what I should call stepping from the sublime to the ridiculous. Please go on, Mr. Courtney, and don't mind her nonsense."

"Indeed, Mrs. Ernest, I feel obliged to your daughter for so appropriate an illustration of the great principle of interpretation which must guide us in deciding upon the meaning of such passages. She has shown us that not only in Scriptural usage, and in the poets, but even in common talk among the very children, *one mode* of wetting is sometimes figuratively employed to designate another mode; and that a person or thing that is as thoroughly *wet* as though it *had been* dipped, may be appropriately and beautifully said *to be dipped*.

"But now to return to the subject of our conversation. I have proved to you, by the united testimony of Mosheim, Neander, and Moses Stuart—of Luther, and Calvin, and Whitby, and Taylor, and Baxter—by Drs. Ypeig and Durmont, Coleman and Bossuet, to whose testimony I might have added that of many others of the highest authority, both among the ancients and the moderns, that immersion was the practice of the early churches, and continued to be the only practice, *except* in cases *of supposed* necessity, for MORE THAN THREE HUNDRED YEARS. I have showed you further, how 'pouring' was first practiced irregularly, and without authority from the Bible, or the Pope, in some rare cases of extreme sickness, till the Monks of Cressy obtained the sanction of the Pope (not of Christ) for its use in these *extreme cases of sickness*, more than seven hundred years after Christ, and how immersion and pouring were at length declared to be indifferent by the Pope and his Council (not by the Scriptures) at Ravenna, in 1311.

"I have showed you also how John Calvin and the Westminster Assembly of Divines were the means of bringing sprinkling into the English and Presbyterian Churches of Scotland and England—whence it came over to America with the Colonists.

"I have showed you also that as this change was made by the Pope and the Papal Church, so it is confined to those countries which are, or have been, under Roman Catholic rule, and that the Eastern Churches, which never acknowledged the dominion of the Pope, have continued to practice immersion even to the present day. I have showed you all this, not by the testimony of *Baptist* witnesses, but by that of members of sprinkling churches—by Lutherans, Episcopalians, and Presbyterians; and these not men of doubtful character, and unknown to fame, but of world-wide celebrity, both in regard to their religious and their intellectual character. He who, after this, will not believe that immersion was the baptism of the early churches, would not believe though Paul himself should return from the dead to testify."

"But, Mr. Courtney," said Mrs. Ernest, "what if it was? Must we be immersed, because the old Fathers were immersed? I thought you Baptists were opposed to old traditions."

"We are opposed, Mrs. Ernest," said he, very solemnly. "We are opposed to the substitution of the *traditions of men for the teachings of the Word of God.* We have ascertained from the Word itself that it was immersion which was commanded by Jesus Christ. It was thus the early Christians understood it. It was this which, for many hundred years, they practiced; but at length the man-made ordinance of sprinkling and pouring was introduced by the authority of the Pope and his councils. You have adopted *this*—your church almost universally practices it—you have no other authority for it, as I have proved by your own writers, but that of the Pope. Is it not true, therefore, that you are in your church 'teaching for doctrines the commandments of men?'

"I did not refer to the usage of the early churches as the *authority* for immersion. If I could not find it in the Bible, I would not receive it, though it had been practiced from the time of Noah. Tradition is no authority in matters of religion. I may use it to confirm the teaching of the actual commandment, but where there is no express precept or example recorded in God's Word, I owe no obedience in matters of religion."

"But why, then, did you go into this long investigation of the practice of the church?"

"I did it, madam, for the satisfaction of Professor Jones and your daughter, who seemed to have a sort of silent conviction that the simple fact that sprinkling

was *so generally practiced*, was in some way or other
sufficient evidence that it must have been commanded
in the Scriptures. I, therefore, traced immersion back
to Jesus Christ, and showed where he commanded it.
I have now traced *pouring* back to Pope Stephen II.,
and showed where he allowed it in cases of necessity,
and to the Popish council at Ravenna, and showed
where they allowed it in other cases; and I have traced
sprinkling, properly so-called, back to John Calvin, and
showed where he commanded it in his Book of Prayers
and Sacraments, published at Geneva. I have, therefore, founded immersion on the *rock* of God's Word,
and at the same time convinced you all, I trust, that
pouring and sprinkling rest only on the *sand* of human
invention—not having even a credible *tradition* to rest
upon."

Uncle Jones listened with some uneasiness to this
long speech. He felt its force, and recognized its
truthfulness, but he was doubtful of the effect it might
have upon his sister. In fact, he was afraid of an
explosion.

Affection for her daughter had, however, been working wonders in the mother's mind within the last two
days. She found that Theodosia *would* examine, and
she desired that she would do it *quickly*. She found
she was likely to be *convinced*, and she began to excuse
her by considering the weight and invincibility of the
arguments. Now, she saw that she *was* convinced, and
every additional reason for such conviction was a
comfort to her maternal pride, as it was new proof that
her daughter was not such a simpleton as to believe
without the most convincing evidence.

She had not the most distant idea of being convinced
herself. She did not hear or weigh the testimony for
herself—she heard and thought only for Theodosia—and

since her daughter *would* become a Baptist, she **was** gratified that it was nothing less than the most *unanswerable arguments* that compelled her to do so.

So far, therefore, from looking angry, she seemed rather pleased with this conclusion of the schoolmaster's arguments; and she herself suggested that he should enter upon the other branch of it, by reminding him that he had promised to show that the American Baptists did not originate with Roger Williams any more than the European Baptists did with the Mad Men of Munster.

"That is one of the easiest things in the world to do," replied Mr. Courtney. "Even granting that Roger Williams established the *first* Baptist Church which was ever known in this country, yet it would not follow that all the Baptists, or *any* of the Baptist Churches received their baptism from him; for there have been, every year since his day, more or less regularly immersed Baptists, and regularly ordained Baptist ministers coming to this country; and even though he had founded the church at Providence, and that in an irregular manner, before any other Baptist Church was founded—that would not invalidate the regularity of any other of the thousands and thousands of Baptist Churches, unless it could be made to appear that they were all colonies from that. I need not, therefore, spend any time upon this point. Of all the thousands of Baptist Churches in America, there are none whose pastors and members have had any manner of dependence on the church founded by Roger Williams. They have many of them received baptism from the *Dutch* Baptists, of whom Drs. Ypeig and Durmont testify that they belong to a body of Christians who can trace their origin down to the very times of the Apostles. **Many** of them received it from the *Welsh* Baptists, who can trace their descent back to the sixth or seventh century. Many of them received it from the English Baptists, who have been the victims of proscription and persecution from a very early day. But *none* of them received baptism from Roger Williams, or the church said to have been established by him at Providence. The truth is, the society established by Roger Williams, Holliman, and others, soon died out. It never planted any other church. It cannot be proved that any Baptist who received baptism in that body and by their authority, was ever concerned in baptizing any founder of other churches."

"I have often heard of Roger Williams," said Theodosia, "as the founder of the Baptists in this country. Please tell me what was his relation to them."

"Roger Williams adopted at one time Baptist sentiments, at least, in some particulars," replied Mr. Courtney. "He desired to be immersed. There was no Baptist minister at hand. He consequently immersed one of his followers, who, in turn, immersed him, and then he considered himself competent to immerse others. The little company, thus irregularly baptized, called itself a Baptist church; but, in about four months, Roger Williams himself changed his opinions and withdrew from the society. The so-called church soon died out, and the present Baptist Church of Providence was founded on an independent basis, separate and distinct from that. It seems probable, however, from recent historical researches, that the *oldest* Baptist Church in the United States, is that at Newport, in Rhode Island, founded by John Clark, against the regularity of whose baptism there has, so far as I know, been nothing alleged. Though, as to that, even if *this and all the other churches of Rhode Island*, had been, and were still, irregular up to the present time, it would not affect the standing of the great body of the churches in the United States, since very few of them derived their baptism directly or indirectly from Rhode Island—and *not a single one of them from Roger Williams.*"

THE SEVENTH NIGHT'S STUDY.

IN WHICH IT IS CLEARLY PROVED

BY THE SCRIPTURES THEMSELVES

AND BY THE

TESTIMONY OF THE MOST LEARNED

AND

EMINENT PEDOBAPTIST MINISTERS,

THAT

INFANT BAPTISM

WAS NOT

COMMANDED BY CHRIST OR THE APOSTLES:

INFANT BAPTISM WAS NOT PRACTICED

OR

SANCTIONED BY CHRIST OR HIS APOSTLES.

SEVENTH NIGHT'S STUDY.

THE attentive reader may have observed that Mr. Percy has not favored us with his presence for the last three nights. Though he seemed so greatly interested in the subject, yet with the third night's study he apparently abandoned it. Since that time he had not visited Mrs. Ernest's cottage, or held any communion with its inmates. He did not know what progress Theodosia had made in her investigations, nor what assistance she had received from Uncle Jones or others. The remark made by Mr. Courtney, as they were about to separate on that occasion, " that he would find it much easier to satisfy his mind that sprinkling and pouring were not baptism, than he would to abandon his church connections and be baptized according to the commandment of Jesus Christ," had opened his eyes. He had, till that moment, looked upon the subject merely as one of curious speculation. It was till then a mere question of fact, to be decided by testimony. As such, its investigation greatly interested him. It was congenial to his logical and discriminating cast of mind, and he had been study ing it as he would a case of law. But he now saw that it was a *practical* matter. If he decided that he had not been baptized, consistency would require that he should at once apply for baptism. This would break off his connection with a large, and wealthy, and influ- ential body, and tie him down to a little company of obscure and ignorant laborers and mechanics—for of such was the newly-organized Baptist Church of which we have been speaking chiefly composed. This was something he could not think of. His natural pride had never been humbled by the grace of God, and he was not at all prepared to resign a position at once honorable and profitable, for one of comparative insignificance and contempt. He thought of these things as he was going home that night, and at once resolved that he would have no more to do with the subject.

In this resolution he had been confirmed, by a visit next morning from Colonel White, one of the members of the Session, who was a wealthy speculator in lands, and one of his best patrons. After some conversation about matters of business, Colonel White carelessly remarked: "They have it rumored, Squire Percy, that you are on the eve of leaving our church and becoming a Baptist."

"Let me assure you, colonel, that there is not the slightest foundation for such a report. I have, indeed, spent a few hours in the investigation of the mode of baptism, but it was for the mere purpose of fortifying my mind with the best arguments in favor of our position on that subject. I found, indeed, that the immersionists have much firmer ground to stand upon than I imagined; but I have never for a moment entertained the idea of leaving the Presbyterian Church."

"I am glad to hear it, Mr. Percy, for I prefer, and so do several of our best firms, to employ you to attend to our business, and we had all about concluded that we could never trust our interests in the hands of one so fickle minded as such a change would prove a man to be; and, besides this, since the death of Deacon Smith, there has been a vacancy in the Church Session, which we have been desirous to fill with some talented and efficient *young* man, since the rest of us are now beginning to be somewhat advanced in years. We were talking of you, and the only objection seemed to be, that you were yet unmarried. I took the liberty to say that I thought *that* difficulty would be removed in the course of another month, as I understood the wedding-day was fixed. It is no secret, you know. But then, rumor says also, that Miss Theodosia is going over to the Baptists; and that her mother, with all her authority, has not been able to dissuade her from the investigation of the subject, though she sees very plainly where it will lead her."

"It is very true," said the young man, "that she has been engaged in the study of this subject, but I do not know to what conclusion she may come. For my own part, I have concluded to have nothing more to do with it."

"It is a delicate matter, Mr. Percy, and perhaps I ought not to mention it, and nothing but my regard for your future happiness, and the honor of our church, could induce me to do it; but would it not be wise in you to use your influence (which I know must be very great) to induce her to pause before she takes a step which will cause your house, always after your marriage, to be divided against itself? I know I have no right to advise, but I take the liberty of a friend to you, and a friend to your father before you, to merely suggest such a thought. Perhaps, on reflection, you may think it advisable, either to see her immediately, or write a little line, stating your own determination, and whatever else you may think most likely to operate upon her mind, so as to prevent such a terrible event as it would be to you and all of us, should she so far disgrace her name and dishonor her profession as to leave the communion in which she was born, and by which she has been nourished and taught—in which her grand parents lived and died—and of which she is herself the ornament and pride, and throw herself away, with all her loveliness and intelligence, by uniting her fate to that ignorant and obscure sect, with a mechanic for a preacher, who have started up here like a mushroom in a single night, and will probably pass away again in a day."

Mr. Percy was about to reply, when the colonel anticipated him by rising and grasping the young man's hand very warmly in both of his. "Pardon me," he said, "I ought not to have spoken thus. Forget that I have said it. But don't forget my case in the Supreme Court. I have entrusted it entirely to you. I want you to have all the honor which will accrue from a decision in your favor. Good morning. You will need all your time to make preparation for next week's Circuit Court—you start on Saturday, I believe?"

"Yes, sir."

"Well, good luck to you," and the colonel was gone.

Mr. Percy walked his office with a restless, undecided air, for some time, and then set himself resolutely to work in the preparation of some cases for the approaching court. But he could not banish the subject from his mind. He sometimes thought he would go at once, and have another conversation with his betrothed upon the subject; but when he remembered her earnest and conscientious truthfulness of soul, he feared to lower himself in her estimation by presenting to her any but the real reasons for his abandonment of the investigation, and these he hardly dared to own even to himself. This was on Wednesday morning. He learned on Thursday that Uncle Jones had been conversing with Theodosia on the subject; and, on Friday, that both he and Mr. Courtney had been at the cottage; and Mrs. Tattle had told young Dr. Woodruff, who was his intimate friend and confidant, that, on the coming Sabbath, Miss Ernest was to be baptized.

Early on Saturday morning, he was obliged to start to a distant county-site to attend a session of the Circuit Court. Before his return (if this story were true) the die would be cast. If he would prevent it at all, he must do it now. He determined to write what he felt he could not speak. The letter read thus:

"DEAREST:—I must leave town to-morrow, and shall be gone a week. I have been so pressed by business, that I have not been able to call in again, as I intended when I saw you last. I cannot come to-night, but I cannot leave without expressing to you once more my earnest love. You know, dearest Theodosia, that the happiness of my life is bound up in yours. I have no wish or hope in the future but those of which you form a part; and, if what I am about to say should be unpleasant to you, I beg you will remember that it is dictated by the tenderest and most ardent affection. It is because I value your happiness even more than my own, that I venture to say what I am about to utter. I have learned from rumor that you have already determined to abandon our church, and unite with that contemptible sect of Baptists. I do not know if this be true or not. I hope and pray the rumor may prove false. I will not say these Baptists are not right about the mode of baptism. It may be they are. But whether one mode or another be correct, baptism is not essential to salvation. It is a mere outward form, and I cannot, for the sake of a mere external and nonessential ceremony, abjure the church of my fathers. I fondly hope that she, whom I love more than all else in life, will agree with me in this. I cannot bear the thought that one so beautiful, so lovely, so accom-

13

plished, so fitted to shine and *lead* in the highest circle
of our society—one, too, who has the unbounded confidence and affection of her brothers and sisters in the
church—should bring such dishonor upon her father's
name, such sorrow to her mother's heart, and such
regret to his, who rejoices in the hope that he will be
the companion of her life, and the husband of her love,
as to prove recreant to her Christian faith—forsake
the church of the mother who offered her to God in
infancy—of the teachers who instructed her childhood
—of the pastor who prayed with her in the time of her
conviction, and rejoiced over her at the time of her
conversion ; and may I not add of him who, trusting in
the solemn promise of our betrothal, expects to spend
his life in promoting her happiness? How can you, my
dearest love—how can you disregard such considera-
tions as these? I know that you are conscientious in
every step you take, and I beg you to reflect whether
these things should not have some influence with you.
I know that you mean to do right, and I entreat that
you will consider if such a course will not be wrong.
I know I have no right to dictate, but, oh! I do beseech
you, if you have any love for me, that you will not so
mortify and distress, not me alone, but all who love
you, as to unite your fate with those boorish, uneducated, and bigoted people, called Baptists.

" Your distressed, but still most affectionate,

"G. W. PERCY."

This note he hardly trusted himself to read, so he
sealed it up, and despatched a messenger to carry it to
Mrs. Ernest's. Its immediate effect on Theodosia we
have already seen. When she had reached her own
room, she threw her head upon her mother's bosom,
and, sighing as if a heart-string broke with every

deep-fetched sob that came, gave free expression to her uncontrollable distress.

It was long before the mother became sufficiently composed to read the letter, and learn what it was that had occasioned such a terrible heart-sorrow to her loving and sensitive child. Terrible she knew it must be, for never in her life had she seen Theodosia exhibit such unutterable distress. The young lady herself did not know precisely what the letter contained. She had loved Mr. Percy with all the fervor of a first and only love. The day was fixed only a few weeks in the future for their wedding. The preparations for it were even then begun. To be what Mr. Percy would approve, was to her the highest point of earthly ambition. She prized her peerless beauty, not for its own sake, but because Mr. Percy praised it. She valued her accomplishments, chiefly because Mr. Percy thought them desirable. With all her independence of thought and originality of mind, she had learned to think that she was wrong, if Mr. Percy did not think her right.

In this investigation he had gone with her step by step, so long as he had taken any part in it. She had, till now, not the very slightest suspicion that he would not *act out his convictions*, as well as herself—much less did she imagine that he would so fearfully disapprove of her obedience to what she now was fully satisfied was the plain and unmistakable command of her Redeemer.

The first influence of this communication was like that of a heavy blow upon the head. It staggered, and then stunned the mind. She only felt that some great and terrible calamity had fallen on her heart and crushed it. She could not recall the language of the letter, but only a general impression of its contents. But there was, here and there, a word which was burnt into her very brain. With all its protestations of affection, she felt (for love is jealous in such things) that if she became a Baptist, she forfeited his love.

To her mother she could speak words no other's ear might hear—and when her sobs had somewhat ceased, and she had been persuaded to lie down, and try to be composed, she drew her mother's face to hers, and while their tears mingled together upon her cheek, she whispered, "I did not think *he* could have cast me off for seeking to know and do my duty."

"My precious child, he has not cast you off—he says again and again, that he loves you dearly, and hopes to spend his life in rendering you happy."

"But, mother, does he not say he cannot *bear to think of my becoming a Baptist?* Does he not call them, whom now I do believe are the true church of Jesus Christ—does he not call them *that contemptible sect?* Does he not say that because he *has no right to dictate*, he *entreats* me not to *mortify* him, not to *distress* him, by becoming one of that little company of boorish, uneducated, and bigoted people? No, no, mother, I see it all. If I become a Baptist, I must resign his love—I must give up all the most cherished hopes of my life. After such an expression of his dislike to these poor and humble disciples of Jesus, I would not dare, if I were one of them, to become his wife. I must choose between him and my Saviour—I see it all—but I can't choose now. Oh! my mother, pray for me—pray for me! *You* will not cast me off, my mother : *you* will love me still. Will you not, my mother? *You* can love, even though I do mortify and distress you, can't you mother?"

"Yes, yes, darling—don't look at me so wildly. I will love you always—I will love you dearly. And so will Mr. Percy, even though you do mortify and distress him. He can't help loving you, my sweet child.

No one, who knows you, can do any thing but love you."

"No, mother, *he can't love as I must be loved*, were I the wife of his bosom. But I dare not think of that now. I must pray—I must ask wisdom—I must get strength from heaven. Leave me now, mother, but don't forget to pray for me."

The mother went away—and, kneeling down, poured out her heart in a sincere and fervent prayer, that God would indeed give comfort to her poor child's loving and smitten spirit. While she, the dear, sweet child, lay still upon her bed, and only prayed with those groanings that cannot be uttered, for *strength to bear*, as well as *energy to do*—her mind grew calmer and clearer, and when her mother came, an half hour after, to bid her good-night, she was in a deep sleep, with something almost like a smile upon her face. This may seem strange to one who does not know that one effect of sudden, deep, and terrible sorrow is quickly to exhaust the nervous energies and predispose to heavy slumber. There is, therefore, a most affecting beauty in the language of the Evangelist, when he says of the disciples, whom Jesus had left only a little time, while he went to pray, that he returned to them, and found them *sleeping for sorrow*. No other language could so perfectly express the deep, intense, and soul-exhausting *agony of mind* which they had felt on learning that their beloved Lord was soon to perish by the hands of his enemies, and that one of their number should be the wretch who would betray him into their hands.

So Theodosia might now be said to be sleeping for sorrow. She did not wake till after her ordinary time of rising in the morning. When she first became conscious, there was a feeling of weight upon her eyelids which prevented her from opening them; and as she lay there, motionless, the events of the past evening began to come back, like the dimly-remembered imagery of some fearful dream. At first, she was only conscious that something terrible had befallen her, and it required some little effort to remember what it was. . Then came to view the letter, just as it looked when her mother handed it to her as she sat in the parlor. She could see every mark of every letter of the superscription. Then the open letter was before her; and she read some of the lines as they had marked themselves with terrible distinctness on her brain; others she could not *see*, but only a dim impression of their sense came up in her remembrance. When, as she ran thus in her mind over the letter, she came to where it read, " I know I have no right to dictate—but oh! I do beseech you, if you have any love for me, that you will not so mortify and distress, not me alone," etc., the tears flowed freely, and she was able to open her eyes.

Her mother had, at that moment, come in, and was bending over her.

" My poor child," said she, as she saw the tears start even before she seemed to be awake—" how do you feel this morning ?"

" Is it morning, mother ? I have been asleep—I have had a terrible dream—or was it all reality ? Do, mother, tell me, did you bring me a letter last night from Mr. Percy ?"

" Yes, my child, you are not quite awake. It was no dream ; but the reality is not so terrible as you imagine. Let me give you this cup of coffee, and you will feel refreshed."

" Theodosia sat up in bed and sipped the coffee—and shortly afterward got up, and went and sat beside her mother and engaged in some worsted work which she had begun the day before. When her mother went out, she followed her, and stood beside her till she returned; so she continued all through the day, accompanying her as constantly and almost as noiselessly as her shadow. She did not speak—she did not weep—she sometimes *tried* to smile, but it was pitiful to see the effort made to divert her mother's mind and make her think she was not *so very bad*. In this condition we must leave her for the present, and go to the dwelling of Professor Jones, where Mr. Courtney and the Rev. Mr. Johnson are waiting to engage in the discussion of the subject of infant baptism—which discussion, if it should prove to be less entertaining than this little narrative of what transpired at Mrs. Ernest's, will, we trust, be more instructive.

"If I understood you correctly, Mr. Courtney," said Professor Jones (when they were all assembled), "you asserted that there was in the Scriptures not the slightest authority for the baptism of infants, and that baptism received in infancy is not valid baptism."

"You are *nearly* correct," said Mr. Courtney, smiling. "I did not *assert* that there was no such authority, for it is not my habit to deal in *mere assertions*. I said that I would *prove* that this was so."

"But how will you set about proving such a negative?"

"By offering the only testimony which the nature of the case admits. Our authority to baptize any one, infant or adult, is derived *only* from the *commandments* or *example* of Christ or his apostles. All they said and all they did which is of any authority to us, is recorded in the Word of God. Now if I can't find, and you can't show me, *any single place* where an infant was commanded to be baptized, or *any single place* where one is said to have been baptized, then I think I may venture to say that *there is no authority there for infant baptism*."

" I think so too; but I am certain we can show you a number of such places. Can we not, Mr. Johnson?"

" Certainly we can. It has always been my understanding that the baptism of the infant children of believers is explicitly commanded by both Christ and the apostles; and what was required by their precepts, they enforced by their example. They both commanded and they practiced it."

" Very good. Here then is the point on which we are at issue. *If the places are in the Book, you can show them.* I will not be unreasonable. I do not ask even for two witnesses—I only require *one.* Show me *one solitary instance* of either precept or example, and I will give up the case."

" I have been accustomed to think," said the Professor, " that the commission itself, as recorded in Matt. xxviii. 19, and in Mark xvi. 15, 16, contained all the authority which was given to the Christian Church to administer the ordinance of baptism; and I had supposed that the authority to baptize infants was to be found in what Christ said on that occasion—' Go ye into all the world, and preach the Gospel to every creature. He that believeth and is baptized shall be saved; but he that believeth not shall be damned.' "

" That," said Mr. Johnson, " is what Mark says. Get a Testament and see how it reads in Matthew. I think it is somewhat different. Here it is—' Go ye therefore and teach all nations, baptizing them in the name of the Father, and of the Son, and of the Holy Ghost. Teaching them to observe all things whatsoever I have commanded you: and lo! I am with you always, even unto the end of the world.' "

" Very good," said Mr. Courtney. " You have the

law all now before you. Is there in it a single allusion,
even the faintest, to infants? Did Christ say, as you
Presbyterians do, Go baptize believers and their infant
children—or believers only? Matthew says, *teach* them
and *then* baptize them. So they must be such as can be
taught. But can a little babe, 'mewling and puking in
its mother's arms,' be taught the doctrines of salvation
by Jesus Christ? Mark says—'He that *believeth* and
is baptized;' so that he speaks of none baptized but
those who had first *believed.* Can little infants, who
do not yet so much as know their right hand from
their left, exercise faith in the Saviour of souls? *You*
will not, I am sure, venture to say they can, though
there have been some *Doctors of Divinity* who were silly
enough to make such assertions. And Matthew, in fact,
says just the same that Mark does; for 'the word rendered *teach* here, is not the one that is usually so translated in the New Testament. This word properly means
disciple, or *make disciples of* all nations.'—(*Barnes'
Notes, In. loc.*) So also says that eminent and good
man, Dr. Doddridge, author of the 'Rise and Progress
of Religion': 'Here it is to be observed, *first,* certain
things are enjoined, viz.: to *disciple*—to baptize—to
teach. Secondly, these things are enjoined in a *certain
order,* viz.: the order in which they stand in the divine
commission.'—(*Dod. Lec.*) So says also that other
great and good man, the pious Baxter, author of 'The
Saints' Rest':

"'Go *disciple* me all nations—and as for those,' he
continues, 'who say they are discipled *by* baptizing and
not *before* baptizing, they speak not the sense of the
text, nor that which is true or rational, if they mean it
absolutely as so spoken, else why should one be baptized
more than another?' 'This text is not like some occasional historical mention of baptism, but it is *the very*

commission of Christ to his apostles for preaching and baptizing, and purposely expresseth their several works in their several orders. Their *first* task is by teaching *to make disciples*, who are by Mark called *believers*. The *second* work is to *baptize* them—whereunto is annexed the promise of salvation. The *third* is to teach them all other things which are afterward to be learned in the school of Christ. To contemn *this order* is to renounce *all rules of order*, for where can we expect to find it, if not here?' 'I profess,' he goes on to say, 'my conscience is fully satisfied from this text that it is one sort of faith, even *saving* faith, that must go before baptism; and the profession whereof the minister must expect.'—*Dis. on the Right to Sacrament*, pp. 91–150.

"Dr. Hibbard, a Methodist, in his Commentary on Matt. xxviii. 19–20, says—'It is well known that our English version does not give a satisfactory view of this passage. The word rendered teach in the 19th verse is altogether a different word in the original from that rendered teach in the 20th. It should read, Go *disciple*, that is make *converts* to Christianity of all nations,' etc.

"Neither of you, gentlemen, nor any other Greek scholar, will dispute that *matheteusate*, in the first part of this commission, means make disciples, as certainly as *didaskontes* means teaching in the last part of it Nor can you, or any man of common sense, pretend that any are commanded to be baptized, but those who have first been made disciples. Now what is the New Testament meaning of a disciple? Jesus Christ himself shall answer: Luke xiv. 26, 27, 33. 'If any man come to me and hate not his father, and mother, and wife, and children, and brethren, and sisters, yea, and his own life also, he *cannot be my disciple*. And whosoever doth not bear his cross and come after me *cannot be my dis-*

ciple. So likewise, whosoever he be of you, that forsaketh not all that he hath, *he cannot be my disciple.*'
Do little infants, who do not even know the name of
Christ, and scarcely know their own, so love Christ that
the love they have to all others is like hatred compared
to that they feel for him? Can little infants forsake all
for Christ, and do they daily take their cross and follow
him? Then they are his disciples, and are commanded
to be baptized. But no sensible man who is not a
Doctor of Divinity would ever think of such absurdity.
You do not pretend to baptize infants on any such grounds.
You do not ask in them for any evidence of penitence,
or piety, or faith, or love, or any thing else that goes to
make a disciples of Christ."

"No," replied Mr. Johnson, "we baptize them on the
faith of their parents."

"But this commission says nothing about baptizing
the *children of believing parents.* By it the ministers
of Christ are commanded to baptize *disciples* (according
to Matthew) and *believers* (according to Mark); but in
regard to the *children* of these disciples and believers,
they are both as silent as the grave."

"It was not necessary," said Mr. Johnson, "to put
the authority for the baptism of infants *in the commission,* since the matter is fully provided for elsewhere.
I grant that it is not in *this* passage, but it does not
follow that it is not in the Bible."

"Oh! no—certainly not," said Mr. Courtney. "I
am easy to be satisfied; show it to me *in any other
place,* and it will do quite as well."

"But, I do not feel disposed," said Professor Jones,
"to give up this passage so easily. Does not the term
'*all nations*' include infants as well as adults?"

"Certainly, but they were not to *baptize all nations,*
for this would include *all unbelievers* and *their* children,

as well as *believers* and *their* children. They were to
Go to *all* nations (not to the Jews alone, as they had
been used to think); and among all nations they were
to make disciples, as many as they could—and those
disciples who believed they were to baptize."

"But, Mr. Courtney, let me put in another plea for
the infants. I am very anxious to get them into this
commission, for I have always thought they were surely
there. It is evident they are not included in the expression 'all nations,' since it is true, as you say, it
will include all infidels, idolators, profligates, and mur-
derers, as well as the infant children of unbelievers—
but are they not included in the word disciples? May .
they not, in view of their innocence, and purity, and
evident fitness for heaven, be properly called the disciples of Jesus? Did not Jesus himself compare his
disciples to them, and say that none could enter
heaven who did not become like one of them? I will
therefore, put it on this ground: None but disciples are
to be baptized, but infants are already by nature disciples—and therefore infants are to be baptized."

"But," said Mr. Courtney, "the disciples who were
to be baptized were *not* disciples *by nature*. They were
to be *made* disciples. They were to be *believing* disciples, and capable of learning, for they were to be
taught. Now as infants are not *made disciples* by hearing the Word—as they are incapable *of faith* or of
instruction in the things that Christ commanded, they
cannot be included in the term disciples."

"Yes, but infants have the natural *capacity to believe
and to be taught*, which will in time be fully developed."

"Very true; and so when these capacities *are* fully
developed, and they *actually have believed,* they will
have become disciples. You know very well that children do not ordinarily grow up the disciples of Jesus,

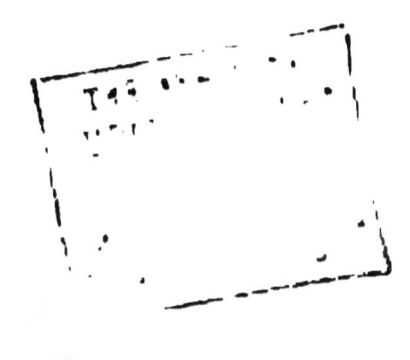

Theodosia Ernest.

PAGE 210.

Theodosia Ernest.

but the servants of sin, and all of them need conversion after they come to the development of their faculties, be fore they can be disciples. They are in infancy *in some respects like to disciples*, but they are *not* disciples, but are by *nature* the children of wrath even as others'— and as soon as they are old enough, they show it very plainly."

"Well, I fear we must give up the commission. But tell me this, if infants are not fit subjects for baptism, how can they be fit for heaven?"

"Those only are fit subjects for baptism, whom *Christ commanded to be baptized.* The Gospel has nothing to do with infants. There is in it no command addressed to them, nor is any act, either of mind or body, required of them in order to their salvation. They are no more required to believe than they are to be baptized. They are saved without either. *You* are required to do both. To *you*, God says *believe* and be baptized. You profess to have *believed*, but you have never made the slightest effort to be baptized. What was done to you in infancy, without your knowledge or assent, was no *act of yours.* You are still living in open disobedience to this law. Jesus Christ did not command *your parents* to *have you* baptized—putting the responsibility on them, but he commanded *you* to be baptized for yourself; and that not *before* you believed, but *afterward :* ' He that believeth, and [then] is baptized, shall be saved.' "

"It seems to me, Mr. Courtney," said the pastor, "that you are rather early in your application of the subject. We have granted, indeed, that the authority for infant baptism is not in the commission by which we are directed to baptize adult believers, but it may be found elsewhere. A recent writer on this subject, the Rev. Dr. Summers, has very expressively said: 'That the New Testament ABOUNDS with the proofs of infant baptism.' "

" Then, sir, it will be very easy to find at least *one text* which teaches it."

" Certainly it will, not only one, but many."

" But I only ask for *one ;* and if you have several, give me that first which you most rely upon."

" Well, sir, you have the Testament in your hand, please turn to Matthew xix. 13, 14: 'Then were brought unto him little children, that he should put his hands upon them, and pray. And the disciples rebuked them. But Jesus said, suffer little children to come unto me, and forbid them not, for of such is the kingdom of Heaven.' Do you not see some authority for infant baptism in that ?"

" Indeed, sir, I cannot—can you ?"

" Yes, truly. It is to my mind perfectly satisfactory. And I do not see how it can fail to convince any candid man who reads it."

" Your mind, Mr. Johnson, must be easily satisfied then, for I can't see *one word* about baptism in it."

" Oh! I do not say that baptism is *expressly named* in it; but, sir, the *inference* is irresistible, that these children were brought *to be baptized*, and that the people were *accustomed* to bring their children for that purpose, and that Jesus commanded his disciples *never to forbid it*, as you, Baptists, have done, but to suffer the little children to come to him, and make a part of his visible church."

" Is it possible! Pardon me, Mr. Johnson, if I say, that to my mind there can be no *inference* about the object or purpose for which these children were brought, because *it is expressly and very definitely stated in the text.* They brought them, that he should *lay his hands on them, and pray.* This was all they came for, and this was all he did. He did not baptize them. He did not command them to be baptized. He merely (verse 15th) 'laid his hands on them, and departed.' But there *is* an irresistible inference that I draw from this text, and that is, that *the disciples had never been accustomed to infant baptism.* If they had been in the habit of *baptizing* children, they could never have objected to their coming to *be blessed* by Jesus. They would have regarded it as a thing of course. But if they had, like the Baptist Churches, received *only adults*, and them only on repentance and profession of faith, it was not at all strange that they should reprove those who brought the little children, who could not believe. And there was a beautiful propriety in the lesson which Jesus taught them, viz.: that though children were *not to be baptized*, and were *not members of his church*, yet they were to be objects of *intense interest* and deep solicitude to his people. Though they were not to be baptized, *they were to be prayed for.* Parents, therefore, ought to bring their little children to Christ by *faith and prayer*, for *that* he has commanded, but *not* by baptism, for that he has forbidden, by requiring those who are baptized first to believe."

"But you cannot deny, Mr. Courtney, that by the kingdom of heaven, in this passage, is meant the *visible church*, and that Jesus expressly mentions children as members of it?"

"Indeed, Mr. Johnson, he mentions no such thing. It does not matter at all whether the kingdom of heaven means the church visible or invisible. He does *not* say that children are members of it, but that *its members are like children.* He does *not* say his church is com-posed of children, but of *such* as are *like* children. For in the corresponding passage in Luke and Mark, he goes right on, and explains by saying, ' Whosoever shall not

receive the kingdom of God as a little child, shall in no
case enter therein.' Mr. Barnes, in his Notes on this
text, says: 'Of such as these—that is, of persons with
such tempers as these—is the church to be composed.
He does not say *of those infants*, but of such as resembled *them*, or were *like* them in temper, was the kingdom
of heaven made up. It was proper, therefore, that he
should pray for them.'—*Notes, in loc.* Olshausen, of
whose Commentary, Kitto, a brother Pedobaptist of his
and yours, declares that it is, on the New Testament,
the best now in existence—Olshausen says on this text:
'For entering into the kingdom of God, there is enjoined that child-like feeling which enables us most
easily to discern the gifts which have been bestowed
upon each, and, consequently, puts us in circumstances
to fulfill our calling.' He goes on to say: 'Of that
reference to infant baptism, which it is so common to
seek for in this passage, there is clearly *not the slightest
trace to be found.*' And Bishop Taylor, another eminent Pedobaptist, says, in substance, that 'to rely upon
this text as proof of infant baptism, proves nothing so
much as the want of a better argument.'"

"I think, Mr. Johnson," said Professor Jones, "that
we had better, for the present at least, let this passage
stand aside. It certainly gives no *direct* testimony in
our favor, and even the inferential is somewhat doubtful. We can afford to let it go, as you know we have
many others, about the meaning of which there can be
no question. Let us take this, for instance, Acts xi.
38, 39: 'Repent and be baptized, every one of you, in
the name of Jesus Christ, for the remission of sins.
And ye shall receive the gift of the Holy Ghost, for the
promise is unto you *and to your children,* and to all that
are afar off, even as many as the Lord our God shall
call.' Here, most undoubtedly, the parents and children

are both included, and that so expressly and plainly, as to leave no room for even the shadow of a doubt."

"That is, indeed," replied Mr. Johnson, "one of the strongest passages, if it be not the very strongest that we have."

"And yet," said Mr. Courtney, "it has not, in fact, the very *slightest value* in favor of your faith or practice, but, on the contrary, furnishes at least a very strong *inference* against them; for if infant baptism was either recognized or practiced, it is incredible that Peter should not have said, 'Be baptized,' not only 'every one of you,' but you and your children. All that is said of baptism, is only to those who are commanded to repent. Those who are commanded to be baptized, are *first* commanded to *repent;* and none are to be baptized but those who *have repented*—not the penitents *and their children."*

"True, Mr. Courtney; but you forget the last part of the text: 'the promise is to you and your children.'"

"The promise of what? Mr. Johnson. What promise is Peter speaking of? Evidently that in the Prophet Joel: 'It shall come to pass in the last days I will pour out my Spirit,' etc. On the faith of this promise, Peter says: 'Repent and be baptized, every one of you, and you shall receive the Holy Ghost. For this promise (that is, of the Holy Ghost,) is unto you and to your children, and to all that are afar off,' etc. It was no promise of baptism, but the promise of something that should *follow* their repentance and baptism. But even if the promise *did* refer to baptism, the subjects of it were not *infants*, for its application is expressly limited to those who can be *called* into the repentance and faith of the Gospel: 'Even as many as the Lord our God *shall call*,' (and no more). Does God call little unconscious infants? If not then they are not the persons spoken of."

14

"What, then, do you think is the meaning of the word children?"

"Simply their descendants In the next chapter, Peter says to these same people, who were all grown men and women: '*Ye* are the *children* of the prophets.' And nothing is more common in the Scriptures than to speak of the Jewish nation as *children* of Israel. They were not a *nation of babies*, nevertheless.

"But even granting, for the sake of argument, that it was *little* children—infants—that were spoken of, then if *they* were to be *baptized* without repentance and faith in Christ, so also are all the aliens and idolators among the Gentiles, for they are included in the term 'all that are afar off.' And there is the same authority to baptize these as the children. They are equally included in the 'promise:' '*You and your children, and all that are afar off.'* Unless you will admit the promise thus to embrace 'all the world, and the rest of mankind,' you must limit it, as Peter did, by confining it to those 'of you,' and of 'your children,' and of the Gentiles *whom the Lord our God shall call.* If, therefore, this is the strongest, or one of the strongest passages you have, your case is a desperate one indeed. The text contains a command and a promise. It commands men *first* to *repent*, and then to be baptized—just as Jesus commands them *first* to *believe*, and then to be baptized? And, of course, unless unconscious infants can repent and believe, they cannot be baptized. Then it promises the 'gift of the Holy Ghost' to those who *have* thus *repented* and *been baptized :* for Peter makes this the condition of their receiving it: 'Repent and be baptized, and ye shall receive the gift.' And as *they* might receive the *gift* of the Spirit on these terms, viz.: baptism and repentance, so might their *descendants*, and so might even the idolatrous *Gentiles,* who were now afar off—even as many of them as the Lord our God should call."

"That is indeed entirely satisfactory," said Professor Jones, "and I am only surprised that I did not see it in that light before. But the truth is. because I saw *baptized* in one part of the passage, and children in another part, I took it for granted (since it was one of the proof-texts quoted in our confession of faith) that it was the *children* who were to be baptized. I see now that it was only those who repented; and I am ready candidly to acknowledge that there is no authority for infant baptism in *this* text, but there are surely many others."

"Oh, yes," said Mr. Courtney, "you know 'the New Testament *abounds* with proof of infant baptism.' And if you will turn to 1st Cor. vii. 14, you will find one which has been relied upon even more confidently than the one we have just disposed of: 'For the unbelieving husband is sanctified by the wife, and the unbelieving wife is sanctified by the husband; else were your children unclean, but now are they holy.'"

"Well, I should like to see how you will set aside a passage so plain and appropriate as that is," said Mr. Johnson.

"I simply say," rejoined Mr. Courtney, "that there is not *one word* in it about baptism, either of infants or adults. It has not only no mention of baptism, but not even the most distant *allusion* to it, direct or indirect."

"Why, sir, does it not say that the children of but one believing parent are *holy?* and if they are *holy*, are they not fit subjects for baptism?"

"You know," replied Mr. Courtney, "that the words *holy* and *sanctified*, among the Jews, were used in a physical or ceremonial sense, as well as in a moral sense. If the Apostle used them here in a *moral* sense, he stated what *was not true*, for in this sense the infidel husband or the infidel wife *was not made holy* by the other's faith. The faith of the husband did not make a *saint* of his wife, nor did the faith of the wife make a *saint* of her idolatrous husband. They might have been, and doubtless often were more sinful afterward than before the other party was converted. Nor does the faith of *both parents combined* render *their children holy*, in this sense of the word: for you know and every other man knows, that the children of believers *grow up in sin, and need to be converted*, just as much as the children of unbelievers; and without such conversion, will just as surely be lost as the children of the vilest. Did David's faith take the incestuous Ammon and murderous Absalom to heaven? You and your wives are both believers: are *your* children, in this sense, holier than other children? Do you not daily pray for God's converting grace to *make* them holy? It is evident, therefore, that the words sanctified and holy (which are equivalent terms) must here be understood in their other sense. The expression is indeed one of those *Hebraisms* in which Paul abounds. Its real meaning is very clearly stated by one of your best Presbyterian Commentators, Dr. McKnight—for more than twenty years the Moderator of the Presbyterian General Assembly of Scotland:

"'I think, therefore,' says he, 'with Elsner, that the words in this verse have neither a federal nor a moral meaning, but are used in the idiom of the Hebrews, who by *sanctified* understood what was fitted for a particular use, and by *unclean* what was unfit for use, and therefore was to be cast away. In that sense the Apostle, speaking of *meat*, says, 1 Tim. iv. 5, *It is sanctified* (that is, fitted for your use) *by the Word of God and prayer.* Ver. iv. *Every creature of God* (fit for food) is *good, and nothing* fit for food is *to be cast away* as unclean. The terms of the verses, thus understood, have a *rational* meaning, namely, that when infidels are married to Christians, if they have a strong affection for their Christian spouses, they are thereby *sanctified* to them—they are fitted to continue married to them ; because their affection to the Christian party will insure to that party the faithful performance of every duty ; and that if the marriages of Christians and infidels were dissolved, they would cast away their children *as unclean*—that is, by losing their affection for them, they would expose them, after the barbarous custom of the Greeks, or at least neglect their education ; but by continuing their marriages, their children are *holy* ; they are preserved as sacred pledges of their mutual love and educated with care.'

"Hence he thus paraphrases the text :—' For the infidel husband is sanctified—is fitted to remain married .to the believing wife by his affection for her ; and the infidel wife is sanctified to the believing husband by her affection for him ; otherwise certainly your children would be by you neglected as unclean, whereas indeed they are clean ; they are the objects of your affection and care.' "

" I do not know," said Mr. Johnson, "that we are bound to admit Dr. McKnight's exposition of this passage merely because he was a Presbyterian."

" Certainly not ; but one would naturally suppose that if there were any infant baptism in the passage, a learned and eminent Presbyterian Doctor of Divinity would be the man to find it. Perhaps *you* can show it to be there, though *he* could not."

" I do not say, Mr. Courtney, that infant baptism is *commanded* in this passage, but only that it is *recognized*. These children were not *morally* holy—that is self-evident. Yet they are called ('*agia*') holy, by the same term which is sometimes used to designate the *saints;* that is, the members of the church. Therefore, they must have been church members; and as none were church members but those who had been *baptized*, it follows that they must have been baptized. That is what I call a demonstration."

"And if it be so," replied Mr. Courtney, "then the infidel wife and the infidel husband had also been baptized, and were members of the church, for they are called (*hagiarai*) 'sanctified,' the same term which in this epistle (1st chapter and 2d verse) is applied to the members of the church: 'To them that are *sanctified* in Jesus Christ, called to be *saints*,' etc. And again, in the 6th chapter and 11th verse, 'But ye are washed, ye are *sanctified;* but ye are justified in Christ,' etc. These *sanctified* ones called to be saints, and these *sanctified* ones who were washed and justified in Christ, were, most undoubtedly, members of the Corinthian Church. It was as such that Paul addressed them; and as the same term (*sanctified*) is applied to the infidel and idolatrous husband and wife who had a believing companion, it follows, of course, that, infidel and idolatrous as they were, they *must* have been members of the church; and as none are church members but those who have been baptized, they must certainly have been baptized. That is what *I call*, not a demonstration, but a palpable absurdity; yet it stands *precisely* upon the same ground with your demonstration."

"We must give it up, Mr. Johnson," said the Professor, "at least so far as this text is concerned, for if it proves any thing, it proves *too much*. It will be better for us to give up the children than to take the unbelieving and idolatrous adults. If we ground our practice of baptizing infants on *this passage*, we must baptize the unbelieving *wife* on the faith of her husband, and the unbelieving husband on the faith of his wife, as well as their children on the faith of either. This we have never done, and would not dare to do, so we must look for some other passage to sustain our views."

"Not quite yet," said Mr. Courtney, smiling; "I have wrested this weapon out of your hands, and I will now turn it against you.

"I will prove, *by this very passage*, that there was no such thing as infant baptism known in the Corinthian Church, or in the mind of Paul, when he was writing to them; but that, on the contrary, the Corinthian, and, of course, all the other churches of that day, were *Baptist Churches*, in which neither the *children*, nor the unbelieving companions of believers, were baptized, or in any sense regarded as church members. If the unbelieving husband or wife had been baptized and made a member of the church, the question to which the Apostle is evidently replying could never have been asked. The Jews, as we learn from Ezra x. 3, were not permitted to continue in the marriage relation with their Gentile wives. Now the question had come up in the Corinthian Church whether a *Christian* should not, under a similar regulation, separate from an unbelieving and idolatrous companion. But if such unbelieving consorts were by *the other's faith entitled to church membership*, and had, consequently, been baptized, such a thing as separation on this ground would never have been thought of. It is evident, therefore, that the infidel husband or the infidel wife were not baptized or made church members. There is in the Scriptures not the slightest allusion to any such church *members* made by the faith of *others*, and not by their own. These persons were, therefore, in every sense, outsiders. They had no more connection with the church than any other heathens had. But the Apostle says to their Christian companions, You have no more reason to discard them on this account than church members have to discard *their children*, for they are also unbelievers, and without the pale of the church. The unbelieving husband and the unbelieving wife, and *your* children, not *their* children, stand in the same category. They are *all* without the church—all unbaptized—and thus far, all equally unfit associates. But as your children, though not in the church, are *holy to you*—that is, fit to associate with, so is the unbelieving husband or the unbelieving wife, although they are also out of the church.

"That this is the sense in which the Apostle uses the terms sanctified, and holy, and unclean, is evident from the fact, that this is the *only* sense in which what he says of the parties can be *true*, and this sense corresponds perfectly with the common Scripture usage of the words. Those things and persons among the Jews were called *unclean* which a holy person might not lawfully touch, use, or associate with. It seems, from Gal. ii. 12, that they considered it very criminal to associate or eat with Gentiles. Peter, it seems, had the opinion that only certain *food* was fit to eat, and that all other was unclean. And he said: 'Lord, nothing common or *unclean* hath at any time entered into my mouth.' And Paul, 2 Cor. vi. 17, says, quoting from Isaiah: 'Come out from among them, and be ye separate, and touch not the unclean thing,' or, more properly, 'touch no unclean person,' 'and I will receive you,' etc. Things unfit for holy persons to use were, therefore, to them said to be *unclean*. Food which such persons might not eat, was called unclean food. And persons which they might not associate with, were called unclean persons. In this sense, therefore, neither the unbelieving children, nor the unbelieving husband, nor the unbelieving wife, were to be regarded as unclean. They were all equally sanctified—fit for the companionship and affection of their believing parents and consorts."

"That is all plain enough, Mr. Courtney; but I do not see what it has to do with infant baptism."

"Simply this. The infidel consorts of believers were not church members—they had not been baptized. When Paul was asked by the church, if the believing husbands and wives must separate from such, he says no; it is as lawful for them to live together as it is for *you* to live with *your children*. But *your children* are *holy* [fit associates] to you, and so their companions are *sanctified* [fit associates] to *them*. Now there was no force or propriety in the comparison, unless the children were in circumstances similar to the unbelieving consorts—that is, they must *all* have been alike out of the church, and *all unbaptized*; and if the children of believing parents were unbaptized, it was a Baptist Church; and if the church at Corinth was a Baptist Church, then all the churches planted by the apostles were Baptist Churches."

"I do not feel inclined to grant all that," said Mr. Johnson, "but we have wasted too much time on this text already; let us proceed. But I see it is of no use to argue with you, for you are disposed to construe every passage so differently from what we have been accustomed to consider their true meaning, that the most conclusive texts have no weight with you whatever."

"But pardon me, Mr. Johnson; do I not construe them according to the natural and necessary meaning of the language? I appeal to Professor Jones to say if I have shown any disposition to present any other than the straightforward and obvious sense of the passages which we have examined."

"I begin to think," rejoined the pastor, "that my

brother Jones is himself more than half a Baptist, which
accounts for his being so easily convinced."

"Not at all, Mr. Johnson. I was very desirous to
find infant baptism in the Scriptures; I confidently
believed it was there; I expected we could have pointed
to it without the slightest difficulty; but I acknowledge
that I can't see the slightest trace of it in these proof
texts which our church has been so accustomed to rely
upon. But though we have no *command* to practice it,
we have authority which is quite equivalent, and that is
the *practice* of the Apostles."

"Certainly," said Mr. Johnson. "I did not expect
to find any such absolute command as could not be
explained away. It is chiefly on the examples that we
rely."

"I hope, Mr. Johnson, you will do me the justice to
acknowledge that I have not explained away any command to baptize infants. I am sure I would not willingly even attempt to explain away any command of
Jesus Christ, or his Apostles, on this or any other subject. I asked you to show me a command to *baptize
infants*, and you pointed to the commission as a command to baptize those who are the *believing* disciples of
Jesus. You pointed, then, to an incidental command,
to let the children come to Christ, that he might lay his
hands on them and bless them. But as the children
were not in the other command, so the baptism was not
in this. It was not for baptism, but for quite another
purpose that he bade them to come. You pointed then
to a command and promise given through Peter, but the
command was *Repent*, and *then* be baptized, which, of
course, excluded infants. And the promise was not a
promise of *baptism*, but of the gift of the Holy Ghost to
those whom *God should call* to repentance, faith, and
baptism, which excluded infants from the promise as

well as the command. You then pointed to the place
which we have last examined, which certainly contains
not even the shadow of a command to baptize infants;
and so far as it teaches any thing upon the subject,
teaches that they were no more to be baptized on the
faith of their parents than unbelieving husbands are
upon the faith of their wives. You have not found the
commandment, because it is not there; I do not like to
discourage you, but I assure you, you cannot find the
example for the very same reason. This has been conceded, over and over again, by the most learned and
most zealous advocates of infant baptism. They rest it
on different grounds.

"Dr. Wall, the most eminent of them all, distinctly
declares: 'Among all the persons that are recorded as
baptized by the Apostles, there is no express mention
of any infants.'

"Bishop Burnet says: 'There is no express precept
or rule given in the New Testament for the baptism of
infants.'

"Richard Baxter says: 'I conclude that all the examples of baptism in the Scripture do mention only the
administration of it to the professors of saving faith;
and the precepts give no other direction.'

"Martin Luther, the great reformer, says: 'It cannot
be proved that infant baptism was instituted by Christ,
or by the first Christians after the Apostles.'

"Erasmus, another of the Reformers, says in his Notes
on Rom. vi. 14: 'The Apostle does not seem to treat
of *infants*. It was not the custom for infants to be baptized.'

"Olshausen, the famous Pedobaptist commentator,
says: 'There is altogether wanting any conclusive
proof passage for the baptism of children in the age of

the Apostles, nor can the necessity of it be deduced from the nature of baptism.'

"Limbroch, another distinguished Pedobaptist professor of theology, and the author of a 'System of Divinity,' says: 'There is no express command for it in the Scriptures. Nay, all those passages wherein baptism is commanded, do immediately relate to *adult* persons, since they are ordered to be instructed, and faith is a prerequisite as a necessary qualification.' And again: 'The necessity of infant baptism was never asserted by any council before that of Carthage, held A. D. 418. We own that there is no precept, nor undoubted instance in Scripture of infant baptism.'

"Dr. Hanna, editor of the North British Review, says: 'The baptismal service [of the English church] is founded upon Scripture, but its application to unconscious infants is destitute of any express Scriptural warrant. Scripture knows nothing of the baptism of infants.'

"Dr. Knapp says: 'There is no decisive example of infant baptism in the Scriptures '

"Neander, the great Pedobaptist historian, says: 'It is *certain* that Christ did not ordain infant baptism.'

"Even your Presbyterian Doctor Miller, of Princeton Theological Seminary, says: 'The fact is, that during the whole threescore years after the ascension of Christ, which is embraced in the New Testament history, we have no hint of the baptism of infants born of Christian parents.'

"So says your able defender, Professor Moses Stuart: 'Commands, or plain and certain examples relative to it in the New Testament, I do not find.'

"So says also your other celebrated writer on this subject, Dr. Leonard Woods: 'The New Testament is silent respecting the subject of infant baptism.' 'It is evident that infant baptism is not introduced as a subject of particular discussion. It is neither explicitly enjoined or prohibited, and neither is the practice of baptizing children, nor the absence of it, expressly mentioned.'"

"I declare, Mr. Courtney," said the Professor, "this is very discouraging. If such men as these, all of whom are on our side of this controversy, and all members of churches that are in the habit of baptizing infants—most, if not all of whom, received their own baptism in infancy—many of whom were eminent ministers, and in the habit themselves of baptizing infants—and some of the most eminent of whom were *authors*, who, like Stuart, and Miller, and Wood, wrote expressly upon this subject—if such men cannot find the 'command,' or the 'example,' it seems hardly worth while for *us* to look for it."

"I do not know," said Mr. Johnson, "what they considered a plain command, or an undoubted example, but I conceive that these statements which Mr. Courtney has quoted so glibly, were (to say the least) very '*unguarded expressions*,' which were by no means justified from the facts in the case. I grant that there is no express *command*, but there are many examples, which, if not plain enough to satisfy *Baptists*, are such as will satisfy any candid inquirer after the truth."

"I only ask you, gentlemen," said Mr. Courtney, "to show me *one* which you will YOURSELVES *say is an undoubted case*, after we have examined the testimony. I only ask you to show me *one* which your own theological writers and teachers will agree upon as an undoubted case—or one which they will all agree upon as even a *probable* case. I do not wish to dissuade you from the attempt, but you could not find *one single solitary instance* if your very lives depended on the effort."

" Certainly, Mr. Courtney," said the pastor, " you are speaking without due reflection, for you must know perfectly well that such examples are as numerous as the household baptisms recorded in the Acts or referred to in the Epistles."

"Not at all," said Mr. Courtney. "I understand what I am saying, and I desire to be distinctly understood to mean that as there is not (as we have already seen) any *command*, so neither is there a solitary *example*, either among the ' *households*' *or any where else*, in which baptism was administered either to an infant or to any one else who did not first profess faith or repentance. From the first of Matthew to the end of Revelations, you may examine every passage in which baptism is mentioned or alluded to, and you not only will find no infant plainly spoken of as baptized, but you will not find so much as an allusion to any such a class as the ' Baptized children of the church.' "

"Surely," replied Professor Jones, "you must be mistaken in this. I am sure I have always thought that there was no more doubt about the Scriptures teaching infant baptism, than about their teaching the divinity of Jesus Christ. I am certain it must be somewhere in the Scriptures."

" Many people are certain that things are in the Scriptures that neither they nor any body else can find there," said Mr. Courtney. " Your Doctors of Divinity have told you it was there, and you took it for granted that they told you the truth. But if it is there, *you* can find it and *show* it to me. And ever afterward you will know how to *give a reason* for the faith that is in you on this subject."

" But Mr. Courtney, we have not time to read over the whole Bible to-night, to see if there is not some case mentioned; and if we do not, we may overlook some case."

"That is not necessary. Your Doctors of Divinity have done it for you; and if they have found any case that had even the remotest squinting toward infant baptism, they have paraded it before the world. Your pastor here is doubtless perfectly familiar with every case that has the slightest bearing upon the subject, and which presents even the shadow of a proof in favor of the practice of your churches. But if you doubt his information, or if he is unwilling to trust to his memory in the case, suppose you take a Concordance, and refer to *every place* where baptism is mentioned. Here is Butterworth's Concordance. It will doubtless mention every place where the words occur; and we can thus test the matter at once."

"Certainly," said the pastor. "I greatly prefer that to a reliance upon my own memory; for though I can without any hesitation refer you to several examples, as in the cases of Lydia, and the jailer, and Stephanus, and Cornelius; yet as I might forget some place, I would leave our defence less perfect than I desire."

"We will then work by the Concordance, and will come to each of those cases in their proper order," said the Professor.

"Very good," said the schoolmaster. "Now what is the first place?"

"It is," said the pastor, 'Matthew iii. 7—'John saw many of the Pharisees and Sadducees come to his baptism.' We must admit there were no infants there, but then you know we do not consider John's baptism to be Christian baptism, which was not practiced till after the death of Christ; and so it does not matter who John baptized, or what class of persons were baptized before the ascension of the Saviour as it was only then that *Christian* baptism, properly so-called, began to be administered. I am willing to grant, therefore, that there was no mention made of the baptism of any infant until after that time."

"That will," said Mr. Courtney, "save us considerable trouble—but it will deprive me of the advantage of at least one very convincing argument against any inference for infant baptism. I think I could easily prove to you that not only John's baptism, but Christ's baptism (I mean that which is *called his*, though John says Jesus himself baptized not, but his disciples), was just the same baptism which *He* commanded after his death —and that since John required repentance and works meet for repentance as preliminary to *his* baptism, and Christ is expressly said to have first *made disciples* of those whom *he baptized* (John iv. 1), unconscious infants were of necessity excluded, and would be, as a matter of course, *considered as excluded* until an express command was given to include them. But we will pass it by, and the first case of baptism that comes up after the commission had, in your view, fully established the Christian ordinance, was that on the day of Pentecost, Acts 2d chapter. Suppose, Mr. Johnson. you just turn to the chapter, and see if you can find any thing about infants there."

"Oh, no. We do not pretend," said the pastor, "that those three thousand were any of them infants, or even children. There were evidently none among them who could not understand the preaching of Peter and the rest, for they *gladly* received his word (41st verse) before they were baptized, and continued steadfastly in the Apostles' doctrine and fellowship afterward. They were all adults, and we must admit also that they were all professed believers."

"Very well," said Mr. Courtney; "then we will go on

to the next case; but I cannot help remarking by the way that it is *very extraordinary* if they *ever* baptized infants in those days—if *they* were considered as included in the commission. I say it is *very remarkable* that all these three thousand should have been old bachelors or old maids, or, to say the least, all unmarried, or if married, all childless. Yet such must have been the case, for not a word is said about the *duty* of bringing their children for baptism—nor among them all was there a single one who brought his little ones that they might be baptized at the same time with his parent. I have been present several times when a number of persons joined *your* society, and there were always among them more or less who brought their children with them. I do not suppose that you ever recorded in your church the baptism of twenty adults, but that they brought some children with them, yet you pretend that the Apostles practiced infant baptism as you do, and still admit that here are three thousand adults and not a single child—but go on to your next case."

"It is," said the pastor, who glanced at the Concordance, Acts viii. 12 : "'But when they (the people of Samaria) believed Philip preaching the things concerning the kingdom of God, and the name of Jesus Christ, they were baptized.'"

"It seems, then," said Mr. C., "that these were adults too; for they were able to hear preaching, and exercise faith. They believed the preaching before they were baptized, and none were baptized who did not first believe. But you did not read all the verse : does it not go on to say, that they were baptized, both the men, the women, *and their children ?*"

"No," said Mr. Johnson, with a very perceptible

15

degree of petulance in his tone, "it only says, 'both men and women.'"

"So then, here is another case, where a large company of men and women were baptized, not one of whom were heads of families. It is *very remarkable*, for if the Apostles taught and practiced infant baptism, Philip had doubtless' instructed them that '*it was their duty and their privilege*' to bring their infant children into the kingdom with themselves. This is what *you* teach, and this is what *your converts* do. If Philip taught as you do, his converts were a 'peculiar people' truly. But let us pass on to the next case, which was that of Simon the magician, in the next verse; but as you won't imagine any infant baptism there, we may pass to the next."

"That was," said the pastor, "the case of the Ethiopian Eunuch (Acts viii. 13); and the next that of Saul (Acts ix. 18); and the next that of Cornelius and his friends, which I have sometimes considered as a case of household baptism, but on examination I do not see that there is any mention of infants (Acts x. 47)."

"Please read it, Mr. Johnson," said Professor Jones. "I have, I am sure, always looked upon this as one of the proof passages."

"I had such an impression myself," said the pastor, "but I see it cannot be relied upon. 'Can any man forbid water that these should not be baptized *who have received the Holy Ghost as well as we*? And he commanded them to be baptized.' Now it is true that Cornelius had a *family*, and he had called together his kinsmen and near friends; and it seems *most likely* that there would have been among them some children, but still it does not seem absolutely certain. It is, I should say, a *probable* case, but I do not present it as a *certain* one."

"How *can* you, Mr. Johnson, I was ready to say how *dare* you, as a minister of the Gospel of truth, even pretend that there is any *doubt* about the case at all? Could little infants in their mothers' arms 'receive the Holy Ghost,' and 'speak with tongues,' and 'magnify God,' as these are said to have done in the 44th and 46th verses? The *persons*, and the *only* persons, who were commanded to be baptized, were those who spake with tongues and magnified God. And it was on this evidence, and only on this evidence, that 'God had granted repentance unto the Gentiles,' that they were admitted to baptism at all. He who could see a probable infant baptism in this, might see it just as well, it seems to me, in the baptism of the three thousand who received the word with gladness, on the day of Pentecost; or the five thousand who received it a few days after; or in the case of the Samaritans, who believed in the Gospel preached by Philip. If *they* heard, repented, and believed, *these* did all that and more, for they received the miraculous influences of the Holy Ghost *before* their baptism; whereas the others received them *after* it, when they received them at all. These did all that those did, and moreover spake with tongues, and 'magnified God,' and yet *you talk about their being unconscious infants.*"

"Oh, well," said the pastor, "you have no need to become so eloquently indignant. I said I was willing to pass by this case. I will admit that it is not even a *probable* instance, if that will satisfy you. We shall find certain ones enough, so we can afford to be liberal in this. You will not be able, I trust, to dispose so easily of the next, which is the baptism of Lydia, Acts xvi. 15—'And of *her household*;' which, as a matter of course, would have some children in it."

"I do not see how Lydia's household should necessarily have children in it. I am acquainted with several households in this town that have no infants in them. You have none in yours. You have children, but none too young to repent and believe, make credible profession of their faith, and lead a Christian life; and if you should all be convinced, in the revival which I believe God is now beginning to send upon our little Baptist church, that you have never been baptized—and should all give us satisfactory evidence of true piety—we would gladly do for you just what Paul did for Lydia. We would baptize *you and your household;* but you would not insist that we had baptized any unconscious babe."

"But, Mr. Courtney, you must admit the principle that the 'household was baptized on the faith of its head.' Lydia *believed,* and she *and her household* were baptized. Now, whether they were large or small, they must have been baptized on their mother's faith."

"No, Mr. Johnson; it is that principle which I especially condemn and deny. What I say is this—No one under the Gospel is to be baptized, or to be regarded as in *any sense* a member of Christ's church, or to enjoy any of the privileges of that church, *who has not first repented and believed for himself,* and in his own proper person: and if you will *show* me *any case* where any one, either old or young, male or female, bond or free, adult or infant, was by the Apostles baptized, who had not first given evidence of his repentance, faith, and conversion, then I admit you have gained your point. I grant that Simon Magus was baptized while yet unconverted, but not before he *professed to be,* and gave such evidence as was satisfactory at the time. For Luke says Simon also *believed* and was baptized. Now Lydia was baptized and her household was baptized; but there is no evidence that her household were children. There is no proof even that she was married, or ever had been. She may or may not have had a husband:

she may or may not have had children; she may have
been a widow, or she may have been an old maid. The
record says not a word on these points. It only says
that her name was Lydia—that she came from a distant
city, called Thyatira—that she was engaged in the business of selling purple, which we know, from other
sources, was a very respectable and profitable employment. We learn, also, that she was keeping house, and
living in such a comfortable way that she could afford to
give the Apostle and his companions a home at her
house during their stay. It appears also that she had a
family (*oikos*), but whether they were children or servants, or both, is not declared; but *one* thing is certain,
whether they were her offspring or servants, they were
grown men, for in the end of this same chapter (verse
40) we read that as soon as Paul and Silas were libera-
ted they *returned to the house of Lydia and saw the
brethren and comforted them.* They were therefore
men, who could be comforted, and not little children.
They were also *believers*, for otherwise they would not
be called brethren.

"Hence the celebrated commentator, Dr. Adam Clarke,
very properly remarks: '*She attended unto the things.*'
'She believed them and received them as the doctrines
of God, and in this faith she was joined by her whole
family, and in it they were all baptized.' And again—
'The first members of the church of Christ, at this place,
were Lydia and her family, and the next in all probability were the jailer and his family.'

"So far, therefore, from being certain or even probable that the household of Lydia were infants, it is placed
past all doubt by the Scripture itself, that they were *men
and brethren*, who believed and were baptized; for though
their *faith* is not specially mentioned, yet it is necessarily
implied by the calling of them brethren."

"But is it certain, Mr. Courtney, that these *brethren* were the same who composed Lydia's family? Might they not have come in there merely to meet the Apostle?"

"No, Mr. Johnson; Lydia and her family were the *only* converts until the Apostle was arrested and thrown into prison. While there, the jailer and his family were converted, and these two families were all the followers of Christ—*all the brethren* that were in the place. But those at the jailer's house Paul and Silas had just left, when they came to Lydia's house, and saw and comforted the brethren there."

"I think, Mr. Johnson," said Professor Jones, "that we may as well let this case go. We can afford to do it, as we have so many others. And it evidently, so far from aiding us, testifies directly against us. The same difficulties cannot exist in that of the jailer and his family, recorded in the same chapter. I have always heard that referred to as a most undoubted example."

"Yes," said the pastor. "The jailer was a man in the prime of life, as is evident from the impulsive character of his behavior. He drew his sword, called for a light, and he *sprang* in, which indicates that he was a man of activity and energy. Now such a man would be almost certain, if he had a family at all, to have among them some little children. I consider, therefore, that this is an unquestionable case. The evidence amounts almost to an absolute demonstration."

"It is a great pity," said Mr. Courtney, "to spoil such a beautiful and perfect demonstration; and if we had time, I would spare it for a few minutes, that we might at our leisure admire its beauty and its ingenuity. But as we probably have several other places to examine, we cannot afford to trifle over this. You read, in verse 33, that 'he was baptized, he *and all his*, straightway.' Now you say that '*all his*' must include one or more infants. I only reply, that if so, they were infants who could *hear* the preaching of the gospel, and could *believe* it and *rejoice* in God. For, verse 32, Paul *preached* to him and *all his*. And, in verse 34, he rejoiced, believing in God, *with all his house*. Now, there is not in the record the slightest intimation that there was a child on the premises. There was a *family*, but whether of adults or children, servants or relations, is not said; but it *is* said, that they all *heard* the Word, all *believed*, and all *rejoiced*, just as certainly as they were all *baptized*. There is the same testimony of the hearing, believing, and rejoicing as of the baptism. The Baptists will baptize all the children in town, if they will come to them believing and rejoicing in God—not, however, on their parents' faith, but on their own. Your next case is in the 18th chapter, is it not?"

"Yes," said the pastor (glancing at the Concordance which he still held in his hand), "and the 8th verse. 'And Crispus, the chief ruler of the synagogue, believed on the Lord, with all his house. And many of the Corinthians hearing, believed, and were baptized.'"

"Does it not say that their children were baptized with them on the faith of their parents?"

"I read the whole text," replied the pastor, gruffly.

"Then you must consider it a *very* remarkable text," said Mr. Courtney, "for it declares that among these *many* Corinthians, there was not a man or woman who had an unconverted child; for if there had been one, it would, if Paul had taught as *you* do, have been brought up for baptism. These early Christians were strange people. There were three thousand of them at one time, five thousand a few days after in Jerusalem, a great multitude in Samaria, and many more here in Corinth—*all childless;* for it is incredible that *if they had children*, and had been instructed that '*it was their duty and their privilege*' to have them baptized, that *some* of them would not have done it. Nay, all of them *must have* done it, or have stood in open *disobedience* to the requirements of the Gospel. We read of their believing, of their rejoicing, of their breaking of bread, of their assembling for worship, of their ministering to the saints—but never a word of their bringing their little children to be baptized. They evidently did not obey this command, if any such command was given them. And there is never an intimation of any reproof of such inexcusable disobedience."

"I must say, Mr. Courtney," rejoined the pastor, "that you are the most unreasonable man I ever tried to argue with. I have given you, at least, two plain and unquestionable instances in which the *families were baptized with the parents*, and yet you say that out of these eight or ten thousand converts, there is not *one* who had his children baptized. To use an expression of your own, I do not see how you can *dare* thus to trifle with the Word of God!"

"I know, Mr. Johnson, that you gave us cases were *families* were baptized, and you can give us more; but you have not shown that these *families contained a single infant child*, and *that is the point on which the whole argument turns*. I reply to you in the language of you own Pedobaptist historian, the celebrated and acute Neander: 'We cannot prove that the Apostles ordained infant baptism, from those places where the baptism of a whole family is mentioned, as in Acts xvi. 33; 1 Cor. i. 16. We can draw no such conclusion, because the inquiry is still to be made *whether they were in these families any children of such an age that they were not capable of any intelligent reception of Chris-*

tianity, for this is the only point on which the case turns.'
Ch. Hist. p. 198.

"I might retort by saying that you are exceedingly
unreasonable in your mode of argumentation. You
say that the Apostles baptized infants. I ask you to
prove it. You reply by saying he baptized *families.*
Now if there *was never a family without infants,* your
argument would be complete. But your own family
has no infants in it. It consists of two grown sons, a
daughter nearly grown, and a servant. My family has
no infants in it: it consists of myself, my wife, and my
nephew, who assists me in my school. The family of
our friend Mrs. Ernest has no infants in it. It consists
of her daughter, Miss Theodosia, of her son Edwin,
and her old servant, Aunt Chloe. All of whom are
old enough to believe and rejoice in God, as the jailor's
family did. Should they all determine to obey the
commandment of Jesus Christ and be baptized according to the Gospel order, you can say of her, as Luke
does of the jailor and of Lydia—She was baptized, and
her household. You see, therefore, that if you would
make your argument worth a straw, you must go one
step further, and prove that there *was an infant* in the
families. It will not do to say that it is *probable* there
was one. It is just as probable that there is one in
yours, or mine, or Mrs. Ernest's, yet you know there is
none. You must, if you build an argument on the
infant as being there, first *prove that it was there.* If
you can't do this, the judgment goes against you of
course. I need not prove that it was not there. The
burden of proof rests on you. If you go into court
and claim property as the heir of a certain woman's
child, you must prove that there was *such a child.* If
you should prove no more than that the woman was
married and kept house, and had been heard to speak

of *her family*, the court would laugh at you. That she was married, kept house, and had a family, you would be told, was not the slightest legal proof *that she had a child*. And this is the point on which your whole claim rests. Peter had a family, though so far as we are informed it consisted only of his wife and his wife's mother. And so Crispus, the chief ruler of the synagogue, had a family: who they were, we do do not know; whether children, grand-children, nephews, or servants. His father and mother, and the father and mother of his wife; his own brothers and sisters, or the brothers and sisters of his wife his clerks or apprentices, if they had lodged in his house and eaten of his table, would have been called—his family, *his house;* but whosoever they were, they ' *all believed on the Lord*,' and so were not unconscious infants."

"Have we not some other case, Mr. Johnson?" inquired the Professor.

"There is only one other," replied the pastor, "and that is that of the family of Stephanus, mentioned by Paul, 1 Cor. i. 16—'I baptized also the household of Stephanus.'"

"And that need not detain us long," said Mr. Courtney, "for your own Presbyterian Doctor of Divinity, McKnight, in his excellent Commentary, says, ' The family of Stephanus seem all to have been *adults* when they were baptized; for they are said, chap. xvi. 15, *to have devoted themselves to the ministry of the saints*.'

"We have now examined *all* your ' examples,' and the infants are not yet discovered. Lydia's family are called ' brethren.' The jailer's family are said ' to believe and rejoice in God.' That of Crispus ' believed in the Lord.' And that of Stephanus ' addicted themselves to the ministry of the saints.' And, Cor. xvi. 16, the church is directed to ' submit itself unto such.' You have not only failed to prove that there were any infants, but I have proved (though by the rules of debate I was under no obligation to do so) that they were all adults, or at least old enough to hear, believe, obey, and rejoice in the Gospel. I leave it now for you to say yourselves, whether there is, in any of these instances, a *single certain example* of the baptism of an unconscious infant?"

Mr. Courtney paused, but neither of the others felt disposed to answer; after waiting a moment, he continued:

"But I am not willing to pass so readily from these passages. You are accustomed, Mr. Johnson, and so are all your ministers, to present these as proof-texts for infant baptism. You will probably go and do it again, though I pray that God may give you a better mind. They stand as proof-texts in your 'Confession of Faith,' and yet, in truth, neither they nor you *have ever believed them to be such*, or else you are more inconsistent in your conduct than sensible men are often found to be."

"Why, sir, what do you mean? Do you intend to insinuate, sir, that we Presbyterian ministers teach as God's truth what we do not believe?"

"I mean to say, Mr. Johnson, that you teach for God's truth what you do not *practice*—and you know a good man's practice *ought* to correspond to his belief. You teach that the *families* of believers are to be baptized on the faith of the *head of the family*. Out of the thousands and thousands of people who are recorded as having believed and been baptized, you find three or four instances in which a whole family believed, and were baptized at the same time, and they are mentioned as a certain man and his family. Now you say if these three or four *families* were baptized, *all* families of believers are entitled to baptism. This is what your argument amounts to, if it has any force at all. Now, in every one of these instances the *whole family*, every member of it, is said to have been baptized."

"Very well," said Mr. Johnson, "so much the better for our cause—so much the more likely that it included *the infants.*"

"It may be so much the better for your *cause*, but it is so much the worse for your *consistency*. You teach that *all* the family were included in these baptisms, but *you do not baptize all the family*. Are not my wife and my nephew members of my family? but you would not on my faith baptize either of them. Is not old Aunt Chloe a member of Mrs. Ernest's family? yet you never have baptized her, or urged on Mrs. Ernest the duty of bringing her *servant* as well as her children. Are not children of ten or twelve, or fifteen or twenty years of age, as much members of the *family* as the baby is? If these passages prove that *one* member of the family may be baptized on the faith of the head, they prove equally that every other member may be; and your only consistent ground is that occupied by Mr. Barnes in his Notes on 1 Cor. i. 16—'Household (*oikon*) the house, the family. The word comprises the whole family, including adults, domestics, slaves, and children.' * * 'It was the custom doubtless for the Apostles to baptize the *entire household, whatever might be the age, including domestics, slaves, and children.* The head of a family gave up the *entire household* to God.· If you and Dr. Barnes *believe* this, you ought to *practice* it. If Paul baptized *all* the children, and all the domestics, and all the slaves, and all the other members of the family, of *whatever age*, you ought to do it too. You are unworthy to have charge of a Christian church, if you do not, at least, *attempt* to do it. You

ought to urge upon your members the 'duty and privilege' of bringing their *slaves*, where they have them—
their men servants and their maidens—their domestics,
male or female, '*of whatever age,*' and all their children,
whether infant or adult, to be baptized upon the faith
of the head of the family.   Nor do I see how you could
well omit the *wife*, for although Dr. Barnes has not included her, she certainly belongs to the *family* as much
as the 'domestics.' If they refuse to perform this duty,
which was thus enjoined, as you believe, by the Apostles, you can not do less than call them to account for
their neglect. If they will still prove obstinate, you
must exclude them as disobedient to one of the 'undoubted' ordinances of the church of Christ.   They are
certainly under as much obligation to bring *all* as to
bring the infants."

"Yes," said the pastor; "but where they have come
to years of discretion, we think it best to leave them to
come themselves, as an act of personal obedience."

"But you have no *right* to leave them, even if you do
think best.   Lydia did not, according to your account
of the matter, leave hers to come when they pleased.
The jailer did not leave his—he brought them all
straightway.   If the head of the family is to have his
household baptized, on the authority of these examples,
he is not at liberty to leave them to come of themselves.
It is his bounden duty to exert all his authority as husband, father, and master, to bring his whole family at
once to the baptismal basin; and it is your bounden
duty, as a minister of Christ, if you believe such things,
to urge the subject upon their attention.   Call upon
them for the immediate performance of their obligations;
and it is the duty of the church to deal with those who
neglect or refuse.   But this you never have done.
There are none of your ministers who do it; and I ven-

ture to say that Mr. Barnes himself has never done it. You never will do—you, none of you, dare to do it. Your own consciences would recoil from the introduction, in this way, of infidels, and blasphemers, and irreligious men and women, into the church of Christ, on the faith of their father or master. As you would be afraid to do it yourselves, you do not believe in your hearts that the Apostles did it. It is altogether inconsistent with every thing we know of their character, and the nature of the churches they established; and it would therefore be fair to infer that these families which were baptized were families of believers, even if they had not been called brethren in the case of Lydia, or said to believe and rejoice in God in the jailer's—to speak with tongues and glorify God in that of Cornelius—to believe in the Lord Jesus in that of Crispus, and to give themselves to the Christian ministry in that of Stephanus."

"I did not expect when we commenced," replied Mr. Johnson, "to be able to convince you of your errors in regard to this subject. I have often observed that the more one reasons with a Baptist, the more firmly he fixes him in his baptistical notions. I have, therefore, had no desire for any such controversy as this. It was only to satisfy my friend and brother, Professor Jones, that I engaged in it at all—and I must now beg leave to decline any further argument upon the subject."

"Pardon me, Mr. Johnson, if in the heat of debate I have made use of any expression that has seemed improper, or in any degree disrespectful to you. I did not intend to do so, and regret most sincerely if my feelings have led me to overstep the bounds of gentlemanly discussion."

"Oh, I do not," resumed the pastor, "decline further

disputation on that ground; though I might, I think, fairly complain of some of your expressions. I merely do not wish to continue a discussion which is not likely to result in any good."

" Permit me to suggest," said Professor Jones, "that if we leave off here we acknowledge ourselves to be completely routed, for it is certain that we have not yet been able to produce a single undoubted precept or example of infant baptism from the Scriptures. But since such men as Woods, and Wall, and Stewart, and Coleman, and Neander, concede this, and yet are the firm advocates of the baptism of infants, *there must be some other ground* on which it can be sustained."

" That is true, sir," replied the pastor. "And I have purposely reserved our strongest argument for the last. But I am sure it will have no influence on Mr. Courtney, nor any other Baptist."

" But, Mr. Johnson, it may have some effect on *me*. And I hope you will do us the favor to present it for my benefit."

"We will not have time to-night," replied the other, " and for the present at least I am tired of the subject. Perhaps you will hear something at church to-morrow that will satisfy your mind " And with this intimation the Rev. gentleman took his leave, and the parties separated.

THE DAY AFTER THE SEVENTH NIGHT

---◦◦---

THEODOSIA IS BAPTIZED

ACCORDING TO THE COMMANDMENT,

AND THE

EXAMPLE OF THE LORD JESUS CHRIST

16

THE DAY AFTER THE SEVENTH NIGHT.

WE left Theodosia in that most distressful condition, in which duty, struggling with inclination, distracts and rends the mind with agonizing efforts to decide one way or the other.

With her this was not a slight or momentary strife. It was the terrible agony of one who struggles for his very life. Dearer to her than life was Mr. Percy's love; it was her first love; it was her only love; it was a pure and holy love; it had been sanctioned by her mother's fond approval; it had been sanctified by their formal espousals; the day had been set for the consummation of their happiness; she had fully given up her whole heart to it; it was the great, controlling, soul-absorbing passion of her being; all the hopes of life were centered here. To tear such love from out the heart, was to rend the heart itself. Yet she felt it must be done; and God gave her strength to do it. All day long, as we said, she had crouched at her mother's side, or followed her like her shadow. She seemed to feel that something terrible impended over her, and that she was safer in her mother's presence. Not one word was spoken by either of them on the one subject which occupied the minds of both. Mrs. Ernest observed that, as the day advanced, her daughter's face became more natural in its expression. The lines of agony began to disappear. The eyes no longer looked so strange and restless; nor did they turn so her, as in the morning, with that beseeching gaze of agony which almost broke her heart. But still, she noticed that her lips often moved, though she uttered no word ; and when she spoke to her about the business of the household, it was some time before she answered, and then slowly, and often in such a way as to show that she had not fully comprehended her meaning. Her mind was evidently far away.

About three o'clock she laid down her worsted, and taking up the Testament which lay upon her work table, turned to the fourteenth chapter of Luke, and read: " If any man come to me and hate not his father and mother, and wife and children, and brethren and sisters, yea, and his own life also, he cannot be my disciple ; and whosoever doth not bear his cross and come after me, cannot be my disciple. For which of you, intend ing to build a tower, sitteth not down first and countett the cost, whether he have sufficient to finish it, les: haply after he hath laid the foundation and is not able to finish it, all that behold it begin to mock him, saying, This man began to build, but was not able to finish. Or what king going to make war against another king, sitteth not down first, and consulteth whether he be able, with ten thousand, to meet him that cometh against him with twenty thousand ? or else, while yet the other is a great way off he sendeth an ambassage, and desireth conditions of peace. So likewise whosoever he be of you that forsaketh not all that he hath, he cannot be my disciple."

" Mother," said she, looking up, and speaking as though her mother had known what she was reading, " you will not make it necessary for me to forsake *you* too ?"

" Why, what do you mean, my daughter ?"

"Jesus says here, that if I do not forsake all for him, I cannot be his disciple."

"Yes, my child, but that has nothing to do with baptism. It means that you must give up all *to be religious.*"

"To be religious, mother, is to *obey Jesus Christ.* 'If ye love me,' he says, 'keep my commandments.' One of the plainest and most positive of those commandments is, '*Believe* and *be baptized.*' Baptism is commanded as much as faith. It makes, indeed, a part of the *sar command.* I trust I have believed; but I *have never been baptized.* Even if the sprinkling which I received in my childhood had been baptism, *it was no act of mine.* I have not obeyed: *I—must—do—it!*" She pronounced these last four words slowly, with a slight pause between each of them, as though each cost her heart a pang to speak it, and yet it must be said.

"Well, my child, if you must, you must."

"But, mother, you will not forbid me? You will not make it needful to disobey you as well as to——" But she could not finish the sentence, and left her mother to guess her meaning.

"No, my dear child, I will not absolutely *forb'd* you You know what I think about these things. Ba;..ism is not essential to salvation, and I had much rather you would remain where you are. I cannot bear to see you sacrifice all your prospects in life for a mere whim, for I don't see but what one baptism is just as good as another. And if you were not in such distress, I would certainly oppose you, but I see it would do no good; and though it will mortify and distress me, I will not forbid you. And if you are determined to do it at all hazards, and it will relieve you of a single pang, I give you my consent."

"Thank you, mother! You do not know what a load

you have taken off my heart." And she buried her face
in her mother's lap, and wept aloud for several minutes
Then she arose, wiped her eyes, and went into her own
room and closed the door.

Shall we invisibly follow her there; see her on her
bended knees pour out her soul to God; hear her cry
for help with those inarticulate groanings which the
Apostle speaks of; see the resolve take form and substance in her heart; see her arise with that same strange
calmness which we observed after she had prayed the
day she came up from witnessing the baptism in the
river; see her open her little writing-desk, and select a
sheet of paper; take her pen and write, "My Dear Mr.
Percy;" then pause, lay down her pen, cover her face
with her hands, pressing upon her eye balls, as if to
shut out some terrible vision, while a strong convulsive
shudder quivers through her frame? It is past; she
uncovers her face; looks up beseechingly to heaven;
composes herself; takes up her pen, and writes as follows:

"I received yours on Friday evening. To say that
its contents gave me *very great pain*, would but feebly
express the truth. I was not only distressed, but most
grievously disappointed; for I had supposed you were
as sincere and earnest in your desire to know and do
your whole duty in regard to this subject as I was myself. Your letter undeceived me. I do not complain
of it. I am thankful for your expressions of interest in
my welfare, and of affection for myself. I will not deny
that I had no higher ambition, so far as this world is
concerned, than to secure your approbation. But I
cannot, *even to please you*, venture to disobey my Saviour
I intend to be baptized to-morrow. I am aware, after
what you have said, that by doing so, I shall not only

'mortify and distress' you, but I shall renounce all
claim to your love. When you return, therefore, I shall
be to you but as one dead. I pray you so to consider
me; it will be better for us both. And if you will spare
me further pain, I do entreat you never to solicit a re-
newal of our engagement. It will not give you as much
pain to read this as it does me to write it; but I have
weighed it well. I say every word deliberately, though
sorrowfully. I will not cease to pray for you   And
will you not sometimes pray for her who *was* your
"THEODOSIA."

This letter she folded, enclosed, sealed, and directed
to Mr. Percy's lodging place, and called the old servant,
Aunt Chloe, and directed her to take and leave it there.

This done, she returned to her mother with something
almost like a smile of joy upon her face. The peace of
God was in her heart; and if she was not *happy*, she
was no longer wretched. With a low, but calm and
almost cheerful voice, she told her mother what she had
done, and asked her to make suitable preparation for
her baptism. At night she sent a line to Uncle Jones,
requesting him, if he could, to be present; and another
to Mr. Courtney, announcing her intention to ask for
baptism. She spent most of the time in her own room,
alone, until the hour of rest, and then slept sweetly till
morning   When she awoke, her first thought was expressed in the language of the Psalmist—" I laid me
down and slept; and I awoke again, for the Lord preserved me." She felt now that she was, in a peculiar
sense, in the care of God. She had given all, and had
obtained all. She had given up self, and obtained Jesus
in all his fulness, and God in all his boundless power
and love. Jesus was *her* Saviour; God was *her* God
Yes, the mighty Maker of the worlds, the omnipotent

Ruler of the Universe, was not only her *God*, but her *Father*. She felt this morning that she might ask what she would. And yet such was the overwhelming conviction in her heart, that her loving Saviour and her kind Father knew so infinitely better than herself what she most needed, and what would be really best, that she could only pray: "'Thy will be done;' I leave it all with thee. Do what thou seest best. Give joy or sorrow; give comfort or affliction; give life or death. Thou knowest best—thou dost all things well. I trust myself—my soul and body; my happiness here and hereafter; all I am, all I have; all I feared, all I hoped for—I give all up to thee. Thou only art my portion now; and I am thine—*all* thine; I *delight* to do thy will, oh, my Beloved. I have now no other love but thee, my Saviour, my Father, my Friend. Thou art my all. Jesus is mine, and I am his. What can I want beside? Blessed Saviour, may I never leave thee—may I never grieve thee any more. Lord, thou knowest all things. Thou knowest that I love thee. Yes, I love thee, and I will keep *all* thy commandments. Show me thy ways. Thou shalt guide me by thy counsels, and afterward receive me into thy glory. Yes, me—even me—poor, lost, rebellious sinner that I am. Thou wilt love me freely. Thou wilt save me through thine own infinite mercy. Mercy, all mercy. Not for works of righteousness which we have done, but of his own mercy, he saves us. Jesus, I thank thee. Oh, make me love thee more."

With such incoherent ejaculations of trust, and praise, and prayer, she rose, and prepared for church.

It was strange how the news had got abroad, yet it had spread like wild-fire through the town that Miss Theodosia Ernest would that morning apply for baptism. At an early hour the school-house was crowded to its utmost capacity, and before the services com menced, even the windows and the doors, and every place was occupied from which one could hope to catch a glimpse at what was going on within, or hear a word of what was said.

The church bells began to ring. Mrs. Ernest had all the morning been distracted between affection for her lovely child, which prompted her to go to the school-house, and pride, which urged her to go and sit in her own pew as though nothing had happened. Curiosity to see and hear what Theodosia would do and say, and what sort of people these Baptists were, joined with affection in pleading for the school-house; and a sort of indefinite dread of what *Mr. Johnson* might say, came to the help of pride. And, it may be, there was something like a mistaken sense of religious duty which spake on that side also. However this may be, the first few strokes of the costly and solemn-sounding bell which had been accustomed to call her to church, seemed suddenly to decide her.

"I want you to understand, Theodosia," said she, "that though I do not forbid, yet I do not altogether approve of what you are about to do, and I cannot sanction any such proceedings by my presence. I don't know what Mr. Johnson would think of me, if I should forsake our own dear church to wander about after these new comers."

This was a new disappointment to the sensitive child. She had greatly relied on her mother's presence to sustain her in the untried scenes through which she was about to pass. She had also hoped that Uncle Jones would call and go with her, but he had not come, and she was *alone.* Yet she was *not alone*, for she looked up as her mother was speaking, and in her heart said again, "Not my will, but thine be done!"—And the Spirit replied, "Fear not, for *I am with thee;* and be not dismayed, for I am thy God!" "When my father and my mother forsake me the Lord will take me up."

I do not say that she felt no natural misgivings, no modest shrinking from going alone into a house filled with strangers, with the consciousness that every eye was on her, and every heart full of curiosity to see how she would look, what she would do, and what she would say; but she thought much less of this than my reader would naturally suppose. The peace of God was in her heart, and it gave to her mind and her manner a quiet yet determined calmness, and a collectedness of thought and perfect self-possession which was surprising even to herself.

She set out therefore *alone ;* for Edwin had not returned from Sabbath-school. Two or three times the mother turned and looked after her as she went, and wished she *could* consistently, and without displeasing Mr. Johnson, have gone with the dear child.

Mr. Courtney had taken it for granted that Uncle Jones or some of the family would accompany her, and when he saw her coming by herself, he hastened to meet her, and conducted her to a seat.

The preacher was not the same who had been there before, but a stranger who had providentially been sent to fill his place. He was a man about forty years of age, rather below than above the ordinary size; his complexion dark, his hair slightly silvered with gray, and the top of his head almost bald. His eyes, and indeed the whole expression of his face, were somewhat peculiar. He seemed to have been long in feeble health, and his face was marked with lines of suffering. Its habitual expression was one of *sad and sorrowful resignation.* The casual observer saw in it no evidence of lofty genius, or of even extraordinary talent—and yet he was an extraordinary man. Though he had but

slight acquaintance with the technicalities of logic, he was
a clear and powerful reasoner. Though he knew little
of the scholastic theories of theology, he was wonderfully familiar with the teachings of Jesus and the
Apostles. Though he professed no acquaintance with
the metaphysical subtleties of mental philosophy, he
knew full well how to convince the understanding and
move upon the hearts of his hearers. He was not
familiar with the ancient classics, yet his style was pure
and strong, and not entirely void of elegance. His
tones and gestures were not formed by any rules of
oratory, yet he was sometimes very eloquent. When
he first rose, there was a slight rusticity in his manner,
and something in his dress which for a single moment
struck Theodosia unpleasantly; but there was, also,
such an air of trusting meekness, that this impression
was removed almost as soon as made. His text was
John xv. 14—" Ye are my friends if ye do whatsoever I
command you." And the main object of his sermon
was to show the vast difference which there is between
the so-called obedience which springs from hope, or
grows up from fear, and the willing and *true* obedience
of the Gospel which is produced by *love*. It was a deep,
heart-searching discourse, and must have left on every
attentive hearer's mind the sad conviction that genuine
Gospel obedience is much more rare than is commonly
imagined. We cannot follow him through all his argument; but we may not omit one portion of it. "The
obedience of *love*," said he, "makes no division of
Christ's commandments into essential and non-essential.
'Ye are my friends if ye do *whatever* I command you,'
whether *you* think it important or not. We know that
we love him when we have respect unto *all* his commandments. The obedience of *hope* says, how much
must I do to be permitted to enter heaven? The

obedience of *fear* asks, what may I omit to do, and yet escape from hell? The obedience of *love* simply inquires, 'Lord, what wilt THOU have me to do?' It does not ask, what *must* I do? but what *can* I do to show my love for Jesus? It does not ask how far I *can venture to disobey*, and keep my hope of heaven? How far off can I follow Jesus, and yet not be disowned of him? Oh, never, never! He who will obey Christ no farther than he may fancy is *essential to salvation*, has never obeyed him at all. Love of self, not love of Christ, is his controlling motive. He is striving not to *please* his Saviour but to secure his *own personal happiness*. Love teaches a different way. Love *delights* to do his will. Love delights to do *all* his will. Love never asks, what is *essential to salvation?* but what did Jesus Christ *command?* Love never asks, how little *may* I do? but how much *can* I do? If *he* commands, that is reason enough. He is no *loving* child who will obey his father only in those things which he must do, or be disowned and disinherited. He is no *loving* child who will do all he dare to grieve a doting parent whom he believes will pardon all, and love him though he grieves him. He who truly loves him will obey his *slightest desires* as well as his most peremptory commands. He who truly loves will *study* to know *all* his will, and in his very heart *delight* to do it—*not* to avoid disinheritance—not to secure his estate—not to enjoy his father's bounty, either present or prospective—but simply because the father *wishes, asks it*, or commands it.

"And yet men call themselves obedient children of God, while they refuse to do what he commands, because he does not add to the command a promise of heaven or a threatening of hell. Oh, it is terrible to think how fearful will be their disappointment! Obeying *only* to secure salvation is itself sufficient proof that they have not obeyed unto salvation. Omitting all but what they think essential to salvation is of itself sufficient proof that they have omitted all that *is essential* to salvation. The faith of the Gospel *works by love*, and love is obe dient to *all* his commandments, so far as it is *able* to know and to do them. When, therefore, Christ Jesus gives a plain command, as that to 'believe and be bap tized,' love will not be content merely to believe. It will do both. It will do *whatever* Christ commands, and he who stops because there is no penalty of hell fire attached to the last, as there is to the first part of the command, is no friend to Jesus. He does not obey from love to *Jesus*, but from love to *self*. And further, the obedience of love takes the command as it is given. It obeys in the *same order* that Christ requires. It not only does the very acts which he commands, but does them in that very *way* that he requires them to be done. If Christ commands *first* to believe and *then*, when thus prepared, to be baptized, the obedience of *love* will never venture to *reverse* Christ's order. It will not seek to be first baptized and then believe. And as the command requires *personal* obedience, it will never seek to substi tute obedience *rendered by another*. Christ commands *you* yourselves in your own right, and for yourselves, to *believe*, and then to be *baptized*. It may be you have not done either. Oh, what a fearful state! Not to have even begun to obey! It may be you have believed, but are fancying that an act done by your parents, and your pastor, without your knowledge or consent, and which *they called* baptism, has released you from the obliga tion to obey yourself. But do not mistake. The religion of Christ is a *personal* religion. The obedience it re quires is an intelligent and personal obedience. You must be baptized for yourself. It must be an act of your own. He that believeth and is baptized, shall be saved. The one is to be your *own* act as much as the other. But this command you have never even *tried* to obey. You have never made the slightest effort. Oh, if you *love* Jesus, will you not at least *try* to obey *all* his commandments?

"One thought more. The obedience of *love* does what HE commands. 'Ye are my friends, if ye do whatever *I* command'—not what others may put in the place of it—not what you may fancy would do as well. You are not to 'teach for doctrines the commandments of men.' Jesus is the sole Lawgiver of his church. *His* commandments, given in person or by those who spake as they were moved by his Holy Spirit, we must obey. If he was immersed in Jordan, then John's baptism was immersion. If John's baptism was immersion, then the baptism administered by Jesus and his disciples was immersion; for John says, Jesus went into a certain place, and there he tarried and baptized. And John also was baptizing in Ænon at the same time. And the Pharisees heard how that Jesus made and baptized more disciples than John. Whatever one did the other did. It was the same *thing*, because it is called in the same connection by the same name. And if Jesus and John immersed, it was immersion that he commanded. Yet *men* have done away with what HE commanded, and substituted sprinkling in its place. To believe and be sprinkled, therefore, is not to *do whatever he commands*, but to teach and practice for his commands the doctrines of men; and of those who do such things he says, 'In vain do they worship me.' Don't call me bigoted for reminding you of this. They are not *my* words, but the words of Jesus Christ. It is *he* who says it; and I believe that he *means* just what he says. Popes and cardinals, bishops and priests, have met in solemn con clave and *changed* the ordinance of Jesus. *They* have substituted the sprinkling of infants for the immersion of believers. This was ordained by Christ, and that by anti-Christ. Yet there are many professed believers, men who would be grieved if I should intimate that they did not *love* the Saviour—who in his name and as *his* ordinance practice these *commandments of men.* The very time and place when and where these changes were thus made by popes and councils is recorded by them· selves. They claim to have *authority* as the vicegerents of Christ on earth to make such changes But the obedience of love will never recognize *their* rule. It obeys *Jesus Christ.* It does whatever HE commands. And whenever professed religious teachers, whether Catholic or Protestant, teach other commandments as a substitute for his—it rejects them with disdain."

After the sermon, he came down from the little platform which had been erected for his convenience, and announced the church as ready to receive applicants for membership—requesting if there were any present who desired to unite with it, that they would come forward while the brethren sang a hymn, and take a seat allotted for that purpose.

The brethren immediately commenced singing the hymn—

> " 'Tis religion that can give
>   Sweetest pleasures while we live;
>   'Tis religion can supply
>   Solid comfort when we die."

Before they had completed the first couplet, Theodosia arose and walked to the appointed seat. And when they had finished, the minister asked her to give to the church some account of her religious experience, that they might be able to judge of the nature of her faith and hope

My reader, who is familiar with her strength of mind, firmness of purpose, clearness of conception, and habitual command of the most appropriate language, can form little conception of the surprise which was excited, as much by her manner as her words. She did not wait to be questioned, and simply answer yes or no, as is customary on such occasions; but modestly arose and turned her face to the audience, and began to relate in a low, but still in a perfectly audible voice, her experience of grace before she made any profession of religion. The house was still as death. Every eye was fixed, every ear attentive to even the slightest modulation of her voice. After describing, in her modest and simple, yet most impressive style, her conviction and conversion, she paused a moment, as if to think of the propriety of saying what was yet upon her mind.

"And why," inquired the minister, who was ignorant of her history, "did you not *then* unite with the people of God?"

"At that time," she continued, "I had rarely been in any other but a Presbyterian house of worship. I regarded Presbyterians as the true church of Christ. Perhaps I would not be going too far if I should say, that I regarded them as the *only* true church, or at least as the only church that was not involved in some most important error of doctrine or practice—it was my mother's church;" and her voice faltered, and eyes filled with tears, as she said it. "It was the church in which God's truth had been made effectual to my conversion I had no shadow of a doubt that it was *the church*, if not the *only* church, and with them I *did unite*. Nor until last Sabbath, did I ever have a doubt that I was right in doing so. Last Sabbath, you will recollect, one of your number was baptized. I had the curiosity to go to the river. As I saw her plunged beneath the water, the thought impressed itself upon my mind, *if that is baptism, I have never been baptized;* for whatever baptism may be, it must always be the same—'One Lord, one faith, one baptism.' I went home and commenced a careful and thorough investigation of the subject. I found that it was immersion, and not sprinkling, that Jesus commanded. It was this which HE himself, as our Example, submitted to in the river of Jordan. It was this which his disciples practiced in his life. It was this which he commanded after his death. It was this, therefore, which he required of me. I have not yet obeyed him, but I *desire* 'to *do whatever he commands me.'* Mine is, I humbly trust, the 'obedience of love.' I have come here to-day, and it is the first time in my life that I have ever been in a Baptist Church. I have come to ask you to *baptize me,* if you think me worthy, according to the commandment of the Lord Jesus."

"Why, this is wonderful!" exclaimed the minister, as she resumed her seat.

"It is the Lord's doing," rejoined Mr. Courtney, "and it is wonderful in our eyes."

"Brethren, what will we do in regard to this application?"

"I move," said one, "that she be baptized, and received into the fellowship of the church."

This was, of course, unanimously determined on.

"When will you be baptized, my sister?" inquired the minister.

"As soon as it may suit your convenience, sir. I am ready now."

"Then after prayer we will at once proceed to the water's side. Let us pray."

They kneeled, and offered up a short and fervent prayer that God would own the ordinance about to be administered in his name—bless her who was to be its

17

recipient—fill her with the comforts of the Gospel—make her a faithful and useful Christian, and at death receive her into his heavenly kingdom.

When Satan finds that he cannot prevent the performance of a religious duty, he often strives to render its performance as distressing as he can. Theodosia had not yet left the house before she began to be assailed by the most terrible temptations. First came the magnificent church, with its soft light, its cushioned pews, its richly carpeted aisles, its tasteful and costly pulpit, its deep-toned organ, and its well-trained choir, which had all her life been the accompaniments of her public devotions. And she could not but contrast their rich, luxurious elegance and comfort, with the rough platform, the naked, dirty floor, the hard benches, and harsh, unskillful voices which had surrounded her to-day. In that splendid church she saw her mother weeping over her daughter's apostacy—her brother showing no interest in her fate—her uncle, whom she loved as a father, and upon whose approbation she had confidently relied, yet he had not come near her, though she had earnestly requested his presence—her pastor, who had taught her in childhood, and prayed over her at her conversion—and there was yet another, whom she now scarcely dared to think of. They were all there—all happy, all united. She only was a poor outcast from all—yes, yes, from *all she loved.* With her own rash hand she had cut the ties which bound her to her kindred and her friends. She had left all the *elegance* so congenial to her delicacy and refinement of taste. She had left all the affection so necessary to the very life of her fond, clinging, loving heart, and here she stood *alone* among these *strangers,* whom, she felt instinctively, with one or two exceptions, had scarcely a sentiment or taste in common with her own. Then, as she was walking to

Theodosia Ernest

PAGE 268.

the river, they passed the *very spot* where she and Mr. Percy stood on the previous Sabbath; and in a single moment, what visions of affluence and ease, of elegant *social* enjoyment, · of domestic bliss—all the happiness of the loved and loving *wife*, extending down through many long and blissful years—came vividly before her mind. She could see nothing else. She forgot for a moment where she was, and why she came there. She walked on unconsciously. Unconsciously she took the offered arm of the minister as he came to conduct her into the river. The touch of the water recalled her to herself. She paused, and suddenly withdrew her arm, clasped her hands together, and looked up to heaven, and so stood for some moments, lost in silent prayer Those who could see her face, observed the expression of distress and terror (which they attributed to a natural timidity at entering the water) suddenly gave place to one of joy and confidence as she again placed her arm within the minister's and walked on. Jesus had heard her prayer—"Oh, Lord, save me! Give me strength to make all this sacrifice for thee! Thou art my Saviour. Thou hast commanded this. I do it in obedience to thee. Oh, leave me not. Help, Lord—I have no other helper—thou art *now my all.*" And as she prayed, the visions of earthly bliss vanished from before her, and she saw Jesus stretched upon the cross in dying agony, and he seemed to say, " I bore *all this* for thee." And she thought of the words of the Apostle—" He died for us." And as she walked along, she remembered what Jesus said—"*Blessed* are ye when men shall hate you, and when they shall separate you from their company, and shall reproach you, and shall cast out your name as evil, for the Son of man's sake. Rejoice ye in that day, and leap for joy—for your reward is great in Heaven." "And every one that hath forsaken houses, or brethren or sisters, or father or mother, or wife or children, or lands, for my name's sake, shall receive an hundred fold, and shall inherit everlasting life."

So fully was her mind occupied with this delightful thought, that she felt no further anxiety, and not the slightest fear. And as she was lifted from the liquid grave, she could not help exclaiming in an audible voice, *"Jesus, I thank thee!"* And then, as they turned toward the shore, such a gleam of heavenly peace and holy joy illumined her beautiful face, that several of the brethren and sisters who stood upon the bank, simultaneously exclaimed, "Blessed be the name of the Lord!"

"Yes," she exclaimed, "blessed be his holy name!" And suddenly she stopped, and with a voice which was naturally sweet and powerful, and had been carefully cultivated, and now was rendered deeper and more expressive by intensity of feeling, she commenced singing:

"Jesus, I my cross have taken,
  All to leave and follow thee ;
  Friendless, poor, despised, forsaken,
  Thou from hence my all shall be.
  And whilst thou shalt smile upon me,
  God of wisdom, love, and might,
  Foes may hate, and friends disown me,
  Show thy face, and all is bright.
  Man may trouble and distress me,
  'Twill but drive me to thy breast ;
  Life with trials hard may press me,
  Heaven will bring me sweeter rest.
  Oh, 'tis not in grief to harm me,
  While thy love is left to me !
  Oh, 'twere not in joy to charm me,
  Were that joy unmixed with thee !"

The effect upon the audience was electrical. Tears streamed from every face; many sobbed and wept aloud Among these was a voice which instantly fixed her

Theodosia Ernest.

PAGE 272.

attention.   She looked up among the assembly, and was
surprised to see that it had increased since she started
into the water to a great multitude.   The congregations
from several other churches had hurried to the river as
soon as they were dismissed from their several places
of meeting.   Foremost among the crowd stood Uncle
Jones, with her mother on one side, and Edwin on the
other.   It was she that she heard; for when she saw her
daughter standing thus alone, and heard her sing,
" Friendless, poor, despised, forsaken," she lifted up
her voice and wept.   Nor did she weep alone.   Strong
men, who were not professors of religion, and who were
thought to care for none of these things, stood and
gazed at that sweet face, all radiant with the love of
Jesus, as though it had been the face of an angel; and
as they looked, the big tears chased each other down
their unconscious cheeks.   The brethren and sisters of
the church wept; old men and mothers in Israel wept
Young men and maidens wept.   But Theodosia heard
none, saw none but her mother.   As she came to the
water's edge, that mother rushed down to meet her, and
clasped her closely to her heart.   The brothers and sisters of the church, who were approaching to give her
the hand of fellowship, stood respectfully aside.

" Oh, mother, do you—can you forgive me ?"

" Don't talk so, my child; I have never blamed you
You have done your duty; you have done right.   You
have obeyed your Saviour—he will bless you.   I wish I
had the courage to follow your example."

" God bless you for those words, my mother!   Oh !
how full of joy my heart is.   He maketh my cup run
over.   Surely goodness and mercy hath followed me all
the days of my life.   Uncle, dear uncle, it is *blessed to
obey*.   Can't you give up *all* for Christ ?

" Mr. Courtney, I thank you for your teachings.   Now

I *know* I am baptized. I have now done just what Jesus commanded. I have left all and followed him; and, blessed be his name, I have already that peace which passeth understanding." And as the brethren and sisters came crowding round to welcome her into the communion of the church on earth, she sang again with that sweet, soul-thrilling voice, to which the intensity of her feelings and utter self-abandonment gave tenfold power:

"Children of the living God,
   Take the stranger to your heart—
Let me dwell in your abode,
   Never more from you to part.

"Can you love me? Will you help me?
   Help me on my way to God—
Can you love me? Will you help me?
   Help me keep his precious word."

While singing, she continued to give her hand to one after another as they came up; and as she finished the strain, a sister standing by sang:

"Yes, come, thou blessed of the Lord,
   No stranger art thou now—
We welcome thee with warm accord,
   Our friend and sister thou.

"The hand of fellowship, the heart
   Of love we offer thee;
Leaving the world, thou dost but part
   With lies and vanity.

"In weal or woe, in joy or care,
   Thy portion shall be ours;
Christians their mutual burdens bear,
   They lend their mutual powers."

The minister pronounced the benediction, and they led her up the bank, and then each went his way rejoicing.

Uncle Jones went home and dined with Mrs. Ernest. When Theodosia had changed her dress, and returned to the parlor, he went up and took her hand as she came in, saying, " My dear Theo., why did you not tell me you were going to be baptized to-day ? I would have gladly gone with you to your meeting."

" Then you did not mean to cast me off?" said she, her eyes filling with tears. " I thought you too had forsaken me. I sent you a line last night, entreating you to be present—but you did not come !"

" I did not get it, nor did I know, till after church, that you intended any such thing to-day. I missed you from your accustomed seat, and inquired of your mother as soon as the meeting was dismissed, and learned that you had gone to be baptized. We hurried to the river, and fortunately were just in time to see you go into the water."

" Oh, uncle ! I am so glad. I thought that you, and mother, and *all* who loved me, so disapproved of what I was about to do, that you would none of you be present. God is already giving me back my friends."

      *   *   *   *

There was preaching again at three o'clock,—and as the school-house could not hold half the people, it was thought best to adjourn to the court house. At night the court house was filled to overflowing, and the preacher requested those who were concerned about their souls' salvation, and desired the prayers of the people of God, to take a seat in front of the congregation. More than a dozen came forward at once, among whom were several who had been a long time professors of religion, and some were members of the Baptist Church. On inquiry, these professors stated that they had been *trying to get to heaven*, and with this object in view had endeavored to lead in some degree religious lives. They had gone to church, partaken of the Supper, sometimes prayed, or tried to pray—but took *no pleasure* in religion ; and from what they heard in the morning, were convinced that whatever obedience they had shown was the obedience of fear, or hope, and not of love. *For if they could have got to heaven without religion, they would have willingly dispensed with it.* They had abstained from open sin, because they knew that those who lived in open sin would *surely be lost.* They had endeavored to perform certain duties, because they considered the attempt (at least) to do such duties to be *essential to salvation.* What they did not think thus essential, had little weight upon their conscience Now they saw that they had been fearfully deceived, and desired to seek for the obedience of love—not the obedience which seeks to merit heaven, and continually looks for its reward—but that which receives all mercies as the *free gift* of God in Christ, and yet longs, and strives, and prays to do *all his commandments*, because it thus and only thus can exercise, exhibit, and gratify the *love of God that fills the heart.*

The minister did not try to give them back their hopes, and make them think that they had no occasion for alarm. He knew full well that Christ will say to *many*, "Depart from me, I never knew you," who here on earth *called* him Lord, Lord, and professed to be his disciples. He greatly feared that there were thousands and thousands who had a respectable standing in the church of Christ, who never asked, with the converted Paul, "Lord, what wilt THOU *have me to do ?*" But only with the yet unconverted jailer, "What must I do *to be saved ?*" This last he knew was most important, but it was not *enough.* It was a needful and common *preparation* for religion, but it was not *religion.* It might lead to *seek* for faith, but it is not the *result* of saving faith, for THAT *works by* LOVE—and through LOVE purifies the heart—and through LOVE brings forth good works in the life.   He was convinced, moreover, that it was infinitely better for many of God's true children to suffer temporary anxiety and alarm, than for one false professor to be confirmed in his delusive hope.

It was determined at the close of this meeting, to appoint one for Monday night, and probably continue to have preaching every night during the week.   Whether they did so, and what was the result, we will learn hereafter.   It is time for us now to return to our study, which at the close of the Seventh Night (the attentive reader will perhaps remember) was about the Scriptural authority, or rather about the utter *want* of all Scriptural authority for infant baptism.

THE EIGHTH NIGHT'S STUDY.

— ∞ —

NEW CHARACTERS AND NEW ARGUMENTS

INFANT BAPTISM IS VIRTUALLY FORBIDDEN

IN THE WORD OF GOD.

THE COVENANT OF CIRCUMCISION

FURNISHES NO GROUND OF DEFENCE

FOR INFANT BAPTISM.

EIGHTH NIGHT'S STUDY.

HE Reverend Mr. Johnson had, early in the preceding week, commenced the preparation of a discourse, which was intended, at once and forever, to put an end to any further defection among his flock. He was a fine declaimer, and was, in the pulpit, accustomed at times to deal in the bitterest denunciation of those who differed from his party in their religious opinions and practices. He had more power of sarcasm than of reason, and hence, found it easier to denounce the opinions of others than to defend his own. His discourse upon the Sabbath through which we have just passed, was that which we saw him preparing at the commencement of our Third Night's Study. It was designed to be a scornful, bitter, and withering denunciation of all those weak minded and credulous, or fanatical, persons who, in this day of light, and surrounded by such advantages as were possessed by *his* congregation, could be by any means induced to wander away from the sacred pale of Presbyterianism. We will not trouble the reader with even a synopsis of this remarkable sermon. It had been prepared with evident labor and care, and it was delivered with great energy and feeling. Under other circumstances, it might have produced the effect that its author intended, which was to deter any other persons from any investigation of the subject of baptism, or indeed any other religious subject, except for the purpose of confirming their faith in the doctrines in which they had been instructed from their childhood. To have

(281)

fully answered his purpose, he should have preached i at least a week sooner. Now, it was universally under-stood to be expressly aimed at certain individuals, whom it was well known had been investigating the subject of baptism, and *might* possibly be considering the pro-priety, or rather the conscientious *necessity*, of a change of church relationship. Many a glance was turned, during its delivery, to the seats occupied by Uncle Jones and Mrs. Ernest. The latter felt that it was an uncalled-for abuse of her absent child, whom she knew had been impelled to the course she had taken by the sternest and most distressing conviction of indispensa-ble duty ; and though she wept as she listened, her tears were tears of mortification and anger. That sermon did more to destroy her faith in Pastor Johnson, and her affection for her church, than all the anti-Presby-terian arguments she had ever heard. So also it did more to fix the attention of the congregation upon the work which was going on among the Baptists, than any thing which *they* could have done or said. Many were willing to go and learn at the Baptist meetings what those terrible and seducing doctrines were which could so excite the ire of their venerable shepherd.

After preaching, he gave notice that a meeting of the Session would be held at three o'clock, at the parsonage, to attend to some business of importance, and gave a special invitation to the *resident ministers* (by whom he meant the President of the college, and those of the professors who were also preachers) to meet with them.

Neither Uncle Jones nor Mrs. Ernest said any thing of this ominous announcement to Theodosia, for both had some indistinct conception that the business to be done related to her case.

Uncle Jones, as one of the ruling elders, and a member of the Session, felt it his duty to be present. He was a little after the time, however; and when he arrived, he found that they had already entered upon the discussion of the business on hand. There was an awkward pause in the conversation when he came in, until the pastor remarked that the matter which they were considering might be an unpleasant one to him; and if so, there would be a quorum present should he think best to retire.

"If your business relates in any way to my niece," said the Professor, "I prefer to witness all you have to say or do."

"We were indeed speaking of her," said the pastor; and though it gives me pain to say it, I have felt it my duty, also, to make some mention of your own case, as of one aiding and abetting error in another, if not yourself entertaining opinions which are inconsistent with your obligations as a ruling elder in the church."

There was a slight flush passed over the manly face of Professor Jones, as the pastor, with evident reluctance, thus gave him to understand that *one* object of the meeting was to inflict the discipline of the church upon his recreant niece, and another to take steps to depose him from the eldership; but he answered very calmly:

"Don't let my coming in interrupt your order of business. You will take up one case at a time. I will be present when you take action on that of Miss Ernest. When you are ready to consider mine, I will retire."

"We understand," said the pastor, "that Miss Ernest, while her name was still standing as a member upon our record, has gone to a Baptist society, solicited immersion, and has actually been immersed by a Baptist preacher. By this act, she has undoubtedly severed all connection with our church, and must of necessity be excluded from *our communion*. The only question is whether we are bound to make the usual citation to appear and answer to the charge."

"There can be no doubt," replied Professor Jones, "that we are bound, according to our rules, to give the ten days' notice of citation, with a copy of the charges preferred against the accused. But, in this case, I will take it upon myself to answer for my niece, that she would prefer the quickest and the simplest mode of excision. She has no wish for farther connection with us. She regards herself as already separated from our communion, and will probably make no answer or defence to any charges not affecting her moral or Christian character, which you may think fit to bring against her."

After some consultation, it was decided that it would not be proper to dispense with any of the stipulated formalities of the rules of discipline; and consequently, all that could at this time be done, was to take order that a copy of the charges preferred against her, the names of the witnesses by whom they were to be established, and a citation to appear and answer ten days thereafter, should be issued and served upon Miss Theodosia Ernest. A committee, consisting of the pastor and clerk, was appointed to carry these measures into execution.

"You are now done with Miss Ernest's case for the present," said Professor Jones, "and I will retire, that you may feel perfect freedom in speaking about mine."

"Oh, no," said the President of the College, the Rev. T. J. McNought, D.D., LL.D., who was present on the invitation of the pastor. "We were merely speaking of what it *might* be necessary to do in a case such as our brother Johnson conceived yours would *eventually become*, should you continue to progress in the direction in which he imagines you have started."

"Brethren," replied the Professor, "let us not misun-

derstand each other. You know me well. I am a plain,
blunt man. I will have no concealment on this subject.
My niece has carefully studied the Word of God, which
our standards declare 'IS THE ONLY RULE OF FAITH AND
PRACTICE.' I assisted her in the investigation. We
both came to the conclusion, as I think every right-
minded man must do, that the baptism commanded and
spoken of in the New Testament, is neither sprinkling
nor pouring, but dipping, or, as it is commonly called,
immersion. This I now firmly believe. This I am
ready to prove from the Holy Word to you or any one
else who feels inclined to inquire into the matter. I will
prove it by the very meaning of the *word* baptize. I will
prove it by a reference to the *places* selected for baptism.
By the going down into the water, and the coming up out
of the water, said to have preceded and followed baptism.
I will prove it by the nature of the *allusions* to baptism,
as a *bath*, as a *planting*, and a burial. I will prove by
the testimony of the Fathers, that it was for centuries
the *only* baptism, and by the testimony of *our own ablest
writers*—such as Wall and Stuart, Neander and Colman
—that it continued to be the *common* baptism for more
than thirteen hundred years, even in the Roman Catholic
Church, and the churches derived from her, and *still* continues the only baptism in the Eastern churches. I will
show you the very time and place when and where the
change was made by authority of the *Pope and his council.* I will show you when and how the new practice
was introduced into England and into this country. I
will show you this, not in Baptist books. These facts
do not rest on Baptist testimony, but on that of *our own*
historians and divines. *You know,* President McNought,
that what I say is true ; and Mr. Johnson knows it, too,
or might know it, if he would look at the evidence in his
possession. Now, if to believe these things on such testi

18

mony makes one a heretic, I wish you distinctly to un
derstand that I am decidedly heretical.   Though I assure
you, on my honor as a man and a Christian, that I am
ready and willing to see and to acknowledge my error,
if *any one of you* can point it out.   On the subject of
infant baptism, I am not fully convinced.   I am satisfied, as any one can easily be who will make a critical
examination of the Scriptures, with this object in view,
that *there is neither express commandment nor example*
to justify the baptism of *any but believers, to be found in
the Word of God.*   Pastor Johnson and myself have
together searched diligently to find either the precept or
the example, and he, as well as I, was compelled to
grant that it *is not there.*   But Woods and Stuart, and
others of our most eminent divines, while they have
granted this, still contend for infant baptism.   There
must, therefore, be *some other Scriptural ground* on
which it rests.   I will be thankful to any one among
you who can point it out."

There was a moment's pause.   The Session were not
prepared for such a confession of his faith and no one
knew what to reply.

"I will now retire," continued he.   "You have the
case before you, and can adopt such measures as you
may think best."

After he had gone, "I told you," said the pastor,
"that he had become a Baptist in all but the name.   I
don't believe his niece would ever have left us, but for
his encouragement and that of her mother."

"They must have felt," said Colonel White (the lay
member whom we have had occasion to mention once
before), "they must have felt to-day, if they had any
feeling left.   I would not have been in their places for
the best farm in the country.   It made my very ears
tingle to hear how you belabored them.   But it don't

seem to have done him the slightest good. I doubt if there is but one argument that can be brought to bear upon him, and that is the same that so easily convinced my young friend, Esquire Percy."

"What is that?" inquired President McNought.

"It is the *argumentum ad pocketum*. I have heard rom doctors that the pocket nerve was the most sensitive nerve in the whole body. Convince a man that his bread and meat depend upon a correct belief, and he is very apt to believe correctly. This may not be always true of a *woman*, but I have never known this argument, when prudently and skillfully presented, to fail of convincing *a man*. You may appoint a committee to confer with brother Jones, and endeavor to convince him of his errors. It is, perhaps, essential that you should; for this will give him a pleasant and honorable opportunity of recalling his heretical expressions, or at least, of explaining them away. But before you do this, let me intimate to him that the Board of Trustees (of whom you know I have the honor to be the President) will greatly dislike to dispense with his *valuable* services in the college—but that it is a Presbyterian college; and however much they may esteem him as a man, and value him as a teacher, yet we can retain no one whose orthodoxy is openly doubtful. Believe me, brethren, you will then find him much more pliable, and ready to be convinced that he is wrong."

"You may try it," said the pastor, "but I don't believe you will succeed. I know him better than you do. He has always been one of the most *conscientious* men I ever knew. He will *act* as he *believes*."

"No doubt of it," rejoined the speculating elder. "He will act as he believes; but he will believe that it is *wrong* to make any change in his church relations, or to meddle any farther with the subject of baptism, unless it is in the defence of our opinions. Professor Jones is a poor man. It is not generally known, but it is true, that he has for several years greatly assisted in the support of Mrs. Ernest and her children. He has thus lived fully up to his income. He has now a growing family. He expects to provide for them out of his yearly salary. It is all he can do. Take away this; turn him out of the house he now occupies, rent free; let him feel that he stands suddenly not only destitute, but without employment and friendship—and he is something more or less than man, if he can look upon his helpless wife and children and refuse to hear to reason."

The Session appointed the pastor and the Rev. T. J. McNought, D.D., LL.D., as a committee to see and labor with their brother Jones, and endeavor to convince him of his errors, especially in regard to infant baptism, as on this point he seemed likely to be most accessible, and then adjourned to meet again at the call of the pastor.

Colonel White considered himself a committee of *one* to make matters easy for the committee of two. Early in the day, on Monday, he called at the house of Professor Jones, at an hour when he knew he was absent, for he felt the necessity of all the assistance he could obtain, and relied upon Mrs. Jones and the children as his most efficient allies.

"Is the Professor in this morning, Mrs. Jones?"

"Not just now, sir. He has a recitation at this time. He will be in in half an hour. Take a seat, colonel."

"No, I thank you, madam. I called to see Professor Jones about some important business. I will meet him at the college. There is a matter afloat, which I fear is going greatly to injure him in his future prospects; and I merely called, as a friend, to suggest some plan by which the ruin—for ruin I fear it will be—may be averted."

"Why, Colonel White, what *can* you mean?" asked the lady, in just that tone of distress and alarm which he desired to hear.

"Oh," said he, taking a chair, and sitting down where he could look right into her face, "it may be nothing after all. Indeed, I don't really believe it will amount to any thing; but still, there is, I *fear*, some danger that he will lose his situation in the college. There is a rumor abroad, you know, that he is about to become a Baptist—or, at least, that he has a little tendency that way; and there are *some* of the trustees who are disposed to be *very particular* about such things—too much so, as I may say. Now, for myself, I am disposed to be liberal; and I shall do what I can—in fact, I may say I have done what I could—to influence their action. You know I have always been in favor of Professor Jones I know him to be a worthy man, and a very superior instructor; and I know he has the confidence—the implicit confidence, as I may say—of the whole community. And what if he *does* entertain some heterodox opinions about a matter not essential to salvation? says I. Why, he is a good man, and that is enough for me. But you know, Mrs. Jones, people don't all think alike; and I am dubious about what the trustees may take a fancy to do. But I can't stay," continued he, rising, and going toward the door. "I could not do less, as a neighbor, than just to call and tell you my fears. I will try to meet Professor Jones himself, and consult with him about what is to be done."

He sallied out, and about the time that Professor Jones was starting for home, placed himself in the way as he came from the college building.

"I am sorry," said he, "brother Jones, that our

pastor used such expressions as he did yesterday. I don't wonder that you became excited; I could not have borne it half as well as you did. But I am afraid you dropped some expressions that will injure you with the trustees. Some of them have been talking with me this morning. They say that you as good as declared yourself a Baptist, and they don't see what further use a Presbyterian college has for your services. But I said, wait a while. Jones is a man of impulse. His feelings were touched yesterday, and he said more than he intended. He is as much a Presbyterian as I am. He will be all right in a week. I took the liberty to say thus much for you. I have always been your friend, and I mean to stand by you through thick and thin, so long as I can be of any service to you. I don't advise you to conceal or falsify your opinions. I know you are incapable of doing *that*; but I merely suggest, since so much depends upon it—your own living, as I may say—that you will be a little more careful and prudent in your expression. Think what you please; but you are not obliged always to *tell* all you think. You understand? I felt bound to give you this little hint. There may be more in it than you are aware of."

Such thoughts as these had already intruded into the Professor's mind. His wife had several times suggested something of the kind. Till now, however, the danger had seemed distant and undefined. It was indeed a dark cloud, but it hung low on the far-off horizon; now, it lowered above his very head, and covered all the heavens with its blackness. Nothing but utter ruin stared him in the face. He walked along home, almost blinded by the rush of fearful thoughts. He sat down in silence to his dinner. His wife seemed even sadder and more distressed than he was. Scarcely had he begun to eat, when she inquired:

" Have you seen Colonel White this morning? he was here looking for you. I *told* you how it would be, when you first begun to meddle with this subject of baptism; but you could not be satisfied. And we are now to lose our pleasant home and all our means of support, and be turned out destitute upon the world, just because you would not listen to your wife, and let well enough alone."

" Oh, not so bad as that I hope, my dear."

Well, I don't know how any thing could be worse Colonel White says the trustees are going to declare your professorship vacant, or something like it, because you have turned Baptist. And of course we must leave this house, which you know belongs to the college, though we have fitted it up for ourselves just as though it belonged to us. And you know you have never saved a dollar of your salary, though I am sure I never spent the half of it. I never could tell what became of it; and how we are going to live, I should like very much to know. If you depend on those ignorant and stingy *Baptists* for a support, any body can see we must come to starvation. They could not do much if they would, and they would not do any thing if they could. I'm sure I hate the day they came here, to disturb the peace and quiet of our town. They have brought nothing but trouble to me."

" But, my dear wife, things may not turn out so badly after all. I did indeed see Colonel White, and he told me, as a friend, that some of the trustees are a little piqued at my entertaining opinions on this subject different from their own; but with his influence exerted in my favor, I hardly think I shall lose my situation, at least till I can make other arrangements."

" His influence! Why, he is the very soul and body of the whole business. You don't know that man as I do. He can't impose on me with his soft words. I could see the evil intention in his eye while he was talking about it to me. As soon as he saw how much it distressed me, I could see it did his very heart good. He is the very man that is working your ruin. And all I wish is that you had not yourself placed in his hand the club to beat your brains out with. If I were you, I would go to the trustees myself, and set the matter right."

"What can I say to them, my dear?"

"Say? Why tell them, that though it is true that you have given a little time to the investigation of this subject, you are as good a Presbyterian as any of them, and have no more thought of leaving the Presbyterian Church than President McNought himself. I know you *love our church*. I have often heard you say so. It was good enough for your father and mother to live in and die in. It was good enough for Timothy Dwight and Jonathan Edwards to live and die in. It is good enough for Pastor Johnson, President McNought, your brother professors, and all the most intelligent, and influential, and *wealthy* portion of the town, and *I can't see why it is not good enough for you.*"

"If I were only sure it is the Church of Jesus Christ, that would be all I could ask," he replied; "but I must consider further of this matter."

"Yes, I see how it will be; you will consider and consider till the mischief is done and we are turned out of house and home. But I know it's of no use to talk to you. You will just go on your own way. I only wish you may never be as sorry as I am that you ever saw a Baptist."

Night came, and with it came the committee appointed by the Session—the reverend pastor and the reverend doctor. They had previously consulted and arranged

their plan of argument. Mr. Johnson knew it would
not be worth while to go again over the same ground
through which they had already traveled. They had in
vain *searched the Scriptures* to find a single precept or
example to justify the baptism of infants. They concluded, therefore, they must make it out by *inference.*

"I understand," said President McNought, "that
you insist on some *express precept* or *example* for infant
baptism, before you will receive it as a scriptural practice?"

"Oh, no," said Professor Jones; "I am by no means
particular about the *character* of the proof. I only ask
for Scripture evidence that it was either required or
practiced. You may find that evidence in any form you
can. You can't find the *precept* or *example*, that is
certain. We have tried it. If you have any *other* testimony, let us hear it."

"The truth is," said the D.D., "there was no necessity
for the precept or example. The case was so plain, that
the early disciples could not help understanding their
duty, so there was no *need* of commanding it.

"Children had *always* made a part of the *Jewish*
Church, and unless there was something said to the
contrary, they would of course be regarded as making a
part of the *Christian* church. If, therefore, you cannot
prove that they *were absolutely excluded* from the Christian church, it is most conclusively evident that they
were received into it, though there should be no record
of the fact."

"To that," said the Professor, "I might reply by
saying that the baptism of infants, if required at all, is
a positive institution of our religion, something *essentially binding* upon the Christian churches. And it is
difficult for me to conceive how you can make out a
positive obligation to perform a certain Christian duty

in a church capacity, from the mere fact that *not one word is said about it.* Your argument amounts to this. The Jews *circumcised* their male infants at eight days old, because God had again and again positively and plainly *commanded* them to do so; therefore Christians should *baptize all* their infant children, both male and female, *because* the Lord has given *no commandment on the subject,* and further, because we cannot find the slightest allusion to any of the first Christians as having done or refused to do it, nor any intimation that any person was ever expected to do it. Such logic may be very conclusive to you, but I can never be convinced by it.

"But I think I may safely venture to take the very ground proposed by you, and prove that *infants* (according to your own language) *were absolutely excluded,* both by the commandments of the Saviour and the example of the early Christians. While looking in vain for any precept or example to justify the baptism of infants, we found enough both of precept and example to satisfy my mind, since I have come to reflect about it, that *infant baptism* is absolutely and clearly *forbidden.*

"It is forbidden in the commission itself. The command to baptize *believers* is a command *not to baptize* any but believers. The command to make disciples *first* and then baptize them, is a command *not to baptize* any who are not first made disciples. If I tell my servant to go and wash all the old sheep in my flock, it is equivalent to a prohibition to wash the little lambs. If I tell him to cut down all the *dead* trees in a grove, it is equivalent to a prohibition to cut any green and living ones—and if he should disobey me and cut the green ones also, I would not consider it a valid excuse, that I had *last year,* on *another plantation,* expressly ordered him to *girdle* both green and dry. So the command to baptize *believers* excludes all others; and as infants cannot believe, it excludes them from the very necessity of the case. Nor would I like to offer, for the violation of this command, such an excuse as this: Oh, Lord, I know that thou didst ordain *only* the baptism of *disciples* and *believers*—but as thou didst, under a *former* dispensation, expressly command children to be *circumcised*, I thought thou wouldst prefer to have them baptized under this, although thou didst omit to tell us so. Would he not reply, What right had you to make ordinances for me? If I commanded the *Jews to circumcise their children*, it was their duty to do it; and when I command *Christians* to baptize *believers* and *disciples*, it is their duty to do *that*. 'Ye are my friends if ye do *whatsoever I command* you.' 'But in vain do you worship me, teaching for doctrines the *commandments of men.*'

"And as a prohibition may be fairly inferred from the *command*, so it may also from the *examples*. Among all the multitudes who came to John and were baptized of him in Jordan, there was *not a single infant*. John required repentance and faith in the coming Messiah as an indispensable prerequisite. He taught them that the *Father's* faith would not avail in this new dispensation. 'Think not to say unto yourselves, we have Abraham for our father; but bring forth for yourselves fruits suitable to repentance.'

"Those who were baptized by Jesus and his disciples were also adult believers, for the Pharisees heard that Jesus made and baptized more disciples than John. He *made disciples* before he baptized them. Of the three thousand mentioned as added to the church upon the day of Pentecost, there was *not one infant*, nor did they bring an infant with them. Of the five thousand, a few days after, there was not one who was not an adult believer. They were men and women. Of the great multitude who believed and were baptized in Samaria when Philip preached, there was not a single little child. The Evangelist expressly classes them all under two heads, 'both men and women.' And nowhere, in a single case, is there even an intimation that there was a child baptized, nor is any one ever reproved for the neglect to have it done. Now if *this* does not absolutely exclude them by example, I do not see what force there is in ex-ample. I reply to your argument, therefore, first, by proving that even if infants had *not* been *expressly ex-cluded*, there would not be the slightest warrant for their baptism ; and, second, by showing that they *were* absolutely excluded, both by Christ's command and the practice of the early Christians."

"Then," said Mr. Johnson, "you are unwilling to believe that 'baptism has come in the room of circum-cision,' as I have been accustomed to inform my people every time an infant has been baptized in my church for twenty years."

"Oh, no, Mr. Johnson—not at all. I am *very willing* to believe it—I may almost say, I am very desirous to believe it. All I ask is that you will give the *slightest Scripture proof* of it. You are too good a Protestant to ask me to take *your word* for it, or even the often repeated *assertions* of all the clergy in the land. Give me *one text of Scripture* to prove it, and I am as ready and willing to believe as even yourself can wish."

" You know," replied Mr. Johnson, " that we teach 'that baptism is instituted by Christ—that it is a seal of the righteousness of faith, and that the seed of the faithful have no less a right to this ordinance under the Gospel than the seed of Abraham to circumcision under the Old Testament.' "

" Oh, yes—I know *you teach* this. I have heard and read it a hundred times : and I have no doubt most of our people think you have Scripture to show for it. It is not enough, however, for me to know that *you* teach it; I want that you should show me where the *Lord Jesus* teaches it, or where he authorizes *you* to teach it. Where is it *said* or even *intimated* 'that the seed of the faithful have no less a right to this ordinance under the Gospel than the seed of Abraham to circumcision under the Old Testament?' If it is in the Bible, you can show it. If I read correctly, the seed of Abraham had a right, or rather were in duty bound to circumcise their male children at eight days old, *because God expressly commanded it*—to give the children of believers the *same right* to baptism would therefore require an *express commandment* that they should be baptized. But you know full well there *is no such* command. I have heard a great deal of, to me, unintelligible jargon about 'federal holiness,' and 'covenant holiness,' and the 'covenant of circumcision,' and the 'Abrahamic covenant,' etc., etc. There may be a great deal of sense and Scripture in it, but I can't understand it. I want a plain Scriptural statement of the facts. You say that baptism came in the room of circumcision. Show me where the Word says so. Show me any thing like it."

"If you will take the Confession of Faith," replied the Doctor of Divinity, "and turn to the 147th page, you will see the texts upon which this doctrine rests."

"Well, here is a copy. Let us find them This is coming to the point. If any text is mentioned or referred to which gives to the *infant children* of believers the same claim to baptism that the descendants of Abraham had to circumcision, or even intimates that baptism has come in the room of circumcision, I am satisfied. This is all I want."

The book was handed to the pastor, who found the page, 147, and read as follows: Gen. xvii. 7, 9, with

Gal. iii. 9—'And I will establish my covenant between me and thee, and thy seed after thee, in their generations, for an everlasting covenant; to be a God unto thee, and to thy seed after thee. And God said unto Abraham, thou shalt keep my covenant therefore, thou, and thy seed after thee, in their generations.'"

"Stop a minute," said the Professor. "Let me turn to the place in the Bible. We will understand it better to read it in its connection. Here it is, Gen. xvii. 7-9. Why did they leave out the 8th verse—'And I will give unto thee, and to thy seed after thee, the land wherein thou art a stranger, all the land of Canaan, for an everlasting possession; and I will be their God'? This makes it all very plain. God agreed with Abraham that he would *give* his seed the land of Canaan for a possession forever; and as a condition, on the other part, he required (see 10th verse) that every man child should be circumcised. I can understand all that; but what has it to do with baptism or Christianity? No more than the carrying of the bones of Joseph out of Egypt."

"Oh, yes it has, Professor Jones, for we read in Gal. iii. 9——"

"Stop a minute, till I find the place. Now—but let me read it; I will begin at the 6th verse: 'Even as Abraham *believed* God, and it was counted unto him for righteousness Know ye, therefore, that they *which are of faith*, the same are the children of Abraham. And the Scripture, foreseeing that God would justify the heathen *through faith*, preached before the Gospel unto Abraham, saying, In thee shall all nations be blessed.' And now comes your proof-text—'So then they which be of *faith*, are blessed with faithful [believing] Abraham.' Now, I think I can understand this; but for the life of me I can't see one word about baptism in it, or of circumcision either. There is no more allusion to

either, than there is to the lifting up of the brazen ser
pent in the wilderness, or the giving of the law on Sinai,
or the falling down of the walls of Jericho. Abraham
believed God. So Christians *believe*. Abraham was
blessed for his *faith*. It was counted to him for righteousness. So *we*, who believe, are also blessed with
believing Abraham; and that is all. There is surely no
infant baptism here. What is the next?"

"It is Romans iv. 11, 12: 'And he received the sign
of circumcision, a seal of the righteousness of the faith
which he had, being uncircumcised; that he might be
the father of all them that believe, though they be not
circumcised,' etc."

"I have it here," said the Professor, as he found the
chapter; "and to understand the sense, I see it will be
necessary to begin at the first of the chapter. Paul is
proving that justification is by *faith*, and not by *works*.
So he says even Abraham *believed* (third verse), and it
was counted [or reckoned] unto him for righteousness;
and in the tenth verse, he asks, how was it reckoned?
before he was circumcised or after? It was before.
He had the faith, and he received the sign of circumcision as a seal of the *righteousness* of faith. And the
Apostle goes on to argue, that if faith was counted to
him for righteousness, while he was yet uncircumcised,
so it will be counted for righteousness to all who believe
in Christ, even though *they* should not be circumcised.
But what has all this to do with baptism? The subject
is never mentioned or alluded to. The sentiment is the
same which is expressed in Galatians—Abraham believed, and believing, he was blessed. So Christians,
believing as he did, will like him be blessed; and thus all
believers may be counted as *his children in faith*. The
only allusion to circumcision here, is made to show that
it had nothing at all to do with the blessedness of faith

To baptism there is no allusion at all. If you will satisfy me that baptism has come in the room of circumcision, so that the law of circumcision was transferred to baptism, you must give me something better than this; and if there were any thing better, the Confession of Faith would have quoted or referred to it. I take it for granted, therefore, that these are the strongest proof-texts you can present. And if they prove any thing at all, that has any bearing whatever upon the point at issue, it is that *all* the members of a Christian church must of necessity be professed *believers*. The seed of Abraham enjoyed certain blessings (the possession of Canaan) in virtue of circumcision, but the *righteousness of faith* pertained to Abraham, as he was *uncircumcised*, and now belongs to those who are his children, *not by circumcision*, or by any thing that came in the room of it, but by the *same faith* which he exercised. Those who *believe*, and *only* those, are to be partakers of the blessing. Christianity is a *personal*, _individual, and not a *hereditary* religion. In the New Dispensation, *every* man stands on *his own* foundation, and is responsible for *himself* to God."

"I do not see," replied the President, "why you should think it necessary to have any Scripture to prove a familiar and notorious *fact*. It is well known that circumcision was the *initiatory* ordinance of the Jewish Church, and we all agree that baptism is the *initiatory* ordinance into the Christian church. Of course, then, it takes the place of the other. It bears the same relation to the Christian, that the other did to the Jewish Church. *It is the door of entrance.* Now, the church of God is, and has been in every age, substantially *the same*, although existing under different names; and consequently, the character of the persons admitted to membership must have been the same

These persons among the Jews were admitted by circumcision, and among Christians by baptism. They were the infant children of church members among them; and so, of course, they must be among us. We don't need any express *text* to prove this, for it is self-evident from the general tenor of the whole Word."

"Your argument," replied Professor Jones, ' is simply this: Infants were members of the Jewish Church; and, as the church of God is always substantially the same, they must be members of the Christian church. The *door* of entrance is changed, but there is no change in the character of the persons who are to enter it."

"Yes, that is precisely what I mean, Whatever other changes were made, there was *no change in the membership*."

"Then," said the Professor, "you mean precisely what is certainly not true. Jesus Christ, when he commanded the *new door* to be opened, commanded *also* that different persons should *enter* it. To the Jews he said, bring in your male children and servants at eight days old. To Christians he says, bring all who *believe* in the blessed Gospel which I send you to preach. If he made the one change, he just as clearly made the other. Believers—as Mr. Johnson and I have seen in our examination of the word—he plainly commands to be baptized; but he commands *no others*, and no others ever were baptized in all the history which the New Testament records. Neither is it true that Christianity is *substantially the same* as Judaism. It was one of the most earnest labors of Paul to explain and enforce the difference. This difference was substantial—it was fundamental—it was constitutional. The other was a religion of *works;* this is one of faith. That was one of outward forms; this of inward affections. That con

19

sisted of the whole Jewish nation, both the evil and good; this is confined to the truly converted. That was a national establishment, and this an assembly of true believers, from which all are to be excluded but the pious in heart and the holy in life This substantial and fundamental change, we, as Presbyterians, recognize in fact, though we deny it in theory. We *say* that infants are church members, but we do not, in this country, *treat* them as such; we do not *address* them as such; we do not, in fact, consider them as such. You, in your preaching, are continually urging the baptized children who have come to years of discretion, 'to come out from *the world;*' and when they are converted, you urge them *to join the church.* It is true that, by the Confession of Faith (p. 504), you are required to inform them 'that it is their duty and their privilege to come to the Lord's Supper,' whether they give evidence of conversion or not, provided only that they are intelligent and moral. But you *never do it;* and half our members would not believe that we have any such rule. In other countries, however, this is done. Our theory is carried out into practice, and the church is filled with unconverted men and women. This is the legitimate result of infant church-membership."

"I am very sorry," rejoined the pastor, "to hear you talk in this way. I fear you are preparing great trouble for us, and are about to bring down terrible sorrow upon your own head and that of your family. I had hoped, for the honor of our beloved church, that you would have thought better of these things. We have, however, done our duty. The Session deputed us to reason the case with you, and endeavor to convince you of your errors; but we find that you *will not be convinced.* Let us hope, however, that you will consider further, and carefully weigh the unanswerable arguments which

we have presented, and let them have their full influence upon your mind. There may be more dependent
on it than you are aware of. I suppose it is not worth
while to spend more time upon the subject; so we will
bid you good-night."

Professor Jones understood very well the ominous
import of this parting address. He knew that his home,
his employment, his all, depended on the will of a few
men, some of whom would take pleasure in rendering
his condition as wretched as possible, so soon as they
had no further hope of binding him to themselves. And
he knew, on the other hand, that those to whom he would
go, had neither influence to aid him, or profitable employment to furnish him the means of support. As
soon as the reverend committee had retired, he fell upon
his knees, and offered up to God his thanks, that thus
far he had not been tempted to deny his truth, or
falsify the solemn convictions of his conscience. And
then, in view of what he now began to feel would be in-
evitable, he prayed for strength to obey all the Master's
will, and trust God for the consequences:

"Oh, my God! I see before me nothing but trouble
and sorrow. Want and affliction stare me in the face.
Lord, give me strength to welcome them, or at least,
firmly to endure them. Thou canst bring good out of
evil. I commit my destiny into thy hands. I have
trusted my *immortal soul* to thee; why may I not trust
my body and my family? Thou hast promised to save
the one and to provide for the others. Help my unbelief! I must go out like Abraham, not knowing whither
I go. I look to thee, my Father in heaven, to open the
way before me."

As he was rising from his knees, the remark of Theodosia, as she came from the water with her face so full
of heavenly joy, came back to his mind with tenfold

force and beauty—" Uncle, dear uncle ! it is *blessed to obey !* Can't you give up *all* for Christ ?"

"Yes, yes," he unconsciously exclaimed, " I will—I do give up all. I will follow where duty leads, let the consequence be what it may. I will resign my professorship to-morrow. God will provide in some way for my wife and children."

The conversation which we have recorded took place in his private study. On returning to his family room, he was delighted to find there his sister, Mrs. Ernest, and her daughter, and also, Mr. Courtney, who had called to have a little conversation with Theodosia, and finding they were about to start out, had accompanied them on their visit.

Mrs. Jones had been so anxious about the result of the conference with the committee, that she could not enjoy the society of her visitors, nor even exert herself successfully for their entertainment. She was, therefore, greatly relieved when her husband came in and took that task upon himself.

"I wish I had known that you and Theo. were here," said he, " I would have turned the reverend committee who have just left me over to you."

"I do not understand what you mean," said Mr. Courtney.

"Only this. My brethren in the Church Session have learned that I do not any longer believe that sprinkling is baptism, or that any but believers are to be baptized. And they have deputized Dr. McNought and Pastor Johnson to endeavor to bring me back into a belief of their human traditions. Their main argument at this time was on the baptism of infants as founded on the usage of the Jews. Baptism, they said, has come in the room of circumcision ; and as infants were circumcised, so infants must be baptized. What answer would you have made?"

"I would have said: Gentlemen, you do not *yourselves believe* that baptism came in the room of circumcision in any such sense that the same order of persons who were circumcised are to be baptized; or, if you *believe* it, you do not *act out* your faith The law of circumcision included only males, but you baptize both males and females. The child, when it was *possible*, was to be circumcised at eight days old, but you baptize at any other time. The servants and the slaves, whether old or young, whether born in their house or bought with their money, were to be circumcised, but you never baptize them—but only the children. They were to be circumcised by the parents and not by the priest; but you require baptism to be done by the minister. If the law of circumcision is transferred to baptism in *one* particular (without any New Testament authority) it is equally transferred in all the others.

"Then I would have said further: Baptism *could* not come in the room of circumcision, because *circumcision is still in force.* No room was ever made for the second by taking away the first. The truth is simply this: God made a covenant or agreement with Abraham, when he was ninety-nine years old, in which he promised to his seed the land of Canaan. The token or memento of this contract was the circumcision of every male. This was the condition of their entering Canaan. This is *now* the condition of their restoration to it. The promise still stands. The Jews are still a separate people. This is their *mark*. By this they are yet to claim their inheritance. This is its object, and this the sum of its value. The covenant has not been revoked It is still in force, and its seal or token still remains.

"God made with Abraham *another* covenant some

twenty-four years earlier, in which he promised him among other things, 'That in his seed should all the na. tions of the earth be blessed.'—Gen. xii. 3. This is what Paul refers to when he says, Gal. iii. 8—'The *Gospel* was preached unto Abraham, and Abraham believed it.' He trusted in the Christ to come, and so was, in a certain sense, a member of Christ's church. So was Noah—so was Enoch—so were all who like Abraham believed God, and it was counted unto them for righteousness. They were not introduced into it by *circumcision*—nor was Abraham himself—for it was twenty-four years after he heard and believed the Gospel, before he was circumcised. He was a member of Christ's mystical body, and an heir of the *heavenly* Canaan, without the seal of circumcision. By *it* he and his seed became the heirs of the *earthly* Canaan. This was its object, and no more. The blessings of the Gospel are to us, as to him, the result of *personal faith.* Thus, they who are of faith, are blessed with [believing] faithful Abraham ; and thus far, and no further, this first-made covenant with Abraham extends to us. If we believe as he believed, we shall be blessed as he was blessed. This is all that any one can make out of all that is said of the relationship of the Patriarch and believers.

"I should have said to them further: Gentlemen, *you* call the Jewish *nation* the church of God, and tell us that the Christian church is the same under a different dispensation. But Christ calls that nation *the world,* in opposition to his church. The disciples to whom Christ spake, John xv. 19, were men in good and regular standing in the Jewish nation, which you call the church. Yet Christ says, I have chosen you *out of the world*—and therefore the world, that is, the Jewish na tion, hateth you. Paul was not only a member, but an *eminent* member of this Jewish body; but he says that *he was a persecutor of the* CHURCH OF GOD. Nicodemus was a 'master in Israel;' but Christ told him he could not come into *his church* till he had been born again. The Jews needed conversion as much as any, before they could make any portion of the *church* of God. This church God set up for the *first* time when John began to preach. For the first time he organized a visible assembly of penitent, believing, holy persons. There were good men, pious, devoted men and women, among the Jews; but they were not gathered into *a church.* The Jewish nation had some religious privileges; but it was not in the Gospel sense *a church.* And when Christ established his church, he made the terms of membership such as were intended to preserve its purity and separation from all national politics. People were not to be born into it, but to enter it by *faith and baptism.* 'He that believeth and is baptized.' But by the introduction of infant baptism, the object of this arrangement is entirely defeated."

"I have often thought," said Theodosia, "since my attention has been directed to the subject, what disastrous consequences must follow if the theory of Pedobaptism were fully carried out, and infants actually recognized and treated as members of the visible church."

"If you would fully realize what the consequences would be, you have only to go to those States of Europe where this is actually done. You will see men who blaspheme their Maker on the way to church, go and partake of the Holy Supper. You will see them leave the church where they have so partaken, and openly resort to the ball room, the horse race, the drinking saloon, the gambling house, the cock pit, and even to the very lowest and vilest haunts of dissipation. They are members of the church. They were made such at eight days old. When they could say the catechism

they were confirmed, and informed, according to the
directions of the Presbyterian Confession of Faith, that
' it is their duty and their privilege to come to the Lord's
table.' To be baptized in infancy and confirmed in
childhood, are all that is needful to church membership.
That *faith* required by the Gospel, they laugh at. They
call those who profess to know any thing about it in
their own experience, deluded enthusiasts. They know
no more of religion than its external ceremonies. They
have the form of godliness, but deny the power. Such
was the Presbyterian Church to which Dr. Carson
preached in the North of Ireland. ' In the general disregard of religion,' says his biographer, ' the people of
his charge were not behind their neighbors. Horse
races, cock fights, and other forms of sinful diversion
were frequent, and were numerously attended even by
professing Christians. The soul of this pious servant
of God was deeply grieved. He knew well the heaven-
born excellence of Christianity, and clearly understood
what should be the fruits of the Spirit, but he beheld
around him only the works of the devil. He rode into
the throng that crowded the race-course, and saw there
the members of his own church flying in every direction
to escape his sight.' * * ' His church was composed of
worldly people, whom neither force nor persuasion could
bring into subjection to the Laws of Christ.' In Germany and some other European States, *every body* is in
the church. Every body is recognized as a church member. Thieves, gamblers, drunkards, and prostitutes are
members of the church. There is no such thing as the
world. The church has swallowed it up. It has taken
all the infidelity, all the atheism, all the blasphemy, all
the vice, and all the depravity of the world into its own
bosom. This is the natural and necessary result of receiving all the *infants* as church members. The church

has ceased to be the body of Christ, and has become a loathsome mass of hypocrisy and vice. There may be in it some few good and pious believers in Jesus. There are in it many upright, and honorable, and moral citizens: but these, as *church members*, are not at all to be distinguished from the basest profligates that issue forth from the reeking stews of infamy. They have all alike been baptized in infancy and confirmed in childhood, without *any profession of conversion to God*—most of them denying the necessity of any such change, and all sit down alike to the same table of the Lord."

" Surely, Mr. Courtney, you do not mean to speak thus of the *Protestant* churches of Europe! I know it is true in regard to the Catholics; but since the Reformation, it cannot be true of any others."

" Yes, Mrs. Jones, I mean to say this of the Protestant churches, wherever they have become *national* churches, and by the process of infant baptism have absorbed the whole population. It is *necessarily* true of *any* church which receives its members in this way. It would be true in *this* country, if you Presbyterians, and the Episcopalians, and Lutherans, and Methodists could by any means accomplish what you all so earnestly are laboring to attain—viz.: to induce *all the people* to have their children baptized."

" Oh, no, Mr. Courtney. You must have conceived a terribly mistaken idea of what we are all aiming at. We desire, I trust, as much as the Baptists themselves, to keep our churches *pure*, and are as strict in our terms of membership and as rigid in our discipline as *you* are. We want our churches to consist, as they now do, of godly people, and would not for a day permit such as you have mentioned to remain in our communion."

" I know it, Mrs. Jones; but in order to do this you are obliged continually to repudiate your own acts, and deny in practice what you teach in theory. I was speaking of what the result must be, provided you could induce all the people to have their infants baptized, and should then recognize these baptized ones as church members *in fact*, as you do in *theory*.

"Listen one minute, and I will satisfy you that what I say is strictly true. You teach that, as circumcision was the door of entrance into the Jewish Church, so baptism is the door of entrance into the church of Christ. If so, all who are baptized are church members. Now, *you Presbyterians* say all the children of *believing parents* must be baptized. In your churches you baptize all the children of those parents who have been baptized. The Episcopalians baptize *any* child for whom proper sponsors will stand. The Methodists will baptize *all* the children, with or without believing parents. Now, if you could succeed (as by sermons, books, tracts, and newspapers you are all striving to do) in convincing *all* the people that you are right, and prevail upon them to bring *all* their children, and have them thus initiated into the church of Christ—I ask you of whom, *in the next generation*, would the church consist? It would be composed of these infants, then grown to manhood. If that generation be like the present, or the past, it will consist mostly of unregenerate men and women. A few will be converted—many will be moral—most will be wicked, and many will be most vile. They will all, however, have entered into the church of Jesus Christ by the door of baptism, and will every one be members of Christ's visible kingdom."

"Oh, no, Mr. Courtney; we would exclude the wicked and unworthy by process of discipline."

'Who would exercise discipline, Mrs. Jones? This would be a body of *unregenerate* men. They would have no love to Christ or his cause. The power of discipline is in their own hands. If they exclude all that do not give evidence of piety, they will exclude themselves. They will do no such thing. They may exclude the *openly* and *scandalously vicious*, for the reputation of their denomination, while there are several sects striving for the supremacy; but if (as in those countries I spoke of) any *one* sect could swallow up the rest, and by connection with the State become the *national religion*, then a man would hold his right to the Lord's Supper, and all the privileges of the church, by about the same tenure that he held his right to vote or to exercise any other privilege of citizenship."

"But if this is so, Mr. Courtney, why don't we see at least some illustrations of the principle among us now? Why are not *our* churches now filled with unconverted men and women?"

"Simply because you don't act out your principles. Your churches *are* filled with unbelievers, but you refuse to recognize them. You daily repudiate your own acts, and continually falsify your own theory. You baptize infants, and you *say* you do it *to introduce them into the church of Christ.* But you *don't believe it.* You never treat them as church members. You give them none of the privileges of church members. You don't count them in the list of your church members. They do not regard themselves as church members. They do not claim or enjoy any of the privileges of membership. They do not exercise the discipline of the church on others, nor are they considered subjects for its discipline. They are practically as separate from the church as the children of an infidel or a Hottentot. It is thus, and *only* thus, that you retain any degree of purity in your actual membership. Your church consists in *fact*, of believers, and not, as **your** book says, of 'believers and *their children.*' You thus

obviate one of the evils of infant baptism, by a virtual
repudiation of the act and regarding it in practice as a
nullity. Mrs. Ernest does not look upon her son Edwin
as a member of the church. She did not consider you
a member, Miss Theodosia, till about a year ago, when
you professed your faith in Christ, and as they all
expressed it, *'joined the church.'* How could you be
said to *join* it, if up to that time you had not been considered as *separate* from it? The baptized children are
urged, like others, to come out *from the world*, and to
unite with the people of God, when they have believed in
Christ; and those who have thus *believed*, and made themselves a public profession of their faith, you count as
members; and to them and them alone you give the
privileges of members. And this simple fact, that you
are obliged to treat the baptized infants, *when* they
grow up, as though they had not been baptized at all,
in order to preserve the spirituality and purity of the
church, is of itself sufficient proof that your celebrated
historian, Neander, tells the truth when he says 'It is
certain that Christ did not ordain infant baptism.'"

"Well, Mr. Courtney," replied Professor Jones, "is
there any other argument you would have urged upon
the attention of my reverend visitors, had you been
present?"

"Yes, sir. I would have said further: Gentlemen, if
you found infant baptism on Jewish circumcision; if you
declare, that the Christian and the Jewish Church are the
same, but only under different dispensations; and that
because infants were circumcised in the old, infants
must be baptized in the new, how can you get rid of the
necessity for a *national* church? The Jewish Church
was a national church: it united Church and State
The Christian is the same, and *it* must consequently be
a national establishment too. We must unite the Church

and State. For this, every Christian should strive. Of this union, where it exists, no Christian should complain; for there is certainly as much Scriptural authority for it as there is for infant baptism. And further, gentlemen, you must receive and recognize not merely three orders of the ministry, like the Episcopalians; not merely deacons, priests, and bishops, but also a grand and supreme ruler of them all, similar to the Pope. The Jewish polity had its common priests, its chief priests—who controlled certain numbers of the others—and its *High* Priest, who was above them all. So, to correspond, there should be the Presbyters, the Bishops, and the Archbishops, if not the Pope. This has quite as much, and the same sort of Scriptural authority as infant baptism. To this, they would have replied, by saying, that the constitution of the Christian church is to be found in the *New Testament*, and that we learn what its officers were, by seeing what ones were ordered or recognized by Christ and the Apostles; and they neither commanded nor recognized but *one* order of ministers. This is good logic, I do not object to it. But I ask if the *membership* of the Christian church is not designated in the New Testament even more clearly than its *officers?* If baptism is the door of entrance, show me a single instance where any one is permitted, much less commanded, to enter in upon the faith of any but himself. Show me any instance in which an infant was received, or ordered to be received; any in which one was recognized as a church member, or even where there was the slightest allusion to him as such. They cannot find one; and so, upon their own principles, must take the whole paraphernalia of Episcopacy, and Church and State, or give up infant baptism."

"But, Mr Courtney, as you say that among us Presbyterians in this country, infant baptism is a *mere nul-lity*, as we don't count the baptized as church members, or give up the discipline of the church into their hands; as they have, in fact, no more to do with the church than other people, and cannot, therefore, injure its standing or diminish its spirituality, what *harm can it do* to baptize infants?"

"What harm! Alas! madam, I am incompetent to tell the thousandth part of the harm that it has done, is doing, and will continue to do so long as it is practiced. Pardon me, if I decline attempting to answer your question."

"Well, then, if you can't tell what harm it does, why do you talk so much against it?"

"I can't tell! Oh, yes, but I *can* tell. I can tell so much that you would not have the patience to hear. I can tell such things of it, that you would almost think it impolite to mention. And that is, in truth, the reason why I felt disposed to decline a proper reply to your question. If I should speak of this act, which *you* perform as a religious *duty*, as I think it deserves, I should characterize it as a *heinous sin*, an act of daring *rebellion* against God; and this you would think scarcely becoming in me as your guest. If I should tell you all the harm I know of infant baptism, instead of convincing, I should probably make you angry. You have been so long accustomed to look upon it as something sacred and holy, that you could hardly avoid feeling indignant at hearing what I, after careful and prayerful study of the subject, have come to think of it."

"I don't see how you could say much worse things about it than you have already; but I assure you that I will keep my temper, let you say what you may. So you may consider yourself as having full license to say

to me in my own house, any thing that you would feel
at liberty to say to me or any one any where else."

"Yes," rejoined Mrs. Ernest, "do go on and tell us
all you think about it. I have some curiosity to understand just what you Baptists do think of us Presbyterians. I know you have a very mean opinion of us, but
I would like to know just how mean it is."

"Go on, Courtney; you have the ladies' curiosity excited now, and you will be obliged to gratify it. If you
don't *tell* what you think, they will imagine it is something very horrible indeed. For myself, I am satisfied
now that it is a thing *not commanded*, and therefore I
would not practice it; but I don't see what great *harm*
there is in it. It is a simple ceremony, and if not required, a very *useless* one; but I don't see who is *hurt*
by it. We are, however, all of us prepared now to hear
hard things from the Baptists. We don't look for any
thing else."

"I should be very sorry to believe that Baptists were
accustomed to say hard things *of* their opponents, whatever they may feel it their duty to say *to* them. Mrs.
Ernest thinks I have a very mean opinion of Presbyterians. She is utterly mistaken. Many of the best and
most earnest-hearted children of God whom I have ever
known are Presbyterians. I not only esteem them
highly, I love them dearly. I love them not only as
individuals, but as Christians. I count them my
brethren and my sisters in the Lord; but at the same
time, I think they have been educated in error, and are
in some things most grossly deceived. They are to that
extent wrong in their faith, and wrong in their practice.
The more I love them, the more I would rejoice to set
them right. I hate error and wrong in them as in others.
I oppose it; I reason against it; I denounce it in them
as well as in others. It is not their persons, but their

opinions that I war against. In most cases, I do not
even esteem them less for holding these erroneous
opinions; for I know they are sincere and conscientious
They have been deceived by those who have instructed
them. They have never had the truth laid fairly before
their minds. Early education, denominational attachments and prejudices have enveloped their intellects in
such a cloud, that it is hard for the clear light of Scripture truth to find its way into their hearts. I was as
honest and sincere when I believed that sprinkling was
baptism, and that infants were to be baptized, as I am
now. So was Miss Theodosia. Nor were we suddenly
convinced that we were wrong. The light shone in little
by little. What was at first a doubt, became a certainty
by patient investigation. It is not long since I said, as
you do—infant baptism is not commanded. It is not
authorized by the Word of God, but still it is only a
useless ceremony. Let those who will, engage in it. No
good is done; but yet it does no harm. Since that time,
I have studied the subject more carefully. The more I
looked at it, the more fearful it appeared. And I am
now fully convinced, that he who baptizes an infant in
the name of the Father, Son, and Holy Ghost, *is guilty
of a most enormous sin in the sight of God!* And this
is not less true because *good men* have done it, and are
doing it still. Good men have often been ignorantly
guilty of most enormous crimes. That excellent and
holy man of God, Rev. John Newton, was for years after
his conversion engaged in the slave trade. It was *then*
considered a reputable and righteous business. Many
good men of the past generation were engaged in the
manufacture and sale of intoxicating drinks. It was
then considered a legitimate and Christian calling. No
good man will engage in it now. Their ignorance was
their excuse. God forgave them as he did Paul for

persecuting his people—because he did it ignorantly, and verily thought he was doing God service. His conscientious sincerity did not, however, make the act a righteous one. The deed was still one of terrible wickedness and daring impiety. So I say of those who practice infant baptism; so I would say *to* them if I could. They may be good men. Some of them *are* good men —earnest, warm-hearted, devoted Christians; but they are ignorantly *sinning against God.* It may not be becoming in me to *reprove* men older, and better, and more useful than myself; but surely I may entreat them, as my brethren and fathers, to do '*no more so wickedly.*'"

"But what is there so wicked about it, Mr. Courtney?"

"Much, every way. In the first place, if you will excuse me for talking so plainly, *infant baptism, as practiced by Presbyterians in this country, is a continually repeated falsehood!*

"You *say* that 'baptism is a sacrament of the New Testament, ordained by Jesus Christ, not only for the *solemn admission* of the party baptized into the visible church, but also to be unto him a sign and seal of the covenant of grace, of his ingrafting into Christ, of *regeneration*, of *remission of sins*, and of his giving up unto God, through Jesus Christ, to walk in newness of life.' —*Con. of Faith*, p. 144.

"Now, this is either true or false. If it is *true*, then the person baptized *is admitted* into the visible church of Christ. You say it is true, and that you *do thus admit* him; but, at the same time, if I point you to one of these members thus received in infancy, staggering from the grog-shop, and ask you if he is a member, you tell me—*No.* You would be ashamed to think that such a wretch had any connection with your church. Is his father a member? Yes, one of the best men in the

20

church. Did.he have his children baptized? Yes, I
suppose he did. Has this man ever been excluded?
No, you reply, he never *joined* the church. He grew
up a wild and reckless boy, and has always been a
vicious, dissipated man. He was never in the church;
nobody ever thought of such a thing. There is an
amiable young lady, moral, irreproachable in her character; but she makes no pretensions to *religion*—she is
perfectly indifferent to it. Is *she* a member of your
church? Oh, no; our members are all spiritual-minded
Christians. She has never even expressed a conviction
of sin, or even the slightest desire to join the church.
Why do you ask if she is a member? Simply because
I remember when she was *baptized*. Does not baptism
admit persons into the visible church? Yes; but we
never *consider* them as members till they make a profession of religion and join the church again. Then
your baptism is a solemn falsehood, for it does not
admit into the church at all.

"But now, if you take the other horn of the dilemma,
and say we *do* admit them—then I reply, you are guilty
of introducing into the church of Christ wicked and
unregenerate men and women. If you recognize them
as members, and treat them as members, you at once
destroy the distinction between the church and the
world. The church no longer is Christ's kingdom. It
is no more a body of *his* people. It consists, in part
at least, of the wicked and profligate *descendants* of his
people.

"But you say, further, that baptism is to the baptized 'a sign and a seal of his ingrafting into Christ'—
'of his regeneration'—and of 'remission of his sins,' etc.
Now this is true or it is false. You *say* it is true. A
mother brings her babe to have it sprinkled. It is a
beautiful child, and she verily thinks she is doing God

service—and is, herself, a lovely object, as she stands there with the infant in her arms. But now I ask you, Is that child 'regenerated'? Is he a 'branch ingrafted into Christ'? Are all his 'sins forgiven'? In other words, is he a *believer* in Jesus Christ? You say—*No*, it is absurd to think of such a thing. Then, I reply, your baptism *is a falsehood*—for it is designed to signify and seal these things, which, in this subject, do not and cannot exist. To a *believer* in Christ, baptism has all this significancy; but to an unconscious babe it can have none at all. There is not, in fact, in your minds, the slightest suspicion that the child is born again and ingrafted into Christ; and yet you say to the world, that this ordinance is designed to signify and seal the fact that such is actually the case.

"*Is it no harm thus, in the house of God, as a religious act, and in the very name of Jesus, to proclaim such practical falsehoods to the world?*"

"I declare, I had never thought of it in that light before. Have you any other charge to make against it?"

"Yes; I say, in the next place, that *the baptism of an infant is an act of high-handed rebellion against the Son of God.*"

Mrs. Jones and Mrs. Ernest both lifted up their hands in utter astonishment. The former looked at him as though she expected to see him drop down dead after making what seemed to her such an impious announcement.

"That is the most astounding statement," said the Professor. "But I know you would not make it, unless you thought you had the evidence to sustain it."

"What!" said Mrs. Jones, "The evidence to prove that it is *wicked!*—positively *wicked!* to baptize a child; an act of rebellion!—high-handed rebellion! Well, I will try to be quiet, just to see what the

man *can* say. Go on, Mr. Courtney; we are all attention."

"Yes," resumed Mr. C., "I have said it; and I will
prove that it is not only *rebellion*, but rebellion attended
with such circumstances as mark it with a character
of peculiar malignancy. Not only a sin, but a *terrible*
sin; most flagrant in itself, and most terrific in its consequences to the church and to the world."

"Really" said Mrs. Jones, "I am curious to know
how you will make it out."

"You know," said Mr. C., "that you Presbyterians
are accustomed to count some requirements of Christ
as essential, and some as non-essential—or, at least, less
essential than others. Now when Christ came into the
world, *one* great object, if not *the* great object of his
mission, was to *establish his visible church*. He set it
up himself. He instructed his disciples carefully in the
nature of its laws, and especially those organic or constitutional laws which lie at the very foundation of the
whole superstructure. To *these* laws especially he must
have attached great importance. Willful disobedience
to these fundamental rules, which regulated and fixed
the very *nature* of the visible kingdom he established,
must have been regarded by him as a rebellion of no
common order. Now the *most important* of these fundamental rules was that which fixed the terms of membership in his kingdom. This lay at the foundation of
the whole business. The character, the influence, the
prosperity of his new kingdom, must depend upon the
character of the persons of whom it was composed
Now the Jewish kingdom, though it had in it much of
good, and was a beautiful type of better things to come,
yet it had included more of the evil than the good. In
it the wicked dwelt in the land, and the righteous were
among them But now Christ was organizing not a

temporal, but a *spiritual* kingdom. His dominion was to be one of interior rule—by the power of love. The subjects of this kingdom were to be *converted men and women,* who loved God and lived to his glory. No one could belong to it, as he told Nicodemus, who had not *been born again.* This was his church. It was designed to be a permanent and living illustration of the power and the purity of his religion. The members of this church were to be his living epistles, known and read of all, describing the nature and results of his religion in their hearts and lives. No fact is more clearly evident than this. The church is not only commanded to be holy—exhorted to be holy—but it is said to be holy, and addressed as though it was thus holy. It is always and everywhere regarded as a body of professedly converted men and women. As many as were baptized into Christ had put on Christ. They were those who trusted in Christ. They walked by faith. They lived, but not they—it was Christ that lived in them. They had been sinners, but were called to be saints, and now had an inheritance among them that were sanctified. They were a peculiar people, zealous of good works. Not of the world, not like the world, for Christ had chosen them out of the world. Such was the church as he established it, and such he intended it should continue to the end of time. Now to secure to it this character, he determined that none should be admitted into it but those who repented of sin, and believed on him with saving faith. The door of entrance into this church was by the ordinance of baptism. Consequently, when any one repented and believed, and gave evidence that he was born again, he was to be baptized, and henceforth counted among his people. The very nature of the church, and the object of its establishment, required that *no others should ever be admitted*

How then, I ask, can he look without abhorrence and indignation upon *that act*, in which a minister of this church—claiming to act by his authority—subverts the very foundation of his church, changes its nature, and defeats the very object of its establishment, by introducing into it, knowingly and willfully, persons who are confessedly not penitents, not believers, not regenerate, but the children of wrath even as others.

" If baptism converted them—if by the act itself they were regenerated—there would be some excuse for this course ; but no one of *you* will pretend to believe that it has any such influence. You *know* that a baptized child grows up a *sinner*, just as his unbaptized brother does. *Doctors of Divinity* talk about such things ; but no man or woman of common sense believes that the sprinkling of a little water on a baby's face changes its heart, and makes it a new creature in Christ Jesus. If it is introduced by this act into Christ's visible church, it comes in a sinner, as it is born ; it comes in an unconverted, impenitent, and unbelieving sinner—just such a sinner as Christ forbade his ministers ever to introduce. And now what is the consequence ? Let us look at the history of the church. It is enough to make one who loves Jesus and his cause weep tears of blood, to see what have been the results of this rebellious departure from the instructions of the Master. For the first two or three hundred years the church remained what Christ intended. It was a body of professed believers. All history accords to its members a character of singular uprightness and purity. It was a light shining in darkness. But when infants, instead of converts, began to be introduced, its whole character was changed. Its spirituality was gone. Its very ministers were worldly men, contending for wealth, and place, and power. In the course of a few generations, it had, like the national

churches of Europe of the present day, swallowed up
the world.   All the villainy and depravity of the land
was in the church, or in that establishment that *called
itself* the church of Jesus Christ.   No Pagan, not even
the tiger-hearted Nero himself, was so cruel in his persecution of the Christians, as this body of baptized
infants became when it grew up to manhood, and was
invested with the power to kill.   Nothing which the most
infernal hatred could suggest, and the most diabolical
ingenuity could invent, was thought too hard for these
baptized ones to inflict upon those who professed faith
in Christ, yet would not conform to their newly introduced rites and ceremonies.   The most bitter and re-
lentless persecution was directed especially against those
who denied infant baptism.   This has continued through
every age.   It has not been confined to the Roman
Catholics.   It has been practiced by *all* the so-called
churches *that received infant members* (your own included) whenever and wherever they have been able to
obtain the power.   The world has been deluged with the
blood of the saints, shed by these members of the church,
whom men, professing to be *his ministers*, have, in his
name, though against his authority, introduced in their
infancy.   Now I say, the act which thus subverts the
very nature of the church of Christ, and leads to such
terrific consequences, *is no common sin*.   Such perversion of the very fundamental law of his church is no
common rebellion.   It is a great and terrible crime.   It
has led to great and terrible results even in the present
world.   Its consequences, even here, have been so terrific, that our very hearts shudder but to think of them ;
what they may be in the eternal world, we cannot conceive.

"But I will go further.   I said 'the baptism of an
infant was *a sin*—an act of high-handed *rebellion* against

God.' I have proved it. I will now say even more than this. *Infant baptism is impious*—it is an act of sacrilege."

"Be careful, Mr. Courtney, be careful!" exclaimed Mrs. Jones. "This is a solemn subject. You should not thoughtlessly make use of words which convey such horrible impressions."

"I *am* careful, Mrs. Jones. I have chosen these words deliberately, because they are the only words that will fully express my meaning. I mean to say that it is *impious* for a professed minister of Jesus Christ to stand up in the presence of the world, and in HIS name, and by HIS authority, perform, as a solemn and sacred ordinance of HIS religion, an act which HE NEVER COMMANDED OR AUTHORIZED! I regard it as a fixed fact, that there is no such commandment or authority. We have been searching for it carefully; we cannot find it. It is not in the book. And now the question comes up —'Even if it be not commanded, what *harm* is there in it?' This is the question we are endeavoring to answer. I say, *If God has not commanded it or authorized it, then to perform it as an ordinance of HIS religion, in HIS name, and by HIS professed authority, is an act of impious sacrilege!* It can be nothing less. I know your preachers do not so *intend* it; I know that they would shudder at the very thought. They verily believe *they* have the authority. They do it *ignorantly*, as Paul persecuted the church. But though their ignorance may, in a degree, excuse their conduct, it does not change the nature of the act. And for one who has studied the subject, who has looked for the authority and failed to find it, as we have, for such a one thus, in the name of God, to do what God has not required, must require a degree of temerity which I trust few of the professed ministers of Christ possess."

"I declare, Mr. Courtney, it fills me with a sort of horror to hear you talk. I am almost sorry I insisted on your saying any thing about this subject. I don't and can't believe that what you say is true. And yet I shall never be able again to see an infant baptized without a feeling of terror."

"But why can't you believe that I tell the truth? Have I not proved every position by the Word of God?"

"Oh, as to that, any body can prove almost any thing they please by the Scriptures. Unitarians, and Universalists, and Methodists, and Episcopalians, and all sorts of people, find plenty of proof in the Bible for all they teach."

"Then how are God's people to know what he requires of them?"

"Well, I don't see as we *can* know with any certainty. I have been raised a Presbyterian, and taught that they were right; and I believe I had as soon risk my soul on their faith as any other. I don't see as I need to give myself much trouble about it."

"You do not deny, Mrs. Jones, that you ought to obey God rather than man, and that the Scriptures are a perfect and infallible rule of faith and practice?"

"Oh, no, I grant that; but the difficulty is, that I can't understand just what they teach. If I could know what they require, I must believe and do it. But Mr. Johnson tells me one thing, and you tell me another, and the Methodist tells me another; and between you all, I don't know really what I must believe or do."

"I will tell you, then. God will hold *you* responsible for *your own* faith and practice. You are not, therefore, to rely on me, or the Methodists, or on Mr. Johnson, but you are to go to the Bible for *yourself*. If there is any command to baptize infants there, you can find it, and you can read and understand it as well as a Doctor of Divinity. Do not take for granted that what they say or what I say is true, but *search the Scriptures* for yourself. Make use of all the helps you can, but don't let any one convince you that any doctrine is taught, or any practice required, by the Word, till *you can see it in the Word.* You will not find the teachings of the Scriptures to be either doubtful or contradictory when you go to *them*, and are *willing* to believe and practice just what they teach. Doctors of Divinity may contradict each other and themselves, but God's Word is not a book of doubtful oracles. It speaks plainly; it speaks decidedly; and it speaks always the same thing. Try it yourself with reference to this subject. Your pastor tells you that he has authority in the New Testament to baptize infants. Ask him to *show it to you.* If it is there, he can find it. You can see it as well as he can. He will, perhaps, refer you to the commission, Go baptize, etc. ; but you will say, this is only a commission to baptize *believers.* It does not say a word about believers *and their children*, but only about believers. He will then remind you that Jesus said, Suffer the little ones to come unto me, etc You will reply, they did not come to be *baptized*, but to be *prayed* for : 'And he laid his hands on them, and departed.' This is good authority to *pray* for children, and to devote them to God by faith, and seek his blessing on them, but none for baptizing them. He will then remind you that Peter says, the promise is to you and to your children.' You will reply, this is a promise of the 'gift of the Holy Ghost,' not of baptism ; and, moreover, it is limited to those 'whom the Lord our God shall call ;' and God does not call unconscious babes. He will then tell you, that 'the unbelieving wife is sanctified by the believing husband, etc. : else were your children unclean, but now are they holy.' To this, your good sense would reply, that there is here not a word about baptism; and if the *child* is to be baptized because it is holy, so ought the infidel husband and the infidel wife, for they are also sanctified or holy. He will then seek to find some *example*. He will tell you, that there were a number of *families* baptized, and it is *almost* certain there must have been infant children in *some* of them. You turn to each place, and find that they who were baptized are the same who are said to have heard the Word, believed in God, rejoiced in God, spake with tongues, glorified God, ministered to the saints, and, in the case of Lydia's family, are called *brethren*. Finding neither precept nor example in the New Testament, he will turn to the Old, and tell you about the covenant with Abraham, the seal of which was *circumcision*, and was applied to the children. Now, he will say, this covenant includes Christians too; for Paul says, All that believe are the children of believing Abraham. And if his children by nature were circumcised, his children by *faith* must be baptized. To this you will reply, true, his children by *faith* are to be baptized, but who are they? Paul says, they are *believers*, not the infant offspring of believers. You will say, further, the Jewish infants were circumcised because God *expressly commanded* it to be done. But God never commanded Christians to baptize their infants. On the contrary, he directed only the penitent, the believing, the regenerate, to be baptized, which expressly excludes infants; and not a single infant ever was baptized during the period of which we have the history in the Scriptures. He has nothing more to offer. This is the substance and the sum of what *he calls* Scriptural authority. Dare you now, with this light in your mind, consider the baptism of an infant an ordinance of God? I say, then, try it for yourself. Search the Scriptures, as the

Bereans did, and see if these things are so. I do not
ask you to take *my* word for one solitary fact or circumstance. Go to the Book. Go not to cavil, but to learn.
Go not to twist an argument out of it, but to ascertain
your duty. Study it; pray over it. Don't rest till your
mind is *satisfied*. If *you can't find* infant baptism in the
Word, you may take it for granted *it is not there*, even
though all the Doctors of Divinity in Christendom
assert the contrary. If you *do find it*, bring the Book,
and show it to us benighted Baptists, and we will practice it; for we do earnestly desire, if we know our own
hearts, to 'do whatever Christ commands us.' If you
find it, it will be your *duty* to bring it to our notice; for
in that case we are in most woful error. If you are
right, we are most *fearfully* wrong. If God has commanded us to baptize our infants, *we* are living in open
and avowed *rebellion*. But we *desire* to obey; and if
you will show us our error, so far from growing angry,
we will *thank* you for the care that you show for our
good."

"There is much in what you have said," replied Professor Jones, "that strikes me with amazement. I cannot deny, that infant baptism is in opposition to the
Word of God; but yet, I have never conceived of it as
the terrible thing you have represented it. I see, however, that it must be even so. If it does not introduce
people into the church, it is a falsehood on its very face;
for this is what it pretends to do. If it does introduce
them, then it evidently subverts the very foundation of
the church, as a body of believers. And if God has not
commanded or authorized it, it must, indeed, be impious to do it in his name, as though he had. I cannot
deny this; but you made some statements concerning
the results of its introduction, which I do not feel disposed to receive solely on your assertion."

"My dear sir, I don't desire you to receive *any thing* on my assertion. What I do not *prove*, I beg you will consider as though I did not say. I don't intend to make any assertion, that I cannot sustain by the very best of testimony."

"You said that infant baptism was not introduced in the time of the first Christians, nor until several hundred years after Christ. And that all churches, both Protestant and Catholic, who had embraced it, had persecuted the saints whenever and wherever they possessed the power. All this is quite at variance with what I have always regarded as the truth. I do not deny that it is so, but I cannot believe it without the evidence."

Mr. Courtney glanced at the clock, as he replied:

"It is now near bedtime. We will not have time to night; but at any time you may suggest, I will convince you that I did not speak without reason. I will prove to you, by the testimony of the ancient Fathers, by the testimony of *your* own most eminent historians and divines, that what I said is strictly and entirely true. I will show you, that infant baptism was introduced in the same way, and by the same sort of authority, that pouring and sprinkling were—only that it began at a somewhat earlier day. I will show you, too, what were the consequences to the true believers, who refused to sanction the innovation—how they were driven out to dwell in caves and dens of the earth—how they were tortured and tormented—hunted like wild beasts; and that not a few hundreds, or thousands, but millions have gained a martyr's crown—slain for the testimony of Jesus; not by Pagans; not by infidels; not by the people of the world; but by *the members* of the (so-called) churches of Jesus Christ, made members in their

infancy by this '*blessed*' ordinance of infant baptism
Where shall we meet?"

"Oh, come back here," said Mrs. Jones. "I begin to
feel a sort of fearful interest in your strange teachings;
something—if you will pardon the comparison—like I
would expect to feel in the dying speech of some
outlawed wretch, denouncing, on the very scaffold,
all that good men hold dear and sacred. I do not mean
any disrespect, but I cannot think of any thing else
which will so well describe my emotions. I shudder
while you talk, to think that you should dare to speak
of one of the most beautiful and holy rites of our
religion as of a deadly sin; and yet I want to hear all
that you have to say. Sister Ernest and Theodosia
will come over with you again to-morrow night."

"So be it. then. We will meet here to-morrow night '

THE NINTH NIGHT'S STUDY.

---◇---

OF THE TIME AND MANNER

IN WHICH

THE BAPTISM OF INFANTS

WAS SUBSTITUTED BY MEN

FOR THE

BAPTISM OF BELIEVERS,

WHICH CHRIST COMMANDED.

NINTH NIGHT'S STUDY.

HERE was no one of the company that assembled at the Professor's house on Tuesday evening, to continue this discussion, who looked so anxiously for the time of meeting, as did Mrs. Jones. The idea that an act which she had always regarded as one of the most beautiful and holy of all the rites pertaining to our holy religion, was really no part of that religion, but in fact directly opposed to it, and forbidden by it, had haunted her mind continually ever since the last night's conversation. She had awakened her husband at midnight, to tell him that she should ever after be afraid to see an infant child baptized—and all the day she had been anxiously looking at the arguments of Mr. Courtney, as she called them up one after another in her memory, but could see no fallacy in the reasoning, though it led to what she considered such fearful conclusions. One reflection, however, gave her some comfort. Infant baptism *could not be a sin, otherwise good men could not have practiced it.* She was sure, therefore, that there must be some defect in his reasoning, though she could not see it.

And when they had come together, she began the conversation by asking Mr. Courtney if he had not said that he regarded Presbyterian and other Pedobaptist ministers as good and pious men?

"Certainly; I said that I knew some such. Men of God, whom I love as my brethren in the Gospel. And I know personally of no one among them whom I would be willing to condemn as being a worse man than myself."

21   (333)

"But how can you say that, Mr. Courtney, when you know that they all practice infant baptism, and teach others to do so, which you say is not only a sin, but a most grievous sin: not only sin, but impious sacrilege? It seems to me you are the most inconsistent man I ever heard talk."

"Will you permit me, madam, to answer your question by asking several others? Were Luther and Calvin and the Reformers good and holy men?"

"Of course they were, Mr. Courtney. No one has ever doubted that."

"Was Archbishop Cranmer, who suffered martyrdom for his religion, under Mary of England, a good and holy man?"

"Certainly; he must have been."

"Were our Puritan Fathers, who settled New England, good and holy men, deserving our reverential and affectionate rememberance for their Christian principle, which led them to sacrifice all for a conscience void of offence?"

"Most assuredly they were; but what has that to do with my question?"

"You will see, madam, when I have asked one more. Is it not a great and fearful sin to persecute and take the lives of men for their religious faith?"

"Of course it is; and no good man will do it."

"And yet, madam, our Pilgrim Fathers persecuted the Quakers and the Baptists, and condemned them to banishment and death Cranmer, before he was burnt, had been very officious and energetic in bringing Baptists to the stake. (See Neal's History of the Puritans). Calvin procured the condemnation of Servetus for his religion, and Luther urged the princes of his country to persecute those who could not conform to his opinions You see, therefore, that good and pious men may be led by their very piety (under mistaken notions of duty), to do things which are most fearfully wrong and sinful. Paul *verily thought* he was doing Goa service when he killed the followers of Jesus; but his mistake did not make the action right. It was still a most awful sin. He did it ignorantly, and God forgave him. So he will forgive your Pedobaptist brethren who in their ignorance imagine they are obeying him in baptizing little children into his church. But the act is sinful, terribly sinful, nevertheless. You are to take *God's Word*, not the example of those whom you consider holy men, as your standard of right."

"If I did not misunderstand you," said Uncle Jones, "you told us last night, that infant baptism was utterly unknown in the time of the first Christians. Now this is altogether at variance with what our ministers have always taught us to believe. I am sure that they have labored sedulously to make the impression on our minds, that from the very times of the Apostles till about six hundred years ago, no one had ever questioned that infants should be baptized. I am sure that I have been told again and again, from the pulpit and in private conversation, that it was the united testimony of *all* the Fathers that infant baptism was received from the Apostles, and that we not only have no account of the time and manner of its introduction, but no history of any period of the church when it was not universally received and practiced."

"Very likely," replied Mr. Courtney. "Doctors of Divinity often deal in just such sweeping assertions. The same men who assure you that the New Testament *abounds* with proof of infant baptism, though no man living or dead has ever been able to show for it a single precept or example, can well afford to make just such statements about history. And I say to them in this, as in the other case, If there be any record of infant baptism in the first ages of the church, you can *show it*, and I can *see it*. Your mere assertions are not worth a straw—bring in your proof."

"But have they no such proof?" asked Mrs. Jones. "Surely the ministers of our church are as good and as truthful as those of any church, and would not make such assertions without good and sufficient authority."

"I will answer your question, madam, by referring you to the writings of some of the most eminent ecclesiastical historians, who were Pedobaptists, like yourselves, but who would not stoop to falsify history to promote the interests of a creed. Let me ask your attention, and yours especially, Professor Jones, to the testimony of a very remarkable class of these witnesses. Soon after the Reformation, a project was set on foot by the Pedobaptist Protestants of Germany, to collect and embody in a permanent form all the known and reliable facts in the history of the early Christian churches. A great number of the most learned and eminent men of Europe engaged in the work. They had access to all the stores of ancient learning, and were fully competent to explore and appropriate them. Lutheran princes and powerful nobles were patrons of the work, and neither money nor labor was spared to make it a faithful picture of the ancient churches. It proposed to give the history of each century by itself; and as it was published at Magdeburg, its authors are commonly called the '*Magdeburg Centuriators.*' It was executed with great care, and has ever since its publication been regarded as one of the most faithful and accurate records of early church history. Now, I want you to remember that there was not a single Baptist among these men; and then observe their language, which is as follows: 'They [the Apostles] baptized *only* the adult or aged, whether Jews or Gentiles, whereof we have instances in Acts ii., viii., x., xvi., and xix. chapters. As to the baptism of *infants* we have no example. As to the *manner* of baptizing, it was by *dipping* or *plunging* into the water, in the name of the Father, Son, and Holy Ghost, according to the allusions contained in the 6th of Romans and the 2d of Colossians.' Thus they speak of the first century; and of the second century they say: ' It does not appear from any approved authors that there was any change or variation from the former century in regard to baptism.'

" The learned and acute Erasmus, writing about the same time, says, in his Notes on the 6th of Romans: ' It is nowhere expressed in the apostolic writings that they baptized children.'

" John Calvin, the founder of your Presbyterian Church, says: ' It is nowhere expressed by the Evangelists that any one infant was baptized.'

" Ludovicus Vives, a name of high historical authority, says: ' None of old was wont to be baptized but in grown age, and who desired it, and understood what it was.'

" Dr. Taylor, of the Church of England, says: ' It is against the perpetual analogy of Christ's doctrine to baptize infants; for besides that, Christ never gave any precept to baptize them, nor ever himself or his Apostles (that did' appear) did baptize any of them. All that he or his Apostles said concerning it, requires the previous dispositions of baptism, of which infants are not capable.'—*Liber. Proph.*, p. 289.

" Dr. Mosheim, who is universally known and regarded as high Pedobaptist authority, says, in his Ecclesiastical History of the first century: ' No persons were admitted to baptism but such as had been previously instructed into the principal points of Chris-

tianity, and *had also given satisfactory proof of pious
dispositions* and upright intentions.' Of the second
century he says: 'The sacrament of baptism was, during
this century, administered publicly twice a year at the
festivals of Easter and Whitsuntide. The persons to be
baptized, after they had repeated the creed, confessed
and renounced their sins, particularly the devil and his
pompous allurements, were immersed under water, and
received into Christ's kingdom by a solemn invocation.'
Of course they were not unconscious infants.

"Neander, another of your own historians, who has a
world-wide reputation, says expressly: 'Baptism was
administered at first only to adults, as men were accustomed to conceive of baptism and faith as strictly connected. We have all reason for not deriving infant
baptism from Apostolic institution, and the recognition
of it (which followed somewhat later) as an Apostolical
tradition, serves to confirm this hypothesis.'

"Coleman, another of your own writers, and a citizen
of our own country, says: 'Though the *necessity* of infant baptism was *asserted* in Africa and Egypt in the
beginning of the *third* century, it was even to the end
of the *fourth* by no means generally observed, least of
all in the Eastern Church, and it finally became a general
ecclesiastical institution in the age of Augustine,' which
you know was at the beginning of the fifth century.

"Now tell me what sort of consciences your ministers
must have when they assert, in the face of such testimony as this, from *their own most eminent historians*,
that infants were always considered right subjects for
baptism! But this is not all. We have positive proof
that Constantine and Gregory, and a great multitude of
eminent men whose history is recorded, and who are
known to have been born of Christian parents and
reared in Christian communities, were yet not baptized

till they had made their profession of faith in mature
years—while there is not on record a single, solitary
instance of the baptism of *a child* till the year of our
Lord three hundred and seventy, and that was the
son of the Emperor Vallens, which was thought to be
dying, and was baptized by the command of his majesty,
who swore he would not be contradicted; and moreover
this was not a little infant, but a boy of six years old.—
See Robinson's Hist.

"Now, if in the face of this testimony they say that
infant baptism was practiced, let them show the proof.
Let them bring a single case. Let them prove their
own most eminent ecclesiastical historians to be false
witnesses, and we will attach all due importance to their
statements."

"But, surely, Mr. Courtney," replied Mrs. Ernest,
"our ministers cannot be acquainted with these testi-
monies."

"It is their own fault then," said he. "These books
are in their libraries—they quote them on other subjects—and if they do not know what they teach on this,
it is because they willfully close their eyes to the light
in order that they may remain in ignorance."

"You say," rejoined Theodosia, "that these writers,
who make such concessions, are Pedobaptists. They were
members of churches which baptize infants by sprinkling. They were themselves baptized by sprinkling in
their infancy; and yet they state, in most express terms,
that it was not so commanded by Christ—it was not so
ordained by the Apostles—and nothing of the sort was
practiced by the first Christians, nor for several hundred years. How, then, could they conscientiously
remain even for a day in their church connection? I
cannot understand what sort of consciences such men
have."

"Nor can I, Miss Ernest, but I will let them speak for themselves. The learned Curcelleus is one of them, and he says: 'Infant baptism was not known in the world the first two centuries after Christ. In the third and fourth it was approved *by few;* but at length, in the fifth, it began to obtain in divers places; and therefore,' he continues, 'we Pedobaptists observe this rite indeed as an *ancient custom,* but not as an Apostolic institution. The custom of baptizing infants did not begin before the third century after Christ, and there appears not the least footstep of it for the first two centuries.' Or if you prefer a more recent exposition of their reasons, take Kitto's Cyclopædia of Biblical Literature, a standard Pedobaptist theological work, and turn to page 287, vol. 2."

"I have the book on the table here," said Uncle Jones. "Here, Theo., find the place and read. Here it is."

"'Infant baptism was established neither by Christ nor his Apostles. In all places where we find the necessity of baptism notified, either in a dogmatic or historical point of view, it is evident that it was only meant for those who were capable of comprehending the word preached, and of being converted to Christ by an act of their own will.

"'A pretty sure testimony of its non-existence in the days of the Apostles, may be inferred from 1 Cor. vii. 14, since Paul would certainly have referred to the baptism of infants for their holiness; but even in later days, several teachers of the church, such as Tertullian (De Bapt.) and others, reject this custom. Indeed, his church in general (that of North Africa) adhered longer than others to the primitive regulations. Even when the baptism of infants was already *theoretically* derived from the Apostles, its *practice* was, nevertheless, for a long time confined to a mature age.'

"Did you not say that the author of this work was a Pedobaptist, Mr. Courtney?"

"Certainly I did. It was prepared by a number of very learned and eminent Pedobaptist divines, and is regarded by Pedobaptists as a standard theological work."

"Well, I must say, that Pedobaptist theological writers are strange people," replied Theodosia, "but I will read on:—'In support of a contrary opinion the advocates [of infant baptism] in former ages (now hardly any) used to appeal to Matt. xix. 14, Suffer little children, etc.; but their strongest argument in its favor is the regulation of baptizing all the members of a household or family, 1 Cor. xvi. 17; Acts viii. 8; xvi. 33; but in none of these instances has it been proved that there were little children among them. And even supposing that there were, there was no necessity for excluding them from baptism in plain words, since such exclusion was understood as a matter of course.'

"Surely, Mr. Courtney, the man is a Baptist!"

"Oh, no," said Mr. Courtney; "read on. You will come to his strong reasons presently." She read on:

"'Many circumstances conspired early to introduce infant baptism. The confusion between the outward and inward conditions of baptism, and the magical effect that was attributed to it; confusion of thought about the visible and the invisible church; condemning all those who did not belong to the former; the doctrine of the natural corruption of man so closely connected with the preceding; and finally the desire of distinguishing Christian children from the Jewish and heathen, and of commending them more effectually to the care of the Christian community—all these circumstances, and many more, have contributed to the introduction of infant baptism at a very early period.'"

"Now we will come to *his reasons*. He has told us that it is not in the Scriptures; that it was not ordained by Christ; that it was not known to the Apostles; that it was the offspring of that error which attributed a *magical* influence to baptism, and to the mistaken idea that no one could be saved without it—together with numerous other circumstances; and now read on, if you please, and learn the reasons why he, notwithstanding all this, is a Pedobaptist."

"'But, on the other hand, the baptism of children is not at all *at variance* with the principles of the Christian religion, after what has been observed on the separation of regeneration and baptism; for since it cannot be determined when the former begins (the real test of its existence being only in the holiness continued to the end of a man's life), *the fittest point of baptism is evidently the beginning of life.*' 'Nevertheless, the profession of faith is still needed to complete it. Confirmation, or some equivalent observance, is therefore a very important consummation. The *fides infantium* [faith of infants] is an absurd assumption of which the Scriptures know nothing.' 'On the other hand, the baptized child is strongly recommended to the community and to the Spirit of God dwelling therein, becoming the careful object of the education and holy influence of the church: 1 Cor. vii. 14. *Nature and experience therefore teach us to retain the baptism of infants* now that it is introduced.'"

"Oh, yes," said Mrs. Jones, "I always feel a much greater interest in children that have been baptized. It is such a blessed privilege to bring our little ones to God, and dedicate them to him in the presence of all his people."

" For my part," replied Mr. Courtney, " I greatly prefer Christ and his Apostles, to 'nature and experience,'
as my teachers in religion.   It is, indeed, a blessed
privilege to be allowed to dedicate our children to God;
and for doing this, we have full authority in the Word
of God.   We are to dedicate them by faith and prayer,
and bring them up for him.   But, let me say to you, in
the language of Dr. Dwight, one of the most eminent
ministers of your own church: 'Nothing is a privilege,
in the religious sense, but what God has made such; and
he has made nothing such, except in his own way and
on his own terms.   Baptism is a privilege when administered and received in the manner appointed by him,
but in no other.   When this ordinance is received in any
other manner, it is plainly no obedience to any command
of his, and therefore has no promise—and, let me add,
no encouragement to hope for a blessing.' "—*Dwight's
Sermons*, vol. iv. p. 343.

" I am almost afraid," said Uncle Jones, " that you
will think me captious; but I cannot yet feel quite satisfied about this matter.   You have, indeed, shown very
clearly, that many very eminent historians and standard
writers, who, it is well known to all the world, were
Pedobaptists, have conceded—and, indeed, have in some
sense *proved*—that infant baptism did not originate till
the third century, or later.   But yet, it seems to me
that I have seen quotations from the early fathers themselves, which proved that baptism of infants had been
practiced from the very first.   Has there not been recently discovered some ancient manuscript, which throws
light upon this subject?   I am sure I have heard some
rumor of such a thing."

" You are not at all mistaken," replied Mr. Courtney.
"A manuscript of Hyppolytus was found, in 1842, in an
Armenian convent on Mount Athos, in T rkey, by

Minoides Minas, a Greek scholar of celebrity, who was employed at the time by M. Villeman to search for ancient books and manuscripts. This work has been carefully examined by many eminent critics and scholars, and there is now no doubt that it is genuine. Mr. Bunsen, a very noted Pedobaptist scholar, has made it the basis of a book on the early churches, in the preparation of which he consulted also the ancient canons and constitutions."

"But pray tell us who was Hippolytus?"

"He was the pastor or bishop of the church at Pontus, near the mouth of the Tiber, in Italy, and had been a pupil of Iræneus. He lived in the early part of the third century, and probably wrote the work in question about two hundred and twenty-five or two hundred and thirty years after Christ."

"Well, what is his testimony about baptism?"

"He says: 'We in our days never defended the baptism of children, which in my day had *only begun to be practiced* in some regions, unless it were as an exception and innovation. The baptism of *infants* we did not know.' And Mr. Bunsen, his translator and editor, adds (vol. iii. p. 180): 'Pedobaptism, in the more modern sense—meaning thereby baptism of new-born infants, with the vicarious promises of parents or other sponsors —was utterly unknown to the early church, not only down to the end of the second century, but indeed to the middle of the third.'"

"But," asked Mrs. Jones, "is there nothing at all in the early fathers in favor of infant baptism?"

"Not *one word*, madam, for the first two centuries— not even an allusion to it. It had not yet been invented. They had never *heard of it*; nor, so far as we can judge from their writing, had they so much as *thought* of it.

"CLEMENS, who is counted among the first, and is said to have been a companion of Paul, says: ' They are right subjects of baptism, who have passed through an examination and instruction.'

"IGNATIUS, of the same age, who is said to have been a disciple of John, and to have seen and talked with Peter and Paul, says: ' Baptism ought to be accompanied with faith, love, and patience, after preaching The other writers of this century were Clement of Rome, Polycarp, Hermes, and Barnabas (?); but it is admitted by those who have searched for it most diligently, that *not one word* about infant baptism is to be found in any of their works. So also in the second century, Dr. F. A. Cox, as quoted by Orchard, says: ' Justin Martyr, Athenagoras, Theophilus of Antioch, Tatian, Minucian, Felix, Iræncus, and Clement of Alexandria, constitute the Christian writers of this second century ; who, so far from *directly* speaking of infant baptism, *never once* utter a syllable upon the subject.'

"CLEMENT says, indeed: ' The baptized ought to be children in malice, but not in understanding; even such children who, as the children of God, have put off the old man with the garments of wickedness, and have put on the new man.' These are the only children he speaks of as having a right to baptism."

"You mention Iræneus," said Uncle Jones. " If I do not forget, I have heard him quoted as authority for infant baptism."

" I have no doubt of it. Those Doctors of Divinity who consider baptism and regeneration as all the same thing, have discovered in his writings the following sentence: ' Christ passed through all ages of man, that he might save all by himself; all, I say, who are by him *regenerated* to God—infants, and little ones, and children, and youths, and persons advanced in years

Now, this is the *only* allusion which it is pretended that Irænus makes to infant baptism; and *some* have had the temerity, not to say the dishonesty—since they themselves consider baptism and regeneration as the same thing, and because Irænus, in some *other* place, uses regenerate in the sense of baptize—to strike out *regenerated* here and put in *baptized*, and then refer to Irænus as having recognized infant baptism."

"I am sure," said Theodosia, "that the cause must be a *very* weak one which requires such support, and they must be very weak advocates of any cause who could stoop to employ such arguments in its favor."

"So also it is claimed by some, that Justin Martyr recognized the baptism of infants, when he says to some aged Christians that they had been the followers of Christ from their childhood; or, as these men read, from their *infancy*. But it is well known that, in those days, all *minors*—that is, all under twenty-five years of age, for that was considered the limit of manhood—were often called children, and even infants. And we read of some instances of persons becoming bishops while they were *infants*—that is, before they came of age; and of many persons being led to martyrdom while they were *infants*, and making earnest profession of the faith which they felt in their hearts, and sealed with their blood. The Baptists will baptize as many such infants as desire to enter into the church of Jesus Christ. But you will not accuse us, on that account, of practicing the baptism of unconscious babes;* and these mentioned by Justin Martyr, are not said to have been *baptized* in infancy, but to have followed Christ from their infancy. It is not till the beginning of the third cen-

---

* For an immense amount of testimony on this point, see Robinson's History of Baptism.

tary that we find the very first certain allusion to the baptism of children; and these were not babes, but little boys and girls old enough to *ask for baptism*, though yet too young to understand its import.

"By this time, salvation and baptism had begun to be regarded as inseparable, and loving parents began to inquire anxiously, What will become of our children if they die unbaptized? To this, the answer commonly given was, that they must be lost. Why not, then, baptize, and so secure their salvation? It seems that a certain wealthy lady, named Quintilla, who was probably a mother, and felt this very natural anxiety about her little ones, had come to the conclusion that if they *asked* for baptism, they ought to have it, whether they gave evidence of conversion or not; and she wrote a letter to Tertullian, the bishop of the church at Carthage, to get his sanction to this novel doctrine. The answer of Tertullian to this letter has been preserved, and contains the first undoubted allusion to the baptism of children which is recorded in the annals of church history."

"If infant baptism had been a universal custom, as is pretended by some," said Theodosia, "there never could have been any occasion for Quintilla to write to Tertullian on the subject, for children would have been baptized, as a matter of course, whether they asked for it or not."

"Very true; and Tertullian would have replied to her, that it had always been the practice of the church to baptize the little darlings, and she need not even wait for them to ask for it; but he did no such thing. 'Those who administer baptism,' he says, 'know very well that it is not to be rashly given.' The good lady evidently thought that it was enough if the children could *ask* for it, and had quoted the Scripture, 'Give to him that asketh.' To this, Tertullian says: 'What

give to him that asketh! Every one hath a right to it
as to a thing of alms! Nay! say, rather, give not that
which is holy to the dogs; cast not your pearls before
swine; lay hands suddenly on no man; be not partaker
of other men's sins.' It would seem that she had referred to the cases of the Eunuch and of Paul, as having
received the ordinance as soon as they asked for it.
And to this, Tertullian replies: 'If Philip baptized the
Eunuch on the spot, let us remember that it was done
under the immediate direction of the Lord.' The Eunuch
was a *believer* of the Scripture; the instruction given
by Philip was seasonable; the one preached. the other
perceived the Lord Jesus, and believed on him. Water
was at hand, and the Apostle, having finished the affair,
was caught away. But you say, Paul was baptized instantly. True, because Judas, at whose house he was,
instantly knew that he was a vessel of mercy. The con-
descension of God may confer his favors as he pleases,
but *our wishes* may mislead ourselves and others.

"This lady seems to have referred, as you do, to the
words of Jesus, 'Suffer little children,' etc. And to this,
Tertullian says, as Baptists do now: 'The Lord does
indeed say forbid them not to come unto me; and let
them come while they are growing up; let them come
and *learn*, and let them be *instructed* when they come;
*and when they understand Christianity, let them profess
themselves Christians.*'

"In another of his works, Tertullian says: 'Adults
are the only proper subjects of baptism, because fasting,
confession of sins, prayer, profession, renouncing the
devil and his works, are required of the baptized.'

"It is evident, therefore, that at this time, the beginning of the third century, the baptism of children had
just begun to be spoken of.

"Now, strange as it may seem to you, your Doctors

of Divinity are accustomed to base the strongest of all their historical arguments on this letter of Tertullian to Quintilla."

'How is that possible?"

"They say, infant baptism must have *existed*, or Tertullian would not have opposed it. If it existed *then*, it must have existed from the *first*, because we have no history of its introduction, and no account of any previous opposition to it. And it is incredible that it could have been introduced without opposition."

"And what answer," said Mrs. Jones, " can you make to such reasoning as that?"

"We simply say that it did *not* exist before. That this is the *first* proposal to introduce it, and that it *was* opposed."

"Very satisfactory, I declare! But what evidence have you that this *was* the first?"

"The best evidence that is possible: *It is the first on record:* If the advocates of infant baptism *say* there was any previous one, let them *produce* it. But we might put our defence on different ground. We might admit that infant baptism was at the beginning of the third century a generally received and recognized *custom of the churches*, and yet it would not follow, by any means, that it was received from the Apostles or had any Divine authority.

"You do not believe that the Episcopal and Catholic rite of confirmation is of Divine authority, and yet it can be traced back as far as infant baptism. You do not believe that there is any Divine authority for signing the baptized with the sign of the cross, yet Tertullian distinctly recognizes *this* as an existing custom in his day. So he does the giving of the newly baptized a mixture of milk and honey, and anointing them with holy oil. The doctrine of baptismal regeneration

22

and of purgatory both date back to or before this early day, as do the observance of some of the feast days and fast days, and a vast amount of the most absurd and silly mummery of the Romish Church.

"The first we read of these fooleries, they were already in the churches; they had, so far as we know, never been opposed; they were there long before we find any trace of infant baptism there, and yet who of you will dare to say, on these grounds, that Christ and his Apostles ordained that candidates for baptism should be divested of their clothing—should have salt put in their hands—should be daubed with the priest's spittle —clothed in white on coming out of the water—signed with the sign of the cross—anointed with chrism—walk from the water with a lighted taper in their hands, etc., etc.

"The truth is, the simplicity of the Gospel was corrupted even in the Apostles' days; and it was not the least onerous of their labors to prevent and correct unauthorized additions to and modifications of their teachings. *The simple fact, therefore, that we find any doctrine or any practice in the churches at an early day, is no evidence at all that it was received either from Christ or his Apostles.* The Scriptures are our *only guide.* This you as Protestants admit, and by this you are precluded from all recourse to 'the *traditions* of the first Christians,' in regard to infant baptism, or any thing else concerning the doctrines and ordinances of our religion. So that it is nothing to you nor to me if infant baptism *had* existed before Tertullian's time. We have shown, however, that so far from being a general practice before that time, it then was for the first time proposed, and it required all the third and most of the fourth to secure it any considerable foot-hold in the churches, and that it did not become *estab-*

lished as an ecclesiastical institution till the time of Augustine, in the early part of the fifth century.

" It is true, as you may read in almost every writer on baptism, that *Cyprian*, who was the successor of Tertullian in the church at Carthage, received a letter from one Fidus, of whom nothing more is known than that he wrote such a letter, asking *how soon* after birth it might be proper to baptize. This was about forty years after Tertullian wrote to Quintilla on the subject. Cyprian, it seems, did not feel quite able to decide this momentous question, and called a council of sixty-seven of his brother bishops of North Africa, who gave it as their opinion that the ' Grace of God should not be withheld from any son of man, and that a child might be kissed with the kiss of charity *as a brother, so soon as it is born.*' This was in the year A. D. 257. It was this same Cyprian who gave it as his opinion that water poured about a person in bed (if he was sick and could not be immersed) would answer in the place of baptism."

" What was the effect of this decree of the African Council ?"

" It seems to have had none. It is likely that it re-lieved the doubts of Fidus; and infants were probably baptized in Africa to some limited extent, but we have no record of any such baptisms. One hundred years after this, Dr. Wall, the Pedobaptist historian, says complaints were common that mothers could not be prevailed on to put their children into the water at baptism. More than one hundred and twenty years after this, Gregory, the Bishop of Constantinople, gave his opinion on the baptism of infants or babes. These are his words : ' But some say, what is your opinion of infants who are not capable of judging either of the grace of baptism or of the damage sustained by the want of it? Shall we baptize them too? By all means, *if there be any apparent danger;* for it were better they were sanctified without knowing it, than that they should die without being sealed and initiated. As for *others,* I give my opinion, that when they are three years of age or thereabouts (for then they are able to hear and answer some of the mystical words; and although they do not fully understand, they may receive impressions), they may be *sanctified, both soul and body,* by the great mystery of initiation.'

"But neither the decree of Cyprian's sixty-seven bishops, nor the opinion of Gregory himself, seem to have convinced the common people; for in the next generation—at the beginning of the fifth century—the priess and bishops wno had espoused the new practice, which they doubtless found profitable to their own purses, if not to the souls of the little water-made Christians, found it needful to meet in solemn council, and pass another decree, declaring that 'Infants ought to be baptized for the remission of sins, and that all who denied this doctrine should be accursed.'

"Previous to this, great multitudes of believers, grieved and disgusted with the corruptions and innovations which had crept into the so-called Catholic Church, had withdrawn, and formed separate societies of their own. From the arguments and the decrees which were designed to bring these *heretics* back into the bosom of Mother Church, it appears that they were, in some particulars, very much like our Baptist Churches.

"The Catholic bishop, Augustin, represents them as asking, 'What good the sacrament of Christ's baptism could do unconscious infants?'

"And to this question he replies, 'That in regard to that matter, it is piously and truly believed that the faith of those by whom the child is presented, profits

the child.' But as this reasoning did not prove sufficiently convincing, another council was called, which
decreed, 'That it was their will that whosoever denies
that little children by baptism are freed from perdition
and eternally saved, that they be accursed.' And this
decision being affirmed and sanctioned by the *Pope*, in
417, we may from that time consider infant baptism and
baptismal salvation as established doctrines of that body
which historians are accustomed to call the Church.
But the decree, with its appended curse, proved insuf-
ficient to convince the stubborn-hearted Baptists. They
refused to baptize their children, and they disowned the
baptism of the Catholics by refusing to receive them
into their communities till they had been baptized by
themselves. This the Catholics called re-baptism, or
Anabaptism; hence the name of Anabaptists, which has
been applied to us almost to the present day. For these
great crimes, the Catholics turned against them the
strong arm of the secular power. They procured a
decree of the Emperor, that not only those who re-bap-
tized, but those who received the ordinance at their
hands, should be put to death. 'By this law,' says
Gibbon, 'three hundred bishops, and several thousand
of the inferior clergy, were torn from their churches,
stripped of their ecclesiastical possessions, and banished
to the Islands.' From this day down to the present, in
every country where Ped_baptists *have had the power*,
our brethren have been the subjects of bitter and unre-
lenting persecution. We can trace them through the
pages of history by the light of the fires that consumed
them, and by the rivers of blood which they have shed
in testimony of their faith. Millions and millions of
these slaughtered saints are standing now with those
who were beheaded for the testimony of Jesus; slain
not by their pagan foes, but by their so-called **Christian**

brethren! — by people whom your writers call 'the Church,' and whose history you record as the history of the Church!!!

"When this work of death commenced, they reproached Augustin (whom historians call a *saint*) with the death of their pastors, and told him that God would require at his hand the blood of these martyrs at the day of judgment. 'Martyrs!' he replied. 'I know nothing about your martyrs. Martyrs indeed! Martyrs to the devil! There are no martyrs out of the church.' We have not time to trace their history through the coming ages, under the different names which have been given them, as Donatists, Novatianists, Cathari or Puritans, Paulicians, Henricans, Petrobrusians, Mennonites, Albigences, Waldenses, etc.; but let me suggest, if you desire to pursue the subject further, that you read Orchard's History of the Foreign Baptists, which contains in a small space an immense amount of information concerning these persecuted and afflicted disciples of Jesus."

"I do not think," said Professor Jones, "that we need to spend further time upon this point now. I confess, for my own part, I am more than convinced. I only wonder that these facts are not more generally known."

"They are public property," replied Mr. Courtney, "and have long been known to Baptists; but your Pedobaptist friends will not read them or listen to them. And when we absolutely force them upon their attention, they take it for granted there must be some mistake about it, or else they would have heard them from their own ministers. But I agree with you that we have spent time enough in our present conversation; and as there is preaching at the court house to-night suppose we adjourn to meet again to-morrow "

"I hope you will meet here," said Mrs. Jones, "for I have yet one very serious charge to offer against the Baptists."

"Permit me, madam, to inquire what it is, that I may be better prepared to meet it."

"It is your *close communion*. I am almost willing to admit that immersion is the only baptism, and that infants are not in the Scriptures required to be baptized —though even about these points there must be some mistake on your part, for our ministers are certainly as learned and as pious as yours, and yet they have always represented the facts as very different from the pictures you have drawn."

"But you forget, Mrs. Jones, that it is by the testimony of *your own historians* and *your own ministers* that I have established these facts. I have scarcely quoted a single Baptist authority. The men who say that there is no precept or example of infant baptism in the Scriptures, are among the most learned and eminent of *your own* writers. The men who say that the very meaning of the word baptize is to immerse, and that it was immersion only which was for ages practiced by the church, are such men as McKnight and Chalmers, among the most eminent of *your own Doctors of Divinity*. The men who say that it is *certain* that infant baptism was not ordained by Christ or the Apostles, and was not introduced until after the second century, are such men as Neander, Coleman, and Kitto, among the most learned and eminent of *your own ecclesiastical historians* and *Biblical critics*. Such men would not say such things unless the truth compelled them."

"That is very strange, Mr. Courtney; but I can't deny that it is true: and I may be convinced that you

are right in these things; but I am sure I never can be
reconciled to your practice of restricted communion."

"Don't be so certain of that, madam. I have no
doubt I shall be able to show you to-morrow that *you
Presbyterians are just as much restricted in your terms
of communion as we are.* The only difference between
us is on the question, What is baptism? But it is now
time to go to the meeting."

They found the house already filled, and the services
had commenced when they arrived. They had not been
there long, when those who stood near the door saw a
horseman ride up and dismount. It was Mr. Percy. My
reader will remember that, after writing that letter to
Theodosia, he had gone to another county to attend the
Circuit Court. He reached the place on Sabbath morning, just before church time, and attended the Presbyterian meeting. At any other time he would probably
have made the fatigue of his journey an excuse for
remaining at his hotel; but he was very unhappy that
morning, and hoped in church to find some remission
of the feverish anxiety which preyed upon his mind.
He could not feel satisfied that he had done right in
leaving off the investigation of the subject of baptism
himself, or in endeavoring to prevent Theodosia from
acting out her conscientious convictions of duty. He
had wished a hundred times, as he rode along, that he
had never written that unfortunate letter. Yet he
never suspected for a moment the influence it was destined to have upon his own matrimonial prospects
That Miss Ernest loved him most devotedly he was
well assured; nor did the thought ever enter his mind,
that either this or any other event was likely to break
off their engagement, or even postpone their marriage.
But when he remembered the earnestness of heart with
which she regarded every question pertaining to religion,

he felt that he must have occasioned great distress to her; and he bitterly reproached himself that he had permitted his selfishness so far to triumph over his affection.

He had at first congratulated himself that he had made to her such an appeal as she *could not* disregard, and consequently had secured the object which he had in view; but on reflection, he began to feel that he should esteem her more highly and love her more tenderly, if it should prove true that her religious principles were so strong and her sense of duty so predominant, that she would not listen even to the voice of *love* itself dissuading her from the path of right.

He began to hope that she would disregard his entreaties and do her duty. He wished he could return in time to tell her that he would not for the world put any restraint upon her conscience. He comforted himself by the thought that, if his letter had any effect, it would only be to postpone her decision until his return, when he determined to take all difficulties out of her way.

When he took his seat in the church, his heart and his mind were in another place. Could he but know what had been her decision—where she was sitting then—what she was doing! He rose when the congregation stood up to pray—he sat down when the preacher said amen, as did the others, but he heard no sentence of the prayer. They sang an old familiar hymn to an air which he had learned in childhood; he joined in the singing, but when it was done he could not have told what was the tune or the words. When the preacher announced his text, he started as from a dream, and as he repeated it: "To him who knoweth to do good and doeth it not, to him it is sin"—the Spirit at once applied it to his heart. He felt that this was precisely the case with himself. He had examined the meaning of Christ's commandment He was satisfied that he had not obeyed it. He knew that it was his duty to do what Christ commanded, but he had deliberately and willfully refused to do it; and what was worse, he had exerted all the influence which he possessed to induce Miss Ernest to do the same.

The main thoughts of the sermon were, First, that men are always inclined to find excuses for their wickedness.

Second, there is no excuse more frequently offered, or more implicitly relied upon, than ignorance.

Third, that although ignorance, when involuntary and *unavoidable*, may be plead in mitigation of one's guilt, as Jesus taught us when he said that he who knew not his master's will and did it not, should be beaten with *few* stripes—yet those who might learn their duty were *doubly* guilty. Their ignorance itself was sin; and those who knew and acknowledged their duty, and yet neglected or refused to do it, had not even the shadow of an excuse. Whatever doubt there might exist in any other case, their sinfulness was certain, and their guilt was fearful.

As the preacher dwelt upon this last thought, an expression of agony quivered in the muscles of Mr. Percy's face, and the tears started in his eyes. He rested his head on the pew before him, and covered his face to avoid the observation of those about him; and as soon as the congregation was dismissed, hastened to his room at the hotel, and passed the rest of the day in most distressful reflections on his past conduct and present condition Not this one sin alone, but hundreds of others, nay, more than he could count, came rushing back upon his memory. *A lifetime of sin*—sin against light, sin against love, sin against deep and plain convictions of duty; sins of his early boyhood, sins of his

heyday youth, sins of mature manhood, all crowded
aroun.' him and seemed to call down Heaven's vengeance
on his head. He tried to pray, like the poor publican,
God be merciful to me a *sinner*. But his prayer seemed
to be reflected back by the ceiling of the room. It had
no messenger to bear it up to the throne He felt that
he was *lost*. His sin had found him out, and he had no
Saviour His hopes were all gone. He knew not what
to do. Night came, and he sat there on the side of the
bed, without a light, feeling that the darkness of the
night was light in comparison with the darkness in his
heart.

His agony of mind was so great that he could not
think. He could only feel. He would kneel down to
pray, but he had no words to utter. He could only
groan in his spirit. He would rise up again and sit upon
the side of the bed. Thus the night wore away. At
last he threw himself upon the bed, and from mere ex-
haustion fell asleep. When he awoke in the morning,
his head was throbbing with pain, and his eyes were red
and swollen. He excused himself from breakfast, and
had a cup of coffee sent to his room. He felt that he
could not attend to the business of the court, and sent
for a lawyer of his acquaintance, made over to him a
minute of his cases, with instructions to have them postponed if possible, and if not to appear for him. He then
tried to consider what he ought to do in regard to his
own condition as a sinner before God. It was not so
much the fear of punishment that distressed him, as an
overwhelming sense of guilt! "Oh!" he exclaimed,
again and again, "what a sinner! What a sinner I
have been! What a sinner I am! Can there be
mercy for a wretch like me! God have mercy on me a
sinner"

After some hours he ordered his horse, and started

for home. He passed another night of horror on the way—excusing himself for his speedy return, by saying what was very true, "that he did not feel well."

The second day, as he rode along, he found his heart going out more frequently in prayer, not so much for *pardon* as for *deliverance* from sin. He loathed himself for his vileness, and longed to be delivered from the power of sin. And he began to think of Jesus more and more as a Saviour from *sin* rather than from *hell*, until at length he found that he was looking to Jesus to *save him* from *his* sins. "Yes," said he, "he came to save sinners—not the righteous, but sinners. And his name was called Jesus, because he saves his people *from their sins*. Will he not save me? But I am not one of his people. I am an outcast. I have betrayed him in the house of his friends. Can he, will he save *me?*" And the Spirit said, "Come unto me all ye that are weary and heavy laden, and I will give you rest. And *whosoever* cometh I will in nowise cast out." "Surely," he replied, "that includes *my* case. Blessed Jesus, save me. Save or I perish. Save, I cannot save myself. Save, I give myself into thy hands. Yes, I take thee for my Saviour. Thou wilt save me. Thou dost save me. Oh, precious, precious Saviour! Thou art indeed the Lord of my heart. Show me what thou wilt have me to do. I have nothing but sin, but thou hast all needful righteousness to plead for me. Be my intercessor. Be my Redeemer. Yes, thou wilt forgive —thou hast already pardoned. I trust my soul to thee, and I believe that thou art able and willing to keep it to the day of redemption."

His distress was gone. He had found hope—he had found peace—he had found joy. He rode on home with a glad heart. What now had become of all his lofty aspirations for worldly fame and wealth. What did he

care now for position in society, for professioral reputation, for all indeed that but three days ago enlisted
his desires. He counted them as less than vanity and
nothing. One only question now filled all his heart,
and that was "Lord, what wilt *Thou* have me to do?"
He could understand now what Theodosia had meant
when she talked so much about obedience to the Master's
will. It was with these feelings he rode into the town,
ignorant of all that had transpired since he left—knowing nothing of the effect which his letter had produced
on Theodosia; nothing of her baptism; nothing of the
meeting which was in progress. He saw the light
in the court house, and heard the singing—dismounted
and approached the door—and learned that it was a
Baptist meeting. Without further question he went in
and sat down.

The sermon was on the importance of Christians professing Christ before the world. And at its close, the
announcement was made that the church was ready to
receive applications for membership—and candidates
for admission were requested to take a designated seat
while the brethren sang a hymn. They had scarcely
commenced the second stanza when Professor Jones
and Mr. Percy came from opposite sides of the room.
Neither had been conscious that the other was in the
house. Both their hearts were full, and who will wonder that when they met they rushed into each others'
arms, and wept upon each others' necks!

Need I tell how Theodosia drew her heavy vail
down over her face, and how her heart beat audibly
while she listened for the words that should explain
this mystery?

She was not kept long in suspense, Mr. Percy was
the first to relate his experience of grace. He dated
his conversion only a few hours back. "This very day,"

said he, " for the first time I have been enabled to realize the pardon of my sins. I fancied some years ago
that I had been converted, but am now convinced that
I was self-deceived." He then began at his early conviction of sin, and related the history of his connection
with the Presbyterians—his recent examination of the
subject of baptism. Though fully convinced that immersion was the only baptism, he had felt that it would
be ruinous to his worldly prospects to change his church
connections; and he told how it was that his sin had
found him out in a distant town—what agony of mind
he had endured for the past two days, and how it
pleased God to speak peace to his soul as he was coming
home. That he had seen the light in the court house,
and learning that it was a Baptist meeting, had come in
with the determination to ask for baptism.

I need not detain the reader by any account of the
experience of grace which was related by Professor
Jones. Nor need I attempt to describe the emotions
of Theodosia, her mother, or Mrs. Jones, while this
scene was passing. I will simply say that Uncle Jones
and Mr. Percy, with some half a dozen others, were received, and Sabbath morning set as the time for their
baptism.

THE TENTH NIGHT'S STUDY,

---◦◦◦---

WHICH IS MAINLY DEVOTED

TO THE

SUBJECT OF "CLOSE COMMUNION."

N accordance with the request expressed by Mrs. Jones, as her visitors were about to leave on the previous night, our company of inquirers met at her house to hear her complaint about close communion. This subject had now assumed a new and touching interest to her. It had associated itself with her domestic affections. She felt that henceforth, in a very important sense, she must be separated from her husband; and though from the moment that she saw he had *decided* upon being baptized, she had, from courtesy and affection, refrained from any further argument *to him*—yet her heart was full of reasons, which she longed for an opportunity to pour out upon some one else, showing that, in this particular at least, the Baptists were the most bigoted, selfish, conceited, and uncharitable people that ever deserved the name of Christians. Mrs. Ernest, though she had entertained the same opinion until her daughter and her brother had become associated with the people she had formerly so much condemned, yet was now almost ready to admit that they might be right in this, as well as other things. In truth, she was like a great multitude of both sexes in all our religious bodies, who never have any opinion of their own upon any disputed point of faith or practice. She had always had full faith in the learning and the piety of her brother Jones and her pastor Johnson What *they* said was true, she never thought of doubting. They were, to her, infallible as the priest to a Catholic. What had she to do with these knotty questions? Had

23 (365)

not her pastor spent his life in studying them? and was
it not in part for this that he was paid, to do the people's thinking for them, and tell them what was the true
faith and practice of a Gospel church?

But now, when her *brother* doubted the pastor's word,
and even Theodosia had gotten the better of him in the
argument, her confidence was gone; her mind was all
unsettled; she knew not where to look for truth; she
must have time to choose anew her spiritual guide; and
in doing this, she was likely to be influenced more by
her feelings than her judgment.

Mr. Courtney found Mrs. Ernest and Theodosia waiting for him when he called to accompany them to the
Professor's residence; and even Edwin had been diligently studying his lessons, that he might gain time to
go with them and listen to the discussion. On their
arrival, they found that the Rev. Dr. McNought, the
President of the college, had called to take a friendly
cup of tea; and, at the urgent request of both the Professor and Mrs. Jones, he consented to remain and take
part in the conversation. Uncle Jones stepped out
for a moment, and Mrs. Jones introduced the subject
by saying:

"Don't you think it hard, Doctor, that my husband
has placed himself in a position that will forever prevent us from communing together at the table of the
Lord? I declare it almost breaks my heart when I
think of it."

"It does indeed seem hard, madam; but we all know
that Professor Jones has only acted in accordance with
the requirements of his conscience. I do not think that
any one who knows him can find any reason to blame
him for any thing but too great haste in making his decision. If he had taken more time, and examined the

whole subject with proper care, he must have ..... .e to different conclusions."

"No, doctor, Mr. Jones did not act hastily. This is no new subject to him. He has been laboring over it for months, and I feared how it would end. He has examined it with the most careful attention, and decided with cool and prayerful deliberation. He knows every inch of the ground over which he has passed, and can give you a reason for every change of opinion that he has made. He is not a man lightly to change his faith on any superficial investigation; and that is what so much troubles me. I know when his mind is once decided, and he has openly expressed his conviction, he is immovable as the Rock of Gibraltar. I have no hope of ever winning him back. His path and mine are henceforth separate: I am a Presbyterian, he is a Baptist. He will abandon his professorship; he will engage in the work of the ministry. I shall go and listen to his preaching; I shall be present when he administers the Supper of the Lord, and neither I nor his sister here —who loves him more than any one in the world except myself—neither of us can partake of the elements at the table where our own brother and husband is presiding. He will be bound to reject us from the company of those whom he will call the saints of God, as though we were not Christians, and never expected to commune together in heaven."

"As for me," said Mrs. Ernest, "if brother ever becomes the pastor of a church, and thinks that I ought to be baptized, I shall let him baptize me. I suspect he is as competent to judge of the meaning of the Scripture as Mr. Johnson, if he only took the same pains to study into it. But I don't see why the Baptists can't act like other Christians. We always invite them to our table— why should they not invite us to theirs? Don't we all trust in the same Saviour; and are we not all seeking the same heaven? I wonder if they expect there will be two tables up there, and they can sit down by themselves in the very presence of Jesus, and send every one who has not been under the water to another apartment? No, no! we will all commune together there, and we ought all to commune together here. I don't blame brother or Theodosia for becoming Baptists, for I know they were compelled to do it by a sense of duty; but I do blame the Baptists for being so bigoted and uncharitable, and acting as though they thought nobody was good enough for heaven but themselves; and I don't see as they are so much better than other people, after all."

"You place the matter on the right ground," replied Dr. McNought. "Every man ought to be fully persuaded in his own mind, and then ought to be at liberty to act out his own convictions of duty. We demand this for ourselves, we ought to concede it to others. If any one feels that he cannot obey Christ without being immersed, let him be immersed; but let him not say, that because *his* conscience requires immersion, that therefore *every person's* must. I profess to love the Lord Jesus, and I desire sincerely and honestly, if I know my own heart, to obey all his commandments. But while Professor Jones has become fully convinced that the Lord commanded us to be immersed after we believe, I am as fully convinced that he commanded us to be sprinkled while we were yet unconscious babes. My conscience, therefore, is satisfied; and if I should be immersed, I should commit a grievous sin, for I would be doing that in professed obedience to Christ which Christ has never commanded. Now, Baptists have no right to ask me to violate my conscience, nor (I say it with all due respect to you, Mr. Courtney) have they any right to exclude me from the table of the Lord for not doing what I regard as a sin."

"You set the subject in a very strong light," replied Mr. Courtney, "and I am glad you do so. I wish to meet this difficulty fairly and candidly. I seek no evasion, and am willing to submit our faith and our practice, in this and every other particular, to the sternest and strictest Scriptural tests. If we are wrong, no people in the world should sooner hasten to get right than we, who have no law but the Scripture, and no leader but Christ. And now, let us look at your argument. You say that a church has no Scriptural right to exclude from her communion any person who professes to love the Lord Jesus, and desires to obey all his commandments, whether he regards those commandments in the same light which the church does or not. A great many professed Christians seem to see the subject in the same light. They say it is the *Lord's* table; and because it is his, and not ours, the church in which the table is set has no right to exclude from it any who profess to love the Lord, and who desire to approach it."

"Certainly," said Mrs. Jones; "I do not see how any body of Christians could ever have felt disposed to arrogate to themselves the authority to determine who shall and who shall not approach the table of the Lord, or upon what authority they can possibly rest so presumptuous a claim."

"Doubtless, then," mildly replied Mr. Courtney, "you will think it is a great exhibition of personal self-confidence, or of Baptist assumption on my part, when I assure you that I can prove, not only to my own satisfaction, but also to yours and Dr. McNought's—

"I. That every church of Christ has the exclusive right within itself to decide who shall be participants in its communion.

"II. That all Pedobaptists, including Presbyterians, are accustomed to recognize and exercise this right, on the same general principles that Baptists do; and,

III. That *no church can refuse or neglect to exercise that right without being guilty of open rebellion against the positive requirements of the law of Christ.*"

"I don't know," replied she, "what you may be able to do about the first and the last of your three proposi tions; but I am sure you can't make me believe that Presbyterians and Methodists either believe in or prac- tice close communion like the Baptists. You and my husband have proved so many strange things from the Scriptures since he has been engaged in this investiga- tion, that I won't deny that you can prove any thing you say you can, which depends upon *them.* But the faith and practice of our church, I am sure, I know as much about as you do. And I know we have never set any such restrictions around our table, as you habitually set around yours. We have always regarded it as the Lord's table, and we constantly invite to our com- munion all who profess to love the name of Jesus."

" You almost tempt me, madam, to prove my second proposition first, and show you at once that you Presby- terians are as close in your communion as we are, and that the only difference between us is that you are more open in your baptism."

"I wish you would, and I think then I could better attend to your proof on the other points."

" Very well—since you desire it, we will take this up first, and then return to the other. If I did not mis- understand you, it is your opinion that all who profess to love the Lord Jesus should be invited to his table, and that the practice of your people is in accordance with this rule."

" Certainly; it is the Lord's table and not ours. And

we do not undertake to decide on the fitness of those who approach it. Let every one judge for himself. 'To his own master he standeth or falleth;' whoever thinks he has the love of Jesus in his heart, let him come."

"Then of course you invite the Roman Catholic, whom you regard as a follower and subject of anti Christ, the man of sin—the great enemy and persecutor of the church, of whom it was foretold that 'he should wear out the saints of the Most High.' He will assure you that although he loves, and reverences, and worships the Blessed Virgin Mother of God, he also loves her Son and the holy child Jesus. And he will assure you, moreover, that his conscience absolutely demands of him to be the very creature of the Pope, which he is known to be. If he should renounce his faith and practice, he feels that he would be guilty of a mortal sin. Of course, Doctor, you would not exclude him 'for not doing what he would regard as sin.'

"Then there is the Unitarian. He claims that he *loves* Christ and delights in his service, although he denies his divinity, and regards him only as a creature. He is sincere and honest in his faith; of course you make *him* welcome. He says he could not worship Christ without being guilty of idolatry; and no idolator hath any part in the kingdom of heaven. You surely will not reject him for not doing what he *honestly* believes would place his soul in danger of destruction.

"And near him stands a Universalist. You invite him, of course, for he says he loves Christ better than any of us, and has more reason to love him. We can only love him as the Saviour of those who believe and repent, but *he* can love him as the Saviour of all the human race; and he will assure you that he would regard it as dishonorable to God to condemn a soul to endless punishment for the few sins he might be able to commit in this life, that he would feel himself fearfully guilty should he venture in his heart to believe that he will do it. And I am sure, Doctor, you could not, according to the rule you laid down awhile ago, exclude him for not believing what, in his opinion, he could not believe without sin.

"'There are also many people in the world who come to your meetings, who have never connected themselves with any religious society, who, nevertheless, make great professions at times of their love to Jesus. They thank their God that they are so much better than many members of your church. Not only will they assure you that they love God better than you or I, but can boast they have *always* loved him, and never have done much, if any thing, for which they think he can complain of them. Upon what ground can you exclude these: since, according to your rule, it is the *Lord's* table, and every one is entitled to judge for himself of his fitness to approach it? How dare you say that each and all of these shall not come and fill your table every time the cloth is spread, mixing with yourselves as every way your equals, and showing to the world that they are in all respects equally entitled to this great and distinctive privilege of the church of Jesus Christ?"

"Oh, no, Mr. Courtney, I did not mean that. I don't want to commune with Roman Catholics, or Unitarians, or Universalists, or non-professors; and we Presbyterians never have been accustomed to invite to our table any such people. All I meant to say was, that we invite *all those whom we have reason to regard as converted men or women, and who have made an open profession of their faith in Christ.*"

"Ah, madam, that is quite a different thing from in

viting *all who profess* to love the Lord of the table. It seems then, after all, that *you*, not *they*, are to be the judge of their fitness. But will Dr. McNought agree to this new rule? He says, if I did not misunderstand him, 'No church has any right or ought to have any inclination to exclude any one from the table of the Lord who *professes* to love the Lord Jesus, and to desire to obey all his commandments, and who is *sincere* and *honest* in his conviction that his faith and practice is correct, *however widely it may differ from that of the church* whose communion he seeks.'"

"Perhaps I expressed myself a little too loosely," replied the Doctor. "I did not intend to say that the church is to have *no discretion* in the matter; but only that she has no right to exclude any whom she recognizes *as genuine and evangelical Christians.* Now, you Baptists do not pretend to doubt (at least you often say so) that Presbyterians and Methodists, and members of other evangelical churches, are just as good Christians as you are yourselves, and every way as worthy and well qualified for the the table of the Lord as you are, saving only that we have not been under the water; and as we are prevented from going under the water by our conscientious regard to what we understand to be the commandments of Christ, you have no right and ought to have no disposition to exclude us on that account."

"Never mind the Baptists just now, Doctor. We will come to them presently. We are now investigating the practice of Presbyterians, and the principles on which it rests, and we have progressed thus far. *You do not,* it seems, leave it for every one to determine for *himself* in regard to his fitness to commune. *You do not* invite all who may *think themselves* worthy and well qualified, but those only whom *you* have reason to think are con-

verted or regenerated men—and the testimony on which
you regard them as such is the fact that they are members in good standing in any of these churches which
require evidence of conversion as a prerequisite to membership."

"Precisely so, sir," replied the Doctor. "I could not
have described our practice more perfectly myself."

"But there is another thing which you Presbyte
rians require besides evidence of conversion, and which
you will no more dispense with than you will with
that."   ‑

"And what is that, pray?" asked Mrs. Jones. "You
seem to know more about us than we do ourselves."

"You shall yourself answer your own question,
madam. When one not previously a member of any
religious denomination is converted from his sins, re-
pents and believes, and gives good evidence that he has
become a new creature in Christ Jesus, do you at once,
without any further preliminaries, invite him to your
communion table?"

"Certainly we do, as soon as he has made a public
profession and united with the church. We could not,
of course, invite one who was not a *member* of any
church."

"Very good; but in what manner does he become a
member? Is he not received in the ordinance of baptism?"

"Of course—if he has not been baptized in infancy he
must be baptized. Baptism is the door of entrance into
the church, and no one can be a member who has not
been baptized."

"Perhaps, Doctor, you may be more familiar with the
practice of your denomination than Mrs. Jones. Do you
agree with her that no one is recognized as a full member till he has been baptized; or do you invite him at

once to your table as soon as you are satisfied that he is a converted man ?"

" Our rules in regard to this matter," replied the Doctor, " are clearly laid down on pages 504 and 505 of the Confession of Faith, ' ON THE ADMISSION OF PERSONS TO SEALING ORDINANCES':

" ' Children born within the pale of the visible church and dedicated to God in baptism, are under the inspection and government of the church, and are to be taught to read and repeat the Catechism, the Apostles' Creed, and the Lord's Prayer. They are to be taught to pray, to abhor sin, to fear God, and to obey the Lord Jesus Christ; and when they come to years of discretion, if they be free from scandal, appear sober and steady, and to have sufficient knowledge to discern the Lord's body, they ought to be informed that it is their duty and their privilege to come to the Lord's Supper.' ' When un baptized persons apply for admission into the church, they shall, in ordinary cases, after giving satisfaction with respect to their knowledge and piety, make a public profession of their faith in the presence of the congregation ; and thereupon be baptized.' "

"And on page 456," replied Mr. Courtney, "you will find this rule—'All baptized persons are members of the church, are under its care, and subject to its government and discipline ; and when they have arrived at years of discretion, *they are bound to perform all the duties of church members.*'

" It would seem, therefore, that although you are, according to your ' Confession of Faith,' at liberty to dispense with any public profession of faith in the case of those baptized in infancy, you are not to dispense with baptism. All the baptized, whether converted or unconverted, are, when they come to years of discretion, ' bound to perform all the duties of church members

And if the celebration of the Holy Supper is one of the duties of church members, they are bound to commune; but no one whom *you* regard as *unbaptized*, however pious he may be, can be permitted to approach your table, any more than any one whom *we* regard as unbaptized can come to ours. What then is the difference between your practice and ours? In what respect is your communion more open than ours? Simply and only in this: That you, according to page 456 of your Confession of Faith, admit the unreligious and unconverted, who have never even professed to be the subjects of regenerating grace, provided they were baptized in their infancy—while we admit none who have not made for themselves a credible profession of their repentance and faith. I will, however, do you the justice to say, that many of your churches in this country so far repudiate your own rules, as not to invite or require the baptized children to come to the table of the Lord till they have given evidence of conversion; and these bodies and ourselves, therefore, stand on precisely the same ground—that is, we each require evidence of both conversion and baptism, before we admit or invite any to our communion."

"But yet," said Mrs. Ernest, "we can't stand upon the same ground, for *we* always invite *you*, and *you* never invite *us*."

"The reason is not, madam, that we do not act upon the same principle, but that we differ in regard to *what baptism is*, and consequently as to who have been baptized. You consider all baptized who have been sprinkled in infancy. We regard those only as baptized who have been immersed on a profession of their faith. But you no more extend your invitation to commune to those whom you consider unbaptized than *we* do. Your *baptism* reaches further than ours, but your invitation to

commune *never reaches beyond your baptism.* Do you
not see, therefore, that *all* our difference of opinion is
simply about baptism, and not about communion?
Show us that the sprinkling of infants is Scriptural
baptism, and we can, and will at once extend our invitation to the communion so as to embrace you all. But
until you can show us that, you surely cannot ask us to
invite those whom *we* regard as unbaptized, while you
cannot invite those whom *you* regard as unbaptized?

"Except in case of the children of your own church
members, you require both conversion and baptism as
prerequisites to communion. And for the most part, in
this country, though not in Europe, you repudiate your
Confession so far as to require it even of them. You
refuse to commune with Universalists, and Unitarians,
and Roman Catholics, because, although you think they
have been baptized, you do not believe they have ex-
perienced the regeneration of the Gospel. You refuse
to commune with a newly converted person, though
satisfied that he is really born again, till he has publicly professed his faith, and been *baptized.* It was on
this ground that Professor Moses Stuart, one of your
ablest writers and most learned men, said that if a pious
member of the society of Quakers or Friends should so
far forsake his principles, as to desire to commune with
him at the table of the Lord, he must refuse unless he
would be first baptized.

"Precisely so it is with us. We also require evidence,
both of conversion and of baptism. We ask for neither
more nor less than you do. Are you not satisfied? or
shall we spend further time upon this point?"

"I did not," replied the Doctor, "need to be told that
Presbyterians require baptism as a prerequisite to communion. No one has ever doubted it, so far as I have

been informed. I am sure no one ever had any reason to doubt it."

"On what ground, then, do you complain of us so bitterly, since we require nothing more than you do?"

"We do not complain of you for requiring *baptism* as a necessary and invariable prerequisite to communion, but for requiring *immersion*, and thus setting up your judgment against that of the whole Christian world. You will not only have baptism, but you must have *your own baptism*—whereas, we receive that of all other denominations, including yours. How then can you say that we stand on the same ground?"

"I do *not* say that we stand on the same ground as regards *baptism*. Here I know we differ as far as a few drops sprinkled upon the forehead of an unconscious babe, differs from the plunging of a believing Christian man or woman into a liquid grave. But in regard to communion, we agree, at least, so far as this subject under discussion is concerned. That is, we both require baptism as preparatory to a Scriptural approach to the Lord's Table. This much you freely admit You admit also, that no Presbyterian Church is accustomed to invite or permit the approach of those to your communion whom *you* regard as *unbaptized*. You will admit, moreover, that you have somewhere, in what you call 'The Presbyterian Church,' the power to exclude from your communion such as you may deem unworthy. I need not, therefore, dwell any longer on this point. You cannot deny that I have fully established my second proposition, which was, as you will remember— *That Pedobaptist churches, even Presbyterians, are accustomed, as well as Baptists, to recognize and exercise the right to determine for themselves whom it is proper and expedient to admit to their communion.* And I have proved, also, that *you as well as we refuse to admit any one who has not, in your opinion, been baptized.*

"So far we are perfectly agreed; but because you consider many persons as baptized whom we regard as unbaptized, you can invite many whom we must refuse. Here, then, is the gist of the whole dispute. Now, let me ask you one question. Does not the Presbyterian Church claim and exercise the right to decide *for herself* what baptism is, according to her understanding of the Scriptures?"

"Certainly she does," replied the Doctor, "and you may find her decision, with the proof-texts on which it rests, recorded on page 146 of the Confession of Faith: 'Dipping of the person into the water is not necessary; but baptism is rightly administered by pouring or sprinkling.'"

"Why then should you or any one complain if a *Baptist* Church should feel that she had equally the right to decide for herself according to her understanding of the Scriptures, and should give her opinion and the proof-texts on which it rests? And what if she should come to the conclusion, that 'dipping the person in the water *is* necessary,' and that baptism cannot be administered at all 'by pouring,' or 'by sprinkling?' What then? Must she act as though she did not believe it? Must she submit her judgment to yours, and receive as baptism, on your recommendation, what she solemnly believes and declares is no baptism? Yet this is what you so modestly require her to do, when you deny to her the right to exclude from her communion the sprinkled and the poured-on members of Pedobaptist societies. If sprinkling and pouring are not baptism, then they have not been baptized; and if they have not been baptized, then they are not Scripturally prepared for communion."

"But how is it made so certain," asked Mrs. Ernest,

" that no one can be permitted to commune who has not been baptized? I know it is the common practice of the churches of all denominations, but I don't remember any express declaration of *Scripture* on which it rests.'

"It is not necessary, madam, to have any express *precept*, when we have a plain and unmistakable example. But in regard to this point, we have what is equiva lent to both.

" We have the often repeated command—Repent and be baptized, believe and be baptized—showing that baptism was *at once* to follow penitence and faith, without any intervening act. Then we have the unvarying example, many thousand times repeated, showing that this command was thus understood and thus literally obeyed. They believed and were baptized. Baptism instantly followed the profession of their faith, leaving no time for the observance of any other rite between; and then we read, Acts ii. 46, that after their baptism they continued 'in breaking of bread.'

" Moreover, the sacrament of the Supper is a *church ordinance*. It was ordained to be observed by *the church*, assembled together in a church capacity. And of course no one could participate in it but *church members*. And no one has ever been regarded as a church member till he had been baptized. This was the door of entrance, the initiatory rite by which one was received among and united to the people of God, and so became entitled to the privileges of the visible kingdom of Christ. Hence the Apostle, in writing to the ancient churches, frequently alluded to their baptism; always addressing them as baptized persons, who had put on Christ in baptism; who had been buried with him by baptism; who had been planted together with him by baptism; who had been in a certain sense regenerated by baptism; and who were in some sort saved by baptism. This is

so evident that no sect or denomination have ever considered the unbaptized as church members and communicants. The open communion Baptists are, so far as I
know, the first and the only Christians who have advo-
cated the giving of the communion to those whom they
regarded as unbaptized.

"That godly, learned man and excellent commentator
Dr. Doddridge, author of 'The Rise and Progress of
Religion in the Soul,' and many other excellent works,
says: 'It is certain that Christians in general have
always been spoken of as baptized persons by the most
ancient Fathers, and it is also certain, so far as our
knowledge of primitive Christianity extends, that no
unbaptized person received the Lord's Supper.'—(*Mis-
cellaneous Works*, p. 510.) Dr. Wall, the great champion of Pedobaptism, says expressly: 'No church ever
gave the communion to any persons before they were
baptized.' 'Among all the absurdities that ever were
held, none ever maintained that any persons should
partake of the communion before they were baptized.'
Lord Chancellor King, of the Church of England, in
his work on the Church, says, page 196: 'Baptism was
always precedent to the Lord's Supper, and none ever received the Eucharist till he had been baptized.' And
those who might have any doubt about this, he refers to
the testimony of Justin Martyr, who describes the practice of the primitive churches in his famous 'Apology,'
addressed to the Roman Emperor, about the year A. D
138 or 139. You will find a translation of so much of
this memorable document as refers to this subject, in
one of your own historians, Rev. Lyman Coleman's
Apostolical and Primitive Church, page 340. 'After
baptizing the believer and making him one with us, we
conduct him to the brethren, as they are called, where
they are assembled fervently to offer up their common

24

supplication for themselves, for him who has been
illuminated, and for all men everywhere, that we may
live worthy of the truth which we have learned, and be
found to have kept the commandments, so that we may
be saved with an everlasting salvation. After prayer,
we salute one another with a kiss. After this, bread and
a cup of wine and water are brought to the president,
which he takes, and offers up praise, etc.'"

"Oh, that is enough, Mr. Courtney. I did not want
to know what Justin Martyr, or Lord King, or Dr
Wall, or any body else said about it, but only what was
in the Scriptures. If I understand aright, you Bap·
tists claim that your faith and practice rests exclusively
on them."

"That is very true, Mrs. Ernest; but I thought it
might be satisfactory to you to know that the same
Scriptures which have led us to require baptism as an
essential prerequisite to communion, have been equally
able to convince all our most learned and zealous opponents, so that in whatever else we may be found to differ, we agree in this. A sect of the Baptists themselves
are, I believe, the first and only people who have ever
attempted to show from the Scriptures that the communion of the church may be shared with the unbaptized;
and they were led to this evidently from their desire to
be free from the reproach of close communion. They
could not deny that immersion was the only baptism,
and therefore they could not but regard their sprinkled
brethren as unbaptized, and they could only commune
with them by denying that baptism was an essential pre·
requisite to the Eucharist. But not even Robert Hall,
who was the leader, or at least, the ablest champion of
his sect, with all his vast learning and surpassing elo-
quence, could persuade the Pedobaptists that *they*
ought to dispense with baptism in *their* communicant

though many of them and some Baptists profess to have
been convinced that *Baptists* ought to dispense with it
in regard to those who wish to approach their table.
But the great body of the Baptist Churches still agree
with their Pedobaptist brethren in requiring baptism
before communion, and we must continue to do so till
some one can find in the Scriptures some precept or example for reversing the order so plainly established by
Christ and the Apostles, which places repentance and
faith first, then baptism, and then the breaking of bread
and the other ordinances of the church of God.

"It is as evident a any thing can be, that if any Jew
or Gentile had professed his faith in Christ in the Apostles' days, and yet had neglected or refused to put on
Christ in his holy ordinance of baptism, he would
never have been invited to the privileges of a church
member."

"Of course he would not have been," replied the
Doctor, "for there was then no room at all for doubt
about the nature or the subjects of baptism. The Apostles had the act visibly set before their eyes by Christ
himself. And the people all knew what was intended
when they were commanded to be baptized. If any one
refused or neglected to obey, it was *prima facie* evidence that he was no Christian, and consequently an
unfit subject for communion. It showed that he either
did not believe or was disobedient at heart. The early
churches, therefore, were bound to reject all who would
not be baptized. But now the case is very different.
The mode of baptism has now, in many minds, become
a matter of great uncertainty. Some think it is one
thing and some another; and some think it any one
of three things. Now, since good Christians may thus,
while they seek and intend to do right, yet fall into
the wrong, how can any church take it upon herself

to decide that one of these modes is right and all others
are wrong, and so exclude all who do not conform to
her standard? for now a failure to conform is not, as
in the Apostles' days, an evidence of an unbelieving
or a rebellious spirit, but only of a mistaken appre-
hension of duty, into which the most sincere and pious
Christian is liable to fall."

"I acknowledge, Doctor, that this argument has a
great deal of plausibility about it. It is the best that
can be offered in favor of open communion, and has
succeeded in imposing upon the minds of some eminent
Baptists. But now, if you will give me your candid
attention for a few minutes, I will show you *that it is
utterly destitute of any Scriptural foundation or logical
force.*"

"You speak very confidently, sir, and I will gladly
give you the attention you require; but if you can do
what you say, I will concede that you are a master in
logic—for I conceive it perfectly unanswerable."

"I know, Doctor, that it is the best and strongest argument which can be made for open communion; and
yet I am sure I can satisfy you that it ought not to have
the *very slightest weight* in the decision of this controversy—because it has not even the shadow of a foundation in the Word of God on which to rest. But before I
enter upon it further, I will, with your consent, go back
and take up the first general proposition which I pur-
posed to establish when we entered upon this discussion,
and that was, as you will recollect, *That every church
of Christ has the exclusive right within herself to decide
who shall be partakers of her communion.* We have
seen already in what manner your church and others are
accustomed to exercise this right. It is simply the
right to determine who shall be entitled to the privileges
of membership—a right which must of necessity belong

to every such organization in order to preserve its purity or perpetuity."

"I do not," said the Doctor, "feel disposed to dispute with you about this. If a Baptist church is a church of Christ, I am willing to grant that within certain limits it is to judge of the qualifications of its members and communicants."

"What are the 'limits,' Doctor, to which you refer?"

"The requirements of the Scriptures. She is to require only such qualifications as the Scriptures demand."

"But who is to judge of what the Scriptures demand, Doctor, the church or the applicants for her communion?"

"She must, of course, judge for herself. The Scripture is given for her guidance. She must examine for herself, and be governed by her understanding of its instructions. Those who are not of her membership can have no right to dictate to her in the matter of their own reception—that is self-evident."

"But now, Doctor, what if she should, upon a careful examination of the Scriptures, come to the conclusion, as your church has done, that no one is permitted to commune that has not been baptized?"

"Then as a matter of course she will do as we do—admit none who have not been baptized."

"But suppose she should come to the additional conclusion that sprinkling and pouring are *not* baptism, and that, contrary to the decision of your church, *dipping of the person in the water is necessary* to constitute a Scriptural baptism—what then?"

"Why, then I suppose she must admit none who have not been thus 'dipped,' for she cannot recognize any others as baptized."

"Of course she must. That is self-evident. And

now, Doctor, I trust you see the fallacy of your boasted argument for open communion; for if every church is to decide *for herself* who shall commune, subject only to the laws of Christ, and if *she* is to be the interpreter and judge of these laws, and should be led to determine that these laws demand that every communicant *shall have been immersed*, what could she do for those who had been only sprinkled or poured upon? Must she not reject them, however good and pious they might be? They may be sincere and honest—they may be intelligent and learned; but *they* are not to decide this question *for* the church. Those without cannot dictate the terms of communion to those who are within. The church must for herself examine. For herself she must decide, and upon *her own* decision she must act. What if the nature of baptism *be* the subject of doubt to many good and holy men—she as a church has nothing to do with their doubts, unless they are her own members. What if good and pious men, seeking to go right, *do* sometimes go wrong, she as a church is not to forsake what *she* thinks right, and go wrong too, merely to accommodate them. On the contrary, she is to stand firmly, like a great rock in the wilderness, a fixed and settled way-mark, which men may see afar off in their wanderings, and by it be guided back into the old paths. If others, like the mariner at sea without his chart and compass, wander to and fro, being wafted about with every wind of doctrine—she is to stand like the light-house, against whose base the winds and waves beat alike in vain, standing ever erect, and sending far across the ocean of doubts and uncertainties the calm and changeless light by which they may direct their course into the destined haven.

"Now look at your argument again. In the days of the Apostles, every one knew certainly what baptism was, and every church was bound to exclude all who had not been baptized. But now, many good and pious people have become doubtful what baptism is. Some think it one thing, and some another; and *therefore* no church of Jesus Christ ought to have any opinion about it; and every one ought to be received who thinks *himself* baptized. The church has no right to decide even as to what constitutes the very act by which men are admitted to her membership, or as to who shall be permitted to enjoy the peculiar and distinctive privileges of members. This must all be left to the good and pious, *without her ranks*, to determine for her. If *they* have doubts, she must give up her right to determine for herself, and humbly receive those who judge themselves to be worthy and well qualified, although *she* may have no doubts at all. Do you not see, that if the principle on which your argument rests be once admitted, it will destroy not only the independence, but the very organization of the churches? The principle is this—A Baptist Church has decided that certain prerequisites are needful to her membership or communion; but there are certain persons, out of her ranks, who think she ought not to require these preliminaries, and demand the privileges of church members without having complied with them. The church consents to their demand—admits them on *their* terms—abandons her own judgment, and repudiates her own rules—does she not at once lose her distinctive character, and cease to be a Baptist Church? Is she a church at all, when those without make laws for her—decide questions of faith and practice for her, and determine who shall take the place of members at her table, and by what rules she shall exercise her discipline?—for if they determine that she has no right to exclude a member for want of baptism, they can, of course, with equal reason determine that she has no right to exclude any one for any other cause.

"Look at your argument again. It takes it for granted, that because *you* and some other good and pious men doubt about the nature of the *act* of baptism, that therefore NO ONE *can arrive at any certainty* in regard to it; and therefore no church of Christ has any right to take any decisive action in regard to it. If this be true in respect to baptism, it is, of course, equally so in regard to other things; and the necessary result will be, that no church has a right, in regard to *any* subject, to hold opinions, and to *act* upon them, if good and pious people of other denominations chance to differ from them. Your argument, if it is good for any thing at all, destroys all church independence and all church sovereignty, and makes it necessary for every church of Christ to go out and ask those who are not of her membership, and have no special interest in her affairs, what she may believe, and teach, and do; and this in regard to matters which are to her of the most vital importance, involving her very existence, by determining for her who she shall admit to the privileges of membership."

"Oh, no, Mr. Courtney, I did not intend to intimate that the church had no right to deny *membership* to those who might sincerely and honestly differ from her on matters about which good men have not been able to agree. But we were speaking of only *occasional communion.*"

"The principle is the same, Doctor, whether the communion be occasional or continual. If he may commune once, why not twice? If twice, why not a dozen times—and, indeed, every time the table is spread? And if he may, of right, continually enjoy this peculiar and distinctive privilege of church membership, why not every other privilege? If we have no right to exclude you from communing with us *occasionally*, we have none to exclude you *perpetually*—and if we have no right to exclude *you*, who are not a member of our church, we could not, of course, exclude one who is a member for a similar cause. Your right to determine for a church the terms of its communion, includes the right to determine for it any other principle of faith or practice. If you may dictate who shall commune *once*, you may with equal propriety dictate who shall commune all the time. And yet, you modestly require us, because forsooth you and some other good and pious men are doubtful about the nature of baptism, to yield *our* convictions to *your* doubts, and assure us that *we have no right* to decide for ourselves upon the nature of the very act of initiation into our membership—forgetting, of course, that your own church has positively decided for herself, page 146 of the Confession, where she declares that 'dipping of the person in water is *not* necessary;' and on page 431 (chap. vii. of Directory), where she absolutely requires the minister to 'baptize the child with water, by pouring or sprinkling it on the face of the child, without adding any other ceremony.' Presbyterians can decide for *themselves* what baptism is; so can Methodists; so can Lutherans; so can Episcopalians; so can Roman Catholics; so can every body else who will decide that it is sprinkling or pouring. But if the Baptists claim the same privilege, they are counted guilty of the most unheard-of presumption, and all the Pedobaptist world desires to know by what authority they venture, like other churches, to think for themselves, investigate for themselves, and come to their own conclusions; or, if they must think, and investigate, and decide, yet you demand to know how they can dare to carry out their convictions in their practice."

"Oh, no, Mr. Courtney, we do not," said Mrs. Jones, "object to your *deciding for yourselves*. It is to the nature of your decision that we object. If you had decided, like all the rest of the Christian world, that baptism was sprinkling or pouring, or that it was of little consequence which way it was done, no one could object to your exercise of the abstract right to decide for yourselves. But we *do* think it is evidence of either bigotry or self-conceit, when you set up your opinions against the whole religious world."

"Your idea of church independence, then, is simply this: Every Baptist church has a full and perfect right to think and decide for herself on all matters of faith and practice, provided she will always think and decide just as your church does.

"But, Doctor, I have another objection to your argument, which makes me wonder how it could ever for a single moment have imposed upon any thinking Baptist —and that is, that it assumes, and takes for granted as the very basis on which it rests, *that no one now can certainly know what the act of baptism was.* In the days of the Apostles, you say, there could not be any doubt about this, and therefore all who would not be baptized, must of necessity have been excluded; but now it is so very uncertain, that good men, meaning to go right, may yet go wrong, and must not on that account be excluded. Let us look at it again in this light. The Apostles knew what baptism was, for they had *seen* the Saviour himself baptized. The early churches knew, for they had *seen* the Apostles baptize according to the pattern which Jesus showed in Jordan. But we who live in these ends of the earth, are entirely dependent for our information on the *written Word of*

God. The Holy Spirit of Inspiration attempted to convey to us in writing such an account of the organization of a church, and the ordinances of Christ's visible kingdom, that we might continue them to the end of time; but he made such bungling work of it, that it is now absolutely impossible to find out what he meant. We can neither know *who* were the persons to be initiated, nor by what act they are to be brought in.

"It is true, that he commanded people first to *believe* and then to be baptized. It is true, that he never, in a single instance, commanded any one to be baptized *who had not believed.* And that there is not in the record a *single case* in which any but a professed believer ever was baptized, nor is there a single allusion, direct or indirect, to the baptism of an unconscious babe. And yet men say, that no one now can certainly determine that he did not command, and does not now require, that little infants who cannot believe or perform any act of intelligent worship, shall be baptized, and thus made members of his churches.

"True, his people are always spoken of as a renewed and regenerated people; as a holy and peculiar people, zealous of good works. The churches of the Scriptures were addressed as active, intelligent, and pious people. And we know, from sad and frequent observation, that the baptism of an infant does not regenerate it or make it any holier than it was before. We know that baptized children do not, on account of their baptism, grow up servers of God and of his laws, yet no one now can tell that Christ did not require these unconverted children of wrath and heirs of hell, to be brought into his church and counted among its members.

"And then as regards the act of initiation, which the Scriptures call baptism, your argument takes for granted that nobody can now tell what it was. True,

the very word itself declares that it was immersion, if
we should read it as we do in any other book. No
scholar ever dreamed of its meaning to sprinkle or to
pour, in any book except the Bible, nor in any part of
the Bible but the New Testament, nor in any place in
the New Testament where it does not refer to the ordinance. Everywhere else its signification is sufficiently
plain. When Josephus, writing in the same language,
and about the same time with the Evangelists, speaks
of a youth being baptized in a lake till he was drowned,
no scholar ever doubted that the lad was *dipped*. When
he speaks of a ship being baptized in the sea, no one ever
ventured to doubt that he meant to say it was *sunk*.
No one ever doubted what Hippocrates means when he
speaks of the surgeon baptizing his probe into a wound.
No one doubts what Homer means when he speaks of
the blacksmith baptizing a huge pole axe in water to
harden the steel. Those who are engaged in teaching
our young men a knowledge of the Greek language,
never have any difficulty in deciding about the meaning
of this word in any of the poets, or philosophers, or historians of Greece. The Lexicons of the language all
agree in giving ' *to dip*,' ' *to plunge*,' as at least its primary and most common signification; and *no one of
them* gives to sprinkle or to pour—and yet you say, no
one can tell for certain that this word means *to dip*, and
not to sprinkle or to pour.

"It is true, according to the testimony of Dr. Barnes,
that this word is used in the New Testament in the
place of the Hebrew word ' *tabal*.' And Professor Stuart,
one of your own ablest scholars, expressly says, that
this word *tabal* always means ' *to dip*.' It is true that in
the fifteen places where Dr. Barnes says it occurs in the
Old Testament, it is translated ' *dip*' or ' *plunge*,' in every
place but one, and there it is ' *dyed*,' which supposed

a previous act of dipping, yet no one can know that it does not mean to sprinkle or to pour.

"It is true, that your most eminent Biblical scholars, as Stuart, Kitto, Chalmers, and McKnight, agree that it meant immerse, and state expressly that immersion was the act which was performed in the first churches; and yet you say, no one can certainly know what it was which Christ commanded, and the church must now require.

"It is true, the Holy Spirit, as if to obviate the very possibility of any misunderstanding, makes frequent and varied *allusions* to it in the Word, speaking of it as a burial, a bath, and the like. True, he has gone into particulars. so far as to explain that it was done in the 'rivers,' and places where there was 'much water:' and that they went down into the water to do it, and came up out of the water after it was done; and yet we can't know any thing about what it was.

"True, the history of the early churches, written by the sprinklers themselves, as the Magdeburg Centuriators, Mosheim and Neander, clearly shows that, in the language of the *London Quarterly*, devoted to the interests of the Church of England, 'There can be no question that the original form of baptism—the very meaning of the word—was complete immersion, and that for at least four centuries any other form was either unknown or regarded as an exceptional, almost a monstrous case.'

"True, we can show from ancient rituals and church canons, that for more than thirteen hundred years it was the only act recognized as baptism, except in cases of alarming sickness.

"True, we have the most unexceptionable records, made by the sprinklers themselves, showing the very time and manner of the change from immersion to sprinkling, and the very decree of the Pope, on whose authority it was done; and yet you take for granted that no Baptist Church now can tell for certain which it was that Christ commanded. And on this ground you demand as a right that she shall give to those who have submitted to the Pope's ordinance of sprinkling, under the false impression that it was baptism, the same church privileges that she offers to those who have entered into Christ's visible kingdom through the door which he appointed.

"If *you* have any doubts about the nature of baptism or the subjects of baptism, you may plead them for what they are worth before his bar to whom we all must give account; but you must not expect Baptist Churches to participate in them, or to act as though it were to them a matter about which there was even the slightest uncertainty. If there are any two things which they are satisfied are clearly and definitely set forth in the Word of God, they are, that believers are the only persons commanded to be baptized, and that those commanded to be baptized are commanded to be immersed. They have therefore not even the shadow of a doubt that you are unbaptized, and if baptism is a Scriptural prerequisite, as you yourselves believe and teach, then yo. are not prepared and cannot claim communion at their hands, unless you undertake to decide for them whom they shall consider as baptized."

"Oh, we are willing to acknowledge," replied Mrs Jones, "that we cannot demand it as a matter of *right*. But the *courtesy*, Mr. Courtney. What we may not demand as a right, we surely may claim on the ground of Christian courtesy and kindness—I had almost said upon the ground of common politeness. And now I ask you seriously to say if you do not think that you Baptists are selfish and discourteous, to say the least in your refusal to invite any but immersed believers to sit down with you? You admit that others are just as good Christians as yourselves, do you not?"

"Certainly; we do not refuse because you are not pious, but because *you have not been baptized.* And you as well as we believe that the Master does not permit *all Christians,* but only all Christians who are members of a visible church, and who have been baptized. You never invite a person to your communion merely because you consider him a converted man and a good Christian. You wait till he has joined the church, and been baptized."

"But we think," said Mrs. Jones, "that we have been baptized. You will grant that we are as sincere and honest in our opinions as you are in yours. The great majority of the Christian world think *our* opinion better founded than yours: would it not, therefore, be proper and becoming in you to show so much respect to the decision of more than half of Christendom, and so much Christian liberality to those who conscientiously differ from you, as to extend your invitation to them, not of right, but purely out of courtesy and politeness?"

"That can never be properly called Christian courtesy, madam, which asks for the sacrifice of Christian principle—and I am quite as willing to meet the demands of open communion on this ground as on the other. But before we enter into the argument, I would like to go back and call up the third proposition, which I stated at the beginning of this discussion, and that is—*That no church can either neglect or refuse to exercise the right which has been given her by her Head, to preserve the purity of her communion, without being guilty of open rebellion against the positive requirements of the law of Christ.*

"We have already seen that every church possesses this right, and it is plain that the *duty* to exercise it follows from its possession. *Somebody* must decide who shall be communicants; if not, there is no bar between the church and the world. If every one who chooses may not come, who shall decide who may? We answer, the church herself."

"By what rule?"

"By the law of Christ, as laid down in his word."

"May she not neglect or refuse to decide for herself, and leave it to those without to come or not to come, as *they* may think best?"

"No; for God has constituted *her* the guardian of his ordinances, which he has placed within her gates."

"But may she not reverse his order, and give communion first, and then baptism?"

"No; she must, of course, be governed by *his law*."

"May she not dispense with baptism altogether?"

"Certainly not, if *his law* requires it."

"May she not treat all those as baptized who *think themselves* baptized?"

"No; she is to be governed by *his Word as she understands it*, and not as it may be understood by *those without her ranks*. She is to examine and decide for herself. She is to recognize and treat as baptized those only whom she believes to have actually been baptized according to the Scripture model. She is not the law giver, but simply the executor of the laws of Christ. She is not at liberty to set them aside for any whims of her own. Nor is she at liberty to enforce one part and not another. If, therefore, *he requires* baptism as a prerequisite to communion, she *dare* not in any case refuse or neglect to do so also. She *must* see his rules carried out, or she becomes unfaithful to her trust, and a rebel to her Lord.

" **If** you have any doubt that each church *is* constituted thus by Christ the guardian of her own purity,
and of the sanctity of his ordinances as administered
within her doors, I refer you to Romans xiv. 5, and
2 Thess. iii. 6, in which the power of the church to de
termine whom they will receive, and the duty of the
church to withdraw from every one who walked disorderly, is distinctly recognized.   But both the right
and the imperious obligation for its constant, faithful,
and impartial exercise, follows of necessity from the
simple fact, that if the church does not herself exclude
the unprepared and the unworthy, there is no one to do
it and it cannot be done at all.

" I am now ready to answer your question about the
Christian courtesy of refusing to invite the unbaptized
to our communion.   Permit me to put it in proper form
for you, and let us see how it will sound.   We will suppose it to be communion day at the Baptist church, and
that your church in a body comes to our door, and asks
admission to our table—not as a matter of right, but on
the ground of Christian courtesy.   You say to us, very
affectionately and kindly—Dear brethren in Christ, we
are fully persuaded that no unbaptized person, according to the laws of our Redeemer, should ever be permitted to approach his table.   *We* never permit any to
come to it in *our* church whom *we* do not believe to have
been baptized.   We could not do it without sinning
against God.   We know very well, brethren, that *you
act upon the same rule.*   You agree with us that it would
be very wrong and sinful to permit any to approach
your table whom *you* do not think have been baptized.
We know, also, that you believe that we have *not* been
baptized, and consequently that you *cannot permit us to
approach without doing what you would regard as an ac.
of open and deliberate rebellion against the laws of Christ.*
25

But we regard you all as Christian gentlemen and ladies, and quite familiar with the laws of *politeness* and Christian *courtesy*, and it must be very evident to you that *these* laws require you to invite us to your communion. You surely will not be so *impolite* as to refuse us."

"Oh, Mr. Courtney, that is too bad! Surely you have no right to look upon us in such a light as that!"

"I am well aware, madam, that your people have not been accustomed to see in this light your claims that we should invite you to our communion. You are so accustomed to think *of yourselves as baptized*, that you cannot fully realize the fact that others should think differently. But thus the case must always appear to the mind of any well informed Baptist. Nor is this by any means the worst of it.

"It is always and everywhere considered an act of great discourtesy to ask one to do any thing which it is well known he will regard as a moral wrong, though it should be asked of him only as a private individual, and in his personal capacity. But the discourtesy is much greater when you ask him, as a public man, in his official capacity, and in direct and open opposition to his *avowed* and *publicly acknowledged* sentiments, to do what not only *you* know he would consider wrong, but what *all the world knows*, or might know, he would so regard; what he has again and again *publicly declared* that he *could not do* without a grievous disregard of his conscientious convictions of right. To ask, for instance, of a Son of Temperance, whom you *know* is pledged not to drink intoxicating liquors; whom you *know* feels that he is under peculiar and solemn obligations not to drink; yet to ask him not merely to disregard the obligation, which *you* know, and which the *world* knows, that he recognizes as binding upon his conscience; but to ask him to do it *publicly and officially as a Son of*

Tempera ice, in the Division room, would be something such an act of discourtesy, though much less flagrant than it is to ask a Baptist, as a Baptist, in his public capacity as a church member, to disregard his obligations to his Saviour, by which the purity of the church and the sanctity of the ordinances are to be preserved."

"Oh, dear, no! Please, Mr. Courtney, don't think so hardly of us. I am sure none of our ministers or members ever intended any thing of the sort when they invited you to our communion, or complained that you did not invite us to yours. We never thought about its being a matter of *conscience* with you."

"And why should you not have thought of it, when we have preached it in the pulpit, and proclaimed it through the press, and repeated it continually in private conversation? No one *need* be ignorant of the ground on which Baptists stand in regard to this question. Their sentiments have been long and plainly before the world. There is no one who has any occasion to complain of them, who does not know, or might not know, that *they cannot dispense with what they conscientiously regard* as Christian baptism; and that on *this* account, and not from any impoliteness or discourtesy, they are debarred from inter-communion with sprinkled Christians.

"But I have not done with this question of courtesy I want our Pedobaptist friends to see precisely where they stand. After you have asked us to disregard the most sacred obligations, to repudiate our conscientious convictions of duty, and as a church, in our assembled and official capacity, to refuse obedience to what you well know we all regard as the imperative law of Christ, and to perform an act which you well know we earnestly believe he has forbidden; when we respectfully decline to do it, and kindly give you our reasons, you set up a

great and senseless cry of bigotry, of selfishness, of ignorance, and (will you pardon me for saying it?) OF
CHRISTIAN DISCOURTESY; as though it were
more discourteous for us firmly to resist all your solicita-
tions to disregard our Master's Word, than it is for you,
who profess like us to love him, to ask us to do it, or
complain of us for not doing it."

"But we do not ask you to do what *we* think wrong."

"No, you only ask us to do what *you know* WE *think
wrong*, and then abuse us because we dare not do it.
But let it pass.   I should think, Doctor, you would find
some serious, if not insuperable difficulties in your plan
of inter-communion with other denominations, over
whose discipline you have no control."

"How so?"

"Let me explain   The peculiar and distinctive privilege of a church member in good standing in your church,
is the liberty of approach to the Lord's table.   When
you exclude the unworthy, they can no longer be permitted to sit down with you at this sacred feast.   Now
suppose you exclude a member to-day for heresy in doctrine, or irregularity in practice, and he goes to-morrow
and unites with some other denomination, can he not,
according to your principles, come right back, and
claim a seat at your table as the member of another denomination, although you have just driven him away
as a member of your own?"

"That might possibly happen; but I do not think we
have ever been much troubled with cases of that sort."

"That is because your open communion is held in
theory, but seldom reduced to practice.   If there were,
in fact, that inter-communion between you and Baptists,
which many of you profess so much to desire, I can
conceive that it might happen very often, to the utter
destruction of any effective discipline in both bodies

Let us see. You require of all your communicants who have children, that they bring them to the church for baptism, do you not?"

"Certainly; it is the solemn duty of every Christian parent to dedicate his offspring to God in this holy ordinance at his earliest convenience."

"Very good. Now suppose some one of them should take a fancy to ask you for the *text* on which this requirement is based. You might, as you very well know, search all the New Testament, from Matthew to Revelation, and you could not produce a solitary precept or example. You would try to satisfy him with a wordy jargon about the covenant of circumcision, etc. But he might reply, Jewish children were *circumcised* at eight days old, because God commanded it to be done. If Christian children are to be *baptized*, you can show where he commanded that "

"You will say—No, but a command was not necessary; they were to be baptized as a matter of course.

"Very well, then. Of course it *was done*, and you can show me at least *one case* among the thousands of ' both men and women,' in which there was *one* little child But you can't find it. And he begins to doubt the propriety of performing as an ordinance of Christ, what Christ did not command. He cannot be persuaded to bring up the little ones into the church. You exhort him and reason with him in vain; and you are obliged at last to exclude him. I have read of such a case. You exclude him, and he comes to us, and we receive him. Now he holds the same opinions, and is guilty of the same practices. But though you could not commune with him as a member of *your own church*, because he was guilty of the *heinous sin* of denying infant baptism, you will *welcome* him back the very next Sabbath as a Baptist. You urge him to sit down to the same table

from which you have just now formally expelled him
And I suppose, if he should decline to accept, you would
henceforth abuse him as a narrow-minded, selfish, bigoted,
and intolerant Baptist, who thought himself too good to
commune with other Christians.

"The same thing might happen to us, and this
furnishes an additional reason *why we cannot* commune
with other denominations. I have said we could not,
because you were in our view *unbaptized ;* and that is
of itself an unanswerable and all-sufficient reason, if
there were no other. But there is another growing out
of this matter of church discipline. Let us suppose a
case for illustration. A minister in our church has imbibed the idea that the sprinkling ceremony, which you
borrowed from the Roman Catholics, is valid baptism,
and insists upon introducing it into our churches. We
would regard it as a great wrong. We would, for the
peace and purity of our communion, at once expel him,
and deny him the privileges of the church. He goes to
you, and you receive him gladly, and the very next day
he comes back and claims, as a member of *your*
church, privileges which we had just now formally
denied him as a member of *our own.* Do you not see
that this rule, carried out in actual practice, must necessarily destroy the force of all attempts at church discipline ?"

"But how do Baptists now avoid that difficulty
among themselves ?"

"Very easily and simply. The right to our communion never extends beyond the reach of our discipline."

"Then how can members of one Baptist Church
claim a seat at the table of another ; for, if I understand
your church polity, every one of your churches is an
independent body."

"They *cannot* claim it as a *right*, and our invitation

to commune is extended by courtesy only to those whose faith and practice is so like our own, that no person could be a member in good standing with them who would not stand equally well with us.

"The rule adopted by Mr. Wesley (Discipline, sec. 5th), and which is founded alike in Scriptural principles and common sense, is the same in substance as that which regulates our practice. That is, ' no person shall be admitted to the Lord's Supper among us, who is guilty of any practice for which we would exclude a member of our church.' This rule you see at once compels us to deny all who teach and practice sprinkling for baptism, and all who engage in what we regard as the sinful though solemn mockery of baptizing unconscious infants, or any others who have not made a personal and credible profession of repentance and faith, according to the plain requirements of the Word of God, which *always and everywhere* puts repentance and faith before baptism, as it puts baptism before communion. We are bound to this course by that solemn and most impressive injunction of the Apostles, 2 Thess. iii. 6—' Now we command you, brethren, in the name of our Lord Jesus Christ, that you withdraw yourselves from every brother that walketh disorderly, and *not after the tradition which ye received from us.*' "

" I declare, Mr. Courtney," said Mrs. Jones, " I had no idea that you Baptists had so good and satisfactory reasons for your singular exclusiveness ; and I promise you now that I will never complain of you again. In fact, if I ever become a Baptist, I shall be a close communion Baptist."

" I do not see," said Mrs. Ernest, " how any one can take the Scripture for his guide, and be any thing else ; and I have been thinking all the time that there must be some good Bible reason for it. or else Theodosia and

her uncle would not have agreed to it—but now, when I
come to think of it, I have not heard either of them say
a word on the subject."

The reader will recollect, that at the beginning of this
conversation Professor Jones had gone out of the room,
for some cause at that time unexplained. He returned
after a few minutes, but took no part in the conversa
tion, in which indeed he seemed to feel but very little
interest. Mrs. Jones had quickly noticed his abstracted
manner, so different from his ordinary behaviour; and
had several times cast an uneasy glance into his face,
hoping to read there the cause. But she could only
learn that it was in some way connected with Theodosia,
whom he loved with the affection of a father. Each
time she looked, his eye was resting with an expression
of the deepest pity upon his lovely niece, who took no
more part in the conversation than himself. In truth she
had spoken very little to any one since the appearance
of Mr. Percy at the court-house on the preceding night.
His relation of his experience of grace, and his declaration of his desire to be baptized, had placed him in a
new relation to her. She did not know that he had then
never seen her letter—and once (but only for a moment)
the thought intruded into her heart that all this change
had been made for *her* sake, and not for Christ's. She
repelled it, however, in the instant that it came, and all
day long had held herself ready to welcome him back
to his place in her heart as her betrothed, and felt that
she could love him now with an affection even deeper
and more intense, higher and purer and holier than that
which with such agony of effort she had been trying to
strangle in her heart. She thought he would have come
and spoken to her before she left the meeting, but he
did not seem to notice her presence there. She was sure
he would call in the morning—but dinner was on the

table, and he had not come. That letter of hers must have prevented; but surely there was not in it any harsh expression, any single word of unkindness. Did not her heart *ache* with the very intensity of her *love*, while she was writing it? And now she tried to recall it, sentence by sentence, and word by word, to see if there was any thing there which she should not have said.

The afternoon wore slowly away. She sat at the window where she could see the door of his office, but it was never opened. She listened to every foot fall on the pavement, but she heard not his familiar step. Once the latch of the front door was moved, and she sprang from her seat, and felt the blood crimson all her face and neck; but she sat down in a moment, for she knew it was her brother Edwin. Mr. Courtney called after supper. Mr. Percy had not come yet; but she hoped to meet him at her uncle's. He was not there—and her spirit retired within itself; and she sat as mute, and almost as unconscious of what was passing around her, as a marble statue.

When Uncle Jones went out, it was to see Dr. Woodruff, a cousin of Mr. Percy, who was also his most devoted friend and confidant. He was to have officiated as the bridegroom's friend on the expected wedding-day. and had just returned from Mr. Percy's mother's, where he had spent the day with one whose earthly career seemed likely soon to close. He had come in to break the melancholy tidings as best he could to Theodosia.

The facts, as he related them to Professor Jones, were briefly these: The servant who waited on Mr. Percy's office had gone there in the morning, and had found the young man lying upon his face on the floor, with Theodosia's letter in his hand. When the servant entered he seemed to be asleep He aroused him, and raised him up; but his looks were so wild, and his face was so pale, and his words (rather muttered than spoken) so strange and unnatural, that he placed him on the bed and ran for his cousin, the doctor.

When Doctor Woodruff came, and read the letter, he understood how it had been. Mr. Percy, from the time he wrote and sent that distressing letter to Theodosia, in the previous week, had been in a state of most intense mental excitement. Much of the time he had been suffering extreme agony of mind. His physical powers had become greatly exhausted, and his nervous system debilitated and excitable. He had gone from the meeting in the court-house (where he had so unexpectedly had an opportunity to ask for Christian baptism) to his office. There he found Theodosia's letter. He had never till then conceived that his letter would have occasioned such distress to her, or that it would have led her to such a determination. Yet if he had been entirely self-collected, and his mind had not been already exhausted by long continued over-excitement, the shock which the reading of her reply now gave him, would have been speedily followed by calmer thoughts, and an instant determination to see her at once, confess his fault, ask her forgiveness, and set himself right in her heart. But exhausted in body and excited in mind as he was, the revulsion of feeling was too great to be endured. He read on till he came to where she said, "When you return, I pray you to consider me but as one dead. It will be better for us both." The paper seemed to grow black before his eyes. The room was suddenly darkened. He felt a strange, dreamy calmness creep over his brain. He sunk down out of his chair in a deep swoon, or fainting fit, upon the floor. He became conscious after a time, but had not strength to rise, and subsided again into a strange, unquiet sleep, mixed with half-waking dreams, in which he saw a beauteous form, more like an angel than a being of the earth, who came and raised him up, and looked into his eyes so sadly, so reproachfully, and yet so tenderly, that he struggled to tell her how his heart bled at the remembrance of the act which caused her so much sorrow—but he could not speak. He strove to raise his hand and make some sign to assure her that he loved her better for her firm adherence to the truth, but the muscles would not obey the will. He could not move—he could not speak—and she was gone. Oh, how deep and how long was the darkness of that night! She was gone! He felt that she was lost to him forever. The very light of his life was darkness now—and yet he waited and watched for her return. Could she leave him thus? Would she not love him still? Hark! he hears her footstep. The door opens. Some one touches him. He starts from his slumber to greet her with some word of love, but he sees only his servant, who is trying to remove him from the floor to the bed. He stares at him with the strange gaze of incipient madness, and bids him leave him to rest in peace. The doctor saw at once that a long and fearful brain fever was the best that he could hope for; and while his strength was yet comparatively undiminished, resolved to remove him to his mother's house, some two miles in the country. This done, he prepared such remedies as his medical skill suggested, sat down, and watched beside his bed till he was satisfied that there was no immediate danger; and then, at his mother's request, came in to explain to Theodosia the reason why he had not called on her. He had thought best to explain, as we have seen, to Uncle Jones, and leave him to make it known to his niece.

The Professor had been so much occupied with this matter, that he scarcely heard the discussion which was

going on in his presence. He was glad when a pause in
the conversation showed that the parties engaged had,
for the present, at least, exhausted their ammunition,
and were prepared for a temporary truce, if not for a
permanent peace. He turned their attention to some
other subject, and in a few minutes the Reverend Doctor
took his leave.

Uncle Jones walked home with Theodosia. They
walked slowly ; and when Mrs. Ernest and Mr. Courtney had gotten some way before them, he broke the
silence by reminding her that she had not spoken a word
all through the evening ; "and," said he, " I will tell you
why. You were distressed that Mr. Percy had not
called to see you since his return, and wondering what
could be the cause. Will it relieve your mind to tell
you that he is sick ?"

" I will not deny to you, uncle, that such was the
subject of my thoughts. I hope he is not seriously
unwell."

" The doctor does not think him in any immediate
danger, but fears it will be long before he can resume
his business."

" Why, uncle, what can be the matter ? I am sure I
never saw him look better than he did last night. Did
you not notice the brightness of his eye, and the fresh-
ness of his cheek, and how rich and mellow was his
voice while he was telling what God so wonderfully had
done for his soul ?"

" I was myself too much engaged to observe him
closely, but I can well imagine that the unnatural flush-
ing of his cheek, and the unusual brilliancy of his eye,
were but the tokens of that intense mental excitement
which preceded, if it did not produce, the fever from
which he is suffering now."

They had reached the cottage door. Uncle Jones

th ought best not to go into any further particulars, and returned to his home.

That night, if one had passed by the window of Theodosia's room, he might have heard many a sob, mingled with half-uttered prayers. Had she known *all* the truth, h·r sobs might have been louder; but her prayers could hardly have been more earnest.

The messenger who went next day to inquire, returned to say that Mr. Percy was no better; and so it was the next day—and the next. Doctor Woodruff had called in a brother practitioner, but did not reveal to him, nor even to Mr. Percy's mother, the whole secret of his attack. The letter which he found in his hand, he had considerately laid aside, to be returned to him should he recover. Its existence was a professional secret. He attributed his illness to the long and tiresome journey on horseback through the sun, and to such excitement of mind as he had himself publicly described before his strange attack.

On Saturday evening Mrs. Ernest received a line from Mrs. Percy, saying that her son was growing daily worse and worse; and, strange to tell, he had in his delirium conceived a singular fancy that Theodosia had ceased to love him, and had even formally discarded him. This idea, she said, was uppermost in all the wanderings of his mind, and evidently was exerting a great influence upon the progress of his disease; and Doctor Woodruff had suggested that if Theodosia could herself assure him of her continued affection, it might have a soothing, and perhaps a healing influence.

Mrs. Ernest handed the note to her daughter, with the remark, that in consideration of their well-known betrothal, there could be no impropriety in granting Mrs. Percy's request.

" We will go to him a once, dear mother," said Theo

dosia, when she had read the note, with eyes full of tears
" Even a brief delay may be of fatal consequence."

When they reached Mrs. Percy's house, he had fallen
into an unquiet slumber, from which they did not seek
to awaken him. They sat down in the room, and con-
versed in a low tone about the nature of his disease,
and other matters which the circumstances suggested.
Theodosia took but little part in this conversation, except as a most eager listener. She sat down near the head
of the low couch on which he lay, but presently arose, and,
under pretence of shading the patient's eyes, adjusted
the candle so that it should not shine upon her own.
Oh, who can tell the thoughts that then were thronging
in her maiden heart! How changed he was! How
pale—how corpse-like was his cheek! How wasted was
the thin, emaciated hand, which lay outside the cover!
How parched and feverish the lips! How sunken the
eyes! How would they look when he should open them?
Would he know her? Would he speak to her? What
if he *now* should open his eyes and see me here?—and
she almost unconsciously moved her chair back out of
his range of vision as she thought of it. His lips moved:
she reached the spoon in the tumbler of water upon the
little table, and moistened them. He opened his eyes
wide; he looked her steadily in the face; he glanced at
her white dress; he looked in her face again. She
fancied that the expression of wonder on his face gave
place to a scarcely perceptible smile. But he did not
speak; he did not make any sign of recognition. She
sat down again and wept.

" You must need rest, Mrs. Percy. You may go and
sleep, and leave the care of him to us to-night," said
Mrs. Ernest. " We will watch him as tenderly as you
could do yourself."

Mrs. Percy laid down, and Theodosia withdrew to some

Theodosia Ernest.   PAGE 411.

distance from the couch, and sat where she could see every change that passed upon his face. The love which she had for a time endeavored to eradicate from out her mind, had only, like the lofty oak when torn and wrenched by the mighty storm, extended its roots more widely and deeply, and clasped them more firmly round her heart; and now, when the cause which led her to cast it off had been removed, she clung more ardently and devotedly than ever to the hope that he would yet be hers. Again and again during that long night, when she hastened to do some little act of kindness, did he open his eyes and look at her with a kind of wondering tenderness in his gaze ; but yet he did not speak, nor was she sure that he recognized her at all.

He slept more quietly that night than he had yet done, and when the doctor came next day, he whispered in his ear that a beautiful vision had come to him in his dreams and looked at him so lovingly, that he was ready to speak, and ask it whence it came, but feared his voice might break the charm, and it would vanish from his sight.

"You must stay with us, my child," said Mrs. Percy, "till my son gets better. He talked of you continually until you came, but now it seems as though your very presence in the house exerts a sort of magic influence over him, for he is quiet, and does not so much as lisp your name. The doctor says if you could but become his nurse, he may yet recover. Will you not, my daughter ?"

"If my mother thinks there would be no impropriety in my doing so."

"Certainly, Theodosia, I think you ought to return and assist Mrs. Percy in every way you can. But your uncle and I are going to be baptized to-day, and you will not be willing to be absent from the meeting."

This conversation took place in the hall, from which there was an open door leading to the patient's room. He heard Theodosia's voice; he thought he heard her name. He made some sound, which recalled his mother to his side, and looking in her face with a more natural expression than he had since his attack, he said:

"Mother, I thought I saw her spirit here last night, and just now I am sure I heard her voice, and thought that some one called her name. Tell me if she is here."

"Would you like to see her, my son?"

"Oh, yes; I want to ask her to forgive me before I die."

"You do not think you are going to die, my child!"

"I have strange feelings, mother. I do not know what death is, or how he comes; but I am sure I have been very near the world of spirits."

"Do you feel any alarm at the prospect of death?"

"My mind is very weak, mother. I scarcely feel or think at all. I have a blessed Saviour: I remember that; and I will trust him, even though I die. But tell me—did I hear her voice, or was it but a dream?"

"Try to compose yourself, my child. The doctor says that you must sleep awhile this morning. If you wish to see Miss Ernest, I will send for her."

"Do you think she would come?"

"I know she would. So make yourself easy, and you shall see her when you wake."

On returning to her visitors, Mrs. Percy related this conversation, and insisted that Theodosia must remain to be there when he awoke; and as the young lady did not object, Mrs. Ernest went home without her. She laid down on her arrival, and took a short nap, and then taking Edwin by the hand, joined Uncle and Aunt Jones on their way to the Baptist meeting.

When the usual invitation was given to those who desired membership with the church to come forward and make their profession, Uncle Jones was surprised and delighted to see both his wife and his sister go up and ask admittance into the church of God. Neither of them had said a word to him upon the subject, for though both had yielded to their convictions of the truth, that immersion is the only baptism, some days before, and both had been convinced that believers are the only Scriptural subjects of baptism, they could neither of them overcome their repulsion to the practice of close communion, or consent to sever their connections with those to whom they had such strong attachments, until the explanations of Mr. Courtney in their last conversation put it beyond the shadow of a doubt that the Lord Jesus not only commanded believers, and them only, to be immersed, but that he had also forbidden all who had not believed and been immersed to approach his table, and required of those who had in this way become, according to his order, the members of his church, that they should carefully guard the purity and the perpetuity of his ordinances, by permitting no one to partake with them in the peculiar privileges of church members who had not, like themselves, been made members according to the same Gospel order. This difficulty removed, they were now ready to be baptized.

We need not detain you any longer, gentle reader, by describing to you the baptism of these three, who, with several others, followed the example of their Saviour, by going down into the water, and were buried with him in the liquid grave. Nor can we now continue the history in which you have come, we trust, to feel so great an in-

26

terest that you would gladly see the end. We have
finished our ten nights' study of Scripture baptism. We
have examined it in regard to its mode, its subjects, and
its results. We have endeavored to do it plainly and
candidly, but if we know our own hearts, we have tried
to do it kindly—and in the spirit of that "charity"
which "rejoices in the truth."

We are grieved to leave our darling Theodosia in
such distress. But she must remain a little while in the
valley of tears, until, by her own sorrows, she has been
taught how to sympathize with the sorrowful. He was
the wisest man of earth who said, "By the sadness of
the countenance the heart is made better." She needs
the discipline of grief to fit her for the life of eminent
usefulness which lies before her—and the history of
which will soon be given in another volume.

A DREAM,

IN

REVIEW OF N. L. RICE'S

NOTICE OF THE

THEODOSIA ERNEST

.

FIRST SERIES,

BY THE AUTHOR OF THEODOSIA.

PREFACE.

THE only attempted review or extended unfavorable notice of the first volume of Theodosia Ernest, appeared in the St. Louis Presbyterian, from the pen of its Editor, N. L. Rice, D.D. That notice is here given, and a review of Mr. R.'s singular statements reviewed in a dream—and also the natural effect of such a treatment of the best arguments ever produced by Presbyterians or Pedobaptists—the conversion of Pastor Johnson. We regard this review, in connection with Mr. Rice's notice, as the most powerful argument in favor of Baptist positions.

J. R. GRAVES.

Nashville, 1857.

NOTICE OF THEODOSIA.

BY N. L. RICE.

AS IT APPEARED IN THE ST. LOUIS PRESBYTERIAN.

F perseverance and ingenuity were evidences of religious truth, there could no longer be a doubt that *immersion* is the only valid baptism. Long and earnestly have the advocates of this doctrine labored to sustain its claims. The pulpit, the newspaper, the tract, the book, learned argument, and assertion, and ridicule, have all been laid under requisition. Then the whole Bible must be translated anew to make it sustain the Baptist sense. And now we have before us, by the kindness of a friend, a *Baptist novel*, the title of which is "*Theodosia Ernest, or the Heroine of Faith.*" The author has modestly concealed his name, but the work is published by Graves, Marks & Ruthland, Nashville, Tennessee. The book is really instructive and amusing. We purpose briefly to notice a few of its peculiarities.

It displays throughout a consciousness of the weakness of the doctrine it is intended to advocate. 1st. The title betrays this consciousness—"The Heroine of Faith." There is in every Christian's heart a strong sympathy with the struggles and conflicts of a genuine faith, rising above the allurements and persecutions of a wicked world. The author has thought it necessary to take advantage of this noble sympathy. If he had adopted the more truthful title—"*The Heroine of Immersion*"—the book would have fallen still-born from

(419)

the press. There is little that is either noble or roman
tic in the zeal of a professing Christian, young or old
for a narrow sectarian dogma. The author judged,
merely, that the cause of immersion needs the advantage of a title far nobler than itself.

The same conscious weakness shows itself in the choice
of a *heroine* instead of a *hero*, and of a heroine who is
a highly cultivated, sensitive young lady of eighteen.
Who can help strongly sympathizing with such a young
lady, devotedly pious, evidently conscientious, willing
to sacrifice every thing for the truth, conducting an
argument against two or three men much older than
herself? We forget the cause and sympathize with the
girl. We put double weight to her arguments, and feel
gratified at the perplexities into which her antagonists
are thrown. The author of the novel judged rightly
that the cause of immersion and anti-pedobaptism
claims all this sympathy and more. If he had been a
hero, instead of a youthful heroine, his hearers would
have weighed his arguments, instead of being carried
away with sympathy.

The cause needed even stronger sympathy; and,
therefore, Miss Theodosia Ernest is brought in conflict
with the man to whom she was engaged to be married—
a cold-hearted, formal Presbyterian lover—whom she
loves most devotedly. He opposes her joining " the
contemptible sect of Baptists"—(we naturally sympathize with a person opposed). She, poor girl, is thrown
into a paroxysm of grief, sighs, weeps, and prays, and
resolves to break off the engagement, just for the pure
love of immersion! The reader feels his eyes filling with
tears of sympathy for the dear distressed creature who
had also her mother in opposition, and is almost ready
to be immersed himself just to comfort her. Who
would have thought that a Baptist knew so well how

much it was necessary to excite the sympathies of his readers to prevent them seeing the flimsiness of his arguments?

The necessities of immersion were even greater. Although Miss Theodosia is singularly furnished with Baptist arguments, for one who has just reason to doubt the validity of her baptism, Professor Courtney, an accomplished scholar, is called to aid her. He, having been a Presbyterian, and having examined the whole subject, is perfectly at home in the discussion. He understands Greek, and he can read all the learned authors on the subject. On the other side we have, first, Mr. Percy, the gentleman engaged to Miss Theodosia, who is represented as wholly ignorant of the subject; Rev. Mr. Johnson, the young lady's pastor, who is made to talk like an ignoramus and a simpleton; and Professor Jones, the heroine's uncle, who had confessedly never examined the subject, and scarcely had sense enough to keep him out of the fire. With such combatants on each side, immersion may lift its head in bold defiance. We cannot help admiring the author's clear perception of the necessities of his cause. It was exceedingly proper that he should select, as the advocates of Pedobaptism, such persons as Mr. Percy, who "had never had a serious thought upon the question" (p. 13); Mr. Johnson, who said, " I have never studied these controversies much"; and " Uncle Jones," who, though Professor of Languages, had considered it the duty of his parents and their pastor to attend to his baptism, and "had never inquired whether they did it illy or well" (p. 121). It is precisely over such persons, as the author rightly judged, that Baptist controvertists gain the victory. And yet we cannot but wonder that he would so publicly disgrace his cause by selecting such ignoramuses as the opponents of the learned Mr Courtney!

The respective characters being thus selected, the advocates of immersion are, of course, allowed to make bold assertions which are utterly untrue, and to keep out of view the merits of the case, whilst their ignorant and soft-headed opponents gape and wonder. Thus "the heroine of faith" decides, as by intuition, that baptism is *an act*, and that if immersion is baptism, sprinkling and pouring cannot be. Her intellect is too lofty, and her perception too clear, to hesitate for a moment to decide against forty-nine fiftieths of the wisest and best men that have lived both in ancient and modern times. The author rightly judged that this heroine ought to be very self-conceited. Mr. Percy is made to admit, what every tolerable scholar knows to be untrue, that all the lexicons sustain the immersionists. It suited the purpose of the writer to keep out of view the declaration of the learned Baptist, Carson, that "all the lexicons" were against them. "Professor Jones," poor simpleton, is made to express the opinion that immersion was first introduced "by the Mad Men of Munster during the Reformation of Luther." He cannot tell, poor fellow, where he got the idea; but "perhaps he got something of it from reading D'Aubigne's History of the Reformation—perhaps he received it by hearing something of the kind from the pulpit." And the accomplished Baptist, Mr. Courtney, has "seen and heard such statements many times from various sources. They are often recorded in Presbyterian and Methodist newspapers" (p. 160). And the learned gentleman gravely goes to work to disprove this statement, which was never made by any tolerably informed Presbyterian, or recorded in any respectable Pedobaptist paper. The book abounds with such vile misrepresentations.

The book is written with ingenuity—it was necessary

that it should be. It keeps out of view the facts and arguments on which Pedobaptists rely, or caricatures them to make them appear ridiculous. It puts into their mouths arguments they never use. It manufactures history to suit the occasion. In a novel, all this can be done in such a way that the uninformed reader will not readily detect it. We are gratified at observing how distinctly the writer shows, first and last, that the cause of immersion needs very peculiar advantage in order to sustain its claims.

After all, since he was advocating a fiction, he is probably right in adopting fiction as the means of its defence. The only way to find so ignorant and stupid Presbyterians as Percy, Johnson, and Jones, is to *manufacture* them for the occasion; and nowhere, but in the imagination of a zealous immersionist, can such Presbyterian young ladies as "Theodosia Ernest, the Heroine of Faith," be found. The author could not successfully assail *real, living* Presbyterians; and, therefore, being resolved on battle and a victory, he manufactures a few to suit him, and then chooses their weapons for them, and directs them how to use them, so they will be sure not to hurt them. Brave man! Don Quixote was scarcely his equal.

Verily, the cause of anti-Pedobaptism seems to be "on its last legs." If it cannot induce the Christian world to receive an immersionist Bible, and if *novels* will not sustain it, what is it to do?

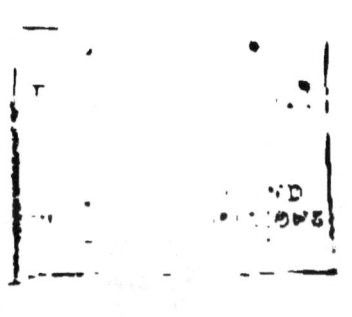

Theodosia Ernest.

CHAPTER I.

A DREAM.

I HAD a *dream*, but whether it was *all* a dream, let him who reads it judge.

Methought in my dream that I was in Pastor Johnson's study. He had in his hand the Presbyterian newspaper, called the Presbyterian of St. Louis. He had just found the article of Doctor Rice on Theodosia. His little gray eyes began to twinkle the moment they caught the caption, "A BAPTIST NOVEL," for, since his troubles with the young lady and her uncle, he has devoured with great avidity every thing which he could find against the Baptists. As he was reading, however, a heavy frown began to gather on his brow, his lips were pressed together with convulsive energy, and the paper shook with the tremulous excitement which pervaded his whole body. He continued to read, however, until he had finished the piece, and then, as if to assure himself that he had not read amiss, he began at the caption and read it every word again. When he had done, he folded the paper carefully, put it into the inside pocket of his coat, looked into the fire for several seconds, then nodded his head three times very significantly, not straight forward with the chin toward his breast bone, but diagonally, with the chin inclined toward the left shoulder, and the back of his head drawn toward the right.

What this peculiar pantomine might signify, I was, in my dream, greatly at a loss to determine, until he had

gone into the room where his wife was engaged in her
domestic duties.

"Mrs. Johnson," said he, "I desire that you will pack
my carpet-bag. I must make a journey to St. Louis,
and to get home before the Sabbath must start this
morning."

"Why, my dear, what in the world is the matter?"

"I want to go and see Doctor Rice, madam; I don't
like the way he talks about me. He has had the auda-
city to call me a *fool*, madam; nay, more, he has even
declared that there is not so great a fool in our whole
denomination. It is too much, madam, for human
nature to endure. I feel it my duty to go and talk to
him as a Christian brother; I want to tell him to his
face that I think he has done me great injustice, and, in
short, has treated me very badly."

Mrs. Johnson seemed instinctively to understand that
delay or remonstrance was out of the question. She
made at once the needful arrangements, and her husband
was gone.

Then I saw, in my dream, that he entered the room
where the Reverend Doctor was engaged in writing.

"I presume this is the Reverend Doctor Rice," said
he. "My name is Johnson, sir; the Reverend Mr. Johnson, of ——, I felt it my duty, sir, to come and see you
about your paper of the ——"

"Ah, I am glad to see you, Mr. Johnson   Take a
seat, sir; I hope you have had a pleasant journey."

"Why, yes, sir, reasonably so; but in fact I have a
great dislike to traveling, and nothing would have induced me to take the journey but a conviction of duty.
I felt it to be my duty, sir, to come and tell you that I
think you have treated me very badly, sir. And let me
say, sir, that you have done more to destroy my confidence an, that of my congregation, in the truthfulness

of our positions on the Baptismal question, than all the Baptist arguments I have ever heard."

"Why, my dear sir, what can you mean?"

Mr. Johnson pulled the paper before referred to out of his pocket, and found the article on Theodosia.

"I suppose, sir," said he, holding it up before the Doctor, "you will not deny that you are the author of that?"

"Certainly not," replied the Doctor, as he glanced rapidly down the column like one who was familiar with the words. "I take credit to myself, sir, as being the first, and, so far as I know, the *only* person who has attempted to answer that peculiar book."

"I have no objection," replied Mr. Johnson, "to your answering the book. In fact, no one could rejoice more than I to see it rightly answered, but I want you to understand that you have done me and those who stood with me in that discussion very great injustice. It was unkind, sir, it was cruel in you to intimate that there was not in all the Presbyterian denomination so great a fool as I, just because I had never carefully examined the subject of baptism for myself, but trusted to Doctor Dwight and Doctor Miller, and our other Doctors of Divinity for my information and my arguments. I have always had a great regard, sir, for *our Doctors of Divinity*. I have supposed they must be pious, and learned, and truthful men. I thought I could *rely* upon any thing I had learned from a *Presbyterian Doctor of Divinity;* I therefore took the substance of their arguments, not venturing to employ a single one of my own, and yet for doing this you count me as a simpleton and called me a fool."

"Ah, my dear brother Johnson, you must excuse me; I did not at first understand precisely who you were. I begin to see it now. Let me assure you, sir, that I heartily sympathize with you on the loss of so lovely a member as Miss Theodosia, and so influential an Elder as her Uncle Jones. I can easily understand, my dear sir, that you were deeply wounded by that event, and still feel a little sore on the subject. But you must not fall out with your friends on that account. *We must* DO SOMETHING *to break the force of the arguments* presented by the author in his silly narrative of that transaction. We must either meet those arguments with sober logic, or we must destroy their influence by *ridicule*. I am sure when you have come to look at the matter calmly, you will not only excuse but even approve what I have said."

"What, sir! excuse and approve your calling me a *fool*, just because I used no better arguments than had been furnished me by *our greatest Doctors of Divinity ! !*".

"Ah, my dear brother, I see that you do not yet quite understand me. I mean to say that, in order to destroy the influence of that silly narrative, we must either fairly meet and logically confute the facts and arguments by which Miss Theodosia and her uncle were convinced that we are wrong and the Baptists are right, or else we must turn attention from them by calling the book a 'NOVEL,' and laughing at the arguments as though they were not worth answering. And now let me say to you in confidence, that it was a great deal easier to insinuate that as a '*novel*' it must be a work unfit for the pious to read, and ridicule and laugh at the book, than to disprove its *facts* or answer its *arguments*. I trust, therefore, you will not take it too much to heart if you come in for your share of the laugh, since you can't help seeing that if I had allowed your arguments and those of your friend, Professor Jones, to be the best we have, our cause is at once and forever irretrievably ruined; but by adroitly representing these as perfect nonsense and foolishness, I make the impression on the minds of my readers that we have some others of most tremendous power, which could not possibly have failed to convince your opponents if you had only known them and brought them forward."

"But, sir," replied Mr. Johnson, "I am sure I brought forward the very best that I could find—I took those of our most eminent Doctors of Divinity, living and dead, the present company only excepted. I would like to know, sir, if any doctor in our church ever stood higher than Timothy Dwight, D. D., and Samuel Miller, D. D., one the President of Yale College, the other an honored professor for many years in our leading Theological Seminary, that at Princeton, New Jersey. I thought, sir, I was safe from the charge of folly when I followed Dwight and Miller, and consequently I took the same ground with these eminent men to show Miss Theodosia that John did not baptize by immersion, but that the Lord Jesus must have been *sprinkled* on the bank of the river. Just turn to volume four, page 349, of Dwight's Divinity—'*It is,*' says he, '*incredible that the multitudes which John baptized in the wilderness were immersed. It will not be mistrusted that this promiscuous assembly were immersed naked. To have immersed them with their clothes on would have exposed them to certain disease and death.*' Now, I did not care to state it just in this way to Miss Theodosia, so I said that they could not have been immersed on account of their great numbers, and for this I had the authority of several Doctors of Divinity. Says Doctor Summers, page 82 of his work on Baptism: '*It was not possible for him to baptize the immense multitudes that came to his baptism by immersing them,*' and gives as a reason that his ministry lasted only a year or less, and in that

time 'he baptized, *perhaps*, two or three millions.' He
thinks, as I did, that they must have stood in rows along
the bank, while the Baptist sprinkled them either
with or without hyssop, he don't know which. So
also Doctor Eagleton, of Tennessee, gives the same
explanation.

"The great Doctor Rice, I know, does not venture to
say, like Summers and Dwight, that it was '*impossible*'
and '*incredible*,' but even he, in his work on Baptism,
page 116, founds an argument on the assumption that
'*it was not very probable.*' And Doctor Miller, whom
some will consider a greater than Rice, expressly says,
'*There is no evidence, and I will venture to say, no
probability, that John ever baptized by immersion.*' Then,
when I wished to prove that the *Apostle* did not immerse
any more than John had done, what better could I do
than follow these great Doctors? Doctor Dwight expressly says, volume four, page 349: '*It is impossible
that those whom Peter and his companions baptized on
the day of Pentecost should have been immersed,*' and
gives as reasons, first, that they had no suitable clothes;
second, there was not time enough, and he plainly intimates that there was not *water* enough.

"So.Doctor Summers says it was impossible, because
there were no places suitable for immersion, and besides
it was impossible for the twelve to baptize such a multitude in the six or eight hours that remained of the
day. So also Doctor Rice himself, page 120 of his
work on Baptism, makes in substance the very same
argument 'Where,' he exultingly asks, 'did the Apostles find sufficient *water* for the immersion of so many?'
And again, 'The number—could the twelve Apostles
baptize three thousand persons in that day?' And
Doctor Miller, whom some will think a greater even
than Doctor Rice, declares, after dwelling upon these

difficulties of the case, 'The man, therefore, who can believe tha, the three thousand on the day of Pentecost were baptized by immersion, must have great faith and a wonderful facility of 'accommodating his belief to his wishes.'

"On these two points, therefore, you see I had the authority of our most learned Doctors, including even Doctor N. L. Rice himself, and yet Doctor Rice calls m a fool because I could not do better than them all."

"Oh, no; excuse me, my dear brother Johnson, but these were not the points to which I particularly referred I grant you had the substance of our arguments on these points, but then that argument of yours based upon *with* as the signification of the Greek preposition 'en,' you must allow that it was rather simple in you to rest so much upon the phrase *with water.*' "

"Not at all, sir; I can admit no such thing. The truth is, sir, this is our *great* argument to the minds of the unlearned. It has more plausibility in it than any other that I have ever read. And, sir, you must let me tell you that though you may now call it silly and rate me as a fool for using it, I did it on the authority of more than one of our Doctors of Divinity. The Rev. Alexander Newton, D.D., in the 'True Baptist,' makes a long and carefully elaborated argument, based upon this rendering of the word. Dr. Summers, page 100, says expressly that 'with' is the proper meaning of the word 'when found in connection with baptism.' And even the great Doctor Rice himself, in his debate with Campbell, page 191, quoted Bloomfield to show that it was 'with water' and not in water that '*en hudati*' should be rendered. How then can Doctor Rice call me a fool for using his own argument, and that of other doctors *almost* equal to himself?"

"I don't deny that I alluded to it," replied the doctor;

27

"but I know too well its fallacy to risk our cause upon it as you did. But it was not for this so much as for your calling attention to those unguarded admissions of Barnes, and Chalmers, and McKnight, that I thought, to say the least, you were somewhat *indiscreet*."

"Why, my dear sir, were not these all Presbyterians? Were they not all DOCTORS OF DIVINITY? Could I not venture to direct an inquiring member of the Presbyterian Church to our own Presbyterian Doctors of Divinity for information? I know those men were counted among the wisest and the best of all our doctors; I took it for granted that they had studied the subject before they wrote about it; I had, I am sure, no suspicion that they would mislead those who trusted to their teaching."

"But when you found which way they were leading your inquirers why did you not contradict and oppose their testimony?"

"I did do my best," replied Mr. Johnson, "but the truth is I am not, like you, a *Doctor of Divinity*, and therefore I could not contradict such men with as good a face as *you* can. If you had been there you migh' have said, 'My dear young friends, it is true that these learned men and eminent masters in the Presbyterian Church *do* teach thus, but they are utterly in error. They have stated what is entirely devoid of truth; you may take *my* word, but you cannot trust to theirs.' But you, no more than I, could have denied that Dr. Barnes admits baptize in Greek to be the same as tabal in Hebrew, and that he says and proves that it in the Scriptures signifies '*to dip.*' You, no more than I, could have denied that Chalmers and McKnight do both un-questionably give immersion as the meaning of the word, and both agree that it was immersion that John and the apostles employed. *That* is too plain for argu-

Theodosia Ernest.

PAGE 435.

ment. But then, as you are a Doctor of Divinity, as well as they, and have been Moderator of the General Assembly one year, as McKnight was for twenty, *you* might have ventured to dispute their word—*you* might have called in question either their learning or their veracity, for if they told what is not true it must have been either from ignorance or falsehood; but it would not have done for a plain and simple pastor like myself to put *my* word against that of any *one* of these great doctors, much less against all three. I assure you, sir, that you Doctors of Divinity have a great advantage over us common pastors in such a discussion as that. When that learned Professor of Theology, Moses Stuart, says that all critics and lexicographers of any note are agreed that immersion is the common and primary meaning of the word baptism, and that the first Christians so understood it, *you* can simply say *it is no such thing ;* but people would expect me to prove it, and that very plainly, too, before they would believe that Stuart lied about it, or that a man of his eminent learning could be mistaken.

"When the learned MARTIN LUTHER says that 'Baptism is a Greek word, and signifies immersion,' and that the etymology of the word seems to demand that the person baptized 'should be wholly immersed, and then immediately drawn out of the water,' as he does in his works, vol. 1, p. 336, *you* could reply: 'Doctor Martin Luther must be egregiously mistaken about this, for I, Doctor N. L. Rice, have examined into the matter, and find it is not true.' When that 'godly, learned man, JOHN CALVIN,' in his Institutes, b. iv., s. 15, says that The word baptize signifies to immerse, and it is certain that immersion was the practice of the ancient church,' *you*, as a Doctor of Divinity, can say: 'Doctor John Calvin was mistaken—this is not true.' When that

very learned and eminent scholar, CASAUBON, says,
'The manner of baptizing was to PLUNGE or DIP them
into the water, as even the word BAPTISM plainly enough
shows,' *you* have only to say: 'Casaubon was either
very ignorant of the matter, or else he lied, for I, Doctor
N. L. Rice, have found it was not so.'

"When the learned BISHOP BOSSUET declares that
'Baptize signifies to plunge, as is admitted by all the
world;' when the famous critic Venema says: 'The
word *baptizien*, to baptize, is nowhere used in the
Scripture for sprinkling;' when the great scholar says,
in commenting on Matt. iii. 6: 'Baptism consists in the
immersion of the whole body in water'—you can simply
reply: 'I know these learned foreigners say such things,
but Doctor N. L. Rice knows better.'

"When such a man as DOCTOR GEORGE CAMPBELL, of
Scotland, the President of a Presbyterian College, says
that 'the word BAPTIZIEN, both in the sacred authors
and classical, signifies to DIP, to PLUNGE, to IMMERSE,
and was thus rendered by Tertullian, the oldest of the
Latin fathers,' that 'it is ALWAYS construed suitably to
this meaning,' that 'it is never in any case, sacred or
classical, employed in the sense of rain or sprinkle,
you have only to say, that 'Doctor George Campbell
differs on these points from Doctor N. L. Rice.'

"When a learned professor of Greek, like the well-
known Charles Anthon, of Columbian College, the
author of some of our most valuable classical school
books, expressly asserts that 'the primary meaning of
the word is to DIP or to IMMERSE, and its secondary
meanings, if it ever had any, all refer in some way or
other to the same leading idea,' that 'sprinkling and
pouring are entirely out of the question,' you have only
to say: 'Mr. Anthon is only a learned *professor* of
languages, and I, a DOCTOR OF DIVINITY, take it upon

myself to assure you that he is entirely mistaken. IT IS NOT TRUE; and whether Professor Anthon is ignorant or false, the world may judge.'

"Now if I, a simple, untitled pastor, should talk so, they would not believe me. I tried it, sir. I asserted roundly, just as Doctor Miller had done. I intended to use his very words: 'Now we contend that this word does not necessarily, or even commonly, signify to immerse, but also implies to wash, to sprinkle, to pour on water, and to tinge or dye with any liquid, and therefore accords very well with the mode of baptism by sprinkling or affusion.' 'I can assure you,' he says in another place, 'that the word we render baptize does legitimately signify the application of water in any way as well as by immersion.' Now I could make assertions as confidently as even Doctor Rice himself, but I found that I was expected to prove them, and that from the Scriptures, and in such a way that the demonstration should be plain to the common sense of an earnest and shrewd, quick-witted girl. I assure you I had rather have tried to satisfy a dozen Doctors of Divinity."

"But why did you not go to the Lexicons, as I did in my Lexington debate? Why did you permit that young lawyer to wrest this weapon out of your hands at the very beginning? Mr. Campbell began to quote the Lexicons on me, but I showed that this was a game at which two could play."

"And yet I am sure, sir, Miss Theodosia would have said that you lost the game, however well you played. The truth is, Doctor Albert Barnes, by pointing to the *places* in the Old Testament where they could find the meaning of the word as it was used among the Jews, had taken away the necessity for any reference to Lexicons, unless it were to prove that Barnes was a false interpreter, and this I did not like to do. But what could the Lexicons have availed for my purpose, even as quoted by yourself? You appealed to eleven of them, and I suppose you gave the most favorable definitions you could extract. Now, you will remember that neither Miss Ernest nor Mr. Percy had taken any such ground as Mr. Carson had done, or as Mr. Campbell did in your debate. No one in our company insisted that *immerse* was the *only* and *necessary* meaning of the word, but only that it was the *common* and *most frequent* meaning, in connection with which it was most *likely* to be employed, and which it must therefore (according to the ordinary rules of interpretation) be understood, *unless the context required some other*. Now you know, as well as I, that the rule of the Lexicons is to give the *common*, every-day meaning, as the primary or *first* definition. And yet, when you attempted to ascertain the meaning of the word baptizo by the Lexicons, what did they testify?

"*Scapula*, according to your own rendering, gives baptizo, to dip or immerse; also to dye, as we immerse things for the purpose of coloring or washing them; also to plunge, submerge, to cover with water, etc.

"*Hedericus* gives to dip, immerse, to cover with water.

"*Stephanus*.—To dip, to immerse, as we immerse things for the purpose of coloring or washing; to merge, submerge, to cover with water.

"*Schleusner*.—To plunge, to immerse.

"*Parkhurst*.—To immerse in, or wash with water.

"*Robinscn*.—To immerse, to sink

"*Schrivellius*.—To baptize, to immerse.

Groves.—To dip, immerse, immerge, plunge.

'*Bretschneider*.—Properly often to dip.

"*Suidas*.—To sink, to plunge, to immerse.

"*Ware*.—To wash, perform ablution, **cleanse**; secondly, to immerse.

"*Greenfield.*—To immerse, immerge, submerge, sink.

" Now, out of all the eleven, you could find but *one*, and that unknown to fame, which does not give *dip* or its equivalent as its first and common meaning. Miss Ernest would have said the testimony is ten to one against you. If you had come into court with ten witnesses against you, and only *one* for you, Mr. Percy, as a lawyer, would have declared your case utterly hopeless.

" But Mr. Campbell, at that time, gave you several other Lexicons, among which was

"*Robertson's Thesaurus*, which defines it to immerse, to wash.

"*Pason.*—To dip, to immerse, to dye, because it is done by immersing.

"*Donegan.*—To immerse repeatedly into a liquid, to submerge, to sink

"*Jones.*—Plunge, dip, baptize, bury, overwhelm.

"*Bass.*—To dip, immerse, plunge in water. Baptisma, immersion, dipping.

" *Stokius.*—To dip, to immerse in water.

" So we have in all sixteen witnesses who depose that this is its primary and common meaning. Sixteen who testify that it must thus be understood when nothing in the context requires another sense. And only one who gives to *wash* as its primary meaning. Mr. Campbell also mentioned several others, whom he said gave it the same sense, and you did not dispute his word."

" But what of all that ?" replied the Reverend Doctor Rice. " I would have set aside all that array of dictionaries by quoting just one sentence from the great Baptist, Doctor Carson, who ought surely to understand what he says, and who was no friend to sprinkling: and yet he expressly says, 'THAT ALL THE LEXI-

CONS ARE AGAINST HIM.' This is testimony enough for me."

"But it would not have been for Miss Theodosia or Mr. Percy. They would have asked to see the BOOK and the place, and would have read it for themselves, and doing so, would have been sure to discover what you must have known before you quoted it, that he does NOT say that all the Lexicons are against the Baptists—he does NOT say that all or any of the Lexicons gives sprinkling or pouring as a meaning of the word—he does NOT say that they do not all agree in giving dip or its equivalent as the primary and common meaning. 'On this point,' he says, 'I have no quarrel with the Lexicons. There is the most complete harmony among them in representing dip as the primary meeting of bapto and baptizo.' But Mr. Carson denies that it has any secondary meaning at all, or that it ever means any thing else but dip or immerse. And it is on this point, that he says, page 55, 'He has all the Lexicographers and Commentators against him.' I could not have satisfied my inquirers with such a misrepresentation, even though my conscience could have permitted me to use it. We all know that the Lexicons give secondary meanings to these words, and in our company there was no disposition to question the propriety of their doing so. But, sir, it has struck me with surprise, since my attention has been turned to the subject, that not a single one of all the seventeen Lexicons referred to and quoted by you and Mr. Campbell give *sprinkle* or *pour* as even a secondary meaning. They give *wash* and *cleanse*, but several of them are careful to explain that it is because things may be washed and cleansed by *dipping* them in water. And I have been thinking, especially since I read your piece, that what *we* are accustomed to call *baptism* is not even *a washing*—for if the

Doctor should tell me to *wash* one of my children, who was sick, with warm water, I am sure I should not feel that I had carried out the prescription by dipping the tip of my fingers in the water and touching them to his forehead. And the truth is, sir—I suppose I may just as well tell it—that since you have made so light of all the arguments which I advanced in our discussion, and yet have given me no better, nor told me to whi h of all our Doctors I can go to find any more forcible or convincing, I begin to doubt whether we are not both mistaken, and that Miss Ernest and her friends had better reasons for leaving us than I can ever find for re-maining where I am."

"Yes," exclaimed Professor Jones (who suddenly made his appearance, unaccountably, as people often do in dreams), "I have often thought how angry we should be if those who owe obedience to us should render it as some of us render obedience to God. Doctor Rice, for example, says to a little servant boy on Saturday night, go *wash* yourself, or go *bathe* yourself, and put on clean clothing for the Sabbath. The servant, instead of bath-ing his whole body, takes a few drops of water in the palm of his hand and pours it on the top of his head. 'You little rascal,' Doctor Rice would say, 'why did you not wash yourself as I directed you?'

"'I *did* wash myself, sir.'

"'You did! Do you call *that* washing *yourself*? Why, you did not even wet your scalp. Come here sir; I'll teach you how to trifle with my commandments.'

"'Please, sir!' exclaims the lad. 'Please sir, don't punish me, I am sure, sir, I did wash myself; I can prove it to you, sir.'

"'Why, you little impertinent. You just now con-fessed that you only put a few drops of water on the top of your head.'

"'I know it, sir; but that was *washing myself*, sir; I can prove it by the united testimony of all your DOCTORS OF DIVINITY, including the Reverend Doctor N. L. Rice.   You may be so angry, sir, just now, that you don't remember it, but in your Lexington debate you said again and again that baptize means to *wash*, and of course wash means to *baptize*, and when *you* and our other DOCTORS OF DIVINITY *baptize*, you only put a few drops of water on the person's head.   Besides, you said again and again, that wash was a '*generic*' word (I believe that was it, sir), and might be performed in *any way*, and as this is the way which all the great DOCTORS OF DIVINITY use when GOD tells *them* '*to wash*' people, I am sure, sir, you could not expect *me* to do more in obedience to *your* command than *you* do in obedience to HIS.'

"But let it pass; I have just called in, Doctor, to thank you for dealing so kindly with me in your article on Theodosia.   It is customary when one has been driven by his convictions of duty to leave some denominations for others for those he leaves to seek by defamation to destroy his peace and injure his usefulness.   It is customary to attack his character and impugn his motives.   And the same course has sometimes been adopted to counteract the influence of a *controversial* BOOK.   When its arguments could not be met and refuted, the moral or Christian character of the author has been assailed with a malignity which argues very little for the piety of the assailants, and of itself affords prima facie evidence that there is something rotten in the system which requires such foul means to sustain it, and breeds such rancorous spirits to contend for it.   But it has gratified me much to see that you speak of me in 'sorrow more than anger;' that you are more inclined to pity than abuse.   You think me weak and foolish, and that is the worst of it. I could expect no less than that, for we all are apt to think disparagingly of the intellect which *cannot* see what seems to ours as clear as light. You thought that my friend, Mr. Johnson, was simple, because he failed to convince my niece and myself; and I might have expected that you would think still worse of me, because I could not be convinced. If Mr. Johnson had used *all* the arguments which he could have found in the works of Presbyterian Doctors of Divinity, you might with good reason have thought him a simpleton indeed.

"He contended, with Doctor Miller and other doctors, that the word baptize means to sprinkle or to pour, as truly as to immerse.

"Like several others, and yourself among them, he denied that John's baptism was Christian baptism.

"Like you and all the rest he denied that Jesus went into the water, or that John baptized in Jordan, but asserted that he sprinkled the people standing in rows on the bank.

"Like you and the other doctors, he denied that there was water enough to be had in Jerusalem to immerse three thousand, or time enough to do it.

"Like you and the other doctors, he made an argument upon the *design* of baptism, as being better symbolized by sprinkling than immersion.

"Like you and the other doctors, he made a very plausible argument upon the Pentecostic outpouring of the Holy Ghost as baptism.

"Like you and some of the other doctors, he made the strongest argument that it is possible to make upon ' *with water*' as the translation of 'en udati.' And he gave to each and every one of these arguments *all* the force to which it was logically entitled, and if they could not stand before the simple, common sense of a strong-minded, earnest-hearted girl, it was not his fault but the fault of the arguments. If he had presented *all* the arguments which he could have found gravely set forth by Doctors of Divinity, little Edwin himself would have laughed him out of countenance. What if, like Doctor Dwight, he had declared that '*Christ himself has expressly taught us that immersion is unessential to the administration of this ordinance.*'

"When he said to Peter, John xiii.: 'He that is washed needeth not care to wash his feet, but is clean every whit,' from which the learned doctor concludes that 'a symbolical washing is perfect although applied only to the feet; as perfect as if it were applied also to the hands and the head, and if this construction be admitted, it must also be admitted that the declaration is general and extends to every other symbolical washing, and therefore to baptism, unless excluded by some plain exception.' See Dwight's Divinity, vol. 4, pp. 150, 157.

"So also another Doctor of Divinity declares, that 'Christ discountenanced the practice of immersion in religious purifications. He that is washed, said he to Peter, needeth not save to wash his feet, but is clean every whit.' John xiii. 9, 10. By reading this text in its connection, we will perceive that so far from introducing the practice of washing the body all over as a religious rite, he discouraged it, by declaring it unnecessary, and by refusing to gratify Peter, who wished to have the water applied to him in a more profuse manner than the Saviour was using it.' See James Wood, D. D., on Christian Baptism, page 35. If Doctor Wood is consistent with himself, he applies the water to the baby's dear little *foot*, for it was the application of water to the '*hands*' or the '*head*' that Jesus '*discountenanced*' and '*discouraged*' I presume, therefore, that Doctor

Wood is not only a Pedobaptist, but a *pedal*-baptist, a foot-baptizer.

"What if Mr. Johnson had said, as more than one of the DOCTORS OF DIVINITY has done, that there is the same proof that the Eunuch immersed Philip that there is that Philip immersed the Eunuch? Yet the great Doctor Miller says: 'There is the same evidence that Philip was plunged as that the Eunuch was.' And Doctor Dwight argues that if '*eis*' means into, and '*ek*' means out of, in the narrative of this transaction, they were *both* plunged *twice* and the Eunuch *three* times. Here are his words: 'The declarations here made, are made concerning the Eunuch and Philip; alike of both it is said that *they went down into the water*, if we render *eis* into; of both also it is said *that when they came up out of the water*, if we render the word *ek* out of. Now let us see what will be the true import of the passage according to this method of construing the words in question, *and they went down both into the water, both Philip and the Eunuch.* That is, *they were both plunged And he baptized him, that is, Philip plunged the Eunuch.* And when they were come up out of the water; that is, when they had both been plunged a second time and risen up from their immersion, *the Spirit of the Lord caught away Philip.* In other words, they were both plunged twice and the Eunuch three times.' See Dwight's Divinity, vol. 4, p. 350, Sermon on Baptism.

"Suppose that Mr. Johnson, like Doctor Wood, had gravely argued that the Eunuch must have been baptized by sprinkling, because he had been reading in Isaiah, and Isaiah somewhere, though not in the passage quoted as that which he was reading, says that Messiah shall *sprinkle* many nations, while every scholar knows that in the Septuagint, which it is most likely he was reading, the word sprinkle does not occur, but '*thaumasontai*' astonish, 'so shall he *astonish* many nations.' And Doctor Adam Clarke says it is the best rendering of the Hebrew. That the *Jews* so understood the Hebrew is evident from their so translating it; and therefore, whether the Eunuch read Hebrew or Greek, he could have found no such word as sprinkle.

"But though your *Doctors of Divinity* had talked volumes of such nonsense, my friend, Mr. Johnson, had sense enough to see that arguments like these could not be expected to stand the scrutiny of earnest, inquiring *common sense*, even in a simple girl, and therefore would not offer them. He used the best you have, and did the best he could with them. I grant that both he and I used some *very simple arguments;* nay, that *all* our arguments were silly as long as we argued against the truth, for every *false* argument *must be foolish*, but neither of us was as silly as some of you DOCTORS OF DIVINITY, and since you have yourself condemned and ridiculed the *very arguments* by which not only he but thousands of your people are deluded and prevented from yielding obedience to Christ, I trust both he and they will see their folly, abandon their errors, obey their Lord, and like my niece and myself, unite with his visible church."

CHAPTER IL

HEN I saw, in my dream, that Pastor Johnson sat with his good old wife, in their own quiet room; but his countenance was sad, and she saw that his heart was troubled, and knew that something had gone amiss with him during his absence. With true womanly tact she sought to find out what it had been without seeming to ask.

"I hope, my dear, you had a pleasant journey, and met with no disagreeable accidents by the way."

"It was as pleasant as I had expected."

"You saw Doctor Rice, of course. I have been told since you started that he is a perfect model of a Christian gentleman, and would certainly explain every thing to your satisfaction. Did you not find it so?"

"Gentleman! Why, yes; I suppose he is what people call a gentleman—a polished, pleasant gentleman—and he made, probably, what he thinks the best apology that the case admits of."

"But you were not quite satisfied with it? Well, I don't wonder. It *was* too bad to call you a greater simpleton than could be found in all the Presbyterian Church. But what explanation did he make?"

"My dear wife," said the pastor, suddenly raising his eyes, and looking earnestly into her face, "I begin to think that our *Doctors of Divinity* are no more to be confided in than other people, and that Miss Ernest, Esquire Percy, and Professor Jones, were right in just casting all their assertions aside, and going to the sacred Word and hunting out its teachings for themselves."

"Why, Mr. Johnson!"

"Yes, my dear; I never mean to trust the bare asser tion of any *Doctor of Divinity* again as long as I live Just think of it now—Doctor Rice *laughs* at my argu ments in favor of sprinkling, and at Mr. Percy's and at those of Professor Jones. He holds them up to the scorn of the world. He speaks of them as though they were almost beneath contempt; and yet you and I know very well that they are arguments which I *borrowed*, EVERY ONE OF THEM, from a *Doctor of Divinity*. They are the *very same* arguments which have been employed by Doctor Eagleton, by Doctor Newton, by Doctor Wood, by Doctor Summers, by Doctor Miller, by Doctor Dwight, and even by Doctor Rice himself. But to make the world believe that we have some stronger and better arguments he laughs at these, as though they were the mere twaddle of the veriest ignoramus in all Christen- dom. But does *he* bring forward any stronger or any better ones? Does he point to the chapter and the page in the works of our Doctors of Divinity, where *they* presented any thing more convincing? So far from it, he was obliged to own to Professor Jones, whom I met at his house, that he had himself employed these very arguments in his debate with Campbell; and the Professor also pointed out to him the volumes and the pages in the works of our *greatest* doctors, where they had employed arguments *so much sillier than mine*, that I would have been ashamed to mention them to a shrewd, sensible girl, like Theodosia. Now, what am I as a Christian man and a Christian minister to do? I have all the time believed that we were right, and, therefore, I so preached and practiced. But you know I would sooner cut off this right hand than use it to sprinkle another babe if Christ does not require *it*. It was because I trusted to the teaching of our doctors

Theodosia Ernest.

PAGE 451.

that I thought he must be right; but when these doctors hold up these very arguments, by which I was convinced, to the scorn of the religious world, and yet give me no better in the place of them, I can't help thinking there is something rotten in the system somewhere.

"I intend, God helping me, to *search* into the *Scripture* teachings *for myself*. I remember that we could not find a single command to baptize infants, nor a single example of one baptized. I remember that our own best commentators, such as Barnes in this country, and Olshausen in Europe, say there is nothing about it in the text I most relied upon, 'Suffer the little children to come unto me.' I remember that we could not find *one single* text, which even our own Doctors of Divinity all agree upon as requiring or justifying the practice— that even concerning the covenant of circumcision, which Doctor McNought thinks is our strongest fortress. Professor Stuart expressly declares, in his commentary on Genesis xvii. and Galatians, that they can afford it *no* countenance whatever; and as to sprinkling, even Doctor Rice himself did not, and dare not say that the Greek word baptize in the Scriptures has ever been truly rendered *sprinkle* by any reliable Lexicon or eminent critic. He only contends that it may be rendered to *wash*, and then says that washing may be done by sprinkling a dozen drops or less of water on the person's head. But *can* it be thus done? If you or I should tell one of the children to wash, not his *face*, but to wash *himself*, would *he* consider it a full and complete obedience if he should only dip the tip of his fingers in water, and touch them on his head, or face, or feet, or hands; for I don't see as there is any more propriety in touching one part than another."

"I don't think we would, my dear," replied the good
28

woman. "And if this be so, I am sure it must be some *wicked* MOCKERY to do that in obedience to *God's* commands, which we would consider as the veriest trifling if it were done in the place of actual obedience to a similar command by us."

"I am afraid, my dear," resumed the pastor, "I am awfully afraid we have been wrong. God knows I *meant* to do right—God knows I verily believed that I was right; but this communication of Doctor Rice has made the case look fearfully dark to me.

"I have thought, and prayed, and thought again, until my brain is dizzy. I can't help seeing Jesus baptized, as Mark says, '*Eis*,' not merely in, but *into* the river of Jordan. I can't help seeing the Eunuch and Philip going down into the water, then the baptism, then the coming up out of the water. I fear our doctors *twist* and pervert the words in trying to make them mean any thing less. I fear some of them almost *prevaricate* to hide the simple and natural meaning of the language. But oh, it is a dreadful thought that we have all the time been wrong; that I, a minister of Christ, have *all my life* been the advocate of error, and have been doing in his name that which he never commanded, and having constantly undone that which he actually did commission all his ministers to do. I must study more about it. I must pray more over it. But if I find it so—much as I love my people, much as I love my church, much as I love my brethren in the ministry, much as I love the doctrines and the ordinances which I have so long taught and administered, I trust I love the truth and love my Saviour better than them all, and I will go down into the water as the Eunuch did, and Mr. Percy shall himself baptize me, as Philip did the Eunuch, and when we come up out of the water I trust to meet the

Theodosia Ernest.

PAGE 455.

Spirit of the Lord ready to find a place for me to labor, and to bless my work."

     *   *   *   *   *   *

Then I saw, in my dream, some few weeks after this, that Mr. Percy had returned from his visit to Nashville and the hill country of Tennessee (an account of which is given in the second volume of Theodosia Ernest), and he was standing in the same place where Theodosia had gone down into the water. The company that stood upon the bank consisted of a great multitude. Many of them had walked in a procession from the beautiful new Baptist meeting-house, which stood near the old school-house where Theodosia had been admitted to the visible company of Christ's people. Many others had come from the magnificent old building, in which, until recently, Pastor Johnson had been accustomed to minister for many years. Many had come from other places of worship, and not a few were there who seldom witnessed any act of religion but one like this, which called them out merely to gratify their curiosity. But vast and various as was the crowd, they were silent, and solemn, and tearful, when the old man stopped at the verge of the water, turned to their expectant gaze, and briefly gave the reasons why, following his Saviour's example, and in obedience to his positive command, which he could no longer misunderstand, he was about to "be *buried* with Christ by baptism."

Those reasons we have not space to tell as he told them that day. It is enough for us merely to state that, after earnest prayer for guidance from above, he had resolved to "*search the Scriptures*" and discard the doctors That he had been unable to find any sprinkling commanded or practiced as baptism. Nor could he and a single text which either commands or justifies the baptism of babes, Presbyterian Doctors of Divinity themselves being judges, since each text that one may claim as teaching it, a half a dozen others will declare has no relation to the case.

"There are," said he, in conclusion, "many of my own former people here. I see their once familiar faces. Some look on me with pity; and could I have continued to practice, in my Master's name, what he has nowhere commanded, I should need their pity.

"Some look on me with heartfelt sorrow; and I see even now the traces which their tears have marked upon their loving faces My friends, I am happier now than I have been for many months. Doubt has now given way to certainty, hesitation to decision—the struggle, the long, agonizing, heart-rending struggle between old attachments and personal inclination, on the one hand, and duty to my Lord and Master on the other, has ceased at length, and I have *peace* with God and *peace* with my own conscience.

"It may be there are some who look on me with *anger*, some who will follow me with bitter words; some who may malign my motives, and seek to destroy my character; some who may send out rumors that their old pastor was *deranged*, or something worse, and that the people whom he served so long were glad to be so easily rid of him. Such things have been said of others, and, doubtless, will be said of me. But, though you may revile me, I will love you still. Though you may persecute me, I will still pray for you, and long and strive to bring you to a knowledge of the whole truth of the glorious gospel of my blessed God. And since you cannot make me hate you, you cannot harm me by your hatred. I part with you all in the love of the gospel, and pray for all, that God will help you see, as I have seen, the sin and danger of setting aside the ordinance of **Christ**,

and teaching for doctrines the traditions and commandments of men."

Then they went down into the water, both Mr. Percy
and the former pastor, and he baptized him; and they
came up out of the water, and I awoke—and behold
it was a dream! And yet, kind reader, *was it* ALL *a
dream?*

THE END

www.ingramcontent.com/pod-product-compliance
Lightning Source LLC
Chambersburg PA
CBHW022023110726
47901CB00006B/1632